DEVIL INCARNATE

THE BOYS OF PRESTON PREP

ANGEL LAWSON

SAMANTHA RUE

FOREWORD

Dear Readers,

This book is not for the squeamish so please read the following content warnings:

If you have a problem selfish, entitled, spoiled, and manipulative men, this book isn't for you. If you're looking for another Reynolds McAllister or Sebastian Wilcox...you won't find it. Even Hamilton Bates isn't a sociopath.

Heston Wilcox isn't just a Devil. He's *THE* Devil. Make no mistake.

If you want a sweet, virginal, Mary Sue-type character, we don't suggest Devil Incarnate. ***There's no cheating here***, but Georgia Haynes likes sex and has notches on that bedpost. A lot. Compulsively. She knows what she wants and how to get it. She puts herself in bad situations to fulfill a need. Which is cool. No judgements here.

If you don't like books with too much sex, welp, maybe try one of our other books.

Content Warning:

Self-harm, hypersexuality, mentions of attempted suicide and other mental health issues, impulse addictions, masochism, and sadism.

***

To keep up with new releases, bonus content, reader talk, and everything else with our books, please join the Angel's Antics group on Facebook!

ANGEL'S ANTICS
READER GROUP

PROLOGUE

GEORGIA

Freshman Year

I look into the camera, testing a crooked smile before clicking the button. I lower my phone to assess the picture, deciding that it's garbage. I try another, this one with my cleavage in the shot. Oh, yeah. That's definitely it.

I add a caption:

Getting ready to crush these lame PhysEd credits. Should I do swim, bball, or track?

#PrestonStrong #killmenow #whyaretheserequiredcredits #Swim-Devils #BallerDevils #RunningDevils

The bench in front of the gym is nice. It's a warm day for March—warm enough that I've abandoned my sweater in favor of undoing a few buttons on my uniform. I get a couple instant responses from people who don't even go here, so I'm scrolling down my ChattySnap when a group of people walk by.

I look up, realizing who it is.

It's *The Devils*, capital T, capital D.

They ignore me, of course. As they should. I'm just a freshman, and they're all juniors. Well, not just juniors. They're some of the most popular people in school. Athletic. Smart. Rich.

Just then, one of them makes eye contact with me. Heston Wilcox. *Oh, god.* He's so ridiculously handsome that my heart instantly starts pitter-pattering. It beats even harder when his steps falter, slowing.

"Hey, you're Georgia, right?" he asks.

I nod, holding back an inner, girlish squeal at the fact he knows my name. *My* name! "Uh, yeah. Hi!" I feel a little cringe at the excitement in my voice, but he just walks back a step, facing me.

Heston's lips tilt into a wry smirk. "You busy tonight?"

I feel a hot blush creep up my cheeks. "Er... me?" A couple of his friends wait nearby, and my eyes dart over. They're all Devils. Hamilton Bates, Ansel Davenport, Emory Hall. There's a girl tucked under Hamilton's arm. Her name is Campbell, but I'm not sure if that's a first or last name.

"Yes, you," he says with a little laugh, amusement dancing in this ocean blue eyes.

I push my shoulders back, trying to adopt a facade of perfect cool. "No, I'm not busy tonight."

He lifts his chin. "I'm having a party. You should come."

Holy shit! Heston Wilcox is inviting *me* to a party! I stammer out, "To your house?"

"Yep."

Blush deepening, I admit, "I don't have a ride."

He glances over at the guys, eyes zeroed in. "Campbell can give you a ride. Isn't that right, Cam?"

Campbell scowls, obviously not pleased at someone telling her what to do, but Hamilton leans down and whispers something into her ear. Whatever he says is enough to smooth her expression. She gives me a look and calls out, "Meet me by the parking lot at eight."

"S-sure," I stutter, trying to look casual as I cross my legs. "Yeah. Sounds great."

They walk off, just like that—as if Heston Wilcox hadn't just socially anointed me.

∽

The ride with Campbell is awkward. I try to strike up a conversation three times, but it falls flat. She barely answers me. I give up, spending the rest of the drive staring at my phone, full of excited nerves. I've been to parties before, but nothing like one thrown by the Devils.

When we arrive, Campbell all but leaves me to scurry after her in my heels. About the only thing that makes me feel a little less like an out-of-place loser is the way Heston looks at me when his eyes find me.

He smiles. "Hey. You made it."

Breathlessly, I say, "Yeah. Hi."

His eyes have that little gloss to them, like maybe he's already a bit buzzed off something. I don't blink an eye when he hands me a beer, a hand landing on my lower back to lead me into a room with a billiard table.

We spend a long time like that; him leading me around the party, talking to people here and there—people I know *of*, but don't actually know. None of them really pay attention to me, but sometimes, Heston will bend down to say something into my ear, like, "You have nice legs," or, "See that guy over there? That's Carl. He can get you anything you want," or, "Want another drink?" Every time he does, I get a small shiver, and the hand resting on the small of my back rubs a little, like he knows.

I wasn't totally expecting it, so it's surprising to find that I'm definitely the girl on his arm for the night. The other girls seem surprised at the way he keeps me at his side too, throwing me the occasional confused or jealous glance. Even when he starts up a game of pool with his boys, he still returns to me, leaning in to talk some whispered smack about Ansel's form.

Never one to be bashful about these things, when the game winds to a close, I play it up, straining to give him a kiss on his cheek for good luck.

When he sinks the eight ball, his eyes find mine, mouth slanting into a wicked grin.

It's such a thrill. Heston isn't just good looking and popular. He's a *Devil*. He's one of the Four Horsemen of the school. He and the other guys have reputations beyond being smart and athletic. The Devils have impossible standards. Each one is rumored to have a 'test' girlfriends are supposed to pass to even be with them. Passing a test, getting 'marked' by one of them, is the fastest way to the top of the social ladder.

But that's not why I'm here. I don't really care about status. I've had my eye on him for a while—there's something magnetizing about him. Dangerous. Sexy. I've heard the rumors about his cock and I'm positively dying to give it a spin.

Sometimes you see the big, life-altering events barreling like a freight train down the track. Other times it happens in a blink, no warning sound, no flashing light, no barricades keeping you off the tracks.

I should know this is one of them, but it's hard to think when his lips are so warm, tasting bitter-sweet like beer when he kisses me, right in front of everyone. It's impossible when he whispers in my ear, "You're so pretty. Want to go upstairs?" And I'm too far gone by the time I'm up in his room, taking in the *boyness* of every-thing; the scent of his body spray, the box of condoms on his dresser, the grinning Devil on the flag hanging over his messy, unmade bed.

"Do you live out here by yourself?" I ask, chills running down my spine from the feel of his lips on my neck. "Not in the main house?"

"I like how it's quiet," he answers, voice deep and smooth. "Private."

It's not quiet now—well, not downstairs. Down there, the party is in full swing; alcohol, skinny dipping, loud music. The bass vibrates through the guest cottage walls, shaking the dresser mirror with every thump and thud. It's a crazy party, one made even crazier by the fact I was invited by Heston Wilcox himself.

He crosses the room and stops in front of his desk, fussing with a laptop. Music streams through the speakers, covering up the rowdy rap from downstairs. The curve of his shoulders, the way he moves—sure and masculine—makes something low in my belly spark.

I know how it is for guys. They have to flirt and put on a bunch of pretenses to get into a girl's pants. I've seen the games.

I'm not here to play.

I know what I want, and I know how to get it. No frills, no bullshit. I want on Heston's dick, like ten minutes ago, and I'm not about to make him work for it.

I take off my sweater and take a quick glance in the mirror to adjust my purple lace bra. The bra makes my tits look fantastic, probably my best feature. Guys are super into them and I know it.

When Heston turns back to me, he blinks once, slow and long, as he takes me in.

My stomach flips at the intensity of his gaze. "It seems so grown-up to be out here alone. No parents, free to do whatever you want." I watch as his fingers tug at the zipper on his hoodie, and he shrugs it off, tossing it on the back of a chair. Next he removes his shirt and I'm treated to his lean and long body. The perfect swimmer's physique. "It's cool that you can have parties like this, even though you're only a junior in high school, and no one cares. My dad is pretty strict—"

His mouth is on mine, cutting me off, tongue pushing through my lips. His fingers move quickly, confidently, under my bra strap. "Fuck, you're stacked," he says, eyeing my tits hungrily. He's right. My tits *are* big. He circles my nipple with his fingers, sending a tremor between my legs. He pinches it and grins. "You like that?"

Electricity zings through my body. Pain and pleasure. I arch back against it. "I do."

"I heard you like it dirty," he says, biting on my earlobe.

I'm distracted by his upper body. The hard lines of his chest and abs. I parse his words and look up, feeling dazed. "What?"

"I heard you like it dirty and *hard*," he says, kissing me, lips rough against mine. One hand circles my waist, thumb digging into my flesh while the other squeezes my breast.

"Who told you that?" I ask, reaching for the button on his jeans. I unzip his pants and pull his cock out. I just about die when I get my hands on him, a slow heat building between my legs. He's long and thick. Big like the rumors. Warm and ready.

His hips buck forward, pushing it into my palm. He shrugs at my question and gives me a smirk. "Think you can take that?"

I open my mouth to answer, to tell him I'm not a virgin and I'm ready to do this, but he kisses me again, harder this time, using his body to angle me to the bed. I try to keep up with his kisses, with his warm tongue, and when the back of my knees hit the mattress, I run my hands down his chest, hoping to slow him down. This isn't like Reilly from Spanish, or Trevor from The Nerd, or Lance from my parents' Christmas party. Being with a guy like Heston is something I want to savor.

"You're so sexy," I tell him, kissing along his shoulders.

He cups my face in his hands and grins down at me, a twinkle in his eye. In that moment, I feel like I'm the only girl he sees. The only one he wants. I feel special. His thumb runs down my cheek, and he bends to kiss me. Sparks ignite across my body, down my limbs, to my fingers and toes. His hand runs down to the hem of my skirt and then back up, fingers twisting tight in my panties. When the kiss breaks, I look at him once again.

"You want this, right?"

"Yes," I admit, but as I say it, something feels... *off*. It's the change in his expression. It's the feel of my panties digging into my sides. It's the dark glaze in his eye that tells me I'm not entirely sure what it is I'm agreeing to.

"Good." He moves faster than I can blink, using his size, power, and athleticism against me. He pushes me back on the bed and before I can bounce, he's on top of me, yanking my panties down my thighs in a sharp motion. His cock presses into me, hard and intimidating. He shifts and thrusts a finger inside, making me gasp. "Jesus, you're tight. Sure you're not a virgin? Is Halloway a liar?"

I blink, trying to follow his words while he fucks me with his finger. *John Halloway?* We'd hooked up a few times over the summer. I'd gone down on him behind the tennis courts at the club and let him fuck me at the Fourth of July party. Did he say something to Heston?

"I'm not a virgin," I gasp out, trying to get into the rhythm. Heston moves fast, hard. It's a challenge to keep up. I sit up to meet him, to find his mouth. He withdraws his finger and plants a hand right into the middle of my chest, shoving me back down flat. He waits for a beat, glancing over to the laptop. From this angle, he's like a magnificent animal, muscle stretched tight, corded and perfected. I reach for his cock, stroking it with my fingers. He looks down on me, his expression shuttered, and falls forward, both hands cinched roughly around my wrists. I grimace but spread my legs, giving him access.

This isn't quite like Reilly, or Lance, or Trevor, or even John, who fucked me hard in the coat closet. There's this spark in Heston's eye, a strange tightness at the corners of his jaw. He's just excited, I think—*by me*—but a dark shadow flickers across his face, and a chill settles in my belly. It intensifies when his grip grows tighter and I say, "Wait, can you—"

His hand loosens, but not to release me. It's just enough to gain leverage so that he can flip me on my stomach. The heavy weight of his hand presses on my lower back and I twist my head to the side. "Heston, I—" but the air stalls in my lungs, pushed out by the weight of his hand around my neck, curling around my throat. Over the music, I hear the tear of foil and the sound of him rolling the rubber down. My heartbeat is like thunder now, but I can't untangle the threads of fear and arousal long enough to decide which wins. I squirm against his hold, and the thing is, I've been with a few guys by now. I've been with the sweet ones and the rough ones. The clumsy ones and the experienced ones. Generally, I'm down to try every flavor.

Absolutely nothing has made me as wet as I am right this second.

A moment later, fingers dig into my hip, lifting me up, and he enters me fast and hard, the sound of our flesh coming together a deafening slap.

It strikes me then what that tight, dark shadow on his face reminds me of.

Like someone who wants to hurt me.

I close my eyes and let him.

Afterwards, when we're pulling on our clothes, he looks different again. Relaxed, calm. Like everything is normal, totally casual. I try my best to mirror this, taking my cues from the way he moves languorously around his room, pulling on a clean shirt, even though there's a lump wedged in the back of my throat.

He says goodbye with a two-fingered wave, goes back to join the party, and barely looks at me again the rest of the night.

An hour later, I'm back in Campbell's car. It's quiet again. I don't try to make small talk this time, instead staring out the window at the passing streetlights, wondering what this knot is that's taken residence in my chest.

It was just sex.

Truthfully, I don't even really mind that he blew me off after. That's what guys do. If they want some more, then they'll start being nice again, paying me attention. I'm used to it. Probably better off anyway, because boyfriends are just drama and a long stretch of same-same boring.

It was just... not the kind of sex I'm used to. Hot, but also cold. It felt good, but also hurt. It was nice, but also mean. Savage. Scary. Heston's a powerful guy—a lot stronger than me. Being at his mercy like that—being hurt like that—should have been repulsive and terrifying, and in some ways, it was.

Mostly, it was the best sex I've ever had.

My cheeks burn with shame, because I might be young, and maybe I've only slept with a few guys, but I'm pretty sure that's not what sex is supposed to be—even casual hookups at parties with older guys. I already hear whispers behind my back at school, that I'm easy. What would people say if they knew I liked... that?

From beside me, Campbell lets out this long sigh. "Are you, like... okay, or whatever?"

I turn to her, blinking in surprise. "Yeah."

"Heston didn't do anything to you, did he?" Her gaze slides over to me. "Something you didn't want? You're not drunk or stoned?"

"I'm not drunk," I assure her. I had a beer, but it was gross and I ended up ditching it halfway through. "And Heston didn't..." I swallow, feeling a moment of panic that maybe she knows. Maybe she's looking at me like that because she's perfectly aware that I'm some kind of sexual freak. Meekly, I finish, "Everything's fine."

Everything's *fine*.

~

"Damn," Emory Hall says, leaning over Ansel's shoulder. They're sitting at their little lunch table, looking at Ansel's phone. I walk by, wedged between trying to catch Heston's eye and pretending like I don't care if he looks at me at all. It's been a month since the party, and although he hasn't outright rejected me, he also doesn't seem like he wants to come back for more.

In any case, I certainly never got an invitation to sit at the table or any of the perks the Playthings get. I'd nearly talked myself into believing it'd been his 'test', but if it had been, then I must have passed.

I *must* have.

"God, he's just drilling her," Carlton says, holding up his own phone. Hamilton glances over and then away with a bored look. Xavier sits with his arm around Skylar Adams—*that's new*—who wrinkles her nose in distaste.

"Are those even real?" Ansel asks. "They're huge."

My eyes skim the room and see that almost everyone has their phone out. The reactions vary—wide-eyed, amused, impressed. I make my way over to a table with the other freshman girls that I know from soccer. Every one of them has their phones out, eyes glued to the screen.

"What's everyone looking at?" I ask, sliding into my seat and placing my tray on the table.

"You've got to see this," Amanda says.

Betsy frowns and puts her phone face down on the table. "This video that just went viral. It's... gross."

"Oh god, is it another video of some guy squirting milk from his nose?" I dig in my bag for my phone and see that I have a dozen notifications—maybe more. People are sharing the video like wildfire. I open up my phone, going to my ChattySnap account. The video is in the top ten spots. I click on one, and although it takes my brain a second to adjust to what I'm seeing, my body reacts differently, going fiery hot and ice cold, all at once. I know instantly, a ball of nausea building when I process what's happening on the screen.

It's a girl face down on the bed, a strong naked guy pounding into her while he holds her down. Neither of their faces are visible. Her hair covers her features, and he manages to stay just off screen. Bile runs up the back of my throat and I swallow it back.

The girl is me.

"Who—who is that?" I ask, pretending to narrow my eyes.

"No clue. Not even sure if it's from Preston. It just started popping up all over today." Amanda peers over at my phone. "Can you see anything identifiable? Like something that would tell whose room that is?"

I've spent all month trying to forget about hooking up with Heston. How off it was. How *bad* it felt afterward, when I was sore and spent, and wishing pathetically for one soft touch. How it was too hard, and too fast, and how despite all that, I've been alternately relieved and confusingly disappointed that he's not like those other guys who wanted to come back for more.

Looking at the video, small pieces click into place. The way he preened toward the laptop. How he kept me down and my face covered. How we didn't speak, how I *couldn't* speak with his fingers around my throat. How, when it was over, he wouldn't make eye contact. No, that's not right. His eyes were dark and emotionless. Cold.

Speculation flows around me, while all I can do is stare at the video, looking for anything that would identify it as me. Thank god my hair looks more brown than red. How long will it be before everyone finds out that it's me? That I let him do that to me? That I *liked* it? I finally shut it off, eyes stinging and every inch of my skin feeling the warm heat of humiliation. The rest of the table is still obsessed, eyes glued to their phones. I glance over at the table of Devils, and Heston's all grins, looking smug and proud.

For the first time in weeks, he meets my eyes.

And winks.

1

FROM THE SWEAT on Mrs. Gilbert's upper lip, you'd never think the guidance counseling office feels like an icebox, an arctic vortex of cold air rattling through the vents. It must be menopause, I think, crossing and uncrossing my long legs.

"Your schedule looks good," she says, ticking off boxes on a sheet of paper. "Even with the time off, you got all your required classes completed, except," she looks at me over her bifocals, "Physical Education."

"What?" I shift restlessly, my skin feeling stretched a bit too tight. "I thought P.E. was exempt since I played a sport."

"P.E. is exempt if you play a *varsity* sport. For two seasons. You only have half of a JV season from freshman year." Her eyes dart up to me and I wait for her to say it. They *always* have to say it. "Which you missed when—"

"I missed a semester. I know." I sigh, reaching down to pluck at the rubber band on my wrist. I barely flinch at the snap and pinch anymore. "Are you seriously going to make me take P.E. with a bunch of underclassmen?"

"Georgia," she says, in that ever-so-patient voice reserved for students whose parents pay seventy thousand dollars a year in tuition to this place. "We discussed all of this last spring. I sent you emails over the summer. I even texted you. There's no getting out of P.E. Every student needs their Physical Ed credits, no exceptions."

"Fine," I say, straightening. "I'll take yoga."

"Yoga is no longer available."

I deflate. "Your text said yoga, volleyball, or swim." Even the thought of the last one makes me cringe. "Why can't I do yoga?"

"Because I sent that text in June. Now it's full." She glances at the computer. "So is volleyball."

"So my only choice is swim?" I give my runner band another hard pull. Just my rotten luck. "Problem is, I'm not a great swimmer."

She smiles placidly. "It's an intro class."

Nervously, I elaborate, "I don't think you understand, Mrs. Gilbert. It's not that I'm *bad* at swimming. It's that I can't. Like, at all."

"You'll be fine," she insists, waving this off. "Coach James is a great instructor. And just think, you'll finally learn how to swim!" She says this like it's some amazing prize.

"Whatever," I mutter. Taking that semester off has been nothing but a pain in my ass ever since. It follows me around like a nasty rash. It was freshman year, for fuck's sake.

"Now that we have all that settled," she says, closing my academic folder, "tell me how things are going."

She gives me another 'look' and now we've entered the mental health checkup part of the meeting. I adjust the silver bracelets on my arm, trying to hide the rubber band. I've been using it since seventh grade. All my counselors say it isn't a healthy coping mechanism, but personally, I think they're wrong. A summer spent on my parent's yacht, sailing the Caribbean, without a single lay is proof of that.

It's not that I'm going cold turkey on sex or anything. I'm just setting boundaries. Limits. Reasonable goals. Four times per year— every three months. It's totally fine. Quality is better than quantity, anyway. It's like that dieting thing—intermittent fasting?—except with dick.

Intermittent dick fasting.

It's not so bad. Sure, sex is all I can think about seventy percent of the time and my skin stopped feeling right about ten weeks ago, but truthfully, I've done great without dick. Totally great. Really, it's been a huge reprieve. With all the time I've saved hunting for nice abs, I've even picked up some hobbies along the way. Calligraphy. Knitting. Beadwork. An ever-growing, finely curated database of all my favorite internet porn.

I pull my rubber band again.

Snap!

If I don't get laid soon, I might fucking *die*.

"I'm good," I say instead. "I spent the summer with my family. No social media, no drama, no problems whatsoever." It'd been a nice vacation from reality. Specifically, the reality of Heston Wilcox's court case.

"That's nice to hear. And your medication? Everything going okay with that?"

I loathe people knowing my business. I know it's part of the deal with them allowing me back in after I took the semester off, but still. I swallow back the irritation. "No changes with my meds. My shrink says they're working."

Mrs. Gilbert frowns at the word 'shrink' and scribbles some notes on her pad. *Jesus.*

"Now, I know a lot of your friends graduated last spring. Are you worried about anything, socially?"

Am I sad most of the Devils have graduated? Obviously. The Devils are my only real friends. I already know things this year are going to be a little harder—a little colder—without all of them beside me. "It stinks, but I still have friends here. Vandy Hall and Caroline Richmond?" Her eyebrows raise and I know she wants more. "I'm excited about my senior year. I'm ready to fill out those college applications and experience all the good things, like homecoming, prom, whatever comes in between."

I told my mother I'm done with having a roommate. Six in four years is enough. She agreed, so I secured one of the suites. Naturally, my twin brother, George, threw a fit about it and demanded one of his own. It's a drop in the hat for them financially, and the least they can do considering the hell I'm going to have to go through this year. My mother is beyond excited about all the senior traditions, and I know I have little choice but to take part in them. The suite is a fair tradeoff, but also painfully ironic.

Figures the year I'd start valuing quality over quantity is the same year I score my very own sex pad.

Snap!

Mrs. Gilbert looks suspiciously at the sound. "I just want to make sure you know that I'm here for whatever you need as you prepare for graduation." She drones on about credits, references, and early admission applications. "Or even just to talk, Georgia. You can always come to me. I want this to be an exceptional year for you."

"Don't worry, Mrs. Gilbert." I smile tightly. "I plan on it being my best."

She assures me she'll send me my updated schedule, and I walk out of her office and cross the campus. Already, the awareness of this being my last year here makes everything feel a little bittersweet. I've been through a lot during my time at Preston—some good, some really shitty. After hooking up with Heston Wilcox that night freshman year, the video of us spread like wildfire. Even though people never figured out it was me—even though Heston remarkably told no one—when the video went viral, I just lost it. I stopped eating, stopped sleeping. I stopped *caring*. I did reckless, stupid things, like three guys at one party. My grades plummeted. I stopped showering, because the thought of being exposed made me physically ill, and my roommate couldn't handle it. She went to the counselor.

But not before I tried to end it all.

Ultimately, I got sent to a treatment program. It was more summer camp than a mental hospital. Located two blocks from the beach, Sunny Hills was a behavioral health center, all dressed up as a luxury resort. Yoga and meditation were daily requirements. We ate all organic, locally sourced food, and at night, when the staff wasn't looking, smoked weed and snuck into one another's bedrooms.

That's where the psychiatrist labeled what happened a 'major depressive episode' and used the term 'bipolar tendencies' to explain away some of my more erratic behavior. To be fair, the meds did chill me out some. The highs and lows evened out, and after six months I came back home, ready to slide back into my mess of a life.

I take the meds, because I do feel better. But there's one thing that the meds, yoga, exercise, or any of the other hippie shit I've tried can't touch.

Nothing manages to stop this intense, bone-deep, fucking *constant*, all-consuming urge to get off.

It wasn't something I revealed until last spring, after I turned Heston in for spreading that video. That's when my doctor added 'hypersexuality' to the list of things wrong with me. Much like my finely curated database of porn, that list is also ever growing.

Everyone likes a good orgasm. The problem is, one doesn't do it for me. Try five. Or ten. People think I want it all the time, but they're wrong. I *need* it all the time. It's this sweltering heat that crawls under my skin until I feel like I'm vibrating at a frequency that everyone can sense. It's worse than an itch. Sometimes, even the thought of not having it *hurts*. Even now, walking across campus, seeing guys walking by, knowing that I could get one of them in the abandoned computer lab, pants around their ankles, sinking down into their lap—doesn't matter who, anyone will do— and finally feel the warmth and hardness deep inside...

Snap!

I spot Vandy leaning against one of the enormous oak trees and walk over. Her blonde hair is even longer now, lighter, touched by the sun of summer, just like the slight freckles dusting the bridge of her nose. She's scribbling in a notebook, which is no surprise. Her mom is a hot-shot journalist, and Vandy wants to follow in her footsteps. I know she's constantly trying to get the newspaper advisor, Mr. Lee, to let her do a deep dive on the dirty underbelly of Preston Prep. Unfortunately, Preston doesn't want its belly exposed. All she ever gets are hard no's.

"Hey girl," I say, walking up and bumping her with my hip.

"Georgia!" Her eyes light up when she sees me. She almost tackles me, flinging her arms around my neck as she squeals in delight. I press my nose into her hair, not bothering to temper my smile. The Devils—Vandy—are home to me now. "I missed you so much!"

"I missed you, too," I say, meaning it. "How was your summer?"

"Fantastic," she says, blue eyes sparkling back at me.

I raise an eyebrow. "Fuck around with Reyn a lot?"

Her cheeks turn pink, even though she throws me a playful scowl. "We spent a lot of time together, yeah."

Those two. Cute as a tragic button. All hot and scarred. A perfect fucking match. If I can manage this whole intermittent dick fasting thing, then I'm probably going to need to live vicariously through Vandy's sex life.

"What about you?" she asks. "How was the Caribbean?"

I flap a hand. "Oh, you know. Daddy was all about the sailing. Mommy was all about the shopping. I was all about the—"

"Hooking up with cute surfer guys." Even though she laughs, I can hear the tension in it. She worries about me. Ever since she found out I was the girl in the video, she's looked at me differently. That's the worst part, to be honest. It's exactly what I always feared. The sex with Heston was rough. Hard. Fast.

Snap!

Either people see me as a victim of assault, or they think I'm a sex freak. Neither is the whole truth, just two mangled halves of it. No one would really understand, anyway.

"No," I correct her, giving her a nudge. "I shopped. I ate. I read a lot of books and got sunburned." I look down at my still pale skin. The curse of being a redhead. "George and my dad fished constantly. It was fun."

Vandy's nose wrinkles at the mention of my twin brother, George. He had a crush on her junior year—until Reyn swooped in and marked her as his own. Literally. She has his Devil's mark tattooed on the inside of her thigh.

"Have you heard from Sugar?" she asks, looping her bag over a delicate shoulder. "I got a few postcards. It looks like she and Sebastian had an awesome road trip. I'm kind of jealous."

Sugar Voss was my transfer roommate from the year before. We became good friends, and then she started dating my other good friend, Sebastian. Wilcox. Brother of Heston.

Yeah, things around Preston tend to get a little incestuous after a while.

"Yes, I got some too," I reply, thinking of the stack of cards up in my dorm room. "And according to ChattySnap, they're snug up at Yale, far, far away from the drama of our little school."

Vandy bites down on her bottom lip. "Come on, after last year, don't you think maybe the drama is over for a bit? Sydney's parents forced her to transfer. Sugar and Bass are happy. Emory is at college. Heston is...well, wherever he is. Jail, I hope." She grins slyly. "And we're going to initiate a few new Devils to make up for the ones that graduated. It's our senior year. It's going to be epic. I can feel it!"

Oh, Vandy. She's so fucking optimistic, sometimes I wonder if she's still popping pills.

"So what are you doing here?" I ask, the two of us ambling slowly across the courtyard. "You didn't move on campus, did you?"

She snorts. "God, like my mother would let me move out of the house. It's going to be hard enough getting her to accept me going to college." Vandy survived a wicked car accident right before our freshman year. It took her a long time to recover, and she still has a significant limp. Her parents and brother, Emory, have been a tad overprotective ever since. But now Emory has graduated, she has a sexy boyfriend who's taking a gap year, and I see the flicker of determination in her eyes as she clutches the notebook against her chest. "I'm trying to get inspiration for an expose for the paper. *Again.* Unfortunately, nothing feels right."

"I'm sure you'll come up with something."

My phone vibrates, and I look at the screen.

I freeze, feeling myself vibrate at that special frequency. It's no surprise that I feel like this—wound tight, trapped inside my skin, nerves firing on all cylinders—knowing that it's so close.

Because my last hook-up was on the final day of my junior year.

Three months ago.

I've spent the entire week approaching this—who I want to match with—as the sophisticated operation it should be. I had an easier time choosing which car I wanted my dad to buy me. I'm not just picking any random Preston guy to break my dick-fast with.

In fact, I refuse to fuck a Preston guy ever again. I'm over all high school guys, actually, with their petty drama and all the shitty comments behind my back. I'm over the way they all fuck, more concerned about getting a quick nut than actually having good sex. I'm over their inexperienced fumbling, completely lacking in assertiveness. I'm *so over* feeling like I have to ask for it harder.

I'm humming so strongly with excitement that I briefly consider telling Vandy about everything. The temporary celibacy. How good I've been. About the fact I'm going to go hog fucking wild on some dick tonight.

But then I remember the tense sound of her laughter before.

I don't want her to worry about me.

"I've got to go," I tell her, sliding the phone back into my pocket. "I have a ton to do before school starts tomorrow."

She waves and I walk off, pulling out my phone once I'm far enough away. I open up the notification and it takes me straight to the app; AcadaNeeds. It's a hook-up app, not a dating site, and it's hard as hell to get verified. This is the better way—vetting someone carefully instead of caving to an impulse.

"Wow," I mutter when I see the attached photo. Over course I've seen the picture on his profile before, but it's no less blood-stirring. It's one of the primary reasons I'd swiped him. My eyes skim over the broad, well-defined chest. It's not one of those cheesy bathroom pics, either. He's waist deep in a clear blue swimming pool, revealing a ladder of impressive abs and a delicious happy trail. He's got a long, lean, well-toned swimmer's body that's already been featured in my late-night relief sessions a dozen or more times.

His screen name is admittedly the epitome of cringe.

HotWetCox

But that photo alongside his bio was a sure seller.

Not looking for any weak bitches. If you can't take a good rough fuck, then don't bother wasting my time. I fuck hard and I make it hurt.

The photo was good, but it's the bio that got me. I've been waiting—hoping, praying—that he'd swipe on my profile, too. I'm not stupid enough to think that one lay will get me through the next three months, but a good, rough fuck will certainly be as close as I could get.

I pause, staring down at the photo, feeling warm heat spread through my limbs. One dick to get me through the next three months, and this is *it*.

Looking around me to make sure no one is watching, I swipe across the screen. Like I told Mrs. Gilbert, I'm ready to make this my best year yet.

Meet me at Underworld. 9pm. You'll be on the list. Wear something red and short.

I tuck the phone into my purse, adjusting the short hem of my dress. Underworld is a shady, lame-ass club that no one at Preston would ever deign to step within five blocks of.

Or, at least, it used to be.

Last time I saw this place, it was full of tweakers and rollers, shitty rave music pulsing from the cracks in the windows. It's been completely overhauled, repainted, new lights, a distinct class of cars parked out front. I step out of mine, gaping up at the glowing 'Underworld' sign hanging over the entrance.

When the hell did *this* happen?

There's a line at the door, maybe two dozen people waiting for entry. I'm not about to go to the end of it. A burly man is guarding the door—bouncer, I assume. A grumpy guy at the front of the line gives me a look as I approach him.

"Oh, come on," he says, the stench of bad cologne hanging around him like a cloud. "If you're twenty-one, then I'm a poodle. Get to the back of the line, little girl."

I hide my nerves with a raised eyebrow, striding confidently up to the bouncer. "I'm RedFox." I'm not vain—not exactly. I just come from a world that understands exactly what it takes to achieve a certain level of beauty. I'm thin but curvy. My tits are big *and* real. My eyes are a deep, emerald green that I know how to flirt with. My hair is a shiny, almost metallic kind of red that people pay a lot of money to replicate. Tonight, I'm wearing a dress that shows off my cleavage and legs. Stacked sandals give me another four inches of height, and I left my long hair down, grazing midway down my back.

I don't need to be on the list to get into this place.

The bouncer shrewdly holds my gaze as he pulls a clipboard from behind him. It only takes one flick of his eyes for his expression to neutralize. "Welcome to Underworld, Miss Fox." I follow the sweep of his arm into the door, shooting the surly cologne man a smirk from over my shoulder.

God, I love rich guys.

Inside, it's both dark and bright. There's still pulsing music—that hasn't changed—but it's less frantic. The club is crowded, but it's still early. There's an energy in the air, like it's still charging, lights jumping around like smoky lasers.

HotWetCox hadn't told me where to find him—or *how* to find him—but I know he'll find me. Red dress. Short. So horny that my back molars ache from grinding. I decide my best bet is the bar, so I weave between a group of rowdy college students to make my way there.

I choose a spot far away from the action and don't bother sitting. I lean my elbows on the bar top and give the woman behind the counter a cool nod.

"Some club soda, please?" I've never had drunk sex worth writing home about. As I wait, accepting the soda with a small thanks, I wonder where this HotWetCox is going to take me. I'm starting to not even care. The static under my skin is getting beyond unbearable. I'd take it in a dirty club bathroom at this point.

I don't have to wonder for long.

Two masculine hands come down on the bar, belonging to the two arms bracketing me from behind. I inhale against the large, ominous presence of him, his biceps brushing my shoulders. I can just barely feel the tip of a nose skimming my hair.

I shiver.

"Here's what's going to happen," a low voice rumbles into my ear, making me freeze. "You're going to take that staircase to the left, walk to the back of the lounge, and go into the office there. You're going to pull your panties off, bend over, and hike that dress up your hips." He leans into me, mouth brushing the shell of my ear. "Then I'm going to fuck you so hard, you'll be limping out of here. Any problem with that, Red?"

My wide, horrified eyes jump to his hands, one long forefinger tapping against the wood. My heart is suddenly vibrating more than anything else, because I know.

I *know* that voice.

Heston Wilcox has me caged in, but I'm not a dumb little Freshman anymore. I reach into my purse, wrapping my hand around the can of pepper spray my dad had insisted I attach to my key ring, and then I whirl around, striking out. My palm meets a solid wall of chest, shoving him back. He barely even moves.

At least, not until he really sees me.

Heston's face shutters and then hardens, body jerking away. "You cannot be fucking serious."

I brandish the pepper spray canister, my keys jangling loudly as I raise it. "Step back, or so fucking help me—"

His nostrils flare wide, jaw ticking. "What the fuck is this?" He swipes out and snatches the pepper spray, key ring and all, in one swift, effortless move. "Did my brother put you up to this?"

I flinch away, both at the quick motion and the way he advances on me, red-hot fury in his eyes. "You're HotWetCox," I realize, disgust roiling in my gut.

"Let me guess. You're recording with your phone," he says, tossing my keys carelessly onto the bar. "Think you can catch me fucking with you so you can turn me in again? Not going to happen." I'm still trying to process the man in front of me. He looks the same—devastatingly hot—but he also looks tired, a little ragged around the edges. There are dark marks under his eyes and his shirt is uncharacteristically rumpled. He gives me a scathing look, lip curling back. "Like I'd ever go for the bitch who sold me out."

Some of that horror holding me prisoner melts away, leaving only the hard exterior of my hatred for him. I snatch my keys from the bar without breaking his gaze. "Don't flatter yourself. I'd rather shove a rusty fork into my eye than be bait for you."

He laughs, but it's flat and barbed, completely lacking in humor. That cold, mean glint in his eyes makes my spine want to jump out of my body and flee. "No, of course not. It's far more believable that you're whoring yourself out on the internet, *Little Red Riding Cocks*."

Bristling, I sneer back. "Shouldn't you be taking a fat one from behind, *in prison*?"

He moves faster than my eyes can process it, a big palm seizing the column of my neck. I gasp, jerking away, but I just knock into the bar, unable to run. His eyes burn into mine, teeth clenched. "You think this is joke, Haynes? You think it's funny that you ruined my fucking life?"

I stare up at him, wide-eyed. The Heston I know is ruthless, cold, and mean. But outside of the rough sex, he isn't the violent kind. That trait fell to the other Wilcox brother. But *this* Heston is ragged and frayed, something else altogether, and it means he's unpredictable. I can tell because I'd know that wild thing sparking in his eyes anywhere. It's probably sparking in mine as we speak.

It's the byproduct of deprivation.

"Go ahead." I swallow, knowing that he feels it against his palm. "Leave a mark on me, Heston. I'll have you thrown back in jail so fast, you won't even have time to close your AcadaNeeds account."

His jaw goes sharper, and he lurches back, snatching his hand away like my throat is fire. "You weren't worth it then, and you're not worth it now." He tilts his head, smirking cruelly. "You can run back to your bitches and tell them I don't take public access pussy. If they want to trap me, they're going to have to find someone who isn't the community cum dumpster."

The glass of club soda is right by my hand and it's more reflex than anything, the way I fling the contents in his face. Distantly, I can hear jeers and laughter coming from the loft above, but mostly I just hear the rush of my charged pulse as I watch him blink the moisture from his eyes. I slam the glass on the counter and don't give that ember of fury in his eyes long enough to fully combust.

I don't run, but it's a close thing.

Even outside, gulping in hard lungfuls of the cool night air, my heart still feels jumpy and off kilter. I press my fingers to my pulse as I dart to my car, willing it to calm. It's like at some point my heart had arranged itself to the throb of the music inside, and now it doesn't know its own rhythm.

It's quieter inside the car, and I can hear my hands shaking when I jam my key into the ignition, rattling the pepper spray canister against the metal. I rest there for a moment, dragging in a series of deep breaths, and I want to scream, because I just keep remembering.

Remembering the way those arms felt, bracketing me in.

Snap!

Snap! Snap! Snap! Snap! Snap! Snap! Snap!

2

I LICK the liquid from the top of my lip, tasting it. It's club soda, so at least I won't have to worry about another goddamn 'contribution to the delinquency of a minor' charge. I'm going to have to talk to Kevin about carding everyone at the door—even my random Sunday night internet pussy.

Shit.

Especially my random Sunday night internet pussy.

I hear the obnoxious, wheezing laughter coming from the balcony above, but I ignore it, reaching behind the bar to snatch a towel from the shelf. We'd drawn some looks with that little show, but I can't focus on anything but the paranoid whirr of my thoughts and the way it's making my stomach burn.

Too tacky and unseemly for my father, and my brother's off at Yale living large on what was supposed to be my life. Sebastian isn't smart enough to come up with that, anyway. Had to be the Preston bitches. Most of them might have graduated, but they still have their little circle of scheming bullshit.

Am I just paranoid because I have—in the past, once or twice—

recorded a few girls without their knowledge? Probably not. Georgia Haynes showing up at my club can't be a coincidence. Not in that sexy little dress. Not after what she fucking did.

The bartender pulls a face when I throw the towel at him, stalking away to the stairs, but he won't say anything. Not if he wants to keep his job. And the thing is, he does. Underworld has been booming since the start of winter.

Since I bought it.

I knew pretty much the second I walked onto campus that college wasn't really my bag. But as the heir to the Wilcox fortune, there were expectations, standards. I played the role for a while, but my patience wore thin quick. I wanted to make money—my *own* money.

My father's money always came with short strings attached. He wanted to oversee every investment, dipping his hands into my goddamn business. Every suggestion I made was wrong. Too risky. Too short-term. "Investment is a long game," he'd say, shooing me aside like an annoying fly. My father's all about tradition, too steeped in the old ways to see the big picture, like me.

My brother, Sebastian, was my first cash cow. He's a fighter, through and through. All about talking with his fists and throwing tantrums. We might hate each other's guts, but even I have to admit the kid excels at what he does. Naturally. He *is* a Wilcox. It was easy to set shit up, to get him into a makeshift ring and bet on him to win a fight. When he moved on to street racing, it was just as easy to exploit that. The kid doesn't have an abundance of brains, but when it comes to speed and hitting things, he's on.

It leaves a sour taste in my mouth as I climb the stairs to the VIP lounge. The bitches of Preston Prep turned me in and got me arrested, just because I recorded a couple videos of us fucking. It was all bullshit, though. Both Haynes and Sydney fully consented to everything that happened in those videos, and they fucking knew it. The whole thing was a stunt to save my dumbass brother from having to fight. The cops didn't really seem to give a shit, though, and neither did my parents. My father cut me off. My mom banned me from the house. I got kicked out of school—not that I can pay for it, anyway. My trust fund is gone. My access to any Wilcox privileges has been solidly rescinded. I lost everything.

Everything except for *this*.

Underworld is the only thing I legally own. I won it in a bet I'd made on one of Sebastian's fights, and now it's my sole asset. It's where I eat, fuck, shower, and sleep. It's the sum of my parts. It's the closest thing I've got to building a future anymore. Almost everything it's earned has gone right back into making it stronger, better, more successful. A year ago, this place was a run-down rave dump. Now, I'm a few weeks shy of setting up valet. The streets are buzzing with the word of it. I took this pile of shit and made it fucking *shine*.

Just one minor problem, though.

"Struck out, eh, Wilcox?" Big Gene throws his arm around my neck as soon as I hit the VIP landing, boisterously dragging me to his usual table. It overlooks the dance floor and bar, and it's exactly where I find his ass parked, every goddamn night, from open to closing. "I thought pretty boys like you could get pussy easier than all that. Must be the new lack of money thing."

I cut him a thinly veiled glare as he slides back into his booth. Despite the name, Gene is short and twiggy, a deceptively small physical presence. "Are you comfortable?" I ask, giving him a haughty grin. "I can have Tara get you another drink." I gesture with two fingers to Tara, who's waiting behind the VIP bar. She knows the routine by now. If I get him nice and drunk, there's a chance he'll leave early. His flunkies, always camped out down below, probably won't, but that's another thing altogether.

He takes the drink, giving Tara a slimy grin. Embarrassing to watch, if I'm being honest. Gene's probably forty-years-old and Tara's barely twenty-one. She doesn't even notice, though, since she only has eyes for me, sliding me a glass of whiskey before she leaves. Big Gene is right about one thing. It'd be easy for me to score pussy. Tara's been gagging for my dick since I interviewed her back in March. She's not really my type though. Too clingy. Plus, she has thick, hardy skin. I have an eye for these things. She doesn't bruise easily.

And anyway, when it comes to business, I don't shit where I eat.

"So what did you do?" Gene asks, spreading his arms across the back of the booth. "You neg her?" At my blank look, he adds, "You know, compliment her with an insult. Negging."

"I know what negging is, Gene." Jesus Christ, I was negging girls when I was in fourth fucking grade. I throw my drink back, swallowing it down in a single gulp. I regret it the second it hits my stomach, increasing the burn. "She's one of the bitches who turned me in last spring. That shitty, anonymous hook-up app matched us. It was a fluke."

Of course I swiped on her picture. In it, she was sprawled out on the deck of a yacht in this little green bikini, head thrown back, red hair tumbling down her shoulders, framing a pair of tits that would make anyone look twice. Even with her face too obscured by the angle and a pair of large sunglasses, I should have known it was her. I've seen those tits. Felt them. Watched them on video and committed them to memory. They're a lot bigger now. More than once, I've heard some guys wondering if she went away freshman year to get implants, but I know better. Georgia's just always been fucking stacked.

He lets out a low whistle. "Daddy's girl doesn't want to ride your carousel anymore, is that it?"

Scoffing, I reply, "I could fuck her if I wanted. Georgia Haynes doesn't discriminate."

"That's not what it looked like to me." He shrugs, taking a tiny sip from his glass. Classic fucking Gene, taking his time, making himself at home in my fucking club. "You know what I think it is? I think you're losing your charm, son. Happens sometimes when men get out into the real world."

I clench my teeth, only barely holding back what I really want to say to this fucker. *I'm not your fucking son.* "Charm has nothing to do with it. Her cunt will fall on anything."

He hums. "Anything except you."

"You don't know what you're talking about, old man," I bite out, fed up. Every night it's the same shit—Gene trying to provoke me, always pushing and prodding. I tolerate a lot of shit from this guy and his flunkies, but after seeing Georgia here tonight, I don't have the patience for it. "For the record, I don't need some balding Northridge failure to teach me how to pull tail. No one negs anymore. Negging's for middle-schoolers who spend too much time on X-Box Live and old fucks who still think hitting on their servers is anything more than a complete waste of time." I give Tara a meaningful look.

Gene stares at me, lips flattening into a tense line.

Well, so much for holding back.

"Fine." He sets down his drink, leaning forward to rest his elbows on the table. From the dark gleam in his eye, I'm already dreading what's about to come out of his mouth. "Why don't we make a wager, then?"

I wave to Tara for a refill, sensing from the way my pulse quickens that I'm going to need it. "A wager on what?"

"Whether or not you can fuck that feisty redhead, of course." He smirks at Tara when she stops to take my glass, sliding me another.

"Fuck no," I say instantly, head shaking. "I start my community service tomorrow, and my PO has been so far up my ass, he can probably smell my breath. The last thing I need is my Ghost of Bad Fucks Past running to the sheriff again."

Gene leans back, thumb tapping the table as he watches me. "If you win, I'll cut your debt in half."

I freeze, drink halfway to my mouth, before slowly putting it down. "You can't be serious." *Fuck.* That's fifty grand off my debt.

"Oh, I can be *very* serious," he insists, and I don't need that cruel slant of a smile to know it.

My eyes narrow suspiciously. "Why do you suddenly care where I put my dick?"

"I don't. I just know you can't do it." He shrugs, looking at me pensively. "You know what your problem is, Wilcox?"

"My problem?" I casually take a crack. "Probably the two years' probation for a variety of bullshit charges. Although," I add, rubbing my chin, "the fact that I owe a Northridge loan shark a hundred grand, and he's holding my business hostage until I've paid off my balance isn't exactly helping matters."

He laughs, low and mocking. "Those aren't your problems, sonny. Those are symptoms of a problem." He looks down at the dance floor, watching the mass of people below. "My Northridge boys always used to say you were a sociopath. Matter of fact, that's why I took a chance on you. Something like that could be useful in a pinch. But I know what you really are, Wilcox." He meets my gaze, eyes hard. "You're a spoiled little brat who doesn't know anything about people. You don't know what it's like to feel responsible for somebody, because no one would let you close enough to find out. You don't know what it's like to feel guilt or regret, because there's nothing you care about more than yourself. You're not a sociopath. Sociopaths are useful. Sociopaths are smart. But you, you're just..." He tilts his head, searching my eyes. "Well, you're just a sad, overrated snob. Imagine my disappointment."

I roll my eyes, wishing I could shut this motherfucker up, just once. "Is there a point buried somewhere under all that self-indulgent navel gazing? Because I actually have shit to do tonight." *Like pack.*

He gives me a sharp smile. "Get the girl to fuck you and I'll reduce your debt by half. I'll even waive the interest—every cent."

I don't even need to think about it, thrusting my open palm at him. "Done."

Big Gene looks at my hand before taking it. "Oh, Wilcox. That, right there?" he says, giving our linked fists a single bob. "That's your problem. You never even asked me what I'd get if you lose. Got those big, dumb, blue eyes of yours so fixed on the prize that it makes you stupid."

"Doesn't matter. I'm not going to lose." I take a sip from my drink, shrugging. "And I already know what you want, but if you want to do the whole dramatic reveal shtick, then be my guest."

"Should have asked that before shaking on it," Gene says, looking far too comfortable for my liking. Regardless, he raises his glass, sweeping it in a gesture toward the room. "If I win, I get you the fuck out of here."

The club.

Of-fucking-course.

"I don't know why you want it so bad," I say, rolling my eyes. "There's no way this place out-earns your hustle."

"That's where you're wrong," Gene says, settling in. "In case you haven't noticed—being one of them and all—my clientele isn't exactly of the paying-shit-back persuasion." He sniffs, eyes taking in the space. "I could do with something legit for a while. Something dependable."

I throw back the last of my drink, muttering, "You taking half of my nightly profits seems pretty fucking dependable to me."

"Aw." He puts a hand to his chest, giving a mocking frown. "That was downright sulky. You're losing your touch." He stands up, leafing through a wallet for two twenties. He tosses them on the table, glancing over his shoulder before leaning down. He keeps his voice low, but I can still hear the gloat in it. "And by the way, I've been fucking that sweet little thing over there for the past month. A full head of hair isn't everything, *young man*. You just remember that." He punctuates this with a soft whack to the side of my head.

My fiery glare follows him across the lounge and down the stairs.

Gene, just like everyone else, underestimates me, and that's the way I like it. He thinks I don't know anything about people, but he's wrong. I know Gene's got this real hard-on for honor among thieves. He takes his losses. And that's exactly what he's about to get, because I know Georgia fucking Haynes even better.

3

I GET myself off in my car first, parked in the darkest corner of Preston's parking lot. It's fast and full of thoughts that I try to scrub from my brain the instant I step out into the night air. I get myself off again once I'm back in my room, standing under the spray of my shower. Again, after getting into bed. I wake up at three in the morning to do it again, and when my alarm goes off, my hand is already tucking itself into my panties, frantically trying to calm the low thrum still building in the pit of my belly.

It's not the masturbation that bothers me.

At least, not today.

Sometimes it does, though. I can go for whole stretches of time where I'm fine getting off once, maybe twice a day—something normal for a teenager. But on other days—on *really bad* days—I have to binge on the swell and climax for hours, needing to get off again and again. Sometimes, on bad days like those, I'll even hide under my covers, still breathless from the orgasm, crying into my pillow because it's still not enough.

Sometimes it's *never* enough.

Today isn't one of those days, but I still want to bury my head into my pillow and cry. In no fucking universe should my brain want to get off to thoughts of Heston goddamn Wilcox. My sex life has always come with its fair share of shame and regret, but today is just...particularly vile.

Even by lunch, I'm still feeling the uncomfortable churn in my gut, heavy with the knowledge that my libido is so heinous that even someone who's hurt me as badly as Heston can penetrate it.

It doesn't help that I'm still horny, completely deprived of the good, hard fuck that was meant to happen last night.

Snap!

"Tell me I can get out of this." I push my barely eaten lunch aside and look imploringly at my friends. "Just...tell me it's not happening."

"Oh, it's happening," Caroline says, grinning. "I can't believe you never took a P.E. class."

I raise a finger. "If anything, that's on Mrs. Gilbert for not making me do it sooner."

Vandy gives me a skeptical glance.

"Fine," I grumble. "Even I'm not sold on that excuse." Mrs. Gilbert is excellent at her job. I'm the one who thought if I just ignored it, everyone would somehow magically forget. Guess not. "It's going to be all underclassmen and nerds," I complain, shoulders falling. "I mean, those Freshman boys won't even know how to handle seeing me in a bathing suit."

"You've seen the school suits, right?" Vandy asks, laughing. "They're the antithesis of sexy."

"Please." I glance down at my boobs and raise an eyebrow. "It's going to take more than cramming these things into red and black Lycra to make them off-putting to fourteen-year-old boys."

Caroline snorts and the three of us shatter into giggles. It's been a strange day. More than half of the Devils graduated—and *all* the guys—leaving the three of us alone. Whoever let them make the nominating decisions left a vast gap in membership. Dumbasses. It feels like losing half a limb—a shield, really. Even not being linked to any of them romantically, like Vandy is to Reyn, they made me feel safe. Protected. People mess with a Devil at their peril. It's only the first day of senior year, and already I hear the whispers starting back up behind my back. No surprise, without Sebastian, Emory, Reynolds, Ben, Tyson, and Carlton sitting at our table. The vacancy is painfully noticeable. One long look from any of the guys—or even Afton—would have everyone shutting their mouths instantly. Now, I swear I can feel them all watching me. Talking in low tones. Throwing me mean smirks. Making crude gestures. Vandy's eyes flick over my shoulder, and I follow her gaze, expecting to see just that.

It's some guy I don't recognize, though. He's tall and lean, standing awkwardly over the empty half of the table. I narrow my eyes and search for the leering gaze, the confident swagger, the evidence that he's looking to make me a conquest. Instead, he looks at us blankly until Caroline asks, "Do you need somewhere to sit?" He nods and she pushes out a chair. "Go for it. We won't bite."

"Speak for yourself," I mutter, taking him in. He's actually pretty cute. Preston doesn't get nearly enough fresh meat. If I didn't have that new rule about not fucking high school guys, he might even make my new shortlist.

Snap!

"Thanks," he says, resting his tray on the table. He drops his leather backpack by his feet, muttering, "Can't take lunchroom table politics today."

"You're new, right?" Vandy leans across the table, offering her hand and introducing herself. Of course, Ms. Welcome Wagon. She points to the two of us. "That's Caroline and Georgia."

"I'm Ozzy," he says after a pause, lazy gaze passing over us. He looks stoned, eyes bloodshot, movements slow and badly coordinated, hair a touch too messy. Briefly, it reminds me of seeing Heston the night before.

Snap! Snap! Snap!

Clearing his throat, he adds, "Collins. Ozzy Collins." The pained expression when he repeats his last name says it all.

Caroline's eyebrows shoot up her forehead. "Wait, you mean like Headmaster Collins?"

"The very one," he replies, stabbing his burrito with his fork. "I don't suppose there's any chance of me sliding under the radar with regard to being the Headmaster's son, is there?"

"Probably not," Vandy replies, grimacing sympathetically. "I didn't even know Collins had kids. Did you just move here or something?"

He heaves a hard sigh and the three of us share a look. "Since I live with my mom, I used to go to Northridge. But everyone thought it'd be a good decision for me to come here for my senior year."

Even I have a lot of questions about that. No one willingly changes schools senior year unless you have a damn good reason, but I stop short of asking. It's none of my business. "Well," I say, pushing my chair back, "I'm going to see if I can talk Coach James into giving me a break. Maybe I can write a paper?"

"On swimming?" Vandy asks, shaking her head. "Good luck with that."

"Thanks." I pass by the new kid, checking him out once more. "Nice to meet you."

Snap!

"Yeah." He squints at the burrito before setting it back down, clearly opting out of the Preston Prep dining experience. At least he's not dumb.

Armed with the bag of low-calorie popcorn from the vending machine, I head across campus, grateful that everyone is in class or at lunch. There's a reason I left early. Fewer people around. Fewer eyes. Fewer whispers. I should be used to it—it's been going on for years—but with all the Devils having my back last year, I'd forgotten just how bad it felt.

Slut. Whore. Skank. Nympho.

It's such a joke. Guys at Preston are historically the biggest sluts around, but you never hear them called anything worse than 'players', and even then, it's never spoken with anything less than jaded admiration. I stare at the name engraved into the plaque above the natatorium: *Bates.* Case in point, Hamilton Bates was one of the biggest manwhores this school has ever seen. He settled down with Gwendolyn Adams and everyone wants to give him an award for it.

Fuck that.

I push open the glass doors and inhale the faint scent of chlorine out in the lobby. I've been to plenty of swim and diving meets here, so I know the coach's office is off the back hallway, toward the locker rooms. The Devils usually came out to support Tyson when he was on the dive team, and plus, what's not to like about seeing a bunch of hot, fit guys in Speedos?

Snap!

I spot the Devil's Swim banner next to a closed door. Another student is already sitting in one of the chairs outside. As I get closer, I have to do a double take when I realize that it's Micha Adams.

"Hey," I say, giving him a grin. "You waiting on Coach James, too?"

Micha's gotten a lot taller over the summer. He's willowy now, and his voice is a little deeper when he answers, "Yep, I'm trying to get out of swim," but there's also something delicately feminine about his new, matured features. His cheekbones are sharper. Curly hair that's been buzzed short at the sides and left long at the top makes it tumble down over an artfully glittered eyelid.

He's fucking gorgeous.

I pause when his words register. "I'm here for the same reason."

Slowly, we size one another up. There's no way Coach James will let us both off the hook. Too visible. Other students would start asking. *Shit.*

"Why don't you want to take the class?" His eyes narrow suspiciously. "Wait, aren't you too *old* for this class?"

Rolling my eyes, I fall into the chair next to him, ripping my bag of popcorn open. "Lame as hell, but I'm short a P.E. credit from when I...uh, studied abroad freshman year. That's half my problem, too. It's going to all be underclassmen." I glance at him, remembering that he's a sophomore now, and extend the bag in offer. "No offense."

Reaching inside, he takes a few pieces of popcorn. "None taken." Micha may be the most confident person I know.

"You barely even look like an underclassman anymore," I add, giving him a sly look as I chomp on my piece of popcorn. "That was quite the glow-up you had over the summer, Adams."

He gives me a sharp look, saying, "Bitch, I've always glowed." The words are without bite, though. "So what's the second half of your problem? Because I doubt Coach James is going to care about you being too cool for underclassmen."

I give him some more popcorn and reluctantly confess, "Uh, well, I'm not exactly a great swimmer. I'm not even a bad swimmer. Basically, I just don't swim at all."

He rolls his eyes. "I follow your ChattySnap, Georgia. Mostly because you post a lot of fine guys, but also, I've seen all the pictures you posted over the summer of you on that yacht. Don't tell me you can't swim."

"I was *on* the boat, Micha. Not in the water." I sigh, letting my head fall back as I chew. "I had this dumb incident when I was a kid, and now I just hate getting into deep water. What's your excuse?" Something occurs to me. "Wait, isn't your sister some kind of swim star at Vanderbilt?"

"Yeah, and?" De-fen-sive. "You know we're not blood-related, right? You can tell, what with her being so *white* and all."

"You're half-white," I point out. "That's not, like, totally outside the realm of logic."

"The point *is*, it's not like we got the same athletic genes. I just never saw the point in learning. It's not like I was ever going to be better than Gwen, so what's the point, right?"

I give him a baffled look. "I don't think that's really how stuff works."

"You sound like you only have one sibling," he says, reaching into the bag for more. "I have four, so let me give you some wisdom; that's the secret to familial harmony. Everyone gets their 'thing'. Mine is dance." He flashes me a winning smile. "That and being fucking awesome."

I purse my lips. "I think you spent too much around Sebastian last year."

"Not possible." Giving me a look that's always been reserved for the fairer Wilcox around this place, Micha shrugs. "The thing is, I spend a lot of time on my hair and makeup. Getting wet always seemed like a waste of all that work."

Well, he's not wrong. I gather my perfectly curled hair up protectively. "Then why are you even signed up for the class?"

"Oh god, it's the worst," he groans. "My mom is on this big self-sufficiency kick. It's all about 'life skills' and a bunch of boring crap she thinks everyone should know. Getting your driver's license, changing a flat, cooking and cleaning. I tried telling her that some things are bound to fall at the wayside in pursuit of the perfect liquid liner technique." He raises his hands to quote, "Apparently that's not actually 'useful' in 'adulthood'. She decided that if I don't learn how to swim at school this year, she won't let me apply to the summer dance program at Julliard."

I grimace at him sympathetically. "Tough break."

The door swings open and reveals Coach James, standing just inside his office. He takes one look at the two of us and sighs. "Adams. Haynes. You're both in my intro class that starts in ten minutes. Is there any reason that you're not dressed out and in the pool area?"

Micha and I both stand, each doing our very best impressions of beleaguered, helpless, pitiful students.

I beg, "Coach James, seriously, is there anything else I can do? Anything other than swim? I can write you the best essay you've ever seen."

Micha shoves himself in front of me. "I can write three of them, and they'll have so many glitter stickers, you'll *die*."

I shove myself in front of him. "I can clean the pool deck."

Micha shoves back. "I'll carry your clipboard."

I give him a look that says just how lame that idea is. "I can boss the ninth graders around, keep them in line."

Micha argues, "I'm on the paper this year! I can get you the best pictures. The swim and dive teams are really so unsung in school media, don't you think?"

"P.E. is a non-negotiable requirement, Ms. Haynes. And Adams, your sister was the best swimmer this school has seen in decades, so you must realize that swimming is an important skill." He looks disappointed in us.

I know it's time for me to admit the truth—that I literally cannot swim. "Look, Coach James, I'm just going to level with you here. I can do a basic doggy-paddle and *possibly* not drown right away, but beyond that, I'm useless." I think back to the party at Reyn's house. I intentionally didn't get in the water. Partially because Reyn's dad was present, hot as hell, and fun to flirt with, but also because *I can't swim.* "It's embarrassing. And scary."

"Embarrassing? Please." Micha scoffs, turning to the coach with big, earnest eyes. "As this school's only genderfluid student, where exactly do you expect me to change, and what exactly do you expect me to wear? Following a long line of tradition set into place by our very white, very male, and very *non-queer* founders, Preston Prep adheres to a gendered locker room policy that fosters a hostile environment for LGBT youth!"

I gape at him, outraged. Outraged! How am I supposed to beat that? The smug jut of his chin tells me Micha knows.

Unfortunately for him, Coach James just smiles. "I've already discussed this with your father. We agreed to give you the option of changing in either room, or my office. You can wear the shorts or the one-piece. Whatever you're most comfortable with."

Micha's face falls. "But—"

The Coach cuts him off. "I'm given to understand that neither of you knows how to swim. Correct?" At our nods, he heaves a loud sigh. "There *is* a remedy to this."

"Really?" I ask. Micha straightens along with me.

"The only technical requirement is that you're able to swim two full laps of a basic stroke. Freestyle, the crawl, backstroke, your choice. Even for a beginner, learning that shouldn't take an entire semester."

"So we could do that and be finished?" I ask, feeling optimistic. "That sounds doable!"

"It should be," he says, eyes tight at the edges. "But there's both good news and bad news."

"Oh! Good news first." Micha explains to me, "The high of good news always helps me process the bad."

Coach James looks between us, something reluctant and heavy in his gaze. "I have an assistant this year who can help you—privately. I can arrange sessions for you during an independent study. It'll be less embarrassing for you, and you'll probably learn faster that way."

I glance at Micha, stunned. "That sounds perfect. What's the problem?"

Grimacing, he stands. "Follow me."

The back door of his office leads to the pool deck. It's stuffy, and the air is filled with the eye-burning scent of chlorine. I sidestep a puddle and look toward the pool, where swimmers cut through the water, completing their laps. Micha and I follow Coach James around to the deep end where someone—Coach James' assistant, going off his red shorts and white Devil tee—is handing out kickboards to a group of middle schoolers. My eyes take in the man's broad shoulders, messy blond hair, and from the angle, a jaw that's seemingly cut from marble. He glances over his shoulder to check the clock and my stomach sinks like a brick.

No fucking way.

"What is Heston doing here?" Micha asks, his narrow eyes watching him.

"Heston is working with me this semester," Coach says with no further explanation.

"He can't be here," I hotly insist. "Right? Not after what he did!" To Micha. To Sydney. *To me.* Not after admitting it in court. I'd left for the summer, and out of my own need for sanity, shut out any information about his case. Seeing him last night was a shock, and I've been avoiding wondering how and why he's free.

But here he is again. Not only free, but free at *Preston*.

What the fuck?

"Headmaster Collins made the decision for Heston to assist me," Coach James says. It's clear he's not a fan of the decision. "I know he's had trouble with a fair number of students in the high school, but he's an excellent swimmer, and we've always had a positive relationship. My plan had been to have him work with the elementary and middle schoolers—he's less likely to have a history there—but you two are asking for special circumstances. Unfortunately, if you want that to happen, it would involve Heston being your instructor."

"You want us to work with him?!" I don't need to look at Micha to know he's sharing my expression.

"I don't *want* you to. It's not required. But know that if you're looking for special treatment, this is all you're going to get. If you want to pass intro quick, it'll have to be done with him. Otherwise, you take the class with everyone else." He shrugs, and for the first time, I think Coach James might be a little scheming. "I need to know your decision by this afternoon so I can make sure it's approved by the office."

He pops his whistle in his mouth and blows, calling out to the kids in the pool. Heston slams the closet door and struts down the pool deck, that long stride of his looking casual and comfortable in a space that's probably more familiar to him than most. I watch him reach out to snatch a wayward pair of goggles from the ground and a shiver rolls down my spine like an avalanche. I can still feel the ghost of his palm around my throat, can still remember the coldness in his eyes as he hissed all those accusations at me. I'd never admit it aloud, but in that moment, I'd actually been afraid of him. I reach out and grab Micha's arm, pulling him toward the doors and back into the hall.

"Are you thinking what I'm thinking?" I say once we're alone.

Micha glowers at the door to the pool. "That there's no way Coach James is expecting us to choose to work with Heston?"

"Yeah," I say, shooting my own glare at the door. "Looks like we're spending the semester in Coach's class after all."

"Speak for yourself," Micha replies, giving me a strange look. "I'm taking the offer."

I blink at him, lost. "What?"

"I'm not scared of that asshole. He pulled a shitty prank on me over two years ago, and he hurt my sister. But he can't do anything to me here." Micha looks over his shoulder, making sure we're alone. "Hamilton said he's on probation or something. If you think about it, one word from either of us will send that jerkoff right back to jail. We've got the power now."

I laugh bitterly. "Micha, that's not how Heston works. He's going to make you miserable."

"Georgia, Georgia, Georgia," he sighs, shaking his head. "Did it ever occur to you that I'm going to make *him* miserable?"

I'm not sure what that evil glint in Micha's eyes means, but I know that it's pointless.

All Heston's ever been is miserable.

"You want to tell me what's going on with your brother?" I snap into the phone while storming across campus. I'd texted Bass the minute I separated from Micha and told him to pick up the damn phone.

"Georgia! My little peach! How are you?" There's a muffled voice in the background, and then Bass adds, "Sugar says hi."

"Bass, don't avoid my question."

"I'm not avoiding it," he answers, still sounding half distracted. "Why would I have any idea what's going on with my brother? Just like you, I spent the summer zig-zagging across our magnificent country with my super sexy girlfriend, forgetting about that asshole."

"Well..." I start, coming to an abrupt stop. I've inadvertently crossed into a game of Frisbee and the disc sails two inches from my nose. "Buck!" I shout. "Dude, come on."

"Sorry, Georgia!" Buck calls out. He gives me a sly grin that makes me think it wasn't an accident. "Saw your ChattySnap pics. Looking good on that boat, girl."

I roll my eyes. Buck and I hooked up at a party at Elena's house two years ago. I was on a particularly destructive streak at the time, and Buck was an easy target. Stalking off, I grip the phone, explaining in a tight whisper, "Bass, I just saw him."

"You saw who? Heston?"

"Where?" Sugar has apparently taken over the phone. "Where did you see him?"

"Here!" I hiss, stomping toward the dorm building. "At Preston, helping with the fucking swim team. He's Coach James' new assistant!"

"Are you serious?" Sugar's voice is low with anger. "They let him go? Jesus ass-fucking Christ. You called it. You all called it."

She sounds so defeated and disappointed, a mirror to my own feelings on the matter. You try to do the proper thing, right a wrong, help the entire female gender by exposing a predator, but what do you get? The same old, misogynistic, protect-one-another bullshit.

"Georgia," Bass says, taking the phone back. He sounds more focused now, voice low and tight. There's a jingle of keys. "I'm going to drive down there tonight, okay?"

"What?" I ask, stopping dead in the dorm lobby. "Sebastian, that's insane! It's a fifteen hour drive here from New Haven!"

"They kept me in the dark about this for a reason," he insists, sounding angry. "He can't just do what he did and get to work at fucking Preston, of all goddamn places." Quieter, he adds, "There's no one there for the three of you," and I know who he means. Me, Vandy, and Caroline. The last remaining Devils.

I deflate just imagining it: Sebastian driving for fifteen hours, just to get here and save me from his brother, like some kind of sad, poor damsel. It's been a long time since everything that happened Freshman year. I've hidden, I've avoided, I've done terrible, harmful things—all to push what happened with Heston as far away from me as possible. I stepped out from under that dark cloud last spring, when I marched into the police station with Sydney to report him. I did it because I was tired of hiding. Sebastian—the Devils—gave me the courage to stand up and take care of myself.

Now it's time to find the strength to do that on my own.

"No." My voice is soft, but final. "You have a life there with Sugar. You guys are happy. It's time for the rest of us to find our own happiness, and that starts with *not* having our friend drive home from college to beat up anyone who's been mean to us."

"But—"

"But nothing," I say, voice sharp. "Let us handle it. Plus, you're wrong. Vandy still has Reyn."

And maybe Micha's right.

Maybe we're less powerless than we think.

Hanging up, I feel a little more determined, but no less seething at the injustice of it all. Making my way up to the fourth floor, I admit to myself that I'm also still pissed about the night before. I'd been so shaken by being matched to him that I didn't make any other efforts to continue my search. Now, I'm stuck snapping this damn rubber band on my wrist every ten minutes, so rattled by the hum of my needs that I'm not thinking straight. Going to Bass was a bad idea.

I pass my floor mates and pause when I get a few feet from my room. A trunk is positioned in the hall and the door is cracked. Loud, bouncy pop-music spills out the open door. Slowly, I step over the threshold and gape at what I find inside. There's a bed where my living room sofa should be, and a desk-dresser combo shoved up by the window. Most notably, a raven-haired girl is rolling up a T-shirt, tucking it neatly into the top drawer of the bookshelf. She doesn't notice me, and I take the opportunity to observe her, taking in her petite body, long earrings, a pair of the same cute shoes I'd seen last week while visiting a boutique with my mother. They cost six-hundred dollars.

"E-excuse me? Who are you?" I ask, so taken aback that the first words come out in a sputter. I turn off the music. "What are you doing?"

The girl turns, her stick-straight hair swinging behind her, and her eyes light up. "Hi! I'm Josephine Wentworth. Everyone calls me Josie." She thrusts her hand toward me, but I just stare at it. Slowly, her hand falls. "It's funny, actually," she says, tucking her hair behind her ear, "there was this whole *thing* at Sparrowood Academy last semester—like a whole scandal with drugs and cheating and blackmail. My parents were just livid when they found out and decided to move me for my junior year at the last minute."

I'd heard about shit hitting the fan at that school. A couple of kids went to jail, if I remember correctly. Sounds like same-old prep school bullshit. Except maybe, unlike Preston criminals, *those* guys are actually still in jail. I cross my arms over my chest. "What does that have to do with you being in my room?"

"Well..." She frowns, looking around the space. "The suites were all taken, and mother didn't think it was appropriate for me to live without a kitchen of my own. Headmaster Collins agreed and," her frown turns into a grin, "I guess we're roommates!"

I stare at her. "Roommates? But this is a solo. A suite. *My* suite."

I have plans for this suite. Lots of plans that don't include some transfer Sparrowood chick sleeping in my damn living room. Like not having to tip-toe around, or be quiet, or having to be considerate like I did all of last year. Is it too much to ask that a girl has a little privacy?

I open my mouth to announce this, but Josie just hands me a sheet of paper with move-in instructions from the housing office. "Sorry," she says, lips quirked in a smile, implying that she's not sorry at all. "But hey, don't worry. I have a feeling before it's all over, we'll be the best of friends."

Will we? Because I have a best friend. A couple of them, actually. And I don't want any more. I stare blankly at her for a few more moments, but she just turns the music back up and systematically fills her drawers with her designer clothing. Who the hell does this girl think she is?

I spin on my heel and go into my room, shutting the door behind me. Falling back on my bed, I glower up at the ceiling. How has everything gone so wrong so fast? First the P.E. fiasco, then the bullshit with Heston. Now this.

Whatever plans I had for having the best year ever are slowly falling apart.

4

THE APARTMENT IS on the back side of campus, past the old gym, wedged up awkwardly against the trees. It's cold, cramped, and has that dusty old-person smell that reminds me of the library in my grandmother's house up in Virginia. It features a cheap, basic living room set, a bare double bed in the bedroom, three plates and five forks in the kitchen, and a shower curtain that smells like a newly manufactured beach ball.

I stand in there, pulling a face at a dark ring around the drain of the bathroom sink, and make a mental note to buy something harder than beer.

For now, I stock the medicine cabinet with four bottles of Mylanta.

I know it's better than a prison cell, but from here, it's hard to see how. Being a Wilcox is all I've ever known, and that's always come with high ceilings, marble floors, my own private rooms, decked-out bathrooms, media rooms, hot tubs, slick luxury cars, and yachts. This apartment makes me feel too big, like I could put my shoulder through a wall at any given moment.

The only good thing about it is the trail that leads down to the lake, but I don't even see that being of much use. The only way to handle this is to do my time and get the fuck out. Preston Prep is the last place I ever planned on returning to.

I walk into my bedroom and grab a clean shirt out of my suit-case. I'll eat my own liver before I bother unpacking here. Too permanent—too much a signal of defeat. When my lawyer offered this deal—probation and community service coaching swim at Preston—I thought he was joking. In fact, I laughed in his face. But here I am, stuffing a frozen dinner into a microwave that's so old, it probably doesn't even pass legal standards anymore. Someone— Headmaster Collins, Coach James, or maybe some Devil with pull, I don't even fucking know—saw fit to take some kind of pity on me with this. Nothing about this pisses me off more than that. I'm Heston fucking Wilcox. I don't take anyone's pity. I don't *need* anyone's pity.

Ever.

I've just pulled the clean shirt over my head when there's a knock on the door. Instead of answering it, I stand by the microwave, waiting for my dinner to finish. No one important knows I'm here. I made certain of that. When the microwave dings, I plop the dinner onto one of the three plates and take my time answering.

"Great," I say when I finally open the door. "It's you."

"Heston." Headmaster Collins is standing on the doorstep, face etched with a frown. Looking back, it's hard to believe I ever found this guy imposing, even as a middle schooler. He's nothing like the powerful icon of authority I used to see him as. Age hasn't done him well. Much like Big Gene, the Headmaster is balding. Unlike Big Gene, Collins hasn't quite accepted it. He's still combing over that patch of scalp, hoping to hide it. "You were supposed to come to my office at the end of the day."

"Oops." I step back into the apartment, leaving the door open. "I must've forgotten." I enter the small kitchenette and open the refrigerator, pulling out a bottle of beer. I hold it up. "You want one?"

He sighs. "This isn't playtime, Heston. You're not in high school anymore, you're an adult. I'm giving you an opportunity to clear your name and reputation."

Guess that answers that question.

I pop off the bottle cap, and it clatters on the countertop. "I've been wondering about that."

"About what?"

"Exactly why you're giving me this 'opportunity'." I take a long swig, letting the cool liquid soothe my throat. "I didn't do much to deserve it. I mean, let's face it. I barely graduated. I caused you a shit-ton of problems. The stuff with the Adamses, the Devil pranks, skipping classes, the videos..."

He gives me an impatient look. "Yes, I recall."

"So why let me back on campus?" I know a trap when I see it. Nothing is free, especially not at Preston. After a pause, Collins shuts the door—a clear indication that whatever he has to say, he doesn't want anyone else to hear. I give him a bland smirk. "Oh, goodie. Here come the strings."

He casually begins, "As you're well aware, I banned the Devils and all secret society activity from this campus."

I snort. "Because of me."

"Partly," he replies. "Unfortunately, in the last year it's become clear that a new reiteration of the club has emerged. They've created chaos at two school functions, embarrassing me and the rest of the administration in front of alumni and guests in the process."

I'm not surprised. I'd heard the rumors about the Devils, and I've seen my brother's tattoo. No one explicitly told me they were back, but they aren't exactly flying under the radar. Every guy I know who'd be involved—Carlton, Ben, Emory—have all graduated. Whoever remains is a mystery to me. Propping myself against the counter, I say as much. "Not that I would rat out a Devil, but all the obvious suspects are already gone."

He nods, adjusting the lapels of his blazer. "Which is why I need you to infiltrate the remaining members and report back to me who's involved."

I stare at the man, that last piece of the puzzle clicking into place. When it does, I bark a flat laugh. "Infiltrate? I'm twenty-one, Collins. I'm an assistant coach. I'm *faculty*. You want me to hang out with a bunch of teenage losers while they gloat about marking some girl in the stairway?"

He pulls a face when I bring up the marking. Stodgy fucker's probably heard the rumors, but never had any confirmation.

"You're right. All the suspected leaders have graduated. Emory Hall. Reynolds McAllister." He levels me with a look, pointedly adding, "Your brother." Personally, I could name at least three other suspects, each of them far more likely than my idiot brother. I don't, though. "The Devils are obviously lacking something of a leadership role, which means it's the perfect time to stop this once and for all."

I raise an eyebrow. "And how exactly do you suggest I do that?"

He lifts a shoulder. "Claim you were sent here to help them regroup. Find out what they're up to. Report back to me."

"So you want me to rat out the Devils." I shake my head. "Come on, Collins. You've got to be smarter than this. Narc'ing isn't my style."

"You have little choice in the matter." He looks unconcerned as he walks around the kitchen, dragging a fingertip over a fine film of dust covering a stool. He rubs it between forefinger and thumb, elaborating, "Your stay here at Preston, which includes a generous application of community service hours, is conditional on your complete compliance."

"My compliance with what?" I narrow my eyes, tracking him. "No one told me anything."

He reaches into his coat and pulls out a folded sheet of paper. He extends it to me, and after I moment, I reach out to snag it from him. It's a copy of my probation contract. Midway down is a high-lighted section, outlining the Headmaster's exhaustive authority over my living situation, work conditions, and legal mandates.

I fold up the paper, tossing it onto the counter. "And if I say no?"

"If you say no, then the contact is void—in which case, you'll have to reappear in front of the judge for a new sentence." He folds his hands behind his back, watching me. "Be smart, Heston. You're done with this place. The Devils aren't anything to you now—you don't owe them any loyalty. This will be a straightforward way to pay off your debt to society."

I look at him, this small, unimportant man who's taking up too much space, and bitterly raise my bottle to him. "You mean this will be a straightforward way to pay off my debt to *you*."

He takes his time making his way to the door. It's the leisurely amble of someone who believes they have the upper hand. "Make the right choice, son."

I stare at the door once he's left, downing the rest of my beer in three hard gulps. The bottle shatters when I spike into the trashcan, and if I try really hard, I can ignore the inferno in the pit of my stomach.

"I'm not your fucking son."

It's a difficult thing to cop to, the way I feel standing on the pool deck, adjusting my goggles, slipping back into the familiar laser-focus. The cool blue water beckons and following is as easy as breathing. I dive confidently into a lane, and as soon as I slice into the water, it rings too true to deny.

Fuck, I've missed this.

My muscles burn with every stroke as I glide through the water, arms and legs reacquainting themselves with the pressure. It's been a while since I did this. More than a year, at least. I still workout regularly, but mostly at the gym. This is something different—more than just a workout. Full body. All power. For eight years, this is where I dominated hardest.

It's a good use of the free period before my independent study students arrive. Two nerds who apparently never learned to swim. Fucking ridiculous. Who doesn't make their kids learn to swim, especially at Preston? It's not like any of these parents couldn't afford an instructor. The kids are probably just lazy, weak little shits, which means I'm going to spend five hours a week dealing with a couple of slackers.

I touch the side one last time and take a deep breath, tugging off my goggles. Looking up, my eyes meet a pair of bare legs. The skin is pale, smooth, a smattering of freckles dusting the knees. I zero in on milky thighs—the kind of complexion that I *know* is perfect for bruising. My eyes travel upward appreciatively, past the hem of cotton shorts, curvy hips, over a set of round, full tits. Her arms are crossed tight across a basic one-piece suit, and her hair, her eyes—

"Jesus fucking Christ," I snap, throwing my goggles aside. "Not this bullshit again,"

My gaze jumps from Georgia to the kid next to her. Micha Adams is in a pair of trunks and a retro T-shirt with a picture of Michael Jackson on the front. He's no longer the scrawny little kid I picked on two years ago. His arms are crossed over his chest too, revealing surprisingly toned arms. It doesn't matter that he's wearing a headband or dark lipstick. This isn't the kid Hamilton busted my jaw over.

I look back at Georgia, feeling the same clutch of fury I had that night at the club. *This fucking bitch...* "What is this, some kind of joke?" I look around, half expecting to see my boys—*my Devils*—laughing in a corner somewhere. The realization that my Devils are gone, that this is a new sort of reality, hits me somewhere in the solar plexus. "The school freak and the county whore just happen to show up in my first class?" Doubtful.

Georgia's jaw tightens, and she might play it off, but I can still see the flinch in her eyes at the word. *Whore.*

Adams's dark eyes narrow. "Yeah, this isn't ideal for us either, Wilcox, but it is what it is. Deal with it." There's a hint of disturbing delight in his eyes, like maybe a part of him finds this funny.

I'm not laughing. "You're really trying my fucking patience, Haynes." I'm tired of getting my balls squeezed by the people at this school. First Collins, now this. I'm not a fucking narc, and I'm especially not a goddamn babysitter.

I lift myself out of the pool and onto the deck. Cool air hits my overheated skin and I grab a towel, wrapping it around my waist. I look across the pool at Coach James, but he's involved with a class. I stop and turn. They're both a few feet away, eyeing me warily. "So this is the set-up?" It has to be. Maybe not by the Devils, but by someone. Two people that I've supposedly 'bullied' or 'harassed' showing up in my class can't be random fucking happenstance. Someone is trying to take me down. Again. *Goddamn it.* I glare down at Georgia, my blood growing hotter with anger when I realize she's staring at my bare chest. "Was this your idea?"

Her eyes snap up, going tight at the corners. "Why do you keep thinking I'm behind some nefarious plan to take you down? Trust me, any proximity to you wasn't even remotely part of my plans for senior year, and now you've popped up twice. If anyone deserves to be pissed off about it, it's me!"

"Twice?" Micha asks, looking between us. Georgia's mouth clamps shut. Good to know she's not announcing to the world about our match-up. If Collins found out about that, he'd throw my ass out of here whether I offer him useful information or not.

"Fuck this," I say, storming away. "I'd rather deal with the judge than be trapped with the two of you in this hellhole."

It's not smart. I should be working on getting between Georgia's thighs, not stomping the other way. But every time I look at her, I'm reminded of that night—of how much she liked it. That bitch came on my dick three times. She loved every second of it. And then she turned around, more than two years later, and used it against me.

I reach the small office Coach James gave me—the captain's office Hamilton and Gwen used during our last swim season. Since competitive swim hasn't started up yet, I'm using it as a place to hole up between classes. I yank off the wet towel and hang it on the hook next to the door. Running my hand through my hair, I try to get a hold of my anger.

Unfortunately, getting rid of my anger for Georgia Haynes is like getting rid of a bad case of the clap.

"You're such a drama queen, do you know that?" she says, storming into the room. "It's just a stupid swim class. I know you can't stand being near us." She gestures to Micha, who's still out on the swim deck. "An Adams Family Freak and the 'county slut'," she sneers at the word, "but we don't have any other options and from what I gather, neither do you."

I walk over and press a hand against the doorjamb, openly using my size to intimidate her. "You're right, Haynes. I am out of options. I wonder why? I wonder who was behind that?" I give a low laugh that echoes off the small office walls. "Was getting me arrested not enough? What else do you want, Georgia? My head on a pike? Me down on my knees begging for forgiveness? Because I've already been tossed in jail, had my reputation smeared, and been completely fucking disowned. I'll be damned if you're getting another fucking thing from me."

Her bright, emerald eyes skim over my chest, cheeks blooming a vivid pink. I've seen her flushed before, so I know exactly how low that blush of her goes—all the way down to her cleavage, her tits, her flat belly.

Bitch is still gagging for my cock, even now, isn't she?

I hear a small series of snaps and my eyes jump down to watch her pluck at a rubber band around her wrist. My eyes narrow on the purpling skin beneath it.

"Don't blame me for your behavior, Heston. Don't you fucking dare," she growls, her green eyes blazing. "This isn't a joke. Micha and I both have to pass a P.E. requirement, and as much as I don't want to spend another moment in your presence, I don't have a choice. Neither does he."

"Join the other class then." This time, the tips of her ears turn red, too. I realize this isn't Georgia being her usual horny self. This is *embarrassment*. "Oh, this is fucking rich. You *need* me to teach you, don't you?" A cruel smile pulls at my lips as I lean forward, goading her. "Why do you need me to teach you, Little Red Riding Cocks?"

From the way her lips are angrily pursed, she knows I know. The way she growls out, "Because I can't swim," is a delightful bonus, though.

I laugh, even though I'm not amused in the slightest. "Seriously."

"I can't swim," she repeats, thrusting a palm toward the pool deck. "Neither can Micha."

My eyes flick out to watch the kid, lost in his own little world as he practices some kind of bouncy dance footwork. "You can't swim. At all."

"Possibly enough to not drown," she clarifies, shifting uncomfortably. "Definitely not enough to pass intro swim."

I cross my arms over my chest, and her eyes track my movements. "So what you're saying is that you're desperate."

She frowns. "Don't be a dick."

"Do you really think I know any other way to be?"

"No." She says it plainly, unapologetic, eyes full of apathy. It almost makes me laugh. I know the rumors about this girl. Hell, I probably started half of them. But I've spent the last three years pretending she didn't exist. Now she's in front of me, vulnerable and desperate.

That's exactly how I like my women.

And it's exactly what I need to win that bet with Big Gene.

"Fine," I say, as though I had another option. "I'll do it, but there are conditions."

"Conditions?!" Her voice reaches this pitch that makes my eardrums cringe. "You don't get to make conditions, Heston. You're the teacher. *Teach*. Or are you such a petty prick that you can't even play at being an adult for five hours a week?"

"Conditions," I grind out, eyes narrowing. "First one being that the two of you will treat me like any other member of the faculty. That means that the next time you call me anything but 'coach' or 'sir', I'll be writing your asses up. Second," I say, stopping before she voices the protest I clearly see building in her expression, "I'm not treating you differently than anyone else. You're not special."

"Good!" She says, balking. "We both know what your special treatment looks like. I think I'll pass."

"And I'm not babying you just because you're both dumbfucks who didn't learn how to swim when you were kids, like normal people." She takes a deep breath in, probably about to argue that no other member of the faculty would ever speak to a student this way. I shut that shit down quick. "And you can't go tattling on me every time I say something that hurts your precious little feelings. If I can play at being an adult for five hours a week, then so can you."

"Fine," she says, clearly holding in an argument against this. "Anything else, *Coach Wilcox*?"

God, that fucking sneer of hers.

I bend forward and whisper in her ear, "Wear a suit that shows off those tits better, Haynes. If I'm going to be forced to do this, I may as well get something out of it." She opens her mouth to say something smart and I close it with my fingertip. "Please, like every guy in this school hasn't seen them already."

I step away, turning my back, effectively dismissing her. I might have been forced into living at Preston, working at Preston, and teaching the snotty-nosed youth of Preston, but when it comes to Georgia Haynes, I'll always have the upper hand.

I plan to use it to my advantage.

5

"Ladies," the woman calls out, getting everyone's attention. She's at the front of the Magnolia Room at the club, standing behind a white podium. "Welcome to the first organizational meeting of the Southern Women's League Ball."

I glance across my half-eaten dessert and sweating glass of iced tea to my mother who's grinning in delight. Vandy is sitting next to me, her mother next to her, then Caroline and her mom. I tug at my collar, trying to get a little extra air.

This is getting bad.

The only thing stopping me from running into the nearest bathroom and shoving my hand down my pants is the thought of my mother sitting so close. It's getting to that tipping point where there's almost no want involved—all *need*.

"If you're in this room, it's because a distinguished woman in the community has nominated you for this tremendous honor. The Southern Women's League has a long tradition of presenting the finest young women during our ball. I am confident that each one of you is worthy."

I reach for my glass, taking a long sip of the sugary tea as the nightmare known as this presentation begins. To my mother's glee, the next few months will be a finely tuned whirr of dresses, escorts, etiquette, and social mores; all the things that make for a perfect southern lady. Just sitting here makes me feel like a fraud on the verge of being exposed.

"God help me," I mutter. If these women knew how close I was to taking one of the caterer's servers to the nearest closet and bending over for him, they wouldn't even let me clear their clean their tables.

Snap!

"Come on, it's not that bad," Vandy whispers. "We'll get new dresses and get to attend an actual ball."

Caroline smashes the rose-shaped pat of butter on her bread plate. "Believe it or not, it really will look good on college and job applications. I know it seems antiquated, but like any old stuffy tradition, there are a lot of networking perks."

I spin my finger. "Whooptie-frickin'-doo."

My mother glances over her shoulder at me, giving a pointed look. I clamp my mouth shut and sit quietly through the rest of the meeting like a good little girl. Because that's exactly what these women expect from elite femininity. Silence, compliance, smiles, chastity, and the complete lack of anything even resembling individuality.

God, I want to get fucked.

Snap!

When the woman up front finally stops talking, my mother turns to me and says, "Have you thought about who you're going to ask to be your escort?"

I slide a little lower in my seat. "Not yet."

The skin between her eyes creases as she thinks. "What about that nice boy who caddies for your father on the weekends at the club?"

"Skip Robinson?" I ask, conjuring up the douchebag. I've hooked up with him twice in the past. He couldn't find my g-spot any better than he can find a ball in a sand trap. "No, thanks."

Snap!

"Oh," Vandy's mother joins in, "how about Paden Mitchell? I hear he's pre-med at Duke."

Paden Mitchell has a micro-penis. There's no fucking way. I offer a fake smile because that's what ladies do. "I think he's too busy with school."

"I guess *technically* your brother could escort you," Mom says.

My jaw drops. "You want me to go with *my brother*? Jesus, mom. I may not have a boyfriend, but I'm not terminally dateless!" It takes a moment for *that* sting to fade away. "I'll find a date, just give me a minute." *To find someone I want to hang out with for more than an hour who also has the potential to be a good lay.*

Since high school guys are out and I'd rather punch myself in the tit than try another online match up, I've pretty much decided this debutante ball is my only chance to land some quality dick. It's feeling like I might not make it, though. The ball seems so far away, and I've been snapping this rubber band so much that my wrist is red and bruising.

And I don't think it's helping anymore.

"You don't have to use such tacky language, Georgia. I'm just trying to help." She looks at Caroline. "If Georgia doesn't want to bring her brother, then you could ask him, sweetheart."

"Mom," I warn, giving Vandy a pleading look.

Her smile in return is equal parts sympathetic and determined. "You'll both find dates. If not, then you know one of the D—*guys* will take you." She stumbles over the aborted 'Devils', but recovers smoothly. "I know Reyn would love it if he had a friend to suffer through it with him. Oh, hey! What about Emory?"

Emory would be a great date, except the part where I wouldn't be getting any dick afterward. Not only is he still dating Aubrey, but after the thing with Sebastian, not fucking Devils is a hard and fast rule of mine. I finally found friends I don't mix sex with, and I like it. It's nice.

"I'll consider it, but I've got a while. I'm sure I can find someone to go with me."

We're excused from the table to go into an adjacent room where one of the formal dress boutiques has set up a display. Vandy flips through the white dresses, mandatory for the ball, stopping on one that has a mermaid bottom. "What do you think?"

"I think it's pretty." I eye the beading at the top. "But if you want to bang Reyn in that thing, you're going to run into issues. You should look for something he can hike up easily."

Snap!

Caroline's cheeks turn red and she scampers around to the other side of the rack, hiding. Vandy's wide blue eyes dart around before she aggressively whispers, "Jesus, Georgia! Not everything is about sex." Despite this, I can't help but notice she re-hangs the dress and moves on to a more sex-accessible style. "Maybe this is why you can't find a boyfriend," she says, suddenly. "You're too focused on sex and not the rest of it."

"It's easy for you to say that," I say, feeling strangely stung. "You're getting it on the reg."

"Yeah, but that's not all we do. We watch movies, hang out with friends, do our homework. You know," she smiles softly at one of the dresses, "couple stuff."

Wrinkling my nose, I insist, "I have zero interest in a study partner. I just need someone who can help take off this edge. It's fucking unbearable." And I'm not even lying. It's getting hard to pay attention or care about anything else. I hate this part of it, feeling like a slave to my urges. I don't think I've gone this long without it since freshman year.

Vandy frowns. "What do you mean?"

"The *edge*. You know, the not-having-enough-sex edge?" She stares at me blankly. "You don't start feeling crazy when you and Reyn go too long without? Like when you went to," I lower my voice, "*rehab*, weren't you dying for it by the time you got back?"

"Well," she says slowly, flipping through another rack, "I mean, I missed Reyn and being close to him. Mostly I just missed talking to him, joking around, cuddling, sleeping—all that stuff. I missed watching him and Emory play HORSE in the driveway and kicking his butt in Call of Duty. Reyn's not just...*that*. He's my best friend, you know?"

I think back to all the guys I've hooked up with. They've been hot or not. They've been funny or quiet. They've been into it, or kind of lame. But none has ever been more than just a hookup. Not even Sebastian, who was my friend both before and after we fooled around. It never moved emotionally beyond that.

Vandy's eyes light up as she spots a dress across the room, calling me and Caroline to follow. I don't go with her, though. I'm too overwhelmed by the gnawing feeling in my belly, the urge combined with guilt. The longing for something that's always just out of reach. Is what Vandy's talking about what I'm missing? The friendship and connection as much as the sex?

No way.

I know boys, and they're terrible. All they want is a good thrust between my legs. If I'm very lucky, they might not even be jerks about it afterward. But otherwise? The only universally good thing men have in common is what's between *their* legs.

I don't need cuddling and all that nonsense. What I need is to get dicked-down. Fast. Otherwise, I'm going to lose my mind.

THE THUMPING MUSIC and nonstop giggles from the outer room penetrate my door, my white noise machine, *and* my headphones. Thanks to some upscale camp she's been attending for the last decade, Josie already knows half the junior class here.

Even though I promised myself I wouldn't, I try again—for the fifth time—grabbing my vibrator and shimmying it beneath the covers. I just need to fucking *come*. One more time would do the trick. Then maybe I can roll over and finally get some damn sleep.

I'm not proud of what my brain conjures. Heston, bare-chested inside the door of that office, looming over me. The way his hand curled into a loose fist as his sharp eyes descended to my chest. Heston has this way about him—always has—where he can somehow manage to feel hostile and soft, all at once. Like maybe he could wrap that broad fist around my throat, fingers digging hard and painful into flesh and tendon, but lick sweetly into my mouth while doing it.

I bite back a cry, feeling myself get closer to the edge. It's no use, though. Hearing six people right through my wall is not conducive to the proper orgasm headspace. At least, not for me. Not since that video got out and went viral. This year was supposed to be my first experience with real privacy. I was supposed to be able to do things like this, stretch out in my bed and just go to town until I wore myself out. Instead, I'm horny and frustrated, so close to release that my muscles are coiled tight, but far enough that my clit is aching and oversensitive.

Damn it!

I turn the vibrator off, tossing it back into my bedside table. I'm still breathing hard and my body is confused, still trembling, teetering on a painful edge. I'm about five seconds from storming out of this dormitory and jumping the first guy I see.

If I laid everything out to my therapist, she would tell me I needed to pull myself out of a high-risk situation and rely on a healthier coping mechanism. I should find a solution, then work out the urges with exercises or some kind of physical activity that does not include another round of failed masturbation.

I spring up.

Yeah, that's it. Something that provides both exercise *and* a solution. What did Coach James say about the swim requirement? I just need to make two laps. How hard can it really be to swim across the pool twice? I may not be proficient in my strokes, but I've watched the Olympics. It's just moving your arms and legs a bunch. Big fucking deal. I don't need anyone to teach me how to do that. Fake it 'til you make it, right?

The more I think about it, the more perfect it sounds. Jittery and anxious, I decide this is the optimal time to try it out, while no one is around. It'll be epic. I'll show up at class tomorrow and swim my two laps, finally done with Heston Wilcox and his abs of steel for good. Bonus? Getting a good workout.

I'm practically a genius.

My shrink would be proud.

I pull on my basic, lame one-piece swimsuit and pay no attention to the cluster of girls Josie has invited into our—*my*—room. It's just one more reason that doing this now is the right move. If I can't work off all this tension, then at least the suite will be quiet again when I get back.

I quickly make my way across campus and into the natatorium. Inside, I make sure no one's around. No janitor. No Coach James. No Heston.

He's the last person I want to witness my attempt at two laps. After confirming that the coast is clear, I shuck off my shirt and shorts, leaving them on the bench by the wall. Excited, I dart across the pool deck and jump in.

The water is a shock to my system, sending my frayed nerves alight. It's refreshing, motivating, and suddenly everything seems clear to me. I start by mimicking the motions I've seen other swimmers do, cutting my arms through the water. It works...

Sort of.

I don't glide like normal swimmers do, and I'm not entirely sure why. My motions grow choppy just to keep me afloat, and it's nothing like it should be. It's not graceful or effortless. It's tiring. Ten minutes in, my legs feel like dead weight. Why don't they propel me forward like they're supposed to?

I stop, gasping for air, feeling the burden of my body as it slowly starts sinking. I look around and realize I'm in the center of the pool—the deepest part—and too far away from the sides.

"Shit," I say, swishing my hands. It causes a wave of water to come toward me, splashing into my mouth. I cough and sputter, taking in more water. A cramp seizes my side and I yelp, bending to ease the pressure. A realization hits me with a startling clarity.

I'm going to drown.

"Help!" I shriek, panicking. It's getting harder to kick. My legs are like noodles, and *Jesus Christ*, I am such an idiot. Two hours of ineffectual masturbation had my legs wobbly and weak even before I subjected my muscles to the water. I try to take in a long breath before my body sinks, but I only manage a small gulp before the water rises over my head, swallowing me whole.

It's different when I'm under. Quiet. Tranquil. It's not like it was when I was seven, falling into the deep-end and freezing up, gulping water into my lungs until my father found me. That experience had been all about fear and shock. But this?

This feels less like I'm sinking and more like I'm being cradled by a million pinpoints of silence and calm. Down here, the urges are too far away to touch me. There is no resonance, no bone-deep pulse of need, no shame, no regret, no ache for a release that won't even sate me. There are no whispers or stares, no ridicule or judgment. I watch one of my last bubbles of air float in front of my eyes, ascending to the soft ripples above, and maybe it's wrong, but the only thing I feel is grateful.

It makes it easy to I close my eyes. To let the silence cradle me. To stop fighting.

This.

This must be what peace feels like.

I sink downward, toes grazing the bottom of the pool, weightless and strangely relieved. I don't even flinch at the tug of my hair, the brush of a hand on my shoulder, the arm that winds around my middle, clamping tight. I'm jettisoned upward with a surge of strength that I know can't be coming from me. I'm not strong. I'm weak. Always, always weak.

I break the surface with an involuntary gasp of needle-sharp air that punches a wet, wracking cough from my lungs. My hair is plastered over my eyes, heavy and cold. It's not until I have a hand secured to the cement lip of the pool that I shove it aside.

Heston, who's got an elbow hooked over the edge, is fully dressed, dripping wet, and from the way he's glaring at me, completely irate. "What the fuck do you think you're doing?"

I flinch at the boom of his voice, amplified by the echo. "I just wanted to—"

"Drown? Make me ruin a good pair of shoes?" A black shoe floats by and he reaches out to snatch it from the water, tossing it out of the pool. "Jesus, Haynes, I knew you were a little crazy, but I didn't realize you had an actual death wish."

"I wasn't trying to kill myself!" I shout, feeling some of that thrum returning. "I just wanted some extra practice, and I thought I was alone!"

"How fucking stupid can you get?!" he barks. "You can't swim! What were you expecting to happen?" He hoists himself out of the pool, revealing his soaked jeans and socks. He looks down at me, nostrils flared wide, and then offers me a hand.

I look away, teeth gnashing. "I'm fine."

"Shut the fuck up." He thrusts his hand closer. "Take my hand, idiot."

After a long moment, I relent, reaching for his wet palm. He yanks me out of the water so hard my shoulder almost dislocates. I watch him wring out the hem of his shirt, clucking in annoyance at the deluge of water that falls from it.

"You didn't give a shit when I was drowning before," I mutter quietly. I'm speaking metaphorically, of course. Not that he would know. I don't even intend for him to hear it at all.

But he does.

His head jerks up, eyes narrowing. "What the fuck are you talking about?"

I shake my head, suddenly feeling exhausted. "Nothing. Forget it." I turn on my heel, storming away. This entire experience was supposed to help me, not plunge me even further into turmoil and frustration.

But I hear his footsteps following me, and just as we reach the office, he grabs my arm, spinning me around. "You know, I'm getting real sick of your whole 'woe is me' act. You know what your problem is, Haynes? You don't take accountability for your own goddamn choices."

I gape as he stalks into the little office, kicking off his other shoe, bending to yank each sock off. "*I* don't take accountability? *Me*?" My voice rises, full of disbelief. "Are you serious right now?!"

He opens up the locker by the wall and strips off his wet shirt, tossing it on the plastic chair in the corner with a heavy slap. "I didn't force you to do a goddamn thing that night." I can't help but stare at the taut muscles in his back and the two perfect dimples right above the waistband of his sagging, water-logged jeans.

When I reach down to snap the rubber band, I realize that it's gone—probably lost in the pool when my arms were thrashing around.

Shit.

He glances back, his ice-blue eyes sweeping over me. "You wanted it. You *know* you wanted it."

Hotly, I respond, "I never said I didn't."

He whirls to face me, eyebrows crouched low. "You sent the cops after me!"

I can't argue with that, but it was never about the sex. It was about Sydney. About him threatening Sugar. About the way he was fucking with Bass. The way he bought and sold whoever crossed his path, acquiring leverage, making bets. "I never gave you permission to record us, Heston, and I definitely never said you could spread it around. Do you have any idea what that did to me? Do you even care?" Scoffing, I add, "Who am I talking to? Of course you don't."

"I didn't tell anyone it was you." He scrubs his fingers aggressively through his hair, sending droplets spraying all over. "And if you'd kept your mouth shut, no one would have ever known."

"I would have known!" I argue, fighting a shiver at the way he's looking at me. "I was fourteen, asshole."

"So what? I was sixteen." He throws his arms wide, veins in his forearm bulging. "I was trying to build a reputation. That's what Devils do." He shrugs like this is acceptable reasoning. If I think there's anything close to an apology coming next, I'm dead wrong. Instead, he stalks toward me, jaw tense. "You know what I think? I think you got a taste of my dick and you *liked* it. I think you wanted more. I think you're being a pissy little bitch because I didn't come back for seconds."

"God, you're so fucking vain." I flick my eyes down to his crotch. His jeans are wet and clingy. The outline of his cock is well defined. I dig my fingernails into the soft skin of my wrist. "I'll admit that I went up there willingly. I'll even admit that I liked it, but I will *never* admit that I wanted to fuck you again. Ever!"

He stops in front of me, face shuttered. "Really."

"Really!"

He tilts his head, thumbing his jeans open. "Then why are your nipples so hard?"

"They're—" My jaw drops, and I cross my hands over my chest. Fuck. They're sharp as the tip of a knife. "I'm wet, asshole. And cold. It has nothing to do with you!"

"You're so full of shit," he says, voice low. "You aren't even looking me in the eye."

My eyes jerk up from his happy trail, nails digging harder into my wrist. "Fuck you."

He drops his pants. He's commando underneath, absolutely nothing hiding the angry jut of his hard cock. I stare at it, slack-jawed and paralyzed, and I must be drawing blood by now with how hard I'm pressing my nails into my skin.

I tear my eyes away, blood rushing in my ears. "What the hell are you doing?"

"You still want it," he says, voice hard and unapologetic. "You've been thinking about it this whole time."

"No." It comes out weak.

"Yes." He almost seems bored as he reaches out to the strap of my suit, and God. If he touches me, he's going to find out how warm I am.

So I slap his arm away, my palm landing so hard that it rattles my shoulder. Even though his hand darts out to catch my wrist in a bruising grip, fire blazes through my veins when I meet his gaze. "No one wants to fuck you, Heston. You're a twenty-one-year-old college drop-out who has no friends, no family, and no future."

He goes eerily still. I watch as a droplet of water slouches down a lock of his hair, landing on the flat line of his eyebrow. His voice is low and full of warning. "What the fuck did you just say to me?"

"You heard me, asshole." I clench my teeth against the way my heart thuds, the pinch of his fingers around my wrist. "You're a pathetic, washed-up loser whose sole accomplishment was peaking in high school. You're *embarrassing*."

In an attempt to pull my wrist free, I strike out with my other hand, but it becomes a frenzied whirr of bone and muscle as he wrestles me back, pushing me against the open door. I fall into it, slamming it closed, staring up into his blazing eyes.

At some point, his broad palm has found its way beneath my chin, fingertips digging into my jaw. "Tell me you don't want it." In a low, hard growl, he demands, "Tell me your pussy isn't wet for me right now. Tell me that if I bent you over that desk and fucked you black and blue, it wouldn't be the best night you've ever had. Tell me, and I'll let you go."

"So help me god, Heston," I whisper, voice sounding just as ragged as I feel. I let my head fall back against the door, eyes sliding closed. "if you don't fuck me at least that hard, I'm going to make you pay for it." There's a moment of tense silence. I don't open my eyes. I couldn't take his viciously smug expression.

He's still pinning me to the door when his hand comes up to roughly yank the straps of my suit down, exposing my breasts. He palms one of them, voice dropping to a deep, harsh octave. "You've tricked all your friends, the cops, my *brother*, into thinking you're the victim, but you're still a whore, aren't you?"

My eyes fly open, wide and incensed. "I'm not a whore! I'm just..." I swallow back the explanation of what I am, why I do his.

I'm just desperate.

But the way he's looking at me makes my heart stop. It's cold and dark. Hungry. Malicious. It's just like that night—the look of someone who wants to hurt me.

I've never been wetter in my goddamn life.

It should make me feel scared, ashamed. But all I can think about is how it felt under that water, when I thought everything might end, and I don't care. All I care about is how alive I feel right now. The way his hands feel on me when he wrenches me away from the door. How his fingers yank my bathing suit over my hips, leaving it bunched at my feet. The way he threads his fingers through my hair and snaps my head back. I hiss at the pain while pushing my hips into him. He spins me, shoving me carelessly at the desk. I go easily, but you wouldn't know it by the way he moves, lurching and turbulent, a palm planted into the center of my back, pressing hard—too hard—making me slam chest-first into the hard wood.

"Shut the fuck up," he says when I yelp, kicking at my ankles, spreading me open. His fingers drag roughly down my bared pussy, and with a wash of humiliation, I know he's realizing just how wet I am for this. "You like it rough—I know you do. Take it like the bitch you are."

"Fuck you," I spit, hips squirming, seeking the hardness against the back of my thigh.

He responds by grabbing my hip, crushing it in his grip to steady me. "Stay still," he growls, lining himself up.

He enters me abruptly, cruelly, making me cry out in surprise. Three months is a long time to be without this. Unstretched, unprepared. It's almost like losing my virginity again, the sting, the feeling of being so full that I have to gulp in a series of slow breaths to adjust to it.

Heston doesn't give me time to. He tangles one fist in my hair, smashing my head down, and curls the other around my hip, pinning me painfully close.

And then he fucks me.

I have to grab the edge of the desk to feel any sense of being grounded. "Oh my god," I gasp. "Oh my god, oh my god." I clench my eyes closed, tethered between two opposing forces—the pleasure of his cock and the pain of his hands, the brutality of him pounding into me with short, deep, thumping shoves. My hips knock into the wood with every hammering thrust, and I know it's going to bruise. The sharp rumbles coming from his chest, the slap of our flesh and muscle, the way he wrenches me back when I shift too far up the desk, snapping out a curt, "Stay still, bitch."

Holy shit.

It's fucking *art*.

My first orgasm is the actual essence of gratification. It explodes through me, taking every bit of thought, every worry, every ounce of tension with it. I know I'm being loud, but I don't care. When Heston snaps his arm up, taking a handful of my hair with it, stinging against my scalp, it just makes it that much better. The burn meets the peak and I hover there, suspended in bliss, before dropping like a sack of bricks.

"Jesus Christ, shut the fuck up," he growls into my cheek, curled low over my back. "I knew you'd get off on this. People think you're a slut for dick, but they're wrong. You're a slut for *this*, aren't you?" He punctuates this with another sharp yank of my hair, slamming my hips into the desk.

I cry out, already feeling the tension building low in my belly, all over again. I open my mouth, lips moving, but I don't even hear what I'm saying. Not until I hear his grunt in my ear—not until I'm filled with the panic that this might be ending.

"Don't stop," I'm chanting. "Don't stop, don't stop, don't stop."

"Shut up," he answers, panting. "Shut the *fuck* up!" But he presses harder, pulls sharper, fucks me violently—like a caged animal—and it's not long before I'm sobbing wet breaths into the wood, coming so hard that my vision goes white, edged in frantic static.

I'm too fucked-out, breathless and boneless, to care when his mouth latches onto my shoulder, teeth sinking into the flesh as his hips punch into me one last time. He grunts, long and ragged into my skin, biting down hard enough that I gasp, flinching away. He just presses harder in response, crushing me beneath his weight as he pulses deep inside.

I can feel his hot come trickle out of me when he drags himself away.

"Oh, god."

No condom.

He fucked me raw.

By the time I get my legs under me, steady enough to lever myself upright, he's already half-dressed and leaving the office.

"Bring a pair of fucking floaties next time, Little Red."

6

"HERE ARE the requirements for the intro class." Coach James pauses, clipboard in hand, and looks at my soaked jeans hanging from the hook by the door. I was running late and hadn't had time to clean up the puddle underneath. "Did you fall in?"

"Something like that," I mutter, tossing a towel over the mess. His eyebrow raises and I sigh. "I came back in last night to get my phone and saw a kickboard in the pool. I thought I could reach it, but I missed."

Coach barks out a laugh. "What I would've paid to have seen that. Heston Wilcox doesn't make too many mistakes."

"You're right. Don't expect that to *ever* happen again."

He gives me an odd look but hands me the clipboard and walks out of the room.

There are no bones about it.

I'm sweating fucking bullets today.

I was supposed to get my dick into that girl and win the bet— get half my debt wiped clean. Easy. Simple. I knew she'd be down for it. It doesn't take a rocket scientist to see how horny Georgia Haynes is and let's face it. I know how I look.

It was her tits. God, it's always been her tits. Her nipples are perpetually erect, the signal that she's always turned on. Georgia Haynes is a filthy whore and begs to be treated like it.

But something in me just snapped. It was that fucking comment about me having no future, no family, no friends. As if she wasn't the cause of it. My brain couldn't decide if I wanted to fuck her or kill her.

So I got as close as I could to doing both.

I've had a lot of rough fucks in my time, but that was some truly next-level shit. I banged her so hard that even *I* have bruises today. If Georgia is looking for a reason to take me down, I just handed it to her on a silver platter.

I couldn't have planned the opportunity any better if I'd tried. I wasn't even thinking about her when I came down here last night. I was still pissed about Collins and the fact I had to sit there and force myself not to smack the slimy, condescending grin off his face. That prick just loves having me by the balls. I only came down to the pool when I realized I'd left my phone in the top drawer of the desk.

And there she was, in all her fucked-up glory, drowning in the pool.

At some point it occurred to me that Big Gene must be right about me not being a true sociopath. Because seeing her sink in that pool, the possibility of letting her drown never once crossed my mind. Irritation, sure. Disbelief. Maybe a little amusement. An overwhelming sense of being completely fucking inconvenienced, because there was no way I could just leave. But never apathy.

I should have let her drown, though. Would've served her snitching, scheming, slutty ass right. I know she's the mastermind behind turning me in to the cops. Sydney wouldn't have had the balls or the motive to do it on her own. That girl is pathetically weak. I only fucked with her to get back at my brother, and I suspect she was doing it for the same reason. But Georgia? She's wanted to get back at me for a long time.

Now she's got my DNA in her cunt, my teeth marks in her shoulder, and my fingerprints bruised into her hips. It would take nothing for her to waltz into a hospital and say I raped her. Everything is on her side—the evidence, my record, motive.

Jesus Christ, I'm a moron.

Mostly, at least.

This thing with my stomach is getting worse, and the worry isn't making it any better. It feels like I've got fucking razor blades churning around in there. I'm tossing back two hard swallows of chalky medicine when a soft knock on the door draws my attention. Georgia stands in the doorway, expression tight. She's wearing that same boring suit as the day before. I don't acknowledge her. I wait for the hammer to drop. No way she's leaving this on the field.

"I need to talk to you before class." She moves to shut the door.

"Keep it open." Christ, I don't need people knowing we're alone in here.

"It's…" She pauses, shifting uncomfortably. "…*personal.*"

"I know you're a skank, Haynes, but I'm not fucking you again." *Ever.* I won the bet. Got the proof. Done and done.

Her pink lips purse together, eyes darting around anxiously. "It's not that."

"Then what? Having second thoughts about last night?" As casually as possible—I won't let this bitch see me sweating—I throw out the very thought that's got my temples throbbing with tension. "Thinking about going to the cops? Should I expect Dewey to escort me off campus?"

"What?" She actually frowns, having the gall to look confused by the suggestion. "No, I just…" But she trails off, cheeks growing pink. Now, I notice the glowing red tip of her nose. Either she has a wicked cold, or she's been crying.

Gross.

I bark, "Spit it out, Haynes. Class is starting in two minutes and you and Adams already skipped one."

There's another long pause before she huffs. "Fine. I need to know if you've been tested."

I raise an eyebrow. "Tested?"

She glances nervously over her shoulder before inching closer, voice lowering. "You didn't use anything. I need to know if I should get tested. You know. For STDs."

I stare at her for a long moment, unable to believe what's coming out of her mouth. "You're afraid that *I* gave *you* something?" I motion between us. "You, the person who's seen more ceilings than Michelangelo, are asking if *I'm* an STD risk. Are you fucking shitting me?"

Her face hardens. "Don't be an asshole, Heston. I might have a reputation, but I also have one hard and fast rule: always use a condom. *Always.*"

I tap my pen on the desk, and her eyes dart to it. My gaze follows and I know just what she's thinking—that less than ten hours ago, I had her bent over this spot right here, slamming my dick so far into her pussy, she could probably taste it. She was tight, too. Shockingly tight. I figured a pussy with as much mileage as hers would be like fucking a sinkhole, but that wasn't the case at all.

"Bullshit."

She blinks, meeting my gaze. "Excuse me?"

I shrug. "There's no way you're going to believe me if I tell you not to worry about it. You're not that stupid. You're going to get tested, regardless. Which means you're in here right now to test the temperature."

She rolls her eyes. "Oh my god, would you just answer the damn question?"

"I haven't been tested in months," I say, not caring about the flash of disappointment in her eyes. "Now, if that's all, we need to get started with class. You can begin by explaining why you're still wearing that shitty bathing suit. I believe we had an agreement."

Her lips press into a tense line. "It's the only one I have. Deal with it."

"That's bullshit, too," I say, pointing the pen at her. "If you're going to lie, be good at it. You're just wearing this to piss me off."

Her face screws up angrily. "No, I'm not. If you absolutely must know, this bathing suit has more coverage than any of my others.

And you should probably show a little more appreciation for it, given the reason I need coverage."

Shit.

The bruises.

I reach up to rub at my mouth, eyes wandering down to her hips. Last night, they'd barely been a shadow. But I still remember that first time, years ago, seeing her the day afterward in Econ, shirt riding up, revealing the palette of red, blue, and purple hiding beneath. Fuck, it'd gotten me instantly hard.

Georgia bruises *beautifully*.

There's no other word for it.

As if in a daze, I quietly demand, "Show me."

"What?" The high pitch of her voice snaps me out of it. "Are you insane?"

I straighten, remembering the mark I'd seen on her last night, when I had her bent over and begging for me not to stop. A Devil's mark tattooed on the base of her neck. Which means she's dating, or has dated, one of the guys. There's no other reason to get marked like that. It's information I filed away for later, but now it makes me uncertain. I don't like not knowing my enemies.

"Go get in the pool," I snap at her, standing. "And try not to drown this time."

She scowls, but walks off, her curvy—*bruised*—hips swaying side to side. My dick twitches and I run my hand through my hair, tugging at the ends. When she's far enough across the pool, I walk over to the bookshelf and remove the small recording device hidden behind last year's All State Trophy. It's been running for two days now—last night included.

There's one thing about a bet; you have to prove it. Is it stupid of me to do the same thing I'm on probation for? Probably. But I record my fucks for a reason. You don't screw girls as roughly as I do without a little insurance to cover your ass.

If Georgia has any plans of framing me, then at least I have this.

I just hope like hell it's got fantastic audio.

～

I CAN TELL they're both bracing for the worst when I meet them out on the deck. "Haynes, put your hair up. Adams," I say to the kid, who's standing there holding his elbow, looking terminally bored. "Lose the shirt."

He argues, "Coach told me I could wear whatever makes me comfortable."

"Did he? That was cool of him." I smile at him, but from the way his face falls, I'm betting he can see the meanness in it. "*This* coach is telling you to ditch the shirt. Now."

Arms up in the air, tying her hair into a knot, Georgia jumps in. "There's nothing wrong with him wearing a shirt with his trunks. You're just trying to humiliate him!"

"No one asked you a goddamn thing, Haynes." I look at Micha, demanding, "Take it off."

"No." There's a flash in his eyes—something angry and troubled. "I got special permission. You just want to pick on me because—"

"You want to know what wet clothes do? As someone who was in this pool last night, fully clothed, allow me to elaborate." I swing my glare to Georgia. "It weighs you down. It tangles you up. For someone who can't swim, it wants to see you fucking *dead*."

He crosses his arms, unblinking. "No."

This little fucker... "You can take the shirt off, or you can get out of my class."

His eyebrows crouch low, and I can tell from the way he shifts his weight from foot to foot that he's conflicted. He probably thought he'd have something over me. He probably thought he could run and tattle the second I said something he didn't like and get his way. He's realizing that this one won't go in his favor. Irritably, he bites out, "Hell no. I'm not showing you my body."

"I couldn't give less of a shit what your body looks like, Adams."

"Heston," Georgia cuts in again, giving me a scathing look. "Let it go."

"No," I refuse, holding Micha's glare. "If you want to cover your chest, you can wear a one-piece." I gesture to Georgia's red and black Lycra monstrosity. "I'm assured they have excellent coverage."

Even though she looks pissed, Georgia blushes, ducking her head.

That just makes him look even more irate. "So you can call me a freak? Tease me? Make me feel like crap for an hour?"

This kid is seriously testing my patience. "You've never had an issue wearing girl's clothes before." I gesture to the empty natatorium. "There's no one else here. And since when do you give a shit what other people think? You're Micha Adams. The eight years I've known you, you've never once worn something just because it'd get you picked on less."

"Things change," he says, shoulders shifting uneasily. It's the first time I've ever seen this kid anything but brutally self-assured.

Shit, maybe I *had* actually hurt his feelings with that prank two years ago.

How utterly disappointing.

"Let's get one thing straight," I say, tossing my clipboard aside. I cross my arms, leveling them with a look. "I have history with the both of you. Maybe you hate me. Maybe I hate you. Maybe I hurt your poor little girl feelings. I don't give a shit. When we're here," I point to the pool, voice hard, "I'm responsible for not letting you *die*. How we feel about each other means jack shit. When this whistle is around my neck, I'm your coach, and I might be a prick, but if there's one thing I take seriously, it's swim. So I'm going to tell you one more time." I look at Micha. "Coach said to wear what makes you feel comfortable. If a one-piece makes you comfortable, then you have five minutes to grow a spine and go put one on. Otherwise, get the fuck out."

I grab the stopwatch around my neck, thumbing it.

After a moment of glaring at me, he heaves a hard breath and storms off toward the locker room.

Georgia purses her lips, head shaking. "I've never met a bigger asshole than you in my entire life." Then she walks off after him.

Nevertheless, five minutes later, they both return. Micha's wearing a one-piece under his trunks—a bit overkill if you ask me, but what do I care—and has his chin jutted out, eyes challenging me to say something.

"Now that you've wasted a whole shit-load of my time, let's get started."

I put them in the shallow end, making them grab the sides and practice their kicks. Micha flops his feet like an over-excited, if grumpy, golden retriever. Georgia's legs are a little longer, a little more graceful. But not by much.

As I watch her, barking out a command now and then, I can't help but wonder if this is really it—If she's not going to turn me in. She still looks pissed at me, but aside from sharing a bunch of sulky, aggravated looks with Micha, she doesn't let it show. I don't think I've ever met a girl who could take a fuck that ruthless. Even Sydney, who was champing at the bit to get pounded by me, was twitchy and distant after—and I held back with her. Not that I cared. She could have said no at any point. Forcing myself on someone who doesn't want it has never been my bag. But I'm not a goddamn mind reader, either.

Fucking Georgia makes me look at all of them, every girl I've fucked, in a new, doubtful light. By comparison, Georgia was unquestionably into it. Un-fucking-questionably. Bitch ruined my life and is going to get what's coming to her, but I can't help but feel a little impressed. This girl can take a seriously brutal dicking-down. It's a shame to let it go to waste.

But I'm done playing with fire.

SINCE COMING HERE, I've only been from the pool to my pathetic excuse for an apartment. I'm not really sure how to handle myself in this place. Back in the day, me and my boys owned this campus. I was a king. A Devil, a legacy, a star athlete. Now I'm some kind of cautionary tale, proof that popularity and wealth can disappear in just a few short years' time.

Food lures me from my routine. Access to the dining hall comes with the job. I've climbed these steps to dinner a million times and nothing has changed; not the look, or the smell, or the cafeteria lady who narrows her eyes at me when I pass through the line. It really hits me when I turn and face the room. For the first time in my life, I have no idea where to sit. No idea where I belong. My eyes jump to the table in the middle of the room—the Devil's table. It's empty.

Maybe Collins is wrong. Maybe they all graduated with my brother.

"Mr. Wilcox, you look lost." I glance down and see Dr. Ross sitting at the teachers' table. "Sit."

"Here?" I ask, just barely holding back a grimace. "With you?"

The way she dips her head, staring at me over a pair of glasses, tells me she heard the scorn there. "You're an adult. It's my understanding you're helping Coach James, which means you qualify as faculty." She nods at the empty seat next to hers. "Plus, you're clogging the flow of the line, and I don't like that."

Her tone drags me back to my days as a student, and I almost expect her to threaten me with detention, even though she can't. At least...I don't think she can. Can she? Can she still make my life hell? I'd bet on it. I slide into the seat across from Mr. Lee and eye his cheap clothes. There are tired lines crowding up against his eyes, something aged and ragged. *Jesus.* Is that what happens to you in this place? Because that's motivation enough to get out of here fast.

I ignore the teacher-themed chatter happening around me—something about staying late at an upcoming conference—and scan the room, trying to figure out who's most likely to be a Devil. It's less that I fear Collins and more that I'm just curious. The LAX guys are still huddled at the same table. As much as I hate them, they're all hot heads like my brother. They've got the right alpha vibe. I recognize two of them, Gus Meyers and Peter Norton, from a few parties back in the day. Buck Smith is sitting on the other side of the table. Peter's got a hot girl leaning into him, ignoring the flirty way she's rubbing his shoulder.

I take a bite of my sandwich, watching some of the other tables. Emory and Reynolds were football players. Maybe some of them are in on it.

Someone new but strangely familiar crosses the room, catching my attention. My interest piques further when he heads straight to the old Devils table, which had been occupied when I wasn't looking by none other than Georgia, Vandy and that super geek, Caroline.

"Who is that?" I ask, interrupting the conversation. Dr. Ross frowns, but Mr. Lee follows my gaze.

"Oh, that's Headmaster Collins' son."

"Collins has a son?" I look again, realizing why he looked vaguely familiar. It's in the face, the line of their jaws, their noses, their eyes.

"Oswald Collins," Mr. Lee adds. "I think he went to another school until recently."

"Oswald," I snort. Loser name. Across the room, this Oswald fucker smiles at Georgia and she grins back, leaning toward him. His eyes dart down to her chest, and I can almost see the wheels turning. He's wondering if they're real.

Hell yes, they are.

I inhale the rest of my dinner and leave the table without another word. I don't think about where I'm going until I'm halfway across campus, the opposite direction from my apartment, and standing under the Devil's Tower. It's not quite dark yet and the sun glints off the old bell hanging up top. I get this brief swell of something that might be called nostalgia on anyone else. I wasn't as well-traveled as the others, but I'd brought a bit of tail up here when I was a student.

There's one way to find out who the Devils are; the tallies on the beam.

Climbing up the stairs, I'm struck by the familiar, imprinted scent. It's part woodsy-outdoors, and part dusty stone and wood. There's another sensation that overcomes me as I get to the top, eyes shifting to the arched window. I'd been leaning there when I got my own mark, a blow job from Jessica Cantrell. A bitter taste fills my mouth at the memory. Jessica was an older, hot, and exceptionally experienced Plaything. She'd had this incident on her horse just before school started, and when the Devils initiated me, they told me to go for it because she was a little busted up, but she was easy—*good*. Too good and busted up, it turns out, for my virgin-self. Her jaw had this crazy bruise, like nothing I'd ever seen before —so dark it was almost navy.

She'd just parted her lips to take me in her mouth when my body seized, cum dripping from her mottled chin.

It was embarrassing as fuck, and I'd vowed never to let it happen again.

I push past my shame to the sins of other Devils, looking up at the scarred beam overhead. I see my own initials with a modest tally underneath, along with Hamilton's, Xavier's, and Ansel's. I still remember the first day we came up here and saw our initials carved into the wood. We hadn't carved them—the senior Devils at the time had. We were all legacies. That's how it worked. We had a place carved out for us since day one.

I see Sebastian's, which to be honest, bro racked up a string before he settled down with that piece of white trash. As I suspected, under the old R.M. for Reynolds there is a fresh slash. The other initials are jumbles of letters I don't recognize until I pause on a G.H.

G.H.?

Georgia pops into my mind first, but then it shifts to her skinny twin, George. Did they really let that loser in the Devils? Jesus, it's worse than I thought.

I jolt when I hear the creak of hinges downstairs, quietly descending the stairs to investigate. A door closes and footsteps echo around the stonework. There's only one door in the Devil's Tower besides the entrance; a locked door on the ground floor. No one that I know of has ever been through it. Until now. I try the handle but it's locked tight, so old and decrepit that it's probably melded to the stone. Maybe I'd imagined it.

I exit the tower and head back across campus, feeling a little adrift. I'd owned this place for four years. Suddenly there's no discernable power structure. People like Collins don't get it—that a place like Preston needs that. It might be petty and juvenile, built on the backs of the less socially fortunate, but a school like this would eat itself from the bottom up without it. I used to think

Hamilton understood. Until he started fooling around with Gwendolyn Adams.

People think we fell out because of injured loyalties, but they're wrong. It was about Preston needing a leader and Hamilton refusing to honor it. It should have been me. I wouldn't have abandoned my responsibilities to the Devils for some second-rate pussy. I would have made us feared. Respected. Powerful.

Instead of leading the Devils, I'm serving time to bring them down.

Fucking stupid.

As I walk back to my apartment to grab my car keys, I see Georgia, Caroline, and Oswald sitting in the courtyard. It's almost dark, but they're huddled around the guy's phone, laughing at something he's showing them. Obnoxiously, I might add. Georgia throws her head back, a peal of laughter drawing stares. Well, isn't she just happy as a fucking peach?

The sight makes my fists curl. I remember her beneath me last night, holding on tight as I fucked her just the way she wanted. I remember that, for most of it, I wanted to wrap my hand around her throat. Take her back out to that pool and hold her beneath the surface, look on coolly as she thrashed around. Make her regret ever fucking with me.

As soon as an opportunity reveals itself, that's exactly what I'm going to do.

I FEEL BETTER when I get to the club. More grounded, like I'm back in my own skin. Last night was the first night I'd left Underworld in the hands of my staff since Big Gene set up shop in my VIP lounge, and the thought makes me restless and annoyed.

Kevin greets me with a firm slap of our palms. "His boys are up there," he says, giving me a look.

I don't react beyond a single nod, walking inside. It's a little less crowded tonight—Tuesdays always are—so it's easy to spot Gene and his flunkies, loitering up in the loft. They stick out like a sore thumb, dressed up in cheap, tacky menswear. These aren't my father's kind of loan sharks. There are no cigars or aged whiskey. Gene's boys are rough around the edges, trying so hard to seem rich and powerful that they look like they're playing dress up in daddy's old clothes.

Big Gene greets me with a slimy grin and an outstretched hand. "Here's our little prince."

I stare at his hand. Instead of shaking it, I pull the USB from my pocket and hold it up. "This," I say, giving it a wiggle, "is half my debt erased."

His smile melts into a hard expression. "You fucked the little princess?"

"It's like I've been saying. She's a whore." Shrugging, I slide into the booth across from him, spinning the drive between my fingers. "I have proof."

When he reaches out to take it, I snatch it away. "Don't be stingy, boy. Share and share alike."

Smirking, I close it in my fist. "I'm not letting this one get out. In case you've forgotten, I already have two strikes for sharing videos."

He raises an eyebrow. "So I'm just supposed to take your word for it?"

I wave Tara over, needing a drink. "We can watch it later. Alone. Without any phones recording."

He grins back. I'm not sure I like it. "Very well. Have it your way." Tucking the drive back into my pocket, I get the tingle of awareness that this is too easy. He takes a slow sip of his cheap vodka, not breaking my gaze, and I bite back a curse, knowing I'm right. This is confirmed when he waves three of his boys over. "Dirty and I were just talking about a new wager, anyway." Gene only calls one of his boys in when the deal is too big to happen without a witness. One flunkie means it's important. Two means the stakes are high. He's calling in three.

Goddamn it.

I look at one of the approaching toadies—Dirty, who lives up to the nickname in every conceivable way. "Is the wager whether he bathes this month? Because I don't like those odds." They slip into the booth when Gene nods at them and I inch away, lip curling up as Dirty takes the space beside me.

"I think you'll like this one," Gene says, smirking. "It's got everything a gambling addict could want. High stakes, intrigue, good odds."

I wonder if my expression looks as flat as it feels. "I'm not gambling anymore."

He looks at my pocket where the USB is hidden and laughs, raising his glass. "Good one."

"That was different."

He flaps a hand. "Sure, you can quit whenever you want. It was just one more hit. This is a new 'you'." He looks at Dirty. "Junkies. Always the same song and dance." Shaking his head, he continues, "You don't have anything to worry about, Wilcox. This is really less of a bet and more of a..." He lifts a palm, tilting it back and forth. "Job."

"I already have a job," *two of them actually,* "and I'm not one of your low-rent minions. I've cleared half my debt and you've already taken ten grand from the business. That leaves me forty in the hole. I'll have it paid off by winter."

He frowns dramatically. "You haven't even asked me what the payout is. No wonder you got a hundred g's into the hole with me. You're terrible at this."

Shrugging, I lie, "I don't care."

There's a reason I never want to hear the payout—the endgame. It's too enticing. Some people call me a gambling addict, but they're only half right. It's not the game I'm addicted to. It's the win. The power. Making the right calls, watching someone else lose. I already know Gene is going to lose. I'm going to pay him back half without interest.

I should have known he wouldn't let that go.

He stares at me for a long moment, calculating in that way of his. "The whore. Georgia Haynes."

Already bored, I look away. "What about her?"

"Haynes," he repeats. "As in Elijah Haynes? As it *just so happens,* the princess's daddy is currently embarking on the campaign trail."

To Dirty, he explains, "He's running for state senator next year, and believe me, daddy makes bank."

I let out a low, humorless laugh, head shaking. "That's why you wanted to know if I could fuck her." *Of-fucking-course.*

His eyebrows bob up and down. "What can I say? Call it research. Now that we know, I'm thinking we should capitalize on this rare opportunity." His face transforms into something that no one at the table wants to see. Stony. All business. "Get close to the girl, find me some leverage against her old man, and you'll get your club back. Better than that, I'll repay you the ten grand I've already garnished from this fine, upstanding establishment. I won't even make you show me that video you've made."

"Jesus Christ," I mutter, head shaking. "Georgia and her brother don't even live at home. They both board at Preston."

"Who else do we know who's boarding at the snotty little rich-kid school?" He hums, rubbing his chin. "Oh, right. It's you. Sounds like round-the-clock access to all a manner of family secrets if you ask me."

There's no losing in this for Gene. Either I don't get him anything and he takes my club, or I get him the dirt he wants and he cons his way into something bigger and better. It leaves a bitter taste in my mouth. There's no sport to it. No kill shot.

"Georgia and I can't stand each other," I tell him. "There's no getting close to her."

He snorts. "If you can fuck her, you can get close to her. She's a young lady, Wilcox. Fuck a young lady often enough, she'll catch feelings. All you have to do is be," he sweeps out a hand, "Prince Charming."

This time, my laughter is plenty amused. "Fuck me, you really don't know this girl at all."

"No," he agrees, eyes sparking. "But you do."

My smile falls, lips pursing contemplatively. There's no loss in this for Gene, but for Georgia? If I try, I can almost imagine it—her being the downfall of her own family. Shunned. Disowned. *Ruined.* Just like me. And all because she couldn't keep her legs closed—not even for the man she finds most repulsive.

That's it.

That's the kill shot.

"Fuck it." I pop a shoulder, lifting my glass. "Why not?"

The worst part is his reaction, all delighted and evilly smug. "Let's toast on it, shall we?" He and the flunkies all clink their glasses, and after a moment, I begrudgingly touch mine to his.

I tip back my drink, already knowing I'm going to find a way to make him lose, too. I know that's the real reason I feel adrift. It's the power structure, and my place in it. Big Gene, Collins, Georgia. They're the ones calling my shots—not me. Nothing since high school has been as easy or clear. It's all muddled out in the world, people climbing haphazardly, with no master or architecture. It's not like the Devils, where a place was just waiting for me to fill it. Adulthood is a bare swath of rotting wood, just waiting for a mark, and no one's about to add one for me.

I'll have to carve it myself.

7

It's a surprise when the familiar black envelope shows up in my locker. The hairs prick on the back of my neck and I glance up and down the hallway. I never knew who sent them in the first place. I assumed Emory, but there were six mysterious, masked people who inducted us into the society last year. Maybe it's been one of them all along.

Even though it's just the three of us, we agree to arrive separately to the tower. Now isn't the time to get lazy. I head down the musty stairs, using my key to get inside. I move a little more gingerly than usual, my hips and shoulder still aching. I try not to think about the pain—about how I got it—but it's difficult. I'm still awaiting the call from my nurse with my test results.

What happened with Heston—it was bad.

"Escalation of reckless and impulsive encounters, such as unprotected sex..." That'd been one predictor my therapist had harped on about. At the time, I hadn't worried about it much. Sure, I have the recurrent and intense sexual fantasies. The issues with establishing rela-

"

tionships. Using sex as a tension reliever. The remorse that follows. But I've always been smart and safe. *Always.*

Until now.

I'm the first one to arrive in the bunker, and as I approach the little table Emory always used to run meetings, I find a curious note.

Devils,

Only three of you remain. Enclosed, you'll find a memory card with the only existing copy of your initiation confessions. Destroy it or protect it.

It's now up to you to replenish the numbers.

Choose wisely.

Choose the strong.

Choose the deserving.

The fate of the Devils rests on your shoulders.

I hear a noise behind me and see Caroline in the doorway. Holding up the note and memory card, I explain, "Looks like someone left us instructions."

Caroline stares owlishly at the memory card. "Is that what I think it is?"

"Our confessions." Nodding, I turn it over in my hand. "And if they're to be believed, the only existing copy."

"Who do you think left it?"

I shrug, loose and unconcerned. "Hell if I know." Her gaze sweeps over me, a frown creasing her forehead. "What?" I ask, touching my hair. "Why are you looking at me like that?"

"Did swim go okay?" Caroline tilts her head, searching, "... Because you look *really chill,* but also like you've been crying."

I hold back a nervous laugh. That about sums everything up. What happened with Heston was bad. It was reckless and impulsive and bordering on self-harm. It was depraved. I'd gone back to my room and stared wide-eyed into space for two hours, unable to look at my own body and the marks he'd made on it. I've barely been able to eat because I keep remembering it, making my stomach churn in shame. I think of the way Sebastian would look at me. Vandy. Sugar. I think of how horrified they'd be if they knew, and it makes me want to crawl into a hole and die there.

But despite this.

Despite *everything*.

I can't stop thinking about Heston's dick.

And god, it was good dick. Fantastic dick. The kind of dick Victorian poets get their tits out to write about. It's not fair that such good dick belongs to someone as contemptible as Heston Wilcox.

But I can't tell her that. They'd have my ass committed.

Again.

"Swim was...embarrassing," I offer. "Heston is a jerk, and God knows he isn't going to make this easy on either of us, but I actually think I might survive. He's weirdly different once class starts."

"Different how?" she asks, expression skeptical.

I think about this, humming. "Very...to-the-point. Focused." Even though he clearly can't help the occasional crude remark, Micha at least seemed to relax pretty quickly once Heston ignored the one-piece. "I think maybe he's taking it seriously. Or at least as seriously as Heston could take anything." Caroline looks doubtful and I can't blame her.

"But you *have* been crying," she notes, and I curse my dumb complexion. My nose always gets neon-red when I've been crying, and there's no covering it up.

"It's nothing," I insist, eyes rolling. "PMS and hallway chatter. Complete overreaction."

Caroline gives me a look that's a bit too full of pity for my liking. I'm guessing she hasn't missed the marked increase in the whispers going around about me.

A moment later we both look toward the door and the sound of Vandy's awkward shuffle inside. She glances around at the empty room and says, "Well, this feels weird."

"Just the three of us?" Caroline asks, taking her normal seat. "Yeah, there's a significant lack of testosterone."

God, tell me about it.

Vandy also sits in one of the empty chairs and nods at the paper in my hand. "What's that?"

"A note from someone—whoever's running this show." I read it out loud, showing her the memory card, and then sit across from them, pulling out a small notebook. "I guess we need to pick a bunch of new Devils. Any nominations?"

"Well, if we're going on legacy, Carter is a sophomore." Carter is Caroline's brother. He plays soccer and is pretty popular. Less nerdy than Caroline, but also less interesting, in my opinion.

I write his name down, but muse, "You now, there's nothing in here about there even needing to be male Devils."

Caroline looks thoughtful. "You're thinking we should go all Playthings?"

"That would definitely be interesting." We all share a devious smile, but I just as quickly admit, "I really want to nominate Micha Adams, though."

"Oh!" Vandy says, clapping excitedly. "I love Micha! Definitely a yes from me. And hey, he's not really like...a *guy*-guy."

"But he's also not a *girl*-girl," Caroline adds. "Anyway, guys can come in handy, right? Remember the rites?"

"Good point." Being marked in the Stairway by another girl—or Micha—wouldn't be terrible or anything, but the breaking-and-entering, the pranks, the element of protection...

Caroline echoes my thoughts, "Some of that brute jock strength might be useful."

"You're right," I concede, giving up on the dream. Nodding, I add his name to the list. "We can just let Micha choose what he wants to be; Devil or Plaything."

"What about that new guy, Ozzy?" Vandy asks, face pensive.

Caroline twirls one of her French-braided pigtails, lips curving into a shy smile. "He's, like, pretty cute, right?"

I give her a look. In all my time here, I don't think I've ever seen Caroline express an interest in anyone. Now she's got the shy smile going on, ducking her head at my raised eyebrow. "Hell yeah, he's cute."

Vandy goes on, "I know he's the headmaster's son but, maybe that could come in handy?"

"Maybe," I agree, tapping my pen on my chin. "Let's find out a little more about him. He could be a narc."

Caroline's smile falls, but she nods. "I *cannot* risk any kind of drama this year. Not with college applications coming up. My mom is breathing down my neck about early admissions and the last thing I need is a disciplinary action just because we invited the wrong person in." Look at her, not thinking with her vag. Respectable.

Teach me your ways.

"Everyone will be thoroughly vetted," I assure her. "Anyone else? We need a couple more people." We spend the next few minutes tossing around names. Buck Smith is one. Gus Meyers and Peter Norton. Caroline suggests Fiona and Vandy balks.

"Are you kidding me? She and Sydney were thick as thieves."

"Well," I say, giving her a look, "so were you at one point. She is a cheerleader and a junior. She's pretty popular despite being friends with Sydney, and when all the stuff was going on with Heston, she did freak out. She wanted her to dump him, so she must not be completely stupid."

Vandy's expression is sour until she raises her eyebrow at me, and says, "What about your new roommate?"

"Josie?" I blurt. "Are you kidding?"

Vandy reasons, "She's pretty. I noticed she's in all AP classes, so she's smart. Obviously rich—"

"And *trouble*," I point out. "She's from Sparrowood. Talk about a narc. She's only been at Preston a few days, she has no sense of loyalty to us. What if she tells them about the Devils? That would fuck up everything." We glare at one another for a moment, until I sigh. "This is hard."

"No wonder they left it up to us," Vandy replies. "Dumbasses."

"Complete dumbasses!" I agree. "How do you recruit zero underclassmen to carry the torch?"

"The problem is that we're too nice," Caroline offers, her expression turning thoughtful. "We want, like, *good* people in the group, but remember our confessions? That first night, I was convinced I'd done something really stupid. I was hanging out with a bunch of liars and cheats and delinquents. But I realized that we all had shitty stuff in our past, and that shitty stuff is what bonded us, you know?"

She looks between us, and I nod. "That night changed my life."

Caroline smiles. "So let's stop thinking about the perfect person and start thinking about the perfect *Devil*. Those may not be the same thing."

"You're right," Vandy says, straightening. "I'm letting my personal grudge get in the way of this."

"Same," I agree. We're looking at this the wrong way. Devils need to be tough, fearless, resilient. They can't be afraid of getting into trouble, and they should have a little bit of a reputation. If Emory or Bass were here, I'd even ask their advice. But they're not. A thought occurs to me. "I mean, there is someone else on campus who was a Devil," I blurt, already feeling my face bloom hot. "Maybe even the best Devil, for a given value."

Vandy frowns. "Who?"

But Caroline knows just who I'm talking about. "Heston? You can't be serious. He helped destroy the Devils!"

"No, right, I know, I know," I say quickly, covering my tracks. "I don't even know why I said it."

But I do know. I know my habits and my cycles. My weaknesses. He was right earlier, about me coming to him to test the temperature. I never would have believed him if he'd told me he was clean. I just had to know what I was dealing with—whether I'd managed to put a wall back up around my libido.

I didn't like the answer.

Just like then, I realize I'm looking for a reason to talk to him. To be around him. To, you know, accidentally have my vagina fall on his cock.

I'm *disgusting*.

"I know you're taking the swim class with him," Vandy says, voice full of caution, "but I don't think it's a good idea for you to be around Heston very much. He's too manipulative and sneaky. I don't trust him."

"I don't either," I agree, glad that I'd chosen not to tell them about what happened in his office. That had nothing to do with trust, but people like Vandy and Caroline...

They're romantics.

They wouldn't understand sex for the sake of sex.

"You're right," I say, smiling tightly. "You're both right. I think just having him around makes me anxious. Like it's better to know where he is and what he's doing than to constantly wonder who he's gunning for next."

"That's reasonable. You two have a past—a really shitty past. No one blames you for being uncomfortable with him being here," Vandy says, slipping into her amateur psychiatrist role. She's the only person I know who's had more therapy than me. "I think the best thing is keeping him at as much distance is possible under the circumstances. You already have to be subjected to him for swim."

Caroline nods and takes the notepad from me. Together we flesh out a list and each pick a few recruits to do some recon on. We agree to come back together in a few days to compare and pick the final nine.

"What about that?" Caroline says, pointing to the memory card.

Vandy looks between us, palms up. "I'm already out about the pill addiction. I have less to lose than the two of you. Y'all decide."

Smirking, I look at Caroline. "Are you thinking what I'm thinking?"

She grins back. "Ceremonial bonfire?"

"Hell yeah!" I glance around the space pensively. "But we don't want to carry it on us, so until we can set a time..." I rifle around, ultimately deciding on an old, non-descript candy tin—Devil's Taffy—to tuck it safely inside of.

As we lock up and leave the Tower the same way we came, one at a time, I realize how glad I am that I still have the Devils—even if we have an impossible task ahead. If I'm going to stop thinking about Heston and what happened between us, I'm going to need as many distractions as I can get.

~

"HAYNES," Heston barks, his cold eyes barely passing over me. "You go to the end of the pool and practice treading water. Adams and I are going to work on the abomination that is his stroke."

Micha gives me a pleading look, like the last thing he wants to be is alone with Heston. I offer a smile of sympathy in return. Heston hasn't been the worst today—I mean, not that the bar is very high—but he does seem particularly impatient.

I take the sloping walk down to the other end, slowly getting deeper and deeper. If I thought my brush with drowning the other night might offer me some magical, water-related epiphany, then I'm wrong. If anything, it's just made me more nervous.

Everything is making me more nervous.

The drowning. Heston being back. Having sex with him. Having *unprotected* sex with him. Waiting for my test results. Wondering if he's telling anyone. Feeling ashamed all the time. Jilling off in a suite that has another occupant. The rubber band being virtually ineffective now.

All of this has sent me into a bit of a tailspin, but Vandy is right. I'm only human. Nothing here is unreasonable. I had a weak moment, but who can blame me?

I suck in a breath once the floor is out of reach, flailing around in an attempt to tread water. I can't help but remember being here before, screaming, aching, sinking. Panic seizes me and I paddle frantically toward the side of the pool, throat suddenly constricted. Once my fingertips graze the cool tiles, I hold on for dear life, panting. I glance back anxiously at Micha and Heston, but luckily neither are paying me any attention. The last thing I need is Heston realizing just how not prepared for this I am. Swimming really shouldn't be this hard.

A drop of water hits my hand, drawing my attention. I look up, seeing a boy I've never met before.

"You need some help?" The guy gives me a winning smile, all sparkling teeth and bright eyes. I'd reach for the rubber band, except then I might sink.

"A little," I say, wanting to get out of the pool more than anything. He offers me his hand and pulls me out, his bicep flexing in the process. I stumble forward and he catches me, fingers lingering on my waist.

"I'm Jase," he says. Water runs down his body, and he flings his hair to the side to get it out of his eyes.

Snap! Snap! Snap!

"Hi, Jase. I'm Georgia."

His green eyes twinkle with the reflection of the water. "You know Gus Meyers, right?"

I tilt my head, trying to figure out if we've met. I can't place him. "Sure. You're friends with him?" He gives a half-hearted shrug, and my eyes skim the hard, flat planes of his abdomen. *Snap!* How have I not noticed him before? "Did you get trapped in this freshman hellhole too?"

"Uh," he blushes. "I *am* a Freshman."

Well.

No *snap!* needed now.

Before I can respond to that, I hear my name echo across the vaulted ceilings.

"Haynes!" My neck pops up and I see Heston storming toward us, scowl firmly in place. Jase drops his hand and lurches away, but Heston ignores him completely. "Since you don't have any interest in learning to swim today, you can stay after and clean up." He points to the storage closet and the disrupted shelves and equipment tossed on the floor. "All of this, plus the filters and the locker room. Showers included."

My jaw drops. "But it's the last period of the day! I'll be here until after dinner. Maybe even later!"

"And?" he replies, uncaring.

I had plans to meet with the girls tonight. I did not have plans that included cleaning the black hole of despair known as the Preston locker room showers. *What the fuck*? "Heston—*Coach*—I was treading water. I was treading water *badly*, but I was doing it. You can ask Jase—" I spin looking for him, but Coach James blew his whistle, and the kid vanished with the rest of his class into the locker rooms. *Thanks a lot, Freshman.* Even Micha bolted. Not that I blame him.

"Get busy," he says, stepping over a big puddle.

I stare at the messy closet. The floor is covered in kickboards, fins, and other pieces of equipment. It's not the worst job in the world. That trophy will definitely go to the showers. It just isn't fucking fair.

Who the hell does he think he is, anyway?

I stomp behind him, bare feet slapping on the tile. "You're doing this on purpose, aren't you?"

"Doing what?" His blond hair is damp—a sign that he'd at some point been swimming.

"Being an asshole to me."

He whirls on me, jaw flexing. "This class is about learning to swim, not flirting with horny little boys."

I gape at him, blinking hard. "You're mad that someone was paying me a little harmless attention?"

"Mad?" He raises an eyebrow. "I'd have to care to feel mad. I just need you focused on class, not shoving your tits in every guy's face."

"So you're a cockblocker now, too?" Not that I was going to hook up with Jase. It's just the principle of the thing.

He shoves a finger at me, prodding it into the skin below my throat. "You're here to learn, not to hook up. This is my time. Don't waste it." He finally turns around and walks back to the closet, adding, "I'm actually your teacher, you know. You're supposed to show a little respect."

"You're kidding me, right?" I laugh, aware that's a touch hysterical. "Respect? There's no one I respect less than you, and you know it. This is all about making a fool out of me. Just admit it. You'd love to see me fail this class. The thought of humiliating me probably gives you wood."

He stops at a shelf in the closet, eyes rolling. "You really think a lot of yourself. I'm here to teach you how to swim, and I can't do that if you're dicking around. So yeah, this *is* about you learning to respect my authority, whether you fucking like it or not." He pauses, looking me up and down. I don't like the way his expression shifts from stony and pinched to this...calculating thing. "That is," he says, propping a forearm against the shelf, hemming me in. "Unless you want to work it off another way."

I freeze, twisting my finger in the rubber band. "Excuse me?"

He steps closer. We're deep inside the closet now. "Don't play dumb, Little Red. You heard me." He looms over me, the light from the closet bright enough to send his features into sharp relief. "You're still coming to class in this ugly thing," he says, reaching down to pluck the strap of my suit.

Snap!

"And you just told me I was shoving my tits in other guys' faces." Gulping, I try to ignore the way my blood is heating. The itch in my fingertips. The rush of warmth between my legs. "Do you really think a more revealing suit is going to help matters?"

He tilts his head, taking me in. "I think I gave you an order and you keep disobeying it."

"I have to wear this one," I say, voice feeling trapped in my throat. "For now."

"Why?" He's looking at me with dark, callous eyes. Probably expecting me to lie.

"You know why."

His eyes grow impossibly darker, trailing over my breasts, down to my hips. "You don't want some pitiful little Freshman dick, anyway. We both know what you really want."

My breath hitches, because the truth is, Heston is right. The sex had been reckless and shameful, but the way I felt during and after? The way I've been daydreaming about it, touching myself to the memory, positively aching for more?

No.

"I can't," I say, looking away from his broad chest. I need to remember the other things. The way I haven't been able to look at myself in the mirror. The churn of my stomach every time I see the bruises. The paralyzing panic that someone might find out.

"It's just a little bargain, Haynes." His voice is innocent, but his eyes are wicked. "You can clean up the closet and locker rooms, or... you can prove your respect to me another way."

Harder, I repeat, "I can't."

He scoffs, turning away. "Have it your way then."

My eyes slam shut, hands clenching into tight fists. So low that I almost hope he doesn't hear me, I growl, "What do you want me to do?"

There's a long pause before I hear the click of the door closing, feel him caging me in against the shelf, smell the scent of him thick in the back of my throat—cologne and chlorine. His voice is a close, quiet hum that makes my eyes drift open to watch. "Hm, I don't know. What do you think? A cock hungry slut like you?" He licks his lips, gaze raking over me. "I think we'd both like you on your knees."

I give him a bland look, ignoring the way his words have my thighs pressing together. "A guy who wants his dick sucked. How original." Of course this asshole wants me on my knees with his cock in my mouth. He'd love getting off like that, towering over me.

Setting his jaw, he tucks his hand down the front of his shorts and pulls out his cock, already hard. "Your choice, Haynes."

I stare down at him, my mouth parting in shock. We're in the equipment closet. In the natatorium. At school. And Heston Wilcox has his hard cock hanging out like it's nothing.

Snap! Snap! Snap!

"Heston," I whisper, knowing that it sounds anguished and defeated, all at the same time. "I *can't*."

His only response is a slow, evil smirk.

Because I'm dropping to my knees.

I wonder if this is what an addict feels like—their brain saying one thing and their actions saying another. I know the second my knees hit the ground, it'll be useless to fight. That it's going to happen. That I might as well.

Because of that, I hesitate halfway down, still slipping into this awareness, prolonging it. His hand lands on my shoulder, pushing me the rest of the way to the ground. His cock bobs in my face, grazing against my cheek, leaving a sticky line of pre-cum.

"Open up, Little Red. Show me how good you are." He tilts my face up so I can meet his dark, hooded gaze. "That mouth, those lips...they're made for sucking cock. Show me."

Deep inside, I smart at the knowledge that he's probably right. That I'm weak and compulsive. A slave to this war constantly raging inside of me. That this is who I am. Maybe it's all I'll ever be. A whore who's better on her knees, on her back, than anywhere else.

Just like always, this notion takes me over that I might as well enjoy it. That I can deal with the shame that's sure to come later. That if I'm going to weather all the negative consequences, then I should at least indulge myself.

Shouldn't I?

I run my hand down his shaft, gripping it at the base. His fingers dig into my shoulder, a silent command.

I open my mouth and give him exactly what we both want.

8

I hadn't planned on being in his position; back against the pool storage room shelves, cock fully encased in Georgia Haynes' glorious mouth. Truthfully, I'd planned on rejecting her. Ignoring her. Making her come to me. That shit always drives girls wild. I'd get her in that office, maybe even my car, perhaps even my bed, and then somehow get her to talk. Seducing Georgia would take almost no effort at all.

I didn't expect the Freshman with a six-pack.

The problem isn't getting Georgia's attention. It's keeping it. Seeing her flirt with that kid set me off in a way I didn't expect. She'll jump on any cock she deems satisfactory, and I can't have her getting what she needs from someone else. Not with so much on the line. I may have been blasé about this to Gene, but the truth is that she's both easily distractible *and* hates me. It's going to take a little work. That's the reason I interfered.

"Slower," I direct, planting a hand on the back of her head, showing her how I want it. Her shoulders tense, but she follows my orders. The hungry, greedy bobs of her head slow to something full of tongue and hard breaths. I shudder out an exhale. "Good girl."

Unable to help myself, I glance down to watch as she pulls back, swirling the pointed tip of her wet, pink tongue around the tip of my cock. I never have sex face-to-face, always from behind. The last fucking thing I ever want to see is some girl looking moonily up at me, like we're equals, seeking something I can't— won't—give. But this?

I kind of like this—watching the bitch who took me down brought to her knees.

Her red hair is in a loose, damp knot behind her head, and I thread my fingers into it and pull. "Look at me," I tell her, I want to see her face while she degrades herself. This bitch owes me more than a fucking blow job. Her green eyes lurch up. "That's right," I rumble, enjoying the way her eyes glaze over when I give her hair another sharp tug. "You're a good little cocksucker, aren't you?" She stares back in defiance, cutting and dark, but her mouth never falters, sucking me down greedily.

She might hate me, but she loves my dick.

My hips buck forward, driving hard into her warm mouth. I hear her own pants, breathy little moans that float around my cock. I look down and see that she's pushed her fingers under the crotch of her suit. I want to be mad that she's not focused solely on me, but the scrunch of her nose and the sucking of her mouth, tits jiggling as she moves, are doing things for me.

I reach down and push the strap of her suit off her shoulder. Her tits, already barely contained by the stretchy fabric, spill out. I graze the top of one with my fingertips, bending over to get a better handful. Her groan vibrates all around me, but that's not what has me frozen, my balls tightening.

From here, I can see the bite mark—*my* bite mark. It's been a few days, but it's still a vivid, dark purple against her fair skin. *Holy shit*. It's so well defined that I could probably count my teeth. I run my fingers over her shoulder, grazing them over the mark—barely a brush against the skin. My shoulders jerk in a shudder and I grab the base of my dick, yanking it from her slick mouth.

She makes a sharp, affronted sound. "Hey!"

I grunt, squeezing the base of my dick to stave off my orgasm. "Get up."

Her eyebrows are knitted angrily together, but she does what she's told, climbing to her feet. My hands are on her bathing suit before she's even upright, shoving it down, over her hips, down her thighs.

I regret doing this in the closet.

Not because it's risky, or because Coach James is probably right across the natatorium, but because the lighting is fucking awful. Even so, the purple marks on her hips are goddamn breathtaking.

"Look at you." Wetting my lips, I reach out to graze a bruise that's still in the perfect shape of my fingers. "Fuck."

"What are you...?" Georgia pauses, realizing in a burst of a whisper, "Oh my god, you're getting off on that!" She punches me in the chest, but I don't even feel it.

Keeping my eyes fixed to the marks, I demand, "Turn around."

She hisses, "No way, you psychopath!" and strikes out again.

This time I catch her wrist, annoyed enough that I wrestle her against the shelf myself, spinning her. Her suit is at my feet and I snatch it up, grabbing her other wrist and wrenching them both behind her back.

As I jostle her into place, tying the lycra around her wrists, I growl, "Stay still and I'll fuck you hard enough that you won't even care about where my eyes are."

She stills, chest heaving, shoulders pulled back against the bind of her wrists. "Damn it," she whines, teeth clenched, fingers wiggling. "You'd better make this worth it, asshole!"

I groan when I look down, because the back of her hips are even better. Two perfectly defined thumb-shaped bruises crown a larger mark—the heels of my palms. Slowly, I put my hands on them, matching them up, soaking in the warmth.

Her shoulders tense, head turning to show me her profile. "Not so hard," she whispers, lashes fanning on a slow blink. "Just...not there. It's still sore."

I stop just shy of telling her to shut up. These marks are mine to look at, mine to touch, but the last thing I want to do is alter them. It's the opposite, actually. I want to take a picture, freeze them in time. It occurs to me it's been a few days now. Maybe they were even better before, although I can't imagine how.

They've already got my dick twitching impatiently.

I grab her by the back of the neck instead, palm pressed against her Devil's mark, and shove her down. "Keep your mouth shut this time."

"Wait!" she bursts in a high-pitched, frantic whisper. "Do you have a condom?"

I answer, "Nope," and then I enter her, hard and fast.

A small sound of surprise escapes her throat, but she plants her feet wide and *goddamn*, she looks good like this; tied up, compliant, full of my dick, wearing my bruises so beautifully.

I don't fuck her as hard as either of us would like, too careful about being quiet to let this twisted, hungry thing in my chest out to play. But I fuck her hard enough, gathering her bound wrists in my hand and yanking her back into my thrust. She makes these tiny, bitten off whines, forehead pressing into the shelf as I pound into her.

I only let myself look at her hips now and then. I'd bust my nut too soon, otherwise. But that bite mark is right in front of me, shifting with the squirm of her shoulder blade, calling to me like a siren. I can't help but bend down to graze my lips over it, tongue peeking out to taste the battered skin. I groan, long and rough into the bruise, knowing that this isn't going to last much longer. It's been a while since I've been able to indulge like this—lay claim to something, mark it up, call it my own.

Georgia comes before I do, seizing so hard that her legs buckle, lips parted in a cry. I stifle it with my hand, clamping a palm over her mouth as I hammer my dick into her. Nothing about this is quiet. Not the sound of our flesh clapping, not the way she's whimpering into my palm, and not the wild grunts being punched from my chest as I fuck myself through her.

I turn to her other shoulder to bite down this time, not caring that she hisses and tries to squirm away from it. I sink my teeth into pale flesh and slam her into the shelves with the force of my thrust, emptying my balls into her tight, wet cunt.

She gasps against my hand, back arching. It isn't until her pussy clenches around my cock that I realize she's actually fucking coming *again*.

"You like that, don't you?" I laugh, low and rough into her ear. "You little freak."

She responds by wriggling her hands free of the swimsuit, grabbing onto the shelf to steady herself as I slip free. She throws me a fiery glare, but I can see that dazed, blissed-out thing happening in her eyes. "Why do you keep biting me like a rabid dog?"

I shrug, pulling my shorts up. "Why do you keep getting off on it like a rabid bitch?"

Her eyes flash, but she's got my come dripping down her thighs and nothing but a rumpled swimsuit to cover it with.

Good luck with all that.

I slip out of the closet, leaving her frenzied, annoyed whisper in my wake.

"Heston! Wait! Where are you going?!"

I SHOVE two fingers under my collar and tug, shifting uncomfortably. The Club requires a tie. I may as well be strung up with a noose, which might actually be preferable. I recognize a handful of people as they come and go, shooting me varying degrees of disapproving looks. I'd sent the attendant to give my father a message twenty minutes ago.

What the fuck is taking so long?

Since he's not taking my calls, texts, or emails, and I've been banned from the estate, this is the easiest way I can think of getting in contact. An ambush at the country club. From the look the attendant gave me, it's becoming obvious that I'm persona non grata around here, too. This shit's getting old.

I lean an elbow on the counter, bored and annoyed, trying to ignore the constant fiery ache in my stomach. I'm almost out of

Mylanta, I haven't eaten yet, and I suspect just being here is enough for my body to rebel. There's an enormous wall of windows past the terrace room, overlooking a large dining veranda. I'd come here on my lunch break, and it looks like a lot of other people had, too. My father, for one. Lawrence Fresco. Paul Travers.

Warren McAllister and Georgia Haynes.

I do a double take at the sight of them. They're at a small, intimate table in the shade of an old oak tree. Georgia's prodding the ice of her sweet tea with a straw, but she only has eyes for the man sitting in front of her.

Reynolds' dad.

"Son of a bitch," I mutter, walking to the window for a closer look. There's only one person in this town who's more of a whore than Georgia, and that's Warren McAllister. This guy used to be legendary—the kind of playboy that teenage boys have always aspired to be. Reyn's dad gets *around*, and it's no secret. It's a long-standing meme around here that nobody should ever leave their girlfriends or wives alone with him. He's probably fucked the mothers of half the students in Georgia's senior class. And here he is, eating lunch with *my* pet comeuppance project.

I'm not surprised to see her here. On the way in, I'd seen a large display of photos on the wall—a collection of portraits of the girls taking part in this years' Debutante Ball. I'd escorted once before for Jasmine Walker. It was a load of pretentious bullshit, but the party was fun enough. The familiar flash of red hair among the bottle blondes immediately drew my attention. I'd know that hair anywhere. I just had it in the palm of my hand yesterday. Georgia Haynes. A debutante. I'd pay to see her walk across the stage in her virginal white dress. Oh, the irony.

Now, Georgia's talking about something, those pink lips moving as she holds Mr. McAllister's gaze. She's still wearing her school uniform, ankles crossed primly, plaid skirt looking a little shorter than usual. Those tits of hers are pushing the boundaries of the Devil-branded, and *very* fitted, red button-down. The tip of her nose is glowing red again, eyes looking just a touch too bloodshot and glassy to play it off as anything but the vestiges of a good crying jag.

Warren nods at whatever she's saying, expression thoughtful and sympathetic. Yeah, sure. Warren McAllister is a *listener*.

Gag me.

I run my fingers through my hair, jaw tightening at the realization that this game is going to be harder than I thought. This girl was convulsing on my dick less than twenty-four hours ago, but she just doesn't stick, does she?

I'm glaring at them, wondering how the fuck I'm supposed to keep her attention, when the attendant finally returns. "Heston," he says, giving me a blank-faced nod. "Sir, Mr. Wilcox isn't able to see you right now. Since The Club is for members only, I'm afraid I'm going to have to ask you to leave." He extends a hand toward the door, like he's happy to show me out himself.

I hold his stare, wondering, "Are you?"

"Am I what, sir?"

I smile. "Afraid."

The attendant smiles back, and even though his expression is perfectly neutral, his response is thick with snobbery. "Not of you." After a beat, he adds a smarmy, "*Sir.*"

Sir? Heston? For years, I've never been called anything but 'Mister Wilcox' in this place. Guess that's Sebastian now.

I give him a cold, calculating look. I wasn't expecting much, but being turned away at the entrance is a bit much, in my opinion. If there's one thing my father's always loathed, it's a 'scene'. Kind of ironic, considering the two men he's raised.

So this is how it's going to be. Ghosted by my family. Turned away at the door. Stripped of my own last fucking name.

Straightening my jacket, I turn on my heel, striding toward the exit, but not before I notice the three people being escorted to the best table on the veranda. It's a nice day outside. Sunny and clear. Slightly breezy. Warm, but not hot. The kind of day that'd lure anyone out of the dark, wood paneled Oxford Room that always smells of cigar smoke and liquor.

I don't pause, knowing exactly what I'm going to do and exactly how I'm going to do it.

The front lawn is flawlessly manicured, an immense bed of flowers and hedges blocking off the side access to the gate that leads to the veranda. I crush a row of peonies under my shoes as I stride carelessly over the flowerbed, effortlessly slipping between two hedges. The veranda is fenced off, but that gate is laughable. I reach between the wrought iron bars, easily lifting the latch and swinging it open.

The elderly couple at the nearest table watches me suspiciously, expressions disapproving. Ignoring them, I march right through the tables, paying no mind to the whispers, the rising tension. Oh, yeah, word of my shunning has gotten around more than Warren over there, hasn't it?

My eyes are fixed on my target; my father and his two business partners.

I deftly swipe someone's mimosa from their table on the way, ignoring their shocked protest. I take an empty chair from another, carrying it the twelve feet to my destination.

Setting it down, I drop smoothly into the seat. "Afternoon, gentlemen."

My father's head snaps up from his salmon, slack with surprise. Almost instantly, his expression morphs to annoyance. "How did you get in here?"

I take a sip of the mimosa. A bit too tart, if you ask me. "The attendant at the front let me in," I lie. There goes his job. "Why, am I not welcome?"

He rolls his eyes. "Well, I'd say you're looking well, but it'd be a lie. You look like you haven't slept in days, and that suit..." His gives a distasteful sniff.

I look down at my shirt front, making a show of trying to smooth out the wrinkles. "It's the weirdest fucking thing, but turns out, our dry cleaners won't accept my business anymore."

Our *dry cleaners.*

My old man sure knows how to burn and salt the earth.

He yanks his linen napkin from his lap, dabbing at his mouth. "What do you want?"

I take my time answering, enjoying the uncomfortable expressions on his partners' faces. "I just came to deliver this." I pull the small box from my jacket pocket, laying it on the table. "Birthday gift for mommy."

He stares at me, unamused. "Your mother's birthday was six weeks ago."

"Oops." I reach across the table to grab someone's croissant.

Looking around the veranda, my father plasters on a mild grin and quietly announces, "You're causing a scene."

"Am I? I hadn't noticed." Shrugging, I follow his gaze to a couple a few tables away. They're watching us with confused, reluctant expressions. I toss Georgia and Warren a wave, raising my voice. "Oh, yeah, Haynes is having lunch with Mr. McAllister. Weird, right? Guess it's only illegal when I'm the one fucking her."

I watch as Georgia's jaw drops, eyes bugging out. She blushes a deep, vivid pink before shielding her face with her hair.

Dragging in a deep breath that's probably meant to be calming, my father turns to his partners. "I need a moment alone with my son." They don't need to be told twice. Uppity corporate types only like drama when it's whispered and dressed up in social mores. Fuck all that. Once they're gone, my father gives me a hard look. "Security will be here at any moment, at which point you'll kick up even more of a fuss, I'm sure. You'd better make it worth it."

"I really should," I agree, tossing half of the uneaten croissant aside. "But nothing is really worth my times these days. Teaching a bunch of spoiled brats how to swim because their parents were too lazy and uninvolved to do it themselves isn't the best use of my skills."

He smiles coolly. "And what, exactly, are these skills you think so highly of? Because you nearly failed out of college, got hauled to jail and charged with reprehensible crimes, and have absolutely nothing to show for the last year of your life." He takes a drink of his sweet tea, but he's not done. "Oh, and that doesn't even touch on your gambling problem. The only skill I see is that you've wasted so much of my money and influence while doing it." He leans back in his seat, gesturing to me with his glass. "If those are your skills, then you're an exceptionally gifted embarrassment."

I lurch from my seat, towering over him, fists curled, stomach searing in agony. *The nerve of this asshole.* All around me, people shift uncomfortably. From my periphery, I can see the hired security coming through the gate, but I don't break my father's dispassionate gaze. "I guess lazy and uninvolved parenting seems to be going around these days."

"Uninvolved?" he says, eyes flashing. "You think someone with a sexual crime conviction could normally serve their community service hours at the local high school?" He picks up his fork, waving one of the security guards his way. "You're just confirming what I've known all along. You've been pampered and protected for so long that you can't even recognize privilege when it's shown to you."

I'm not someone who fights with my fists. That's what my brother does. Sebastian is all about bone and flesh, beating something until it's bloody. It's sleazy and barbaric. The man in front of me taught me that real men fight with their heads. They strike out with ideas, leverage, power. He used to tell me that life is a game, and the second you show your temper, you'll know you've lost. I've always respected that about my father. His hands never get bruised. He always has control.

But right now, I want nothing more than to hit him in the face.

Before I can, a steady hand lands on my shoulder. "Easy now, son," Warren McAllister says to me, voice low. "You don't want this blowing up."

I follow his gaze to the approaching guards, mere feet away. Looking back to my father, I bite out, "I need to know about the Preston Devils."

My father's lip curls. "That's why you came here? To ask about some asinine high school secret society? What about them?"

"Rumor has it they're back in action," I explain.

"Then they're even more asinine than they used to be," he says, returning to his salmon. "Being their downfall, however indirectly, was the only useful thing you ever did."

One of the security guards approaches us, jerking his chin toward the gate. "Time to leave, Heston."

I refuse, "I'm not done here, yet."

But Warren's tugging my elbow, whispering, "Leave it, son."

I rip my arm from his grip, whirling at him. "I'm not your fucking son!" Turning to my father, I thrust a finger in his face. "I'm *yours*. And you can't take my fucking name away."

Sidestepping the security guard, I march through the veranda, dodging scandalized looks and badly veiled, whispered insults. Fucking sheep. I pass Warren's table, where Georgia seems to be gathering up her things, shooting me a dark glare as she stands.

"Happy now?" I growl, not stopping to hear her response.

I storm out the same way I came in, passing the old couple and out the side patio gate. I press my back against the building, waiting for security to pass in their decked out golf cart. Once they're gone, I step out of the flower beds and onto the sidewalk. I shove a fist into my stomach and try to breathe through the churning, fiery ache. Liesel used to say I probably had an ulcer, but it's never been anything like this before. Bad enough that my face screws up in pain.

"He just needs time."

I jerk my head in the voice's direction. McAllister leans against the wall, a cigarette between his fingers. I narrow my eyes, straightening. "What did you say?"

"Your father. He needs time. I know I needed it when Reyn fucked up." He takes a drag on the cigarette and then exhales. "It's painful watching your kid ruin their lives—because you know deep down that you're part of the blame."

I snort. "You really don't know my father at all. He doesn't blame himself for shit."

He shrugs. "Give him time. And a little space." He looks me up and down. "And get your shit together, Heston. Prove that you're not the fuck-up he thinks you are."

Smiling bitterly, I shake my head. "That's where you're wrong,

Warren. I am the fuck-up he thinks I am. And so what, you know? This is me." I hold my arms out. "This is what I am."

"You're a Devil. Devils are never perfect. Hell, we've all got our troubles. But we're also strong. Powerful. Smart. Just because you've forgotten that doesn't mean it's not who you are. Your father," he says, glancing back over to the patio, "isn't a Devil. Not anymore. He wouldn't get it."

"But you do?"

He doesn't answer, turning and stubbing the cigarette on the side of the building, before tossing it in a nearby trash can. I can't help but watch him go, wondering what it would be like to have a father who actually listened, who understood that I'm my own person—that I'm not him.

I laugh darkly at the idea. Even though my father has banished me, one thing is certain. He still owns me, and there's no way to change that.

9

THE ONLY THING stopping my thoughts from spiraling me into a black hole of self-hatred is that I'm in World History listening to Mr. Francis animatedly discuss the French Revolution. Mr. Francis is in his thirties, handsome, and has really nice hands. He moves them a lot and I can't help but watch them, thinking about how they'd be good at different things. The piano, maybe? Art? Other, more personal, actions? A gold wedding ring glints on his finger and I push that thought away. I often wonder how hard it would be to seduce a teacher, even though I'd never have the guts to do it—especially considering what happened between me and Reyn's dad.

But the fantasies—intrusive, captivating, awful things—are difficult to stop. Sophomore year, I went out of my way to be transferred out of Mr. Kent's Art Appreciation class. I couldn't pay attention to a single thing, because my freak of a libido was too hyperfocused on the way he moved. It got so bad that I couldn't even focus in the class that followed it. After dropping Art History, my GPA rose an entire point.

Now it's almost a welcome distraction from seeing Heston at the club a couple hours ago.

A knock on the classroom door interrupts both Mr. Francis and my own disturbing fantasies. A younger student with braces and glasses stands in the entry, a note in her hand.

"From the Headmaster's office," she says, handing the note to Mr. Francis. He opens it and glances up, eyes meeting mine.

"Miss Haynes." He holds up the note. The whispers and giggles start immediately. Speculations about why I've been called to the headmaster, no doubt. No one wants to get disciplined, including me. Especially if I haven't done anything wrong. "You may want to gather your things."

I stand and take the note from his fingers. "Thanks."

The girl who brought the note scurries down the hall in front of me. "Hey," I call out. She turns, looking anxiously back. I wiggle the note. "Do you know what this is about?"

She nudges her glasses up her slender nose. "Uh, they just put the notes in the cubbies and the office volunteers deliver them." Shrugging, she adds, "They don't give us details, sorry."

Sighing, I reply, "Okay, thanks."

Collins' office is down a side hall, adjacent to the in-school suspension room. I take a deep breath and knock on the door.

"Come in."

Opening the door, I cautiously step inside. The last thing I need is to get in trouble for something stupid, especially this early in the year. Especially so close to my debut. *Especially* alongside the rumors that are probably already flying around after Heston's little stunt at the club a couple hours ago. My mother is going to have an absolute conniption.

Collins isn't on the other side of the desk, though. Heston Wilcox is sitting casually in the leather chair, his long, slender fingers tapping an even rhythm on the arm. My heart flips anxiously in my chest.

"Shut the door."

Frozen, I wonder, "What are you doing here?"

His cold eyes land on my hand. "Did I stutter? *Shut the door.*"

I consider leaving, but what if Collins knows he's here? What if I really am in trouble? Heston is faculty now, which means he probably has the authority to punish me. Pushing aside the indignation that rages within at such an unjust thought, I close the door.

The resounding click makes my stomach churn.

Heston leans back in the chair, gazing down his nose at me. "I get the interoffice memos now that I'm an official 'staff' member. Collins is at a conference until five."

Some of the tension drains from my shoulders as I realize what's really happening here. "So you thought you'd hijack his office to harass me?"

"Harass?" His mouth tilts into a sardonic grin. "'Harass', 'assault', 'non-consensual'. You really go for the top-shelf buzzwords when it comes to me, don't you?"

I cross my arms. "If the shoes fits..."

"So," he says, picking up a paperweight and tossing it from hand to hand. "You're fucking McAllister's old man."

"No, I'm not."

"It makes sense," he goes on, not listening. "He's basically King Fuckboy of the forty-somethings. Sure, he's old—plus, your friend's dad, which is kind of gross—but the guy's got experience. I'd expect that from you. And what forty-something fuckboy wouldn't want to pull some busty, young tail?"

"Hello!" I wave my arms. "I'm not fucking Warren."

Ignoring me, he leans forward, face mockingly pensive. "But you've only been eighteen for....what, two months? Three? And that lunch certainly looked cozier than a random one-off hook-up might suggest, which means—"

"That we're not fucking?"

"—that he either fucked you when you were underage, or Warren McAllister is one of those pedo creeps who keeps a countdown clock of some nubile teen's eighteenth birthday." He pulls a grimace. "That's pretty cringe."

I roll my eyes, letting the silence sink in before asking, "Are you done?"

He slowly stands, chair rolling back behind him. Circling the desk, he approaches me, and I get this flash of what a predator looks like right before it pounces. Unfortunately, I don't parse the thought in time to lunge away before he reaches out. One palm lands flat on the door beside my head, while the fingers of the other dip beneath the waistband of my skirt, yanking it down one hip.

"Look at it," he demands, eyes hard.

I flinch away—not out of fear, but out of necessity. Vandy was right before. Being close to Heston is a bad idea. Just not quite in the way she meant. Every time he's close like this, all I can see are the corded muscles in his forearms, the way he holds himself— confident and aloof. The intensity of his gaze does something to me, stirs something so deep inside that I don't understand it. But I know that it's something primal and cavernous and unquenchable.

I know that it wants more.

Swallowing, I look down at my hip. The bruises are fading by the day, but they're still stark and alarming. I look away, refusing to meet his stare.

His voice is sure and smooth. "You liked this."

"No," I reply, head shaking.

"Don't deny it." As if to punctuate this, he curls his fingers around the bone, pressing into the soft, bruised flesh. "You fucking loved it."

I try to hide the hitch of my breath, fixing my eyes to his firm chin. "I liked the sex, not the way you did it. It could have been anyone."

"Is that what you've been telling yourself?" He presses harder, chuckling quietly at the way my mouth parts. "It was the best sex you've ever had, and you know it."

I try to shake out of the fog, meeting his gaze with a raised eyebrow. "Wow, that Wilcox modesty doesn't get much exercise, does it?"

"If the shoe fits..." he says, echoing my words. "Problem is, I don't share. Not with pathetic Freshmen, and certainly not with sad old creeps like McAllister."

I glare at him. "You don't know anything about Warren."

His jaw goes rigid, fingers digging in harder. "I know that I'm not settling for his sloppy seconds."

The thing is, Heston's not entirely wrong. I did make a pass at Warren—last year, at Reyn's pool party. It wasn't a great time for me. I have my highs and lows, and that day was definitely a low. But Warren was sexy and older, distinguished, and the thought of those hands on me had me shaking with need. I found him cloistered in the den, reading something on his tablet, and I made my move. It was common knowledge that Reyn's dad slept around. Plus, I knew how I looked in my little bikini. Even the Devils—some of whom were already in relationships—gave my tits a second or third glance.

But the only thing I got from Warren was a blanket draped tight around my shoulders and his warm, sympathetic gaze.

"That's not what you want," he'd said. *"Take it from someone who knows."*

I had a complete breakdown, right there on his couch. It wasn't the rejection. I couldn't even remember the last time a guy had rejected me, but it didn't sting. No, the thing that made my throat seize with sobs was how he treated me with such compassion and understanding, even though I didn't deserve it. I'd sunk so low that I was trying to seduce one of my best friend's fathers. I knew how Reyn felt about his dad sleeping around. He hated it. And there I was, trying to exploit it.

I told Warren everything, and I might not have realized it, but I think it was because I realized that, in some awful way, he and I might be alike.

And we are.

Nowadays, we just...talk. He listens. Warren doesn't judge me or make me feel bad about my choices. He's the one who encouraged me to tell my therapist about the urges and impulses. When I told him about my dick-fasting, he wished me luck and cheered me on. And this afternoon, when I told him about Heston—without giving names, of course—he told me exactly what I needed to hear.

"You should be kinder to yourself, Georgia. It's your senior year and you're stressed out. Having a difficult time at this point is perfectly

normal. Life isn't always going to be a summer vacation on a yacht, isolated from anything that might tempt you. You might not realize it now, but this is only going to make you stronger."

It's the strangest thing, but now that I know him the way I do, the thought of having sex with him makes me feel sick to my stomach. Not because he isn't still a total hottie, but more because I think I sort of love him now.

Possibly in the way a girl loves a father.

But none of that is Heston's business. I think I'd saw off an appendage before showing him that much of my heart.

"So here's the deal." Heston licks his lips and a warm sensation spreads to my belly. "If you want my dick, you're going to have to show me some exclusivity. No one else, in any way, shape, or form. No kissing, no eye-fucking, I don't even want you thinking about anyone else." His eyes drop to my chest, and for a moment, I'm almost certain he can see my pulse hammering. "Do that, and you can have my dick on tap. Whenever you want. However you want."

I jerk away, snapping, "I *don't* want it. The last time—the last *two* times—they were flukes, okay? Massive lapses in judgment. It won't happen again."

Darkness flickers in his eyes and a smug grin tugs at his mouth. I feel the power rolling off of him. "Even you don't believe that. I bet you're already wet for me."

It's unnerving how well he knows me. Why? How? Did he manage to gather all this from me that one night, all those years ago? From the night in the office? Are the other boys talking about me?

That's another reason I don't do repeats. I don't want any of them to get too close, to know too much about me. But Heston Wilcox seems to know, anyway.

His hand drops to the hem of my skirt and then underneath, knuckles grazing the fabric of my panties.

"Don't," I say, squirming away. I turn to the door but he's bigger, faster. His quick fingers turn the lock and he pins me against it, unyielding. Once again, his hands wander, this time going straight between my legs. "Heston, I mean it. I'll go to Collins."

"No, you won't." He sounds perfectly sure about it. Sure and almost annoyed that he has to say it. "Then everyone will know what you've been doing—*who* you've been doing. And that'd be so...what's the word everyone keeps using? Oh, right. Embarrassing." Breathing a low laugh, he adds, "Oh, but the look on my brother's face will be fucking priceless."

I don't want him to do it because it'll prove how weak I am. How I have no control over my wants and needs. I'm not scared, I'm ravenous. The old familiar vibration is already there, threatening to drag me away.

His head dips down next to mine, nose running against the shell of my ear as he shoves his fingers beneath the crotch of my panties. "Spread your legs or it'll hurt more than it needs to."

I don't move, closing my eyes and holding my ground.

"Closing your eyes won't make me go away." His breath warms my cheek and I sense the brush of his body against mine. He could overpower me easily, *does* overpower me, as two fingers enter me at once.

A long, tremulous shudder rolls through me.

He fucks me with his fingers, curling them deep inside. "Just like I thought," he rumbles into my ear. "So fucking wet for this."

He's relentless and doesn't abate, not even when I reach out to hold on to him, hips bucking mindlessly into his palm. I start to feel the tingling sensation that comes just before the wave of an orgasm, but I bite down on my bottom lip, desperate to stave it off— to not let him win.

"You know how good I can make this for you," he tells me, mouth so close to my own. "Say you'll save this for me, Little Red. Tell me there won't be anyone else, and you can have it, any time, on command." I shake my head and he tenses in response. "Stop pretending it isn't what you want."

"I don't want it," I lie, not sounding even remotely convincing.

I'm not prepared for the feeling of his lips brushing over mine, or for his teeth to tug at my bottom lip, forcing my mouth to part. The feel of his warm tongue is sudden and jarring.

And *so fucking good.*

It adds a whole new wave of pleasure within my struggle to maintain control. His jaw is firm, commanding the kiss. It's been so long, I'd forgotten what kissing Heston is like; an abrupt, thrilling drop. I know it's going to end painfully, but while it's happening—while he's cradling my jaw in his large, warm palm, tongue looping around mine—all I feel is weightless and free.

Without meaning to, I melt into it and everything disappears; my hate, my anger, but most of all, my resolve.

The orgasm is intense, body-wracking, spreading through my core like a wildfire.

He swallows my cry, the heel of his palm grinding painfully into my clit as I ride his hand. By the time the tremors stop, he's basically holding me upright. Heat, both from exertion and embarrassment, scorches my cheeks.

The shame hits me like an avalanche.

Blinking back sudden tears, I reach for the doorknob, but his hand comes down on mine, stilling me. Bitterly, I think, *aren't we done*? How much more humiliation is he going to put me through?

He looks into my watery eyes, reaching up to brush a knuckle along the curve of my cheek. As if in a daze, he softly whispers, "You're beautiful like this."

I feel a tear spill over, tracking its way down my cheek. He blinks as it falls, like the tear has shattered his trance.

"You've never been uglier," I reply, taking the opportunity to twist the handle and bolt out of the room.

THREE TIMES MAKES IT A PATTERN.

I'm used to having patterns—or cycles, really. Textbook bipolar. I cycle in and out, looping in this eternal high, low, happy, destructive manner. It's one of the reasons I don't do repeats with guys. Once I loop through, I need something more. Different. Better. Which makes my weakness for Heston is particularly confusing. I actually hate him. It should be easy to pass him over for someone else. So why do I keep caving?

It has to be the sex. Maybe it's just that good. Maybe denying myself for three months has made me weaker, hungrier. It can't just be about Heston. It's about how the rubber band doesn't work anymore. It's about the stress of senior year, the lack of Devils around to shield me from the mean whispers. It's about me, just having a difficult time.

That's what Warren says, at least.

"Hey, Georgia," Buck calls as I walk into the dining hall for lunch.

"Buck." I grab a tray and get into line. He follows me. "What's going on?"

"Just seeing if you're going to Underworld Saturday night."

Ugh. The last place I want to go is somewhere else I could possibly run into Heston. He was there once before. Who's to say he won't be there again? Despite that, I have to admit that the thought of getting pretty with my girls and dancing this tension away holds some appeal.

"Don't they card at the door?" They hadn't carded me, but I'd been on the list.

Buck looks almost offended. "I got someone who can let us in. No worries."

"Maybe." I shrug.

He slides closer, snaking an arm around my hips, pinning me in. I inhale his spicy cologne. "Well, if you do, will you save a dance for me?"

I give him a flirty smile but don't commit. I don't really enjoy thinking back on that night with Buck. The sex was fine, even if he'd been a bit of a selfish lay. I just wasn't in a good place. A lot like I am right now.

When I turn and start across the crowded dining hall, I see familiar blue eyes watching me. I skip a step, overcome with a moment of paranoia that he's taken to stalking to me or something. But then I remember.

Duh, he's a coach.

This means that he sits with the other faculty to eat lunch. The same coach who I sucked off in the storage room a couple days ago.

The coach who fingered me yesterday. The coach who's fucked me from behi—

"What are you doing?"

I lurch forward, wobbling my tray. I grip it to keep it steady, knowing that my face has probably turned red. Vandy's gaze shifts from me to Heston, who now seems overly interested in his sandwich and phone.

"Nothing." I stride toward our table.

Vandy's voice is cautious, laced with concern. "Sure you weren't looking at Heston?"

"Who's looking at Heston?" Caroline asks, her voice way too loud.

"Shhhh!" Vandy and I both peek across the room, but he's not paying attention. Why would he? It's not like he can torment me here, in front of everyone. "No one is looking at Heston. Especially me."

"You mean Heston Wilcox?" Ozzy asks. He drops his bag on the floor and his tray on the table. He's taken to sitting with us every day, which is something I've been pondering. Usually, a guy only sits with three solitary girls because he wants something.

It's usually not a chess partner.

"You know Heston?" Vandy asks. "How?"

He shrugs and stabs his fork into his ravioli. "I know *of* him. My dad's complained about the Devils since time immemorial." Chewing, he looks at me and asks, "What, did you date him or something?"

"Hell no!" I erupt, wondering where he even got that idea.

Just then, a scrawny little Freshman—can't be a day above fourteen—trips over his laces and falls flat on the floor, right beside the faculty table. The entire lunch room erupts in cheers and laughter, even though we all wince in sympathy. It was a hard hit, face-first into his lunch tray. As soon as he pushes up onto his knees, a rivulet of blood bursts from his nose, dribbling down his chin. The teachers all gasp, scrambling out of their seats to rush to the boy's side. Dr. Ross holds a roll of napkins to his nose, while Mr. Francis clears the area. Mr. Lee is already on the phone, probably calling the nurse.

Heston doesn't spare the gruesome scene a single glance.

He tears a bite from his sandwich and keeps scrolling on his phone.

My jaw drops. "See what I mean?" I toss a hand in his direction. "He's the *worst!*"

I'd been on a video call with my mother all night, trying to clear up that whole veranda debacle. Apparently Kitty Klaus, who's in Irene Babbage's tennis class, heard from Yvonne Pugh that Heston and I had lunch together. Here I'd been worried about Warren's reputation being marred, when the chatterboxes at the club are too stupid to reliably transfer gossip.

Rolling my eyes, I explain to Ozzy, "Heston and I have history. And it's not the fun kind of history, like that time Napoleon got attacked by a horde of bunnies. We're talking the fall of the Roman empire."

"Oh!" Caroline says, looking excited. "We're totally the Visigoths in this metaphor!" She laughs, but I just stare at her, blank-faced and lost.

"Come on, girl. I've got Mr. Francis for World History. Nothing penetrates." I'm way too busy thinking about his fingers. Come to think of it, I might have to transfer out before it reaches Mr. Kent's levels of destructive to my GPA.

Ozzy seems to get it, though, letting out a little chuckle. "Visigoths. Nice one."

Picking at my ravioli, I add, "Anyway, long story short, Heston is garbage and I'm single. *Gloriously* single."

"Are any of you on the AcadaNeeds app?" He looks between us, hopeful.

Oh, yes. Ozzy is putting some serious feelers out here.

Vandy shakes her head. "I'm gloriously *not* single." The look on her face makes me want to barf. It's a miracle she doesn't whip out her phone to show Reyn off. It's obvious she wants to. It must suck to still be in high school when your super hot boyfriend has already graduated.

"I tried AcadaNeeds," I grumble, "but it was an epic fail. Total confirmation that I need to focus on myself this year."

"Oh, yeah?" He looks beside him, to where Caroline is splitting her attention between the food and a textbook. "What about you?"

She looks up, eyes wide and startled. "Me? A dating app?" She gives a nervous laugh, adjusting her tray just-so. "I'm way too focused on school to worry about boys. As it is, I'll probably end up going to the Debutante Ball with Georgia's brother. Or Vandy's brother." Quieter, she mutters, "Someone's always got a brother."

Vandy and I share a sympathetic look. Poor girl. She's way better than that.

"You realize AcadaNeeds isn't really a dating app, right?" He grins at her, trying to catch her gaze. "It's just for hooking up. You know, anonymous, casual fun."

"Oh," Caroline says, cheeks blooming scarlet. "Casual. Like, for sex. That's...um..." Trailing off, she looks majorly uncomfortable.

Ozzy thankfully realizes this, swiftly changing the topic. "So, lasagna, spaghetti, ravioli. Did my dad strike a deal with a pasta wholesaler, or is this Italian cuisine week?"

But when I look back at Caroline, she's shoving her textbook into her bag and suddenly standing. "Um. Bye."

"Wait," Vandy calls. "Where are you going?"

Caroline doesn't stop, and the whole thing bothers me. She's always been shy and prone to getting flustered. God knows, Sebastian spent the first half of last year flirting with her enough that it's a miracle she didn't faint. But it was different. There was never any real heat in the way he'd tug her pigtails and call her pretty. It was the teasing kind of flirting.

I exchange a look with Vandy and she nods. Hopping up, I collect my bag and follow Caroline out of the room. I sense Heston's hot gaze on my back as I pass by his table, but I'm better this time—armed with something better than the rubber band.

I jam the sharp point of a pen into my thigh.

Jab!

It only takes a few minutes to find her, tucked in the periodicals section of the library. Unsurprisingly, she's going over the college admissions books. It's well known among the Devils that this is her happy place.

"Everything okay?" I sit on the couch next to her and she shrugs.

"I'm fine."

I give her a skeptical look. "You don't seem fine."

She shakes her head, face falling. "You wouldn't get it."

"Hey." I nudge her shoulder with mine. "Try me."

She sighs, tossing a book aside. "I'm a still a virgin."

I frown. "So?" I'm not really surprised. This girl is married to getting into an Ivy. "That's not a big deal."

She props her elbow on the arm of the couch, resting her temple on her fist. "I just feel dumb, especially around you and V. She and Reyn are probably going at it like bunnies, and you..."

"I what?" I ask, kind of curious.

She gives me a shy look. "Well, you know..."

I turn to her, folding a leg beneath me. "Tell me."

"There are a lot of rumors about you, Georgia." She looks away, eyes cast down. "And, well...you don't really keep your casual hookups a secret. You're, like, *super* experienced."

There's something in the way she says that—'*super* experienced'—that cuts me pretty deep. It's the inflection. It's the emphasis.

She's calling me a whore.

What is it Heston loves calling me? *Little Red Riding Cocks*. I know people talk about me like this—they always have—but it hurts when Caroline's the one doing the talking.

She rolls her eyes. "Like, who gets to be a Senior without ever hooking up with someone they like? Or even someone they *don't* like?"

"A lot of people." At least, I think that's true. Something comes to me and I perk, poking her. "You got marked for the ritual, right?" It was part of the initiation into the Devils. Each of us had to climb the Stairway to Hell and mark another Devil. For me and Sebastian, that meant some very advantageous oral. God only knows what the others did, but either way, it was clearly sexual for most of us.

This doesn't seem to mollify her. If anything, she just looks even more miserable. "We just gave each other hickies, even though..." She looks at me out of the corner of her eyes, voice dropped to a low, soft octave. "Carlton *really* wanted me to go down on him."

"He did?" At her nod, I cautiously ask, "He didn't, like, pressure you or make you feel bad about—"

She flaps a hand. "No, nothing like that."

"Oh, thank god." I deflate, so relieved that I have to press a palm to my chest. "Because I'd hate to kill him, but I would." We share a laugh, but her smile melts away almost instantly.

"I kind of regret turning him down," she confesses, biting her lip. "He offered to do it to me, too, you know? He was so soft and sweet, and plus, he's cute. He's *nice.*"

I stare at her. "Carlton is a drug dealer, Caroline."

Her eyelashes flutter behind her glasses. "Well, yeah, but he's a *cute* drug dealer."

Shaking my head, I add, "He's not for you. You deserve someone amazing. Someone who isn't always a couple wrong moves away from becoming a felon. Someone who isn't a total space cadet."

"But it would have been some experience," she insists, looking frustrated. "Why does everyone else get to play the field, but I need some amazing, long-term, steady boyfriend?"

I remind her, "A lot of girls aren't into dating around. Look at Vandy and Sugar. Even Afton, who was easily the most popular girl in school, was totally hung up on that older guy. You have plenty of time to figure it all out. There's no rush."

Her bottom lip suddenly trembles. "But what if I want to rush into something for once, Georgia? What if, for once, I want to just go with the flow and not over-think *every single thing*?" She shoves two fingers beneath her glasses, wiping her watery eyes. "You hook up with a lot of different guys, right? It's not a big deal for you. You just do it, right? I don't know why it feels like a big deal for me."

I purse my lips. "I'm not really sure I should be your role model here."

"Why?" She gestures to me, hand sweeping out. "You're totally sex positive! You own your needs and just go for it."

"Not everyone looks at it that way." I grimace, still remembering the way she said those words. '*Super* experienced'. "You said it your-self—there are a lot of rumors."

"And they bother you? The rumors?" she asks seriously.

I gape at her. "What? Of course they bother me. It's fucking awful. You've got the girls, who hate me for being a slut, and then the boys, who like me for being a slut. It's totally lose-lose. "

Her forehead puckers. "Then why do you keep doing it?"

Why?

I give a dark laugh, knowing that what I like doesn't matter. It's about the need. The itch. The compulsion. The all-consuming, ravenous drive.

I'm not ready to admit that to Caroline, though. Especially not in the middle of the library. "I don't want people to think I'm a whore. It's just not fair. Guys can fuck around all they want, with whoever they want, and no one bats an eye. The patriarchy sucks."

"Doesn't it?"

We spend the rest of lunch talking, but even though my mouth moves, my brain is moving faster. It's thinking about all the reasons I have to abstain this year. The soiled reputation. The health risks. The emotional risks. The rumors, the gossip. The way guys treat me. The way *girls* treat me. Every single negative consequence of giving into my urges races through my head.

Maybe I'm lying to myself, but I wonder if it'd all be solved by keeping it to one person. That was my whole goal, wasn't it? One dick every three months? Not one encounter, or one orgasm. Just one dick. When I think of it like that, it's like I never failed to begin with. It's hard to stop the snowball of thought after that.

The thought I can still have sex and keep to my rules.

But only if it's with Heston.

10

HESTON

I STAND inside the open equipment closet and stare at the chaos within, tipping my bottle of Mylanta back. It makes no goddamn sense. I straighten up in here every day. I supervise the idiot little middle-schoolers when I make them put their shit away. I watch from the deck as the high schoolers do the same, and they might be a little careless, but nothing that explains how, every morning, I come in here to complete destruction.

Absolutely ratfucked.

To make matters worse, Coach James has informed me that competitive swim is starting up, which means that I can kiss that sweet private office goodbye. It also means that my 'independent study' class will have to start taking place in the evenings.

I have important shit to do on Monday evenings. Well, obviously I have important shit to do every evening, but Monday evenings are *mine*, and now I have to spend it teaching grown ass people how to kick their legs usefully.

As the shit-cherry on my shitty day, Georgia doesn't show up for class. Micha does. He stands there on the deck, arms folded, looking bored and annoyed with everything.

I stare back, equally bored and annoyed. "Any clue where your classmate is?" I ask.

He inspects his nails—a glittery purple—and doesn't even bother to look me in the eye. "I'm not her keeper. Maybe she didn't want to put up with your crap today."

I take a deep breath and count to ten. "Adams. You're a student. You can't talk to me like that."

He gives me a tight smile. "Maybe she didn't want to put up with your crap today, *sir.*"

I have two students. One is mouthy, the other is absent.

Mouthy I can deal with. "I want fifty walking laps in the shallow end, followed by ten breathing drills."

"Fifty?!" he cries, and then, "Ten?!"

"I can make it seventy-five and fifteen," I offer, knowing that it's probably not possible. He'd be here all afternoon.

Micha's face screws up, like maybe he's doing the math on that. If he realizes it's not exactly tenable, he does us both the favor of not arguing. Smart kid. He snatches his Devil-branded swim cap and tugs it over his head, jumping into the pool.

Yeah, the mouthy student is fine. It's the other that's a problem.

It's possible that I may have pushed things a *little* too far in Collins' office. Sure, she'd said no and pretended like she wasn't into it. That's Georgia's new shtick, I'm realizing. She wants it, but she won't cop to it—not until she's right on the razor's edge. That's why I have to keep bringing her to it.

If Big Gene were here, he'd tell me to change tacks. To be nice. To send her flowers, jewelry, Hallmark cards. He'd tell me to woo her.

But Gene's wrong. Georgia doesn't want romance. She wants a nice, hard, reliable dicking-down on the reg. She's so fucking transparent, she might as well be walking around this campus with a sign attached to her chest screaming, "Need dick, will work."

The other guys here have her pegged all wrong, too. Georgia doesn't want to be used. She wants someone *she* can use.

That's exactly the guy I'm going to be.

It's just a problem—this lack of trust. Pushing her like that may have been a mistake. And now, like it or not, I'm going to have to be the one to test the temperature.

Once class is over and I've worked Micha hard enough that he's too tired to talk back, I head across campus. Georgia lives in Hayden—fourth floor, like the other seniors. I never lived on campus, but it doesn't matter. As I climb the staircase, memories come flooding back. I had a lot of fun here back in the day, sneaking into rooms, sneaking girls out of rooms, smuggling all a manner of booze and drugs inside.

I ignore the looks I get from the girls as I walk down the hall. Technically, I probably shouldn't be here, but I don't have any choice. I need to know if she's going to go to Collins, if I missed my shot with that little fingerbang stunt. The longer I wait to find out, the more my stomach aches. In an effort to create an excuse for being here, I stop a small brunette and say, "I'm looking for Georgia Haynes. Do you know where her room is? She left her phone by the pool."

"Room on the end," the girl replies, staring at me wide-eyed. "The suite."

"Right." I give her a grin. "Thank you."

I shouldn't be surprised that Georgia has the suite. Only the most spoiled get these rooms; Hamilton, Sebastian, etcetera. I never needed Gene to tell me that her family is loaded. Her father's foray into politics is a recent development, but he's owned a huge commodities trading firm for as long as I've known them. I've seen them at the club before, been to some of their parties, have shaken her father's hand at a banquet or two. Plus, she's debuting at the ball this fall. Society girls are always spoiled little princesses. The Haynes are obviously old school. Idly, I wonder what they think about their daughter being a sex-freak.

I knock on the door and hear someone shout, "I'll get it."

A girl opens the door; long dark hair, blood-red lips, and wearing a Sparrowood sweatshirt that grazes the top of her bare thighs. I take her in and consider that maybe Georgia is more sexually liberated than even I gave her credit for. Is she hooking up with this beauty? I wouldn't blame her. Grinning, the girl cocks her head, sending a cascade of hair over her shoulder. "Well, hello there. I don't think we've met. I'm Josephine Wentworth. People call me Josie."

"Heston Wilcox," I reply, peering over her head. "I'm looking for Georgia Haynes. Is this her room?"

"It is." She opens the door wider. "She's in bed right now."

A flash of the two of them wrestling in bed pops into my head. I blink it off and hold up my phone. It's a flimsy excuse that can't tread water any better than Georgia can. "She left this on campus and also missed class today. I thought I'd make sure everything is okay."

Josie's eyebrow quirks. "You're a teacher here?"

"Swim coach," I say. One thing is for certain, at least. Georgia hasn't told her roommate a thing. This girl is absolutely clueless.

Her eyes rake over me like she's trying to see the outline of my Speedo through my clothes. "Oh, I bet you are." She leans against the doorjamb. "I'm new this year and still meeting people. It's just that you look really young to be a teacher or coach."

I shrug. "They wanted the best."

She grins at my smugness. "We didn't have teachers that looked like you at Sparrowood. Or ones who made personal appearances in dorm rooms."

"What can I say? Here at Preston we like to provide that extra touch for our students' success."

Her tongue flicks out and licks her bottom lip. Again, all I can think of is her and Little Red rolling around together.

"Come on in, I'll get Georgia."

Violating what I assume are a dozen different faculty rules, I step into the room. In the corner, against the windows, is a bed and dresser. So this girl definitely lives here, despite it being a single suite.

"I thought the rooms were solos," I say, nodding to her set up.

"I enrolled too late to get my own suite, but Daddy talked to the Headmaster. This was the next best thing." She points at the kitchenette. "Can't live without my coffee first thing in the morning."

"What...?"

Josie and I both glance over. Georgia stands in the bedroom doorway, still clad in her school uniform. Her shirt is wrinkled, and she's barefoot. My first thought is of the way she trembled in my arms as her orgasm rocketed through her yesterday. The second thought comes when I look behind her at the rumpled mess of her bed. Another flash of the two girls jumps to the forefront of my mind. But this time, I'm with them.

Jesus.

All this shit with Little Red is seriously trying my dick's patience.

Georgia's mouth gapes as her gaze pings between me and her roommate. "What are you doing here?"

"Coach Wilcox brought your phone back," Josie says, pointing to where it's clutched loosely in my hand. "Wasn't that nice?"

"My phone," she says, narrowing her eyes. Raising an eyebrow, I give her a look that says she's to play along with the charade. Shouldn't be hard. Georgia's pretty good at bullshitting. Just ask my blue balls.

"Sure, right. You shouldn't have." Voice flat, she doesn't sound convincingly appreciative. She holds out her hand for the phone. Guess I have no choice but to play along.

"A 'thank you' is acceptable."

She looks away before giving a terse, "Thank you."

She seems pissed, but not smug. There's no way she told on me for the incident in Dewey's office. "Care to explain why you missed class today?"

Crossing her arms, she says, "I wasn't feeling well."

"Did you go to the nurse?"

"No."

"Do you have a note?"

"I do not."

Josie watches us like a tennis match.

I hold her stare, not backing down. "Then you'll need to come to my office tomorrow so we can discuss the consequences of you skipping my class."

Her cheeks redden, jaw ticking in a way that suggests her teeth are grinding. "You're kidding."

"You know the standard procedure for ditching class, Miss Haynes. Come to my office and we'll discuss it then." I turn toward the door and then pause, glancing back. "Until then, you may want to keep a better watch on your belongings. I don't know about you, but personally, I hate it when other people touch my things."

"It was nice to meet you," Josie calls out. I give her a smile and a nod before stepping into the hallway. I haven't gone far when I hear Josie ask, "Is he always like that?"

"Like what?" Georgia asks. "Insufferable?"

"Commanding, powerful..." In a lower voice, "...*hot*."

"He's not any of those things," she says, scoffing. "He's just a loser with a whistle."

My nostrils flare angrily as I march out of the dorm, but I know better. Little Red has to tear me down because inside, she's already built me up.

And that's exactly what I need to be if I'm going to win my freedom from Gene.

THE SUN'S just setting when I get back to my apartment. I spend as little time as possible out here. It's cramped and isolated. Too quiet. It has a weird smell. The water pressure is shit. The ambient temperature hovers around 'uninhabitable cinder'. There are at least a dozen other places I'd rather be. As I stand there, staring at it from the patch of grass masquerading as a yard, I get the sense that it possibly used to be a garden shed.

I don't see the envelope until I almost step on it.

It's sitting on the stoop, my name printed on the front. I look around first, half expecting to see its messenger milling about. All I find are trees and nothingness.

I take it inside, flicking on the overhead light that does nothing to brighten the space. Opening the envelope, I find an old, antique key and a note.

"We are what we always were in Salem, but now the little crazy children are jangling the keys of the kingdom, and common vengeance writes the law."

I frown at the inked script. "The fuck does that mean?" Tossing the cryptic note aside, I hold up the key, inspecting it.

There's a pitchfork etched into the top.

I wait until dark to leave my apartment and approach the Tower. I'm not unfamiliar with sneaking around campus. Buster the security guard comes and goes like clockwork, taking the same worn loop as he did when I was a student. When he passes the Tower and heads toward the athletic fields, I duck into the arched entrance, then turn quickly toward the locked door. The iron key is warm from being in my pocket, and it doesn't slide in easily. I have to jiggle it around for a few seconds until the tumblers switch, unlocking the bolt.

I use my phone to guide my way, brightening the stone stairway that leads underground. It's warm outside—still early fall—but down here the temperature drops. At the bottom is another arched door. This one has a lock, too. Annoyed, I dither for a moment, but decide to try the key in my hand. It's still a struggle, but the notches fit. The heavy wooden door creaks as it opens inward, and my light reveals a musty, slightly damp room.

How long has this place been down here? And how did I never know about it?

The walls are covered in Preston memorabilia, some faded and worn, others slick and full of color. Half-melted candles sit on every surface, along with all kinds of Devil iconography. Photos, pennants, banners, stickers and stamps. A red and black blanket has been tossed over the back of a leather couch, and twelve chairs form a circle in the middle of the room. If it weren't for the pyramid of empties stacked against the wall, it'd look like some goddamn basement AA meeting or something.

I approach a table against the back wall and see a stack of photos—clearly more recent. There are no faces, but its images of the scenes Collins told me about. There's proof of them stealing other school's mascots. The homecoming hijack. The basketball game prank. I pause on a stack of pictures featuring freshly inked tattoos. I flip through them, searching for something identifiable, and hit pay dirt with one. A Devil's mark on a broad pectoral. I'd know my brother's obnoxiously shirtless chest anywhere.

Fuck, but all of this would be a lot easier if I could just ask him about the Devils. That bridge has been well and truly burned, though. No skin off my back. Sebastian and I were pitted against each other since the day he was born. No surprise that this is where it's led us.

What confuses me most, as I go through the pictures, is that several are definitely females. There's a smooth inner thigh, a narrow ankle, the soft curve of a hip. I stop on the last picture, the dark inked lines of the Devil's mark at the base of a thin neck.

Georgia.

Was this another ritual? Marking Playthings?

Who would want a girl like Georgia, anyway? Afton Cross, definitely. Vandy Hall? Sure, Reyn's into that virginal shit. But Georgia's the school bicycle. Everyone's taken a ride. She's not the girl you tag as your own. She's the girl you do on the side when the girl you've marked isn't putting out satisfactorily.

It's further evidence that whatever is going on with the Devils, they're making some questionable judgments. Girls like Georgia aren't loyal.

I arrange the pictures back like I found them and poke around a little more. I spot a notebook and flip through it, seeing a list of names. Micha Adams? Ozzy Collins? Buck Smith? Josephine Wentworth?

I can't imagine what those four would have in common.

Satisfied that I've seen enough, I take one last scan of the room. My eyes land on a small, silver box on a shelf. I grab it, flipping the latch and opening it up. Inside, nestled against a silk lining, is a memory card. Impulsively, I take it, tucking it in my pocket. Maybe this will have the dirt I need on the Devils—at least enough to give the Headmaster names and get him off my back.

It's obvious that she's not happy when she arrives in my office the next day—five minutes early, to boot. Since our class has been moved to the evening, the natatorium is practically deserted. But the janitor's still lurking about, as well as a couple of the competitive swim students, trying to get in some extra practice.

She walks in the room, tosses my phone on the desk, and plainly announces, "You get a lot of calls. Who's Gene?"

"None of your business." I narrow my eyes. "Did you answer my phone?"

"No." she rolls her eyes. "Like I want to know what degenerate and illegal stuff you're up to."

I'm not sure I believe her, but I slide my phone in my pocket and say, "About your punishment for skipping class—"

"I'm not sucking your dick."

After a long moment, I give a slow clap. "The debutante, ladies and gentleman." *Jesus.* In some ways it's refreshing to be around a girl who doesn't get shy about sex, but even I could use a little decorum. "I don't want head, Haynes."

She narrows her eyes. "Then what?"

Still, I let her sweat for a moment, swiveling back and forth in my seat. "There's an invitational meet tomorrow, and our swim team is hosting. Coach James left me a list of chores that need to be done before morning and then taken down on Sunday. Since you skipped class, that list is yours. That is, unless you want to barter—and not for sex." I lean back in my seat. "I need information."

She frowns, looking suspicious. "What kind of information?"

"What do you know about the Devils?"

Her expression gives nothing away. "I know you imploded them with your bullying and harassment."

"Hilarious." I roll my eyes. "I'm talking about the *new* Devils."

"What new Devils?" she asks innocently.

"Oh, cut the shit," I snap, leveling her with a hard look. "I've seen the mark on your neck, Little Red. And your initials are carved up in the stairway. You're someone's Plaything. You're going to tell me whose."

I doubt it's McAllister. Emory, maybe. Irritation flickers through me at the idea of the two of them together. Not that I'm jealous. Hell no. I've already proven just about anyone can get in between her legs. I'm pissed that Emory or whoever it is isn't a little more discriminatory. There's nothing to this girl. She's shallow and vapid. Playthings are supposed to be above the rest, not easy lays.

The thing is, it's a problem. If Georgia is loyal to this guy, then the best-case scenario is that she's still fucking him. The worst case is that she actually has some kind of attachment. Neither of those gels with my goals to get close to her.

She hesitates, and for a moment, I actually think she might cave. For some reason, I'm oddly disappointed at the prospect. It's as if being proven right—finding out just how loyal she *isn't*—is sort of bumming me the fuck out.

She purses her lips, eyes unreadable. "I have a tattoo of the school symbol. I've got team spirit." She pumps her fist lamely. "Go, Devils."

So she *is* loyal. Whoever it is must have some kind of hold on her.

Son of a bitch.

Shrugging, I try, "I don't know why you'd bother lying for him. Whoever he is, he's obviously not satisfying your needs."

Her jaw goes slack. "Excuse me?"

"You heard me." I wave a hand at her. "The way you walk around here, always all horny and worked-up. It might not be obvious to other people, but I can see it from a mile away. This guy isn't taking care of his duties."

She drops her arms, hand curling around the pen I realize she's been holding in her palm. "I'm no one's *duty.*"

"You could be mine," I say, eyes drifting down her tight little body. Those soft tits. The full hips, probably still wearing my bruises. Her pussy, always so wet and tight for me. Yeah, this job isn't exactly a burden. "Dick on tap, remember? If you were my Plaything, I'd drop everything I was doing to satisfy you."

She laughs, head shaking. "One? I don't believe that for a second. And two? I'll never be yours, Heston. *Never.*" She's still holding that pen, and she hides it pretty well, but the tremor in her shoulder gives away what she's doing.

She's jabbing it into her thigh.

Hard.

That's when I know this is all but done. Little Red is going to cave. It might be days—fuck, it might be *hours*—but she's going to say yes. She's going to give herself to me.

My dick's already getting hard at the prospect. "Here's the list of things that need to be done tonight. Don't miss anything," I command, handing her the clipboard.

"Wait," she says, staring down at the list. "You're still making me do this? I gave you information."

"You gave me fuck-all, Haynes." I stand and circle the desk, feeling a few pounds lighter. I hadn't realized how much I've been sweating this. It almost makes me laugh. "You can start after class is over."

She gapes at the list, which admittedly is long. I hadn't wanted to do it all alone, so this little situation is a win-win for me.

"There's a football game in an hour," she whines, those big green eyes gazing up at me. "There's no way I can get all of this done in time."

"You should have thought about that before you skipped my class." I loop my whistle around my neck, noticing that Micha just arrived on the pool deck.

"But you—" She swallows back her comment. I know I'm pushing it with her. She could snap and rat me out at any moment, but I know she won't. I've got something on her that no one else does: the shame of her wanting me.

She ignores me during class, shooting daggers in my direction the whole time. I make her do the same walking and breathing drills Micha had done yesterday, and then I send him to the vending machine beside the dining hall to fetch me a bag of chips.

The look he gives me upon his return tells me exactly what he thinks of being my gopher. "I don't think this bag of Doritos is going to help me swim better."

"Sure it will," I argue, taking the chips from him. "If your coach is hungry, then maybe he'll be in a bad enough mood to make you join your classmate with all those drills."

He drops beside me, smartly keeping his mouth shut.

At least for a moment. Mouthy shit. "It was just one absence," he says, watching Georgia. "You're being too harsh."

"Funny," I say, cramming a chip into my mouth. "No one would question Dr. Ross for giving a detention on account of a tardy."

"Dr. Ross is a legitimate teacher." Micha pulls a second bag of chips from his bag—some disgusting low-fat, low-sodium, organic atrocity. "Plus, all we do is give her shit for her tardy policy. And it's not like Georgia's bad. If she skipped out, she had a good reason."

That's beside the point. "What do you know about Haynes being good or bad? She's a Senior. You're a Sophomore."

He shrugs. "I know she had a hard time, up until last year. She was quiet and kept to herself and always looked sad. Then, like overnight, she became one of the most popular girls in school. And it never got to her head. She was never mean or anything." His eyes cut to mine, narrowing. "Unlike certain other popular people."

Ignoring that lame-ass jab, I say, "Wait. What do you mean she got popular overnight?"

He tries to keep that glare up, but eventually looks away, shrugging. "Like one day she was a part of the scenery, and the next she's sitting at the cool table with Afton, Aubrey, and Elena, and the rest of them. You know, the cool girls."

I munch on another chip, watching Georgia duck beneath the water for the seventh time. "Who else was sitting at this table?"

He hums, thinking. "Emory and his sister. Plus, that guy she's dating—Reynolds. Ben Shackleford and...what's his name? Cal?"

"Carl."

"Yeah." Micha nods. "That's right, Carlton. Also the diving guy, Tyson. Caroline was always with them, too."

I roll this around in my brain, thinking this must have been them—the Devils and their Playthings. "What about my brother?"

"Sebastian?" Micha asks, blinking. "I don't know. Sometimes? He mostly sat with the lacrosse guys, though."

Just then, Georgia emerges from the water, wicking the water from her eyes. "That's ten, I'm done."

Once class is over, and she changes, she comes back out and starts on the list. My plan is to help her—or at least supervise, but a text changes everything.

It's from my bartender.

Big Gene and his boys are asking for you. Seems important.

That could explain the calls. Fucking Friday evening and I'm stuck here at the pool instead of seeing to my business?

I don't think so.

Georgia has just started untangling the banners that drape over the ends of the pool when I come out of the office, bag on my shoulder, locking the door.

"No way," she says, pausing her battle with a knotted string. "You're not leaving, are you?"

Smiling, I reply, "Think of it as some of that team spirit you were just telling me about." Her jaw drops. "Oh, and don't forget to turn off the lights when you're done."

"You're a dick! You know that, right?"

I grin, because I know it's killing her that I have the upper hand. She's the one who's fucked up here. Not me.

For once.

11

"Mrs. Gilbert, I don't know..."

We're in the Preston Prep Auxiliary Hall, which is always used for stuff like this; odd, one-off club meetings and events. Every month, Preston likes to extend a hand to the surrounding schools in hopes of us mixing in with the locals. But I *am* a local. Like, basically. Sure, we have three beach properties, a mountain retreat, and a condo in France, but my home address is located a mere twenty miles from Preston.

"It's your last year," Mrs. Gilbert says, looking out over the large, crowded room. "Volunteering as a peer group leader will look good on your applications. Plus, you have some experience with counseling."

Staring at her, I say, "I'm usually on the other side of it, though."

She smiles patiently. "That experience will be useful, too."

"Look," I start, shifting my gaze to a pair of middle-schoolers huddled around a phone. "I'm not qualified to give advice. I'm not sure I'm even qualified to tell someone to *get* advice." The truth is, I'm a hot mess. Now that my rubber band has been rendered weirdly ineffective, my thigh looks like a collage of pen-bruising, and on top of that, I've been hooking up with one of the vilest men this school has ever seen, even though I don't really want to. I'm a hazard to myself on every level. Who am I to tell some kid to face their inner demons or whatever?

"You don't have to give advice," she insists, voice low. "Just be there for someone. Listen to them. Opening yourself up to someone else's problems might help put your own into perspective." She gives me a meaningful look. "I am speaking from experience. Do you suppose I always feel qualified to counsel you?"

I point out, "Your degree probably helps."

Luckily, I spot Micha hovering around the donut table, sipping daintily at a cup of something hot and sweet.

He sighs when I sidle up to him. "You got roped into this, too, huh?"

"Definitely not in my top ten choices of ways to spend a Saturday morning." I'd rather be in bed, finishing knitting the scarf I'd started for Sebastian last week.

He nods. "Did Mrs. Gilbert give you a whole speech about how it'd look good on college applications?"

"You too?"

"Apparently being super queer gives me 'a special insight into the struggles of LGBT youth'. Like I'm some kind of expert." He rolls his eyes, picking a sprinkle off a donut. "It didn't really matter. My mom makes all of us do one personal volunteer project every school year. It was between this and charity construction. Can you imagine me with a power drill?"

"Not so much." I look at the donuts, figuring if I'm going to do this thing, I might as well get something glazed out of it. "So what's the scoop? We just walk up to some poor kid and start a deep conversation?"

Micha is methodically plucking each sprinkle from his donut and eating them. "I was thinking of just standing here and looking all unapproachable." He gives me a dark, sulky look. "Working?"

I snort, nudging him with my elbow. "You look like someone just told you Lakevale got cancelled." It's been brought to my attention, from the way he constantly talks about it during our swim class, that Lakevale is Micha's favorite terrible teen show.

He swings a far more natural glare at me. "Bite your tongue, beeyach! It's bad enough that I have to miss it live because swim class got moved up to evenings."

We chat for a little while longer before Mrs. Gilbert's stern gaze forces us to part. *Sheesh*, I think. *What if I'm counseling Micha?!*

She gives me a slow, disapproving shake of her head.

I take a seat among a row of empty chairs, pushed against the wall, and decide that he has a pretty good idea about looking unapproachable. I'd brought my knitting bag just in case I found myself in the position to work on this scarf, and I pull it all out.

As soon as I get into the rhythm of threading and hooking, something inside of me loosens and calms. Truthfully, scarves are one of only three things I know how to make, but I think I've gotten really good at them. I've already made one for Vandy, Caroline, Emory, and Reynolds. Now I'm working on Sebastian and Sugar's. With the out-of-state Devils all coming home for winter break in a few months, it'll be the perfect addition to all their gift bags.

"Oh, cool," comes a low voice to my right. Looking over, I notice a younger girl—maybe a Freshman—watching my fingers move the needles. "Is that hard?"

Brightening, I answer, "Not in the least. Takes a little practice, but it's easy to pick up if you have the patience."

The girl grimaces, eyes pinging up to meet my gaze before instantly darting away. "I have ADHD, so I'd probably be bad at it."

"What? No way!" Laughing nervously, I add, "If you're like me and don't have *any* patience, then it's also a good way to learn some. It gets me out of my head for a while. Gives me something to focus on."

She purses her lips, nodding. "I guess I could see that."

After waffling for a moment, I reach into my bag, pulling out one of my spare pairs of knitting needles. I hand them to her. "I could teach you some stitches?" The girl's eyes flash in delight as she takes the needles, accepting the yarn I hand her next. "This is a basic slip-knot," I begin.

We spend the next thirty minutes huddled over the needles in our lap. Despite her comment before, I learn that the girl—Eliza, she says—is actually fantastic at it. She picks it up quick, eyes lighting up when she finishes her second row. I quietly explain to her that I'm doing scarves and then tell her some excellent websites and videos for beginners. She softly mutters back that she's going to ask her dad to pick her up some yarn and needles over the weekend because she wants to make a scarf, too.

It isn't until I finish a row and look up that I realize we've attracted a little audience. Two girls and a boy, probably middle-schoolers by the looks of them, are standing nearby, watching us curiously. I blink at them as if I'm emerging from a haze—and I suppose I am. When I do this, everything feels so far away. It doesn't always last long, and the vibrations still exist, but it pushes them into the background, like a gentle hum.

I look at Mrs. Gilbert, who's watching me back.

She throws me two thumbs up.

I laugh in defeat. "Okay, don't just stand there," I tell the kids. "Pull up a chair! We're going to learn some wicked Stockinette stitches!"

I guess I'll bring more needles and yarn next week.

When I get home, I pass out—*hard*.

The first week back at school is always difficult, but between my self-imposed celibacy, then breaking it with the worst person possible, this one has been particularly brutal. It's a deep, dreamless sleep—the kind of sleep I'll be thinking longingly about come Monday morning. It's made all the better by the call I'd gotten earlier informing me that my test results all came back negative.

The only thing that rouses me are the vibrations. I'm so used to the need that my hand is already reaching for my pants before I realize I'm not the one doing the vibrating.

It's the phone I'd wedged beneath my pillow.

Pulling it out, I squint at the screen and realize that it's already seven. *Holy shit.*

"Hey," I answer, voice a little groggy. "I'm up, I'm awake."

"Georgia! I've been texting you all afternoon!" Vandy doesn't get pissed easily, but it's pretty obvious she's annoyed. "What time are we meeting?"

"Meeting?" I sit up and rub my face. Christ, this nap really got away from me. Who knew that teaching four underclassmen to knit would be so taxing?

"Did you forget?"

"Of course I didn't forget," I lie. When she doesn't respond, I let out a sigh. "Fine. I totally forgot. What are we doing tonight?"

"We're going to that new club, remember? Underworld?" I hear another voice in the background. "Caroline is already at my house."

"Shit," I mutter. "That's tonight?"

After doing all the work at the pool the night before, then volunteering with the peer group, I'm beat. None of this is to mention the dread I feel about possibly running into Heston again. It's bad enough when we're here at school, in a supervised environment.

"Yes, it's tonight," she says, sounding exasperated. "You promised we'd have a girl's night."

This is Vandy's first year as anything even remotely approaching independent. Ever since her accident, her family has sheltered and coddled her. Even if she was hiding a pain pill addiction behind their backs the whole time, it wasn't until she joined the Devils that she finally got a taste of what it's like to be a normal teenage girl. Now she's hungry for the experiences.

"Fine, fine," I relent, unable to say no to her. "Give me an hour to get pretty."

Squealing, she says, "Meet us at the old Kmart parking lot, okay? And would you bring me those earrings you wore on Tuesday? All of mine are so...*ugh*. Cute."

An hour later, I'm pulling into the lot, spotting Vandy's compact car and, curiously, her boyfriend's Jeep. "Oh, hell no," I say when I get out of the car. "Vandy, I know you're new to this, but you cannot bring your boyfriend to girls' night out."

Caroline sidles up to me, arms crossed. "They're being gross," she mutters.

And wow, are they ever.

Reyn is leaning against his Jeep, arms hanging loosely around Vandy's waist. She's gazing into his eyes—yuck—and smiling as she whispers something. He gives her a smirk and a slow, disgustingly gratuitous kiss before letting her go.

She turns to us, shrugging. "Sorry, but movie night with my boyfriend was my cover story." Still, as soon as we start toward Vandy's car, Reyn grabs my arm, pulling me to a stop.

"About tonight—"

Groaning, I say, "Let me guess. Don't let her drink. Don't let her leave a drink unattended. Don't let her dance with anyone. Don't let her be seen dancing *by* anyone. Don't let her blah blah, yadda yadda." I give him a slow, hard look, folding my arms. "This is girls' night, buddy! You have no power here."

Reyn stares at me, his handsome face perfectly blank. He reaches into his pocket and pulls out a crisp one-hundred-dollar bill. "I was going to tell you to make sure my girl has a good time." He raises an eyebrow, extending the bill to me between two pinched fingers.

"Oh," I say, blinking in surprise. "Well, yeah. Obviously."

Still.

Aww.

Vandy and Caroline are already waiting in her car. I slide in the backseat and we all wave Reyn goodbye as she starts off.

"Damn, you girls look hot." I peer over the seat to get a better look at Vandy's dress. It's short and sparkly with a low cut front. I whistle my approval. "Reyn's really cool with you wearing that out?"

"He picked it out himself, actually." Her cheeks turn pink. "You know he likes it when I dress sexy."

There's more behind it, of course. He loves the fact she's confident enough now to put herself out there. There was a time when she wasn't. It doesn't hurt that he trusts her.

"Well, when you reject all the guys that are definitely going to hit on you tonight, send them my way. After the last twenty-four hours, I need some kind of distraction." I can't have sex with them, but I'm totally willing to grind up on a nice piece of meat—any piece of meat that isn't Heston fucking Wilcox.

Caroline twists back and looks at me. "So what's going on? Why couldn't you come to the game last night?"

I launch into the whole thing with Heston—well, not the *whole* thing, but enough. I explain how he's using his teacher leverage to force me into doing all his grunt work and that I spent Friday night setting up the natatorium for the swim invitational.

"Which, by the way, is totally stupid," I complain. "You'd think it was prom with all those pointless decorations." Vandy and Caroline share a look, both knowing damn well that I'm a complete decoration whore. I offer, "There wasn't even any glitter. It was all boring banners and dumb ropes with the floaty ball things. And I can tell you now that it's a lot harder to get those ropes across the pool when you can't swim."

"That's bullshit," Vandy says, glancing back in the rearview mirror. "You need to tell someone that he's over-stepping."

"Well, that's not everything," I say, sighing. "He's also been asking questions about the Devils."

Caroline frowns. "What kind of questions?"

"He wants to know who's in and he thinks I know because he's seen my tattoo." I quickly add, "You know, on account of swim."

The girls exchange a worried look.

Vandy asks, "Did he guess that you're a Devil?"

"God, no," I laugh. "But only because he thinks I'm just a Plaything. He thinks one of the Devils branded me like a cow."

Caroline snorts. "Sexist pig."

I laugh, already feeling so much lighter. This night was the best idea we've had in a long time. "Yep. He's going to be shook when he finds out they let girls into his secret society." I tug at the hem of my black, sparkly skirt. "Anyway, when I wouldn't fess up to anything, he made me do all the setup work in retaliation."

"He's such an asshole!" Vandy bursts, forehead puckered angrily. "Why does he want to know all this, anyway?"

Shrugging, I answer, "Hell if I know. He could just be curious. I mean, he was a Devil himself and was pretty much why they got disbanded in the first place." The lights of the club up ahead illuminate the dark street. "But with Heston, you never know. He's always working some kind of angle. I definitely don't trust him."

"You shouldn't," Vandy says. "No one should."

"I still can't believe the school let him come back on campus." Caroline shudders. "He's such a creep. How does he get away with it?"

"Have you seen his face? Or his body?" Vandy asks. Her eyes dart to mine in the rearview mirror. "That level of hotness sways a lot of people."

Caroline bitterly adds, "And a powerful father who has a lot of money."

I know that's probably a part of it, but I can still remember the scene between them at the club that day. Heston and his dad are just as at odds as Sebastian hoped they'd be. It's not like Heston doesn't deserve his epic fall from grace. Seeing him completely shunned by his family was undeniably satisfying.

But sometimes, I think of him standing there on that veranda, all tired and rumpled, looking like his father just ripped his heart from his chest, and satisfaction isn't what I feel. Not exactly. There is a sense of justice, but beneath it lurks something sadder. It's far too cynical to be called pity. It's just that Heston has always been this enormous, untouchable, superhuman force in my life. It's almost as if seeing him so diminished, tossed aside like the Club's trash, makes everything seem a little more vulnerable now. A little less radiant. After all, if a Wilcox can reach such lows, then can't we all?

I tune them out as they go off about how Heston is a monster. He *is* a monster. A manipulative, narcissistic, sociopath. I've yet to see a single redeeming quality from the guy. And here I am thinking about feeling sorry for him.

Even worse, here I've been thinking about his offer—*dick on tap*—and how badly I want to accept.

I dig my fingernails painfully into the soft pit of my elbow.

I'm half-expecting I'll need to use my silly AcadaNeeds name to get us in, but true to Buck's word, we're let in with nothing but a glance at our very fake IDs.

Inside, I'm met with the same energy as the first time I came here. The fast, bouncy music engulfs us as we walk through the door, Vandy and Caroline both taking it in wide-eyed and over-alert. We'd all done some pretty wild stuff last year, but it's our first time really out in the thick of it without the older, far more powerful Devils at our backs, nudging us forward, shielding us.

For the first time, I'm kind of glad they're not here. I look at Vandy in her sexy dress and Caroline in her skin-tight pants, and I think to myself, *We are going to own this place.*

It's crowded, but I can already see people I recognize from school. There are clumps of other people, like overly made-up college girls that I assume are from Saint Mary's. Guys clustered by the bar. All kinds of couples on the dance floor—guys with girls, girls with girls, guys with guys—every possible combination.

"This place is awesome," Vandy cries, her face lit up by the flashing lights. "Hey, do you wanna dance?"

Caroline wrinkles her nose in response, but Vandy is having none of it. She grabs Caroline's hands and pulls her toward the dance floor, laughing in delight. This is another change in the last year. With her injury, there's no way Vandy would have done something like this, but everything is different now. *She's* different.

They wave me over but I point to the bar, calling out, "I'm going to need a drink first!"

I don't want to admit it, but I'm not in the mood for dancing. If it weren't for watching Vandy and Caroline have a good time—a new experience—I wouldn't really want to be here at all. Like so many other times, I just plaster a smile on my face and ask the bartender for a drink.

Leaning back on the bar, I get a good look at the club. There's the dance floor and tables along the sides. There's an elevated area at the back, surrounded by a curtain to provide privacy. I assume it's the VIP area, because what club would be worth going to if there wasn't an air of exclusivity?

I'm taking a picture of Vandy to send to Reyn when loud voices catch my attention. I glance over to the door just in time to see Buck and a few other guys from school walk in. Buck looks good, tall and athletic, but I'm not even feeling that tonight. I grab my drink and slip away from the bar, making an escape to the staircase before he sees me. I pass a couple at the bottom, shoving their tongues down one another's throats and get this moment of white-hot envy that I'm not expecting.

At the top, I wander over to the railing where I have an excellent view of the dance floor below. I watch Vandy and Caroline awkwardly shimmying with one another. Buck leans against a beam, eyes scanning the room, like he's looking for someone. Suddenly his expression changes and he straightens. I follow his gaze to a girl across the room. Josie. Target acquired.

I go to take a sip from my drink, but it's suddenly snatched away.

"Trying to get me arrested again?"

A chill runs down my spine, but I refuse to turn at and look at him. I don't need to. I know Heston's voice better than I'd ever admit.

"What are you talking about?" I wonder, sounding bored.

I feel him move closer, his body sliding up right behind me. "Me, giving liquor to a person underage."

My heart hammers at the feel of him so close. "Then it's a good thing the bartender gave it to me, not you."

I can hear him taking a sip of the drink, forearm brushing my shoulder as he sets his down on the nearby table. "The owner is the one who'll get the citation, though."

"And?" It takes me a long moment to really understand. When I finally do, a sour laugh escapes me. "Of course. *Of course* you own

Underworld. How stupid of me to think I could go anywhere in this town without you lording yourself over it."

He ignores that, peering over my shoulder. "Brought your girls, huh? It looks like they're having fun." His fingers push my hair aside and graze my neck, making me shiver. "I wonder what they would think if they knew what we've been doing?"

I try to ignore the way my pulse is fluttering. The way my legs feel like jelly at the feel of his breath against my skin. The way a lightning bolt of want shoots down my spine, right to my center. "You mean, the fact that you've been blackmailing me and using your position of authority to force me into doing things?" I glance back and fuck, he's so good-looking it hurts. "I doubt they'd be surprised."

"I'm talking about how much you like it." The pads of his fingers trail down my back. His voice is a rough rumble in my ear. "How wet you probably already are."

"I told you no," I say, fighting the tremor running through my body. "It's not what I want. *You're* not what I want."

"No?" He pulls at the hem of my skirt and I feel the press of his hard erection against me. Down below, the song changes to something fast paced. I see a wide smile split Vandy's sweet face. God, she'd be so disappointed in me—in this.

"I don't get you, Little Red." He ducks his head to my bare shoulder, soft lips dragging against the skin in a light kiss. "You want it so fucking bad. I can feel it. Why are you fighting this so hard? Is it the Devil? The one who gave you that mark?" He makes a low, disapproving sound that shoots straight to my pussy. "He's all wrong for you. He let you come here like this, so desperate for dick that you're shaking. Christ, look at you, trembling for me."

"Because I hate you. I hate everything about you."

"Not everything," he responds, lips finding a particularly sensitive patch of skin below my ear. "Not the way I make you feel."

Breathing low and shallow, I say, "I especially hate that." But he can't hear me. It's barely a whisper, already carried away by the beat of the music, lost to the ether.

"All I need is a yes." His hand comes down on my thigh,

knuckles grazing the skin beneath my dress. "Just say yes and you can have it. Who knows? Maybe you'll fuck yourself out of wanting this so much. Don't you want to find out?" His voice is wicked, far too full of the awareness that I'm weak here.

And I am. Weak. Turning his words over in my head, even though I don't want to. Thinking about how he's right—that Heston is evil, but somehow, he knows me. He knows I need it. He knows the exact way I'd talk myself into it. A means to an end.

He knows his lips against the shell of my ear will make my breath hitch.

"Say I did," I rasp out, lights flashing behind my closed eyelids. "If I said yes, you'd have to give it to me, whenever I needed it."

"Think I can't handle your appetite?" He fumbles behind me, unzipping his pants and lifting my dress. "Competitive swimmer, remember? I've got stamina like you wouldn't fucking believe."

I gasp as his fingers find my panties, slowly toying with the seam that's probably already damp. I never really needed him to help me justify this. My brain is leaps ahead, already telling me it's okay. It's not breaking my rules. It's just taking advantage of them, making it so that I'll be stronger.

If I try hard enough—and I really, *really* do—I can convince myself that having sex will actually make me a *better* sex addict.

And in that moment, I truly believe it. "Yes."

In one swift move, he yanks aside my panties, entering me in a slow, deep thrust.

My hands clamp onto the railing, jaw going slack at the feel of him sliding into me. I should have been smarter. I should have bartered—for condoms, at the very least. But right now, all I can think about is how amazing it feels. How much I want to push back into him and feel those broad palms against my skin.

There's a shudder in his voice when he whispers into my ear. "Good girl."

His grip is steady and firm on my hip, the other secured around the railing. His movements are deliciously slow—almost tender— the sweet drag of his hard cock digging and retreating.

His warm punch of breath tickles the skin of my neck. "I could go all night, you know. I could take you into my office and fuck you the way you really want. I could make it hurt."

A shiver runs through me at the way he slams forward, a soft grunt escaping his lips, just a little taste of what I already know he can do. "No," I say, shoving back against him, sinking another fat inch of his cock inside me. Considering how much of a mess I am inside, it's a miracle that my voice comes out remotely even. "I say when we do this—*how* we do this."

His low, humming rumble reverberates from his chest to my spine. "As you wish."

I fight to keep my expression blank as he fucks me, not wanting the rest of the club—Jesus, *my friends*—to know what I'm letting him do to me. Because this is different from the times before, when he had me right against the edge, using my need against me. This is me giving in.

And *fuck*, it's such a relief.

This thing we're doing is sloppy and careless. I've never once done something like this where I'm so exposed. The thought should be frightening, yet another scrap of evidence that I'm escalating, but it's like water through my fingers. I can't focus on anything but the way he feels against, around, inside of me. The slow, sharp build of my approaching orgasm is only heightened by the sounds he makes in my ear, full of harsh, guttural breaths.

"You know the best thing about fucking you?" he asks, fingers digging hard into my hip. From the outside, it probably looks like we're dancing up here, grinding together, eyes fixed on the dance floor below. "It's that I can feel right when you're about to come. Your pussy gets so wet and tight, like it doesn't want to let me go. Did you know that, Little Red? Did you know your body wants me so bad that it's begging me to stay?"

If I thought I was shaking before, then I'm downright quaking now. My knuckles go white as I grip the railing, knowing that he's right. My body *is* begging.

The orgasm is a sweet, intense wave that explodes through my center, arcing out like an electrical storm assaulting my nerves. I can't hold in the whimper, slamming my hand over his on the railing to ride it out, to keep him close.

"Yeah, that's right," he grunts, crushing me hard against the railing. "No one can make you feel this good, Little Red. No *one*." I can feel the pulse of him inside, the warmth of him spilling into me just enhancing the sweet shudder going through my body.

Down below, Vandy and Caroline are laughing, trotting off the dance floor, taking a break. I watch as they stand on their tip-toes, peering around the other dancers, searching for me.

Heston makes a sharp, annoyed sound when I shove him away, his spent dick slipping out of me. "What the fuck," he growls, hurrying to tuck himself back into his pants.

I straighten my dress, shrugging. "I'm done with you." As I walk away, trying not to feel the phantom pang of him inside of me, I toss over my shoulder, "For now."

I GET TO THE STUFFY, humid pool the next morning feeling like a freight train ran me over. I got a drink, once I'd left Heston up there trying to collect the last of his brain cells, but it sort of went to my head. Although I only had the one drink, it must have been strong enough for me to feel it the next day. The only other explanation for the way I'm feeling right now is a lot harder to swallow.

I'm not ready to deal with the shame and regret of saying yes to him.

"Ms. Haynes!" My name echoes off the vaulted ceiling, making me flinch. Coach James strides toward me, his expression grim. "Are you the one that set up the lane ropes for the meet yesterday?"

Lane ropes? *Oh.* "That's what they're called? Um, I mean, yes." I'd spent an hour dragging the ropes from one end of the pool to the other. It'd been time-consuming and physically exhausting, and I never want to do it again.

He doesn't look happy. He looks distinctly *un*happy. Actually, now that I really look at him, he looks furious. "You didn't secure the hooks. Halfway through the first event, they unlatched, disrupting the entire race. Not only was it embarrassing, it delayed the meet and cost us an important win!"

"I-I-" I'm at a total loss for words. All of that because of some ropes? "God, I'm so sorry, Coach. I tried really hard to get them all—"

"I don't want to hear your excuses," he snaps, face stony. "It's completely unacceptable. Those kids trained hard for that meet and you took away their win! What am I supposed to—"

"It was my fault."

Coach James' angry gaze flicks over my shoulder. Turning, I see Heston standing behind me. He's clad in a black hoodie with a tight gray T-shirt underneath. Coach James rests his hands on his hips and says, "Care to explain, Wilcox?"

He shoves his fists into the pockets of his loose, olive-green shorts. "It's my fault Ms. Haynes didn't attach the ropes correctly. I didn't show her how to do it before I left."

I blink, trying to figure out if I'm still drunk. Maybe I'm dreaming.

Except Coach James' mouth forms a tight thin line, and he says, "Heston, you know better than that. Secure ropes are an important part of any meet."

"I do, and I apologize." Heston shrugs, a lock of blond hair falling into his tired blue eyes. "I was in a hurry and didn't make sure the job was done right. That was my responsibility."

Coach James has a few more choice things to say, and to my shock, Heston takes it. Even when the Coach demands Heston *personally* tidy up the entire pool deck when we're finished, Heston just bluntly agrees. I barely hear any of it, though. I'm still trying to process the two words I'm pretty sure I heard Heston just say.

"Wait," I call out to him once the Coach is gone, still feeling dumbstruck. "Am I insane, or did you just defend me *and* apologize to Coach James?"

"Yeah. So?" He runs his hand through his hair, from forehead to crown, sweeping it away from his face. It's such a Sebastian-like gesture that it almost completely disarms me. It's the first time I've ever really looked at him and seen the resemblance between the brothers. Heston usually keeps his hair short. This unkempt messiness, I'm realizing, is completely new.

Baffled, I say, "I don't think I've ever heard you, like...*apologize* before."

He looks unbothered as he shrugs. "The thing with the ropes is tricky and I should have told you. I was just in a hurry to dip. That was my fuck-up. I'll own it."

"First time for everything," I mutter, not missing the way his eyes narrow as they slide to me. "So was that why you were in such a hurry to leave? Because you own Underworld?"

He starts toward the storage room, jaw tense. "Not that it's any of your business, but yes. I had to take care of some shit. This whole thing is basically like having two jobs." He looks the part, too, tired around the eyes and just a touch too disheveled to be manufactured. He takes a large key ring from his pocket, flipping through it.

Watching him, I ask, "When did that happen, anyway? Last I checked, that club was dump."

The lock springs and the swings open the door. "I got it last spring—you know, before...everything." Before we turned him in, he means. Before he got arrested. Before he ended up back here. He ducks into the closet, pausing to quietly add, "I haven't really told anyone." I hear the demand, even if he doesn't speak it aloud.

He'd like it to stay that way.

"Why not?"

He shakes his head, jaw tensing as he reaches for an empty storage bin. "I've been a little too busy to bother, Haynes. But mainly, I don't like people in my business."

By people, I wonder who he means. His brother probably, or maybe the people he likes to gamble with so much. It could be his parents, even. I get the feeling his mom has a lot of problems, and I know from Sebastian that their dad has many high expectations. There's a whole side of Heston I don't know about, and it makes me weirdly uncomfortable. Mostly because I'm curious.

"Well, for what it's worth," I offer, shifting awkwardly, "it's pretty cool."

His blue eyes dart to mine. "What's pretty cool?"

"Underworld," I elaborate, taking the box he passes to me. "Like I said, it used to be a dump. It seems like you've done a good job."

I cringe in a million different ways on the inside. For one, the last thing Heston needs or deserves is praise, and for two, even if he did want or deserve it, it falls flat, sounding more patronizing than anything.

Despite this, he looks at me, forehead creased. When he stands still like that, blue eyes boring into mine, it's almost like he's considering me for the first time. "Thanks?" The question emerges slow and reluctant and more than a little baffled.

Clearing my throat, I follow him across the pool deck. "The parking sucks, though. And the lights are little to rave'y. And the VIP area with the curtain is douchey."

He whirls on me, eyes full of exasperation. "If this is how you give compliments, I'll take a pass next time." He unzips his hoodie, tossing it on the bench next to the wall. His T-shirt has a faded, smirking devil on the front. He points me to the other side of the pool, and I go as directed. He unties the flags on his side, giving me a view of his ripped lower body. I do the same with the flags on my side, wondering how soon is *too soon*.

It's not that I'm disinclined to inconvenience him. God, as if.

I just don't want him to think I'm so eager. "So what are you doing this morning?"

It's horribly fake, and he instantly senses it, eyes narrowing in on me. Possibly a compliment and small talk in the same five-minute span was a bit much.

"Seriously?" He drops the flags and stares at me, brows crouched low. "It's only been ten hours."

Flustered, I loop the cord around my elbow, going round and round until they make a tight lasso. "So much for all that stamina you were bragging about."

He lets out a low, raspy laugh. "Fucking hell, Little Red. I'm at work."

I give him a look. We've fucked three times, and during each of those, he's been at 'work'.

He rolls his eyes, moving to the next rope. "Okay, point taken. Help me pack all this shit up and I'll fuck your brains out like a nice little lapdog."

Instantly panty-soaked.

Hot damn.

We spend an hour methodically packing up the ropes, banners, and decorations. Each time he lifts an arm to grab something, or crouches down to grab something, or—*lord*, just grabs anything, in any way—the vibrations get a little deeper, a little more insistent. I wriggle my shoulders, skin feeling tight as I watch him heave the tall ladder down the deck to the equipment closet. Heston's got these muscles. They're not all big and bulging and obnoxious like his brother's, either. They're subtle. Lean. Efficient. They're the kind of muscles that make you want to run your fingertips over the defined ridges.

He's slotting the ladder into place when I reach the closet, trapping him in.

I give him the demands I was too sex-fogged to consider last night. "I want kissing and condoms."

He turns to me, mouth curling up in confused distaste. "What?"

I cross my arms, cocking an eyebrow. "I'm calling the shots, right? Those are what I want. Kissing and condoms." After a moment of us staring at one another, I add, "And chocolate."

"Chocolate," he repeats, voice deadpan.

Shrugging, I explain, "I just like it."

He chuffs out a humorless laugh, bracing an arm on a nearby shelf to tower over me. His eyes are dark as he pins me with a stare. "Kisses, no condoms, and you get your own goddamn chocolate."

"This isn't a negotiation—" I try, but he barrels right over me.

"I fuck raw, Little Red. Take it or leave it."

Hotly, I insist, "I'm not getting tested every Wednesday just because you refuse to wrap it up."

He lifts a shoulder. "Then don't get tested."

"Yeah, right. I'm not trusting some creep with an AcadaNeeds account to keep it in his pants." Glaring him up and down, I mockingly add, "*HotWetCox.*"

His jaw tightens, right before he pulls out his phone. The screen illuminates the space between us uncomfortably, throwing his crazy jaw line into sharp relief. He taps the screen and turns it, showing me his AcadaNeeds profile.

Then he deletes it.

"Given that you're panting for my dick after a whopping ten hours without it, I'm guessing I won't have time to fuck around with anyone else." He slides his phone back into his pocket, reaching behind me to ease the door shut. "You in, or what?"

The kiss borders on violent, full of too much teeth and bone. His hands clamp onto my hip, spinning me until I'm shoved against a shelf. I make a pained sound, grabbing a thick fistful of his hair and bucking against him.

He's already hard.

He rips his mouth away and wrenches me from the shelf, spinning me, but I stop him, perching on the edge of it instead.

"Like this," I say, already panting in anticipation as I reach for the button on my pants.

He's staring at me with this ice and fire look that makes my belly clench. "Like what?"

"Fucking," I say, giving into another one of those deep, biting kisses. "Like this, facing you."

He rears back suddenly, face contorted in disgust. "What?! I don't want to *look* at you!"

It's like a pitcher of ice water has been poured over my head.

"Wow," I say, stunned by the sheer amount of alarm in his voice —like the thought of looking at me isn't just repulsive, but inspires actual fucking panic. "You want to look at my back?" I ask, jumping down from the shelf, fist clenched angrily. "Then watch this, asshole."

He doesn't even try to stop me as I storm out of the closet, so pissed off that I can't even see past the churn of hatred and mortification fuzzing up my head. He's not even the one I'm mad at. This is

Heston, after all. He has one nature and I know full well how deep it cuts.

I'm angry at myself. Not for thinking that this was anything but a truly terrible idea. Not even for looking at him earlier and thinking that he had some sort of mysterious, hidden depths.

No, I'm mad at myself for actually letting Heston Wilcox hurt my feelings.

12

Heston

I wake to the alarm shrieking in my ear, hard cock pressed against the mattress. "Fuck," I groan.

I dreamed about her again. Usually when I dream about fucking girls, it's just like real-life. Hands gripping the soft flesh of her round ass, fucking her hard and relentless as she's bent over a desk, a chair, a railing. The sight of a bruise purpling tender skin.

The first dreams about Georgia were just flashes of what we've done already. But not last night. In this one she was naked and straddling my hips, long red hair hanging over her shoulders. Her tits bounced as she moved—*riding me*—and I couldn't stop staring at them, her face, or those bright green eyes, trapping mine like barbed wire. In the dream, her eyes weren't filled with hatred as usual. They were full of something so much worse; want and expectation, a horror so quiet and soft that it choked me.

It wasn't a dream.

It was a goddamn nightmare.

People call me a liar, a manipulator, a cheat, and I guess they're not wrong. I prefer the word 'engineer', though. Knowing how people tick, anticipating their reactions, finding their weaknesses; that's how you own them. Some people are better at hiding than others, but it doesn't matter. Look into someone's eyes long enough and you'll get the measure of them.

I know exactly what can happen if you let someone really see you. I know because I've done it myself. If the eyes are the window to the soul, then my ass is buying as many mental curtains as I can. It can't be anything worth seeing anyway—probably a black pit of nothingness. That's always how I've felt, anyway. Even when I was a kid, I didn't feel things the way others did. I didn't react or cope or function the 'proper' way. I knew it then, and I know it now. Which is why this dream about Georgia, this game I'm playing, has me all twisted up inside.

In the dream, she'd seen me. She'd pulled away the curtains and dipped her greedy hands inside. She'd gotten the sum of my parts. The mere memory of it makes me sick.

Sick and inconceivably horny.

It's making my stomach hurt again. I scrub a hand roughly over my face, wondering, "What the hell is wrong with me?"

That dream is what I get for my behavior the day before. For being 'nice'. For letting her think something like that was even on the goddamn table.

I'd shown up to the pool because I knew Coach James expected it. I'd already bailed on Friday night, but when I heard him shouting at her for those stupid ropes, I jumped in. I don't know why they both acted so surprised. It's not like I'm incapable of owning a fuck-up.

So what if I only bother when it suits me?

It just so happened that, on that morning, it did. Georgia and I have come to an agreement, and it took a shitload of work. Way more work than it should have. If I have to eat some crow to maintain the tenuous balance, then I'll do it.

But I'm sure as hell not letting her look at me while we fuck.

I blast the shower as cold as it'll go, but it does nothing to quell the morning wood. Giving up, I crank that shit so hot that it's scalding, closing my eyes to get lost in a fantasy. I don't feel an ounce of guilt as I stroke myself, conjuring up the image of my palm prints bruised into a soft, round ass. Yeah, that's fucking hot, imagining my hand coming down on her cheeks, the sound it'd make, the way she'd whimper and buck back against it. I bet Georgia would like that. None of this stupid 'facing you' bullshit. Just bend her over the nearest flat surface and spank her until she's dripping wet and teary-eyed. That's what we'd be good at. Rough, painful, faceless sex.

My balls tighten and strain, but the orgasm pulls just out of reach. Frustrated, I jerk myself harder, conjuring up a new scene where I'm staring at dark red lips and perky, erect nipples. I remember the dream, the strong rolling thrust of hips, the way her tits felt in my palms. But it's the fucking eyes that get me. Brilliant and green. Trapping me. Burning me from the inside out. Digging inside as she uses me.

The orgasm rocks through me so hard that I have to shoot out a hand to steady myself, smacking my palm against the cool tile wall. After, I keep my eyes closed for a long time, holding onto the memory and sensation. It's just because she asked for it. Because she left me there in that closet, hard and frustrated.

Next time, I'm going to fuck it out of her.

An hour later, I've found a quiet bench outside the dining hall to have my coffee and breakfast burrito in peace. I try not to eat inside if I can help it. Too fucking weird. I'm still closer in age to the students than the teachers, but sitting with them is out of the question—not that I'd want to, anyway. Every day that passes, I get the surreal awareness of how young they all seem. Young and so goddamn stupid. I'd been one of them just three years ago; entitled, stuck-up, king of the world. Being here as an adult is the sickest form of torture imaginable. The middle-schoolers make me want to strangle something and the high-schoolers…

They're the worst.

I'd passed a group of kids clustered by the stairs, recognizing one of them as Haynes' roommate, Josie. I'm not surprised to see her surrounded by a bunch of guys. Back in school, I would have been all over her tail, too. Everyone knows Sparrowood girls are freaks between the sheets.

I'm chewing a mouthful of eggs and bacon when I hear a guy say, "So Wentworth, what's it like living with her?"

Wentworth, I remember, is Josie's last name.

I hear her reply, "What do you mean? Obviously, I wanted the suite to myself, but she's not too bad for a roommate. I've definitely had worse."

"You're not, like, hearing wild sex moans all night or anything?"

"Hell," another boy laughs, "or all day, for that matter."

From the sound of her chuckled, "What?" Josie sounds confused, but happy to play along.

"Come on, you've gotta know, right?" a kid says. "She got that solo so she can whore herself out. Whorgia Haynes gives away more pussy than the animal shelter."

"Seriously?" Josie asks. "I think you guys are full of shit. She's never even had a guy over to the room, except—"

I freeze mid-chew, spine going rigid, but she's cut off by one of the assholes, saying, "I heard she fucked the whole wrestling team last year."

"Nah," someone says, "just four of them."

"I heard she's super into anal."

"And loves to suck cock."

"Georgia's bedroom gets so much traffic, Starbucks is thinking of opening a store there." There's a loud, collective bark of laughter before another guy adds, "Try making 'Georgia Haynes' your password and you'll get an error. *Too easy.*"

Josie groans, "Gross. You guys are pigs." But she's still laughing when she says it. After a moment, she thoughtfully adds, "You know, she does hide in her room all the time. I thought she was just sleeping or studying a lot, but the other day? I could have sworn I heard this weird, mechanical vibrating."

"Oh, shit!" The guys whoop in laughter, followed by the obnoxious slapping of palms.

Really?

"I bet that thing has to be a horse dildo. She's gotta be so stretched out by now."

They all keep laughing and I can't shake this thing that's got my blood buzzing. I take a moment to realize it's annoyance. Never mind that I've been balls deep in that woman and it's some of the tightest pussy I've ever had. This shit isn't even creative.

I smash the rest of my breakfast into a ball, lurch up from my seat, and charge over to them. As soon as they see me, their eyes widen, mouths all clamping shut. I may still blend in like a student, but they all know my position at the school and their expressions reveal it.

I try to keep the building anger from boiling over, but it's not working. "Some of us are trying to eat and don't want to listen to you going on about dildos and stretched out pussy." I shoot the youngest looking kid a glare. "Like you'd have any idea what to do with either of those, anyway."

"Come on, Coach Wilcox," one of them says, grinning. It's the kid who was flirting with Georgia during swim class that day. Jase something. "Tell the truth. My older brother told me all about you. You're a legend."

I eye the kid. "Who's your brother?"

"Gus Meyers." He gives me a cocky grin. God, I know that grin. I've seen it on his brother's big dumb face, and I've seen it in the mirror. He leans forward conspiratorially. "You totally hit that back in the day, didn't you?"

My facade slips, the one I try to wear around campus because I know Collins and Dewey and all the other faculty are expecting me to fail. For a moment, I let the Devil out, flexing my size over him. "I got to be a legend by being the best. By keeping my mouth shut and dominating everyone and everything in this school. I never needed to brag about banging a whore to get there. Do you get me?"

He nods, and I see a flash of red to the side. Glancing over, I realize Georgia is standing a few feet away. Watching us. *Listening* to us. I know just how much she heard. It's in the way her jaw sets, the bitterness in the curl of her mouth.

She spins on her heel and marches off.

With one last glare at the students, I decide to go after her. *Jesus Christ.* One step forward and three steps back with this girl. This shit is quickly becoming a third job.

I follow the flash of her fiery hair as it disappears around the back of the dining hall, where it smells like old grease and bacon. A big dumpster sits close to the wall and I circle around it, looking for her. She's not there, though. I grimace as I look toward the tree line that leads into the woods.

I'm still contemplating if I should go after her or not when a black streak runs from the trees—a cat. Another cat follows its lead, both of them heading straight toward the stack of recycling bins.

A moment later, I hear a sneeze.

Then another.

The cats loudly meow and a voice whispers, "Go away. *Achoo!*"

I walk around the recycling bins and see Georgia squatting against the building, cats circling anxiously nearby. When she looks up at me, her nose is glowing red, eyes watery and irritated. I can't tell if it's from the sneezing or what she just heard.

I raise an eyebrow. "Hiding again?"

"No," she says, rubbing her nose. "Well, not from you. Your brother did too good of a job taming these stupid cats. They won't leave me alone."

I realize then that I'm still holding the burrito. I toss it a few feet away and the two cats, plus another that's still hiding in the woods, rush over and start picking away at it.

When they're occupied, she slumps down the wall, knees tucked to her chest. "Apparently, neither will you."

Scratching the back of my neck, I start, "Listen, I don't know what you just heard, but—"

"I heard enough."

Of course she did. "I wasn't trying to—"

She shoots me a dark look. "Don't, Heston. Nothing you say will make this any better. If anything, you'll just make it worse." She's all red faced and worrying that bottom lip of hers, and for some reason, I find I can't leave.

It's really pissing me off. "How is any of this my fault?" I wonder, tossing a hand toward the dining hall. "You made your own choices. It's not like anyone's spreading lies about you. Own your shit, Haynes!"

She explodes, "You think I don't know that?!" Despite this, a tear falls, tracking down her cheek. She angrily swats it away. "You think I have a fun time looking at myself in the mirror every day? Because it'd be really easy, you know. It'd be so fucking easy to blame it on you and that goddamn video. But I *do* own my shit, Heston. I know it started before that night happened." Sniffing wetly, she looks away, eyes hard. "I know it was the *reason* that night happened. You knew. You even brought it up."

She's right. I knew. Word was all over Preston about Georgia being the girl who would do anything, and that's exactly what I needed. A girl who could take it fast and hard. A girl who wouldn't care if I didn't want to look her in the eye while I was doing it. A girl who wouldn't ask a lot of questions afterward, or make demands, or have any deluded expectations.

I needed a dirty little slut.

And that's exactly what I got.

She rests her forearms on her knees, brows knitted together. "It's not like I ever wanted to be the school slut. I just wanted to have sex." After a pause, she laughs, the sound abrasive and without humor. "That's a lie. I needed it. I *needed* to have sex. Some days, it's all I can think about, like—" Her mouth clicks shut, eyes lurching to mine, "I don't know why I'm telling you this. You'll probably have it on blast before dinner."

"Believe it or not, I actually have better things to do than contribute to the Preston gossip mill. Plus," I move to lean against the wall beside her, staring unseeingly into the woods, "it's not anything I didn't already suspect. You're like a nympho or some-thing, right?" She'd probably have to be to keep coming back to me for dick.

I hear a sniffle, feet shifting against the pavement. "Does it really matter?" she mutters, voice low. "A slut by any other name..."

Rolling my eyes, I look down at her and say, "Oh, so fucking what?" When her green eyes jump up to mine, flashing, I add, "Be the slut. Be a legendary slut. Be the best fucking slut this school has ever seen—the kind of slut people are still talking about ten years later. I don't see the big deal, Little Red. Girls want to be you, guys want to fuck you. So they talk shit sometimes. Who cares?"

She shakes her head. "You wouldn't get it. You're a guy."

"Yeah," I say, snorting. "What the hell do I know about people talking behind my back, calling me names, acting like I'm beneath them. You know the difference between you and me?"

Belligerently, she offers, "You're an evil piece of shit who enjoys hurting people, and I'm not?"

Shrugging, I don't deny it. "Yeah, sometimes I get off on hurting people. But I've never gotten off on hurting myself. That's the differ-ence between us, Little Red."

Her face screws up. "I'm sorry, is the guy who doesn't even want to look at me while we're fucking trying to give me advice on building a better self-image? This is just a lot of irony for one conversation." It comes out just a touch too caustic to be confused for mere sarcasm.

I stare down at the top of her head, realizing that I possibly, somehow, managed to hurt her fucking feelings.

Jesus Christ.

I shift my weight, trying to think of something to say, and it's stupid. Georgia ruined my goddamn life. I should rub it in, make the sting that much sharper. It's no less than what she deserves.

Instead, I stand rigidly against the wall, flustered and off-balance. "It's not about you." I stare off at the cats as they devour my crushed burrito. "I mean, come on. Those tits of yours are legendary. Who wouldn't want those things bouncing around in front of their face?" Unbidden, I'm struck with the memory of the dream. Her riding me. The way her slender throat looked when she threw her head back, drawing my eyes right down to her tits. *Fuck*. I try to shake out of it, huffing as I look down into her confused eyes. "Ask Sydney. Ask Reagan. Ask any girl I've ever fucked, and they'll tell you I did it with all of them the same way."

Those big green eyes flutter with a blink. "Why?"

I break her gaze before curtly saying, "I don't like people looking at me. It makes my dick soft. End of story." I feel her eyes on me, but refuse to meet them. I've given her too much already.

Gently—almost *shyly*—she asks, "You're not just saying that?"

I gape at her, wondering why the hell it matters. It's not like Georgia likes me. Why would she care whether or not I wanted to look at her? "Do I strike you as someone who tells you something to spare your feelings, Haynes?"

Fucking girls, man.

"Oh." There's a long beat of silence. I can hear the birds over the lake in the distance, the far-away sounds of kids laughing. Georgia shifts, legs stretching out in front of her. "You're wrong about me not getting off on treating people badly. If my therapist were here, she'd say I'm being unfair to you. That I'm going to have to figure out how to make lasting relationships and respect other people's boundaries. I can't just keep chasing the same high over and over again. The crash is too hard. I think..." She swallows loudly, worrying at the silver bracelet around her slender wrist, spinning it around and around. "I think that's why it has to be you. Of all the people I can hurt with this, you're the only one I wouldn't feel bad about."

"*Ouch*. A guy can feel a little used, you know." The deadpan look I give her cushions the reply, making her eyes roll.

"Like you don't deserve it."

I take a paranoid look around before dropping to settle beside her against the wall. "I know you're new to this whole revenge thing, Little Red, so let me give you some pointers from a seasoned pro. Fucking a guy until his brains are goo isn't really much of a hardship." I slide my eyes to hers, voice slow. "Especially not when it's some particularly hot pussy."

Despite everything, her cheeks actually go pink. "Shut up."

Because I was serious before about not bullshitting for the sake of it, I bluntly add, "The pussy is tight, Little Red. The mouth could use some work, though."

She stops spinning that bracelet to extend a middle finger.

"You're kind of a bitch, you know," I tell her, watching the cats finish the last of my breakfast. "You did me dirty as fuck. Going to the cops over some bullshit like that was a lame move."

She turns wide, infuriated eyes on me. "I keep telling you! You did this to yourself, Heston!"

I shake my head. There's no way I'm giving her that one. "It was a shitty move. There's no honor in using the law to do your dirty work. But this?" I give her a long look, seeing her in a new light. "Using me like a piece of cheap meat is the only respectable move you've made."

She groans, head falling back against the wall. "Well, that's the last nail in the coffin for my pride. Heston Wilcox is calling me respectable."

"Hate me all you want, but you've gotta admit, I always take care of my own shit. I don't need other people to do it for me like some little bitch."

She tilts her head to stare at me. "Fuck you, Heston."

I shoot her a look. "On whose terms?"

She takes in another wet sniffle, swinging her damp eyes away. "We can do it like that, I guess." Quietly, she mutters, "It's better the other way, though."

I scoff. "For you, maybe." Although it will be a shame not to see those tits bouncing. I reach down to adjust myself, feeling her eyes track the motion, forehead creased.

"Really?" she says, eying the bulge in my pants. Her voice might drip of judgment, but there's a dark eagerness in her expression.

I give it a squeeze. "Girls are hot when they cry."

The eagerness disappears instantly. "Oh, my god!" Most of it, anyway. She still gives my boner a second—a third—glance. "You're a legitimate psycho, you realize."

Shrugging, I say, "Happens to all guys. Comforting a crying girl is a straight shot to boner-ville."

She barks a disbelieving laugh. "That was you *comforting* me? 'Be the best slut you can be'? Seriously?"

"Yeah, a little too touchy-feely for me, too."

Despite her horror, she's still chewing on that lip pensively. Her voice drops. "Do you, like, *want to*?"

"I'm a guy, I always want to." Still, I look around. Georgia might be too horny to consider these things, but I'm sure as fuck not. "Even a gambling addict wouldn't play these odds, Little Red. Maybe later, when I'm not in danger of getting caught nailing a student beside the dumpsters."

She looks disappointed, but nods in agreement.

❧

Monday is bullshit, from the second I wake up to Headmaster Collins banging on my door.

"What have you found?" he asks, that comb-over of his immaculate.

I have to rub the sleep from my eyes before I can glare at him. "Aside from a new and interesting dislike of you? Almost nothing."

He raises an eyebrow. "Almost?"

"Jesus Christ," I groan, pinching the bridge of my nose. "Is this really something we need to talk about at seven in the morning?"

His jaw sets, eyes narrowing. "We'll talk about it when I want to talk about it, Heston. Or have you forgotten the whole reason you're here?"

"Fine," I bite out, folding my arms over my chest. "Benjamin Shackleford and Carlton Wade."

Collins frowns. "What about them?"

"They were Devils."

It's a useless piece of information, and from the look on his face, he knows it. "They both graduated last year. How is this supposed to help me?"

"Look," I start, teeth grinding, "I've been here a week. I'm not sure what you were expecting, but I'm not just going to stumble into a secret society over a single weekend."

It's a lie, of course. I have the key and I know what doors it opens. But I haven't looked at that memory card yet. My laptop is sitting on top of my nightstand. At home. The one I'm banned from even entering. Knowing my father, they've probably already wiped and donated it. I need to pilfer one from the computer lab, I just haven't had the time.

I'm not handing over information until I know what that information is.

"Figure it out," he snaps, leaving in a huff.

The day doesn't get any better from there. I manage to snag some lap time between classes, but when I emerge from the pool and make my way to the office, I realize my clothes have vanished.

Shirt, pants, shoes, even my fucking socks.

I spend the next three hours stomping around the natatorium, interrogating anyone I see. Two middle-schoolers start crying loudly—fucking annoyingly, I might add—when I threaten to write them up. I storm away in hopes of finding someone with thicker skin, but they're all like that. Dumb, sniveling little shits. I have to sprint to my apartment for spare clothes and rush back to make my next intro class, but I don't have extra shoes, so I'm forced to wear my shower slippers for the rest of the afternoon. I skip dinner, not in the mood to listen to a room full of teenagers give their opinions on my choice of footwear, which makes this annoying fucking situation with my stomach even worse.

But the worst part about it is that it's Monday—*my* goddamn Monday—and I'm stuck in this stupid independent study class with Georgia and Micha until eight. I rub at my temples as Micha argues about doing drills.

"It's not really teaching," he's saying, mouth a tight line. "I don't see why we have to be here if you're just going to make us *walk in water*. That's not a useful life skill! Anyone can walk in water. Some of us have better things to do with our night than—"

I snap, "If you're not in that pool in ten seconds, I'm giving you detention until you're forty."

Georgia rolls her eyes, but unlike Micha, this isn't the battle she wants to pick. "If I can get credit for walking in water for an hour, then whatever." She still sulks her way to the shallow end and shoots me a glare as she lowers herself into the pool.

When I'm sure they're occupied, I finally allow myself to kick back, slipping my phone from my pocket. Earlier, I'd heroically liberated a twenty-dollar bill from a seventh-grader, who'd less heroically liberated it from a sixth-grader, who probably liberated it from his mother's purse, and that's how I'd scored the box of Chinese food I pull into my lap. The natatorium is practically deserted, aside from us, so I don't even try to hide what I'm doing. I load up the network's app and press play.

As soon as the Lakevale theme starts up, I dig in.

I hear a swish of water, but don't bother looking up from the screen. Not even when I hear the rapid patter of wet feet slapping against the floor. Not until a drop of pool water falls on my arm, that is.

I glare up at Micha. "Get back in the pool."

"I knew it!" He's staring in shock at my phone. "I *knew* I heard that song! You're watching Lakevale! Georgia!" He swings his head around to look at her, face agonized. "Georgia, he's watching Lakevale!"

"It's Monday night," I point out, not irrationally. "Of course I'm watching Lakevale. Now go finish your drills."

"You can't do this to me," he cries.

"Yes, I can," I disagree.

"You know what?" Micha's nostrils flare as he snatches his bag from the bench, pulling a towel out. "You can go ahead and give me detention. I don't care. I'm not standing in that pool, listening to the new episode of Lakevale over shitty phone speakers." He pulls a wireless speaker from his bag next, thrusting it at me. "Sync it up and shove over, asshole."

It's straight up insubordinate, is what it is. I *should* give him detention. I should send him marching right to Collins. I should tell Coach James that he's flunked—better luck next time.

But the show's about to start, and my phone's speakers really are shitty. "Fine," I growl, thumbing my screen to sync the Bluetooth. "But you'd better sit down and be so quiet that I don't even know you exist."

"What?" Georgia says, having gotten out of the pool, too. "The two of you are seriously going to sit there and watch Lakevale for an hour?"

Goddamnit.

I pin her with a glower. "Maybe it's escaped your notice, but I live on a campus with over three-hundred teenagers. The second I walk out that door," I point at it for good measure, "someone is going to spoil it for me."

"It's true," Micha insists, ripping off his swim camp. "One time my dance class ran late, and I wasn't even out of the parking lot before someone texted me about Peyton Nolan being murdered." He casually explains, "She didn't actually get murdered, it was just a setup so that her sister Flora could—"

"Both of you shut up!" To Georgia, I say, "Either do your drills, or sit down and be quiet. Your choice."

Huffing, she grabs a towel from the bench and joins us. But not before muttering, "I can't believe you're watching a stupid teen show."

I turn a slow, dangerous glare on her. "Stupid?"

Affronted, Micha says, "Lakevale isn't *stupid*."

"And it's not a 'teen show'," I add. "It's a small town political thriller. Its absurdity transcends the bounds of satire all together. Lakevale is a goddamn contemporary masterpiece."

"I can't believe I'm about to say this," Micha says, expression anguished. "But you are being *so cool* right now."

Just then, the opening scene starts up, and Micha and I both shut our mouths. If Georgia has something else completely fucking blasphemous to say about it, she does herself the favor of keeping it to herself.

It's a fucking awesome episode, too—exactly what I needed to wash this shitty day away. Micha whips his phone out during the ad breaks to post his reactions on ChattySnap. Even Georgia seems to get into it, her shoulder brushing against mine as she leans in to see the screen better. I can tell she wants to ask questions, but she doesn't, opting instead to hum under her breath now and then.

For the first time in weeks, my stomach stops hurting.

13

Georgia

"What was that?"

"Hmm...?"

"That. That *look*. What was that about?" Micha kicks off his flip-flops and the accusatory look vanishes for a second when he takes off his shirt. I'm already in my bathing suit, sitting on the bench at the edge of the pool deck.

"I don't know what you're talking about."

"Well, usually you're all foaming at the mouth when you see Wilcox. Whatever that look is on your face? It's not rabid."

I shrug and walk over to the edge of the pool, dipping a toe in to feel the temperature. "Waste of my precious energy, to be honest. Plus, you were the one being so chummy with him yesterday." I raise my voice mockingly. "Oh, Heston! You're so cool for liking Lakevale!" Looking at him, I make a gagging sound. "Barf."

He clutches his chest. "You're misquoting me! I refuse to be taken out of context like this. That's like, libel or slander or something."

"Whatever you say." I peer across the pool again and take him in. He's talking to Gina Neal, the girl's water polo coach. He's leaning casually against the wall, propped on his arm. Something she says makes him laugh, a genuine laugh, and I find myself unable to look away.

Heston has a wicked smile. No, everything about him is wicked. It's as if he was created to entice people into watching the way he moves. Like those illusionists who distract you with one hand while the other pulls off a trick. Everything from his smile, his intelligence, his face, and most definitely his body can be used to stun. It just depends who his target is and what he wants out of them.

The problem is that it's been three days.

It's not like I'm a complete slave to my body's urges. I'm usually good to go for a while after some great sex, and that's exactly what fucking Heston is—great sex. But it's different this time. I'm used to spending that stretch between hook-ups looking for the right guy, then flirting with them, building a tension.

With Heston, the tension always comes built-in. Right now, my brain is wondering what the damn hold-up is. I know who it's going to be—he's standing *right there*—so why am I not on his dick already? I thought keeping it to one guy would make everything easier, but maybe I was wrong. Perhaps having a convenient piece of meat always within reach is just making me more impatient.

He laughs again, glancing over at the lap pool as he does, inadvertently catching my eye. His smile doesn't drop, but my stomach sure as hell does.

"That," Micha says, shivering dramatically. "*That's* what I'm talking about."

"*That* was nothing, Micha." I inch into the pool, letting the cold water hit each part of my skin a sliver at a time. "Stop being weird."

"You're the one being weird. Not me."

I try to keep my eyes off of Heston as he saunters over, but it's difficult. His expression might shutter over when he approaches, but he doesn't look angry, just distant. That's fine. Distance is something I can handle. Given the way my whole being coils in anticipation of having him close, it might be something necessary at this point.

"We're working on backstroke today," he says, grabbing a clipboard from a nearby bench. "You'll take turns guiding one another."

A flutter of panic tickles up my spine. I've made some progress with all this swimming stuff, but being on my back isn't a part of it. The one time I tried had felt strange and claustrophobic, so I encourage Micha to go first.

"Sure," he says, shifting to his back. His form obviously isn't the best, either. With his neck craned up above the water, his bottom sinks.

"Adams, get your head and ass flat."

Micha tosses Heston a tense glare. "But what if the water gets under my swim cap? It'll mess my hair up."

"Lay your head back or I'll get in and do it for you." He paces the edge of the pool, looking annoyed and impatient. "No more messing around. In no universe should it take teenagers this long to learn how to swim. Focus."

Micha raises his eyebrow at me. "So much for the friendship power of Lakevale bonding."

He flattens out, grimacing when the water covers his ears. Heston and I make brief eye contact and for all his bluster, I think he doesn't mind Micha as much as he pretends. It's hard *not* to like the kid. I'd seen the two of them last night, geeking out over that stupid teen show. They were about five more minutes of airtime away from having an actual civilized conversation.

I hover beside Micha, hands just under his back in case he needs a save. He doesn't, though. The truth is, there's nothing keeping Micha from being a good swimmer other than his refusal to learn. He's a cool kid, but chock full of that Adams stubbornness.

Me, on the other hand...

"Good job," Heston says, once Micha has mastered the back float. "Haynes, your turn."

His tone is aloof, which is perfectly appropriate here. Student and teacher, that's what we are. Except my skin prickles under the heat of his gaze as he watches me shift to my back, one hand clutching Micha's arm while the other flails uselessly around in the water.

"Ease into it," Heston says, pausing his pacing to lower into a loose crouch. "Just like you're laying down."

I give a few more flails, breath trapped tightly in my throat. "I can't," I squeak.

Firmly, he insists, "You can."

I shoot him a fiery glare, but it's met with the ice cold blue of his eyes. I blink first. "You promise you won't let me drown?" I beg Micha.

"Of course not." He holds out both hands like that proves something. "How about I stand behind you and hold your shoulders?"

"Okay," I say, chewing on my lip. "That might work."

From the edge of the pool, Heston issues the same directions as he gave Micha. I bend my knees and lower my shoulders into the water. Sensing Micha's presence behind me, I try to relax.

"Now," Heston adds, "push your belly and tit—uh—*chest* up." His eyes narrow at the slip in language. "Butt flat, like a board."

I do as he says, feeling briefly like I can handle it. The water is cool and I can sense the peace, can grasp the *idea* of floating like it might be something natural.

Heston says, "Relax your shoulders. Head all the way back."

I look up at Micha's sweet, encouraging face, and feel a boost of confidence, grinning back at him as I extend first one leg, and then the other.

"Straighten," Heston says, watching. "Straighten. Straighten. Damn it, Haynes, straighten!"

Flinching, I completely lose whatever sense of peace I'd just gained. My ass drops, water whooshing up above my ears as I sink, and I bolt upright too suddenly, heart pounding. The movement makes a wave of water rush up into my face, engulfing me in its tide. It feels just like getting sucked under, water pouring into my mouth when I yelp instinctively.

"Oh god," I choke, gagging on the bitter taste of chlorine and frustration. The water gets lodged in my windpipe, sending me into a coughing fit. Wheezing, I say, "Forget this. I'm done. Totally done!"

"Are you okay?" Micha asks, running his hand along my back. "How did that even happen?"

"You mean how did I almost drown myself in chest-deep water? I don't know, but I'm over it." Lurching toward the side of the pool, I grip the edge for dear life. "I'm done. That's it. No more."

"For the love of—" Heston takes a deep breath, nostrils flared, like he's trying to hold in something mean. "Haynes, it was your first real try. You can do this, but you have to woman the fuck up and find your balls!"

"No part of that made any sense!" I let out a wracking cough, shaking my head. "I can't."

Heston rises from his crouch, pushing his hair back. "Adams, go ahead and head to the locker room. You're done for the day." In a low, begrudging voice, he offers, "Good job."

Micha looks at me, a kind but worried question in his eyes. I nod my head in reply. He doesn't need to listen to Heston berate me for being a loser who can't swim. Brushing my wet hair off my face, I peer up at him.

He's glaring down at me, arms crossed over his broad chest. "So you're just going to give up like some little bitch?"

I slump dejectedly against the edge of the pool, fixing my eyes to his stupid, hideous crocs. "Why not?"

He snaps, "Because you need to do this to pass the class, and I need you to pass the class so I can get the hell out of here."

Rolling my eyes, I look up at him. "That sounds like a *you* problem. Personally, I think high school diplomas are overrated. I mean, you got one and look where you are."

His jaw tightens, a tight ball of muscle ticking at the back. It was a low blow. But when he turns to walk away, I feel enough of a sense of victory that I begin lifting myself out of the pool. However, before I even hoist myself on the edge, he's turned back around, grabbing at the hem of his shirt.

"You know what?" he says, yanking the shirt over his head to reveal his incredible body. "Fuck it. I'll teach you myself."

He jumps in, making the water slosh over my torso. "What? No."

"Obviously, you need the help of a professional." His hand runs through his wet hair, pushing it out of his eyes. It's two shades darker wet, and the rivulets run distractingly down his neck and chest. I get a good look at the tone of his muscles as he approaches me.

"You're not a professional, Wilcox. You're an ex-high school swimmer on probation."

"I know what you're doing," he says, raising an eyebrow. "You think if you piss me off, I'll end the class and let you off the hook just to get you out of my face." He gives me that same wicked grin as before, making my insides twist and turn. "Never bullshit a bullshitter. Shut up and watch me."

Everyone else has left and there's nothing but the sound of the sloshing water and the two of us. One minute he's standing and the next he's on his back, gliding gracefully through the water. Sometimes he uses his arms to propel him back, other times just his legs. He cuts clean through the water like a fish, making it look easy.

Easy and painfully sexy.

"Your turn," he says, rising back out of the water. "Get on your back."

It's a battle to tear my eyes away from the sight of his wet chest, but I do. "I never get tired of hearing guys tell me that," I mutter, still surly.

"Stop stalling." His hand sweeps under the water and lands on my lower back, sending a shiver up my spine. I glance away, afraid to look at his face, but this is Heston. He doesn't let me shut him out. He brushes forward to whisper velvet-soft into my ear, "And I thought we'd already established that I prefer you on your front, Little Red."

I duck my body under water just to cool it off.

When I come back up for air, he's watching me, eyes calculating. "What's freaking you out so much about this?" he asks, resting his hands on my shoulders. His voice echoes loudly, a little too harsh in the soft silence of the natatorium, but his eyes hold only determination and curiosity.

Thinking, I try to explain, "I can't hear anything with the water in my ears, and I can't see anything except the ceiling. It's all...claustrophobic or something. Disorienting?" He's eased me halfway back in the process of my stilted explanation, his knee prodding into the base of my spine. "I-I just don't like it."

"Take a deep breath and relax," he says. I try, feeling the water against the back of my head. He braces my neck with one hand, and as much as I hate to admit it, I feel safe like this—near him, beneath him, being cradled by him. It's only because, despite everything, Heston *is* an excellent swimmer. Plus, he's already saved me from this pool once. I doubt he'd let me drown. His probation officer probably wouldn't look too kindly on that.

Looking up at his face, I'm momentarily struck by his angles. Even from below, he's absurdly good looking, all chiseled jaw and smooth, toned chest. His other hand skims under my back, barely touching me. Heston's hands have gripped me, crushed me, dug bruises into my flesh. But this touch is almost alarming in its gentleness, as if something is suddenly very wrong.

No, not *wrong*.

Just new and jarringly unexpected.

A current races through me like a lightning strike at the feel, the way my body wants to arch into his hand, seeking more and more. I bolt upright, placing my feet on the ground.

Heston grunts as he catches me. "Seriously? You were almost there. You have *got* to chill the fuck out, woman."

I move away, putting some distance between us, trying to find some clarity in the sudden, thick fog of *want* that's throbbing in my veins. "I think you should just fail me on this section."

"No fucking way." He gives me a hard look. "It's important that you learn this."

"Why?"

"If you're ever in trouble in the water, you'll need to be able to float on your back. It saves a lot of energy." There's nothing in his voice and expression but utter sincerity, which just makes me feel dumb.

"Do you not feel this at all?" I ask, gaping at him.

He looks around, brows knitted together. "Feel what?"

I drag both palms down my face. "So that's a 'no'." I don't get it. He enjoyed fucking me. Hell, he goaded me into it. But somehow I'm the only one standing here squirming with lust. The thought of having dick on tap was really appealing to me, but now I'm not sure. He turned me down that day behind the dining hall, and now he's just acting like my regular jerk of a swim coach. What the *fuck*? Groaning in agony, I look him in the eye and angrily confess, "You are *killing* me."

Comprehension comes over his features, flattening his mouth into a thin line. "Oh, that." He sets his jaw and comes toward me, snatching my hand from where it's tugging on my hair. Holding my gaze, he dunks our hands beneath the water, pressing my palm against the hard bulge at the front of his trunks. My mouth falls open in shock and I watch, enraptured, as his blue eyes flick to my lips. "It's about *focus*, Little Red."

Funny, because the only thing I'm focused on now is the massive erection I'm holding in my hand. I fold my fingers around it, giving it a tight little squeeze, and watch as his own jaw goes slack, eyes growing dark.

His voice is full of warning as his gaze pings around the natatorium. "Don't."

Oh, I do.

He visibly bites down on a groan as I stoke him through the fabric of his trunks, chest puffing out with his inhale. "Jesus, you're going to get me fired. Or arrested. Probably both." He only takes my hand away because I let him, eyes meeting mine with a flash of resolve. "You manage to float on your back for five minutes, then maybe we can figure something out for later tonight."

My mind races with the possibilities. "The office?"

But he shakes his head. "The swim captain's been using it, and he gets after-hours access. Not taking that risk."

"Then where?" I'm ashamed to say that I wouldn't necessarily turn my nose up at a quick and dirty locker room fuck.

Heston sighs, dropping down to cover his torso in the water, arms slicing through the surface. "I have an apartment on campus."

He drops his voice, ducking his chin into the water to look at me through wet eyelashes. "It's a single."

"What?" I blink at him for a moment, sure that I haven't heard him right. He closes his eyes when the wave of water I push at him slaps him in the face. I hiss, "You asshole! You're telling me we could have been—and *for days*?!"

He whisks the water from his eyes, smirking at me. "I can't have a student coming around to my apartment at all hours. Be realistic."

"Fine," I growl, knowing that the way he makes me feel is just because I'm horny. "Let's get this over with so I can get some action."

He tilts his head. "You ready?"

"Not in the least," I laugh humorlessly. "But needs must, so get to teaching."

Hoping to keep him from touching me so much, I move faster this time, lying on my back quickly. I still don't balk when he braces my neck, but I do close my eyes so I don't have to look at his face. Or his chest. Or his muscles.

Focus.

"Okay," he says, once I've been floating assisted for a few minutes. "I'm going to let go. Can you try not to freak out?"

"Yes."

"And hey," he says, tapping my forehead. "Open your eyes so you don't run into something."

I blink, hoping maybe he won't be in my line of vision, but nope, there he is. Face. Chest. Muscles. In an effort to get away from him, I move my arms and legs, propelling myself through the water. Finally, I'm able to grasp onto that sense of peace I'd brushed up against before. It's intangible and hokey, but I imagine myself being light as a feather, shaping it into a new awareness of my body and its relationship to the water. Somehow, it works. The sensation is surreal, floating and gliding at the same time. It's not until one leg dips and I crane my neck that I realize I'm in the much, *much* deeper section of the pool. I make eye contact with Heston and yelp, sinking like a stone.

It isn't like before, where I let the calm and silence engulf me, too fascinated by the weightlessness of oblivion to bother being afraid of it. This time, I fight, kicking my legs and whipping my arms frantically through the water. A moment later, powerful arms wrap around my body and drag me back to the surface.

"You okay?" he asks once we're close to the side of the pool. Our faces are inches apart and his breath is warm, strangely cinnamon-y, like he chewed gum at some point. His lips are red and look so soft that I'm briefly mesmerized by them. I'm only broken out of it when his fingers push the hair off my cheek, grazing my chin.

"I'm—" Lost. Horny. Hot. I swallow. "I'm fine." And then, "That was five minutes, right?"

It was not even remotely five minutes.

Heston's mouth curls into a slow, devious smirk. "Sure was."

"How does this sound," Vandy says, holding up a sheet of paper. "After surviving a harrowing accident and struggling with a pain killer addiction, I've become stronger and more capable."

Caroline taps her pen against her lips in consideration.

I stare at the two of them like they've lost their damn minds. "You can't put that," I say. "You *can't*. Especially not the drug stuff! The Deb committee will lose their shit."

"But it's the truth," V says, unapologetic. "It shows my resilience and strength."

"To normal people? Sure. But to sixty-year-old society women, it shows that you're a weak and flawed hooligan with loose morals, *not* proper debutante material." I sink into the booth. We're in the back corner of The Nerd working on our bios, and even though I'm thrumming with impatience to get back to campus and meet up with Heston, I'm trying my best to achieve that whole 'focus' thing. "My mom has been preparing me for this my entire life. Trust me, they want to hear about how perfect you are and what a great wife you'll make. That's all they want to know."

"It's not 1958, Georgia," Caroline says, dipping a couple fries into her milkshake. "We're progressive women."

I hold up the brochure we all received at the first meeting. It's half schedule and half manifesto, filled with various criteria for 'coming out'. "We have to wear white dresses, pearls, and white elbow-length gloves. *White gloves.* And look at this! There's literally a footnote in here that suggests 'the donning of a hoop skirt would be acceptable'. A fucking hoop skirt? Come on. There is nothing progressive about it. They want chaste little Stepford virgins, not individuals. Personalities need not apply."

Vandy slumps, frowning. "Then what do I write about?"

"Cover the accident. Leave out the part about the stolen car. Talk about your struggles, but focus on your successes. You know, like the newspaper and your grades and stuff." I toss the brochure on the table. "Definitely do *not* mention being a Plaything."

They nod at the last one. *That* we can all agree on.

"What about you? What are you writing about?" Caroline asks.

I shrug because my bio was written ages ago. "My service work. My dedication to Preston. My time studying abroad."

Vandy's eyebrow shoots up. "Uh, Georgia? You never actually studied abroad."

"Yeah, well, no one knows that. I mean, except for the Devils, and since they're a secret society, it shouldn't be a problem." Lowering my voice to a discreet whisper, I add, "It's not like I can announce that I had a mental break because a sex video of me went viral."

"It's just so dumb that we can't be ourselves, you know?" V smiles cunningly. "Imagine the three of us just going up on the stage and laying it all out there. God that would be glorious."

I hum, but not really in agreement. I've had my dirty laundry out there before, and it's not fun. It's exhausting. I feel like all my energy is spent running from my truth—running from what I really want, who I am, and what I feel—but being able to put on a white dress and pretend like I'm someone worth having in society is the only plus about this whole thing. It's fake. Blessedly fake.

We work for another hour, but on-campus curfew is approaching, and I don't want to risk being late.

Okay, that's a lie.

I can't risk missing out on Heston's dick.

It's dick that I'm owed—dick that I *earned*. Rationally, I understand that this thing we're doing can't be heading anywhere good. Irrationally, I just don't fucking care. No matter how hard I try to put Heston out of my mind, it doesn't last long. He's right there, like some kind of parasite, sucking me dry and leaving nothing but a vibrating mess of want and bad decision-making.

I tell the girls good night and hop into my car, heading back to campus. It's late, and the lot is full, which means I have to park down by the stadium. There's a path that cuts through the elementary school playground, which is perfect since it goes right past Heston's apartment.

I'm walking around the swings when I hear, "Georgia Haynes!" from the top of one of the play structures. I glance up and see a face in the dark. At first, I think it's Gus, but then he hops down, and I realize that it's actually his brother, Jase. The Freshman who was talking shit about me a few days ago. The one Heston intimidated.

"Hey Jase," I mutter, still walking.

Another kid jumps from the structure, landing with a soft thud. I don't recognize him.

"What are you doing out so late?" Jase asks, walking toward me.

I offer him a fake smile. "I had a meeting off campus."

"Is that what seniors call it? A 'meeting'?" He laughs, and I'm not sure what he's talking about, but I think I have an idea. I ignore him, walking faster.

He moves quickly and so does the other guy, who's behind me one moment, then blocking my way the next.

Noting the two hundred dollar water bottle in his hand, I recognize it as a classic move. I can smell the alcohol from here. "Don't let Dewey catch you with those. He's a hardass about alcohol."

He unscrews the top and finishes it off. "There. No problem." He nods at his friend. "That's Ryan."

Ryan looks a little sweaty and has a piggish nose.

I give him a tight smile and say, "Well, you guys have a good night. I need to get going before Buster makes his rounds. You should, too."

Jase's eyes dart to the other kid's. "My brother says Buster is too lazy to walk all the way down here. Sure you don't want to stick around? I've also got some weed." He gives me this look. It's all puppy dog eyes and low-burning horniness. Sad to think about, but that kind of look used to have me on a guy in a split second, back when I was an underclassman.

Not anymore. "Look, Jase, you're a cute kid and all, but I really need to go."

I push past him, and the flirty light that was in his eyes a moment before vanishes, replaced with a flash of sharp spite as he grabs me. "Don't act all innocent. My brother knows a guy who told him you were the one in that video. Jesus, I've jerked off to that thing more times than I can count."

I yank at my arm, but he doesn't let go. Through clenched teeth, I reply, "Bravo. You like watching illegal videos of girls being recorded without their consent. Getting off to that isn't the humble brag you seem to think it is."

He laughs. "You liked it. I saw your face. I want to see that same look when I come inside of you." He jerks his head toward Ryan. "You ready?"

"Ready?" I ask, swinging my head in Ryan's direction. He has his phone out, and I suddenly realize he's either recording or preparing to. "Oh, hell no! Get off me!"

Jase squeezes my arm, wrenching me toward him. "Come on, girl. I've got a cool five hundred riding on the fact that I'll be the first guy in our class to bang you."

I freeze, looking at him wide-eyed. "What?! There's a bet to see who can fuck me first?"

Wow.

Just. Fucking. *Wow.*

Nausea rolls over me and my heart pounds so hard, I think it may rip through my chest. I've done a lot of things I've regretted, but they've been *my* mistakes. I know what everyone says about me, but this? I'm a game now?

He takes my moment of shock to pull me closer, trapping me against his chest. "Ryan and I can split the win if you're into anal."

"Oh, gross!" I plant a hand in the middle of his chest and push, but he's stronger than he looks—stronger than *me*. "Jase, so help me god, if you don't let me go—"

He grunts when my fist catches his chin, grabbing my wrist in a bruising grip. "Would you calm down? We get it, you like it rough." He gives me a sleazy, booze-scented grin. "I'll give it to you good, baby."

I try to yank away, but he grips me tighter, fighting against it. "I'll tell Collins about this, asshole! You know as well as I do that he's zero tolerance on harassment."

"You think they'll believe you?" He wedges a hand between us and I hear the rake of his zipper lowering. "You think Collins will believe the school whore, or the fine, upstanding young man with the perfect GPA? He even let Wilcox back in the henhouse."

Ryan laughs while Jase shoves me toward the play structure, tearing the sleeve of my shirt in the process. I panic, lashing out as my heart hammers wildly. Frantic adrenaline courses through my veins, so I don't even feel the pain of how tightly he's pressing me against the wood and metal. I just feel what I'd felt earlier in the pool—the urge to fight. The instinct to get out of this.

What Jase doesn't know is that, at the treatment program, I had to take classes, and one of them was self-defense.

And I aced it.

Spinning quickly, I try to kick his feet out from under him. It doesn't exactly work, but while he's off balance, I bring my knee up in a quick, sharp jerk, driving it right into his balls.

The feeling of my kneecap jabbing into soft flesh would have made me cringe at any other time. Instead, I hear the shocked wheeze from Jase, who falls to the ground like a sack of bricks, and just run.

I bolt across campus, chest tight as I dart through the lacrosse field, back behind the bleachers, following the tree line. Once I'm away from the playground and on the backside of campus, I glance back to see if they're following.

Which is exactly when I slam into something, hard.

"Oof!" I fall back, landing on my ass.

"What the fuck?!"

I look up at the person I just crashed into. Heston is frowning down at the brown bag of food smashed against his stomach and then at me. The shopping bags he'd been holding are scattered around his feet. A box of new shoes. New shirts. A Bluetooth phone speaker.

A seed of a notion takes root in my brain, connecting the dots. Heston is a gambling addict, and Jase is making bets. I shoot to my feet, rage rippling through me as I slam both of my hands into his chest. He doesn't budge.

"You son of a bitch! Just when I think you can't get any worse, you pull something like this?!" I give him another ineffectual shove. "What is wrong with you?"

He watches at first with parted lips, blinking in confusion, before his expression hardens. "Yeah, I'm going to need a little more than that to narrow down whatever it is you're being such a bitch about."

"Don't pretend like you don't know." I glance back over my shoulder, but Jase and Ryan aren't there. That doesn't mean they aren't watching or waiting for me to be alone again. "You set up a bet on me, didn't you?"

He stares back at me, voice even when he replies, "I have no clue what you're talking about, Haynes."

"Sure you don't." He gives me a blank look. "The bet? To see who in the freshman class can fuck me first?"

His eyebrows shoot up his forehead. "Excuse me?"

"Yeah, I know all about it." I push up on my toes, like that makes me more intimidating. "God, you're the fucking worst."

"I'm a lot of things, but I didn't set up any bets with the Freshmen." His jaw tightens as he bends down to gather up his dropped shopping bags. "How would that make any sense? Didn't I tell you I'd only do this if you *weren't* fucking other people?" He tucks the shoebox under an arm, fixing me with a glower. "Use your head, woman."

A twig snaps in the distance, and I flinch, whipping around to look over my shoulder. When I turn back, Heston's staring at my torn sleeve, gaze moving over my shoulder for a long moment.

"I think you should come inside."

"I-Inside?" He strides past me and unlocks the door to what I'm now realizing must be his apartment. Nodding, I shove my trembling hands into my pockets and follow him up the stoop, heart only just slowing to something resembling a normal rhythm.

I dart inside once he has the door open, only feeling better once he's shut it behind us. I watch as he drops the bag of food on the coffee table and turns on a lamp. The room brightens, revealing a very basic set up; old, floral-printed sofa, sturdy-looking end tables, a hoodie tossed over a chair. I've actually been in Heston's room before, and it's obvious he hasn't bothered to make his mark on this one. In fact, aside from the hoodie, it doesn't even seem like he unpacked at all.

He shrugs out of his jacket and dumps the contents of the brown bag on the table. A stack of foil-wrapped tacos lands in a pile. "So, who were you running from out there?"

Swallowing, I tuck my limbs in close, oddly anxious about being here. "Just some stupid Freshman on the playground."

"The ones that told you about this bet." I nod and his eyes dart to the tear on my sleeve. "Things get rough on the slide?"

I bite back the explanation that's on the tip of my tongue. I'm not telling him what happened to me out there. Not when he's the cause of it. "It's nothing."

He raises a skeptical eyebrow. "Nothing? You were scared, Little Red." He shoves a taco my way. When I reach for it, it's obvious my hands are shaking. His eyes zero in on it. "Strangely enough, you still are."

"It comes with the reputation," I say, teeth grinding. "Guys think just because I like sex, it means they're entitled to it."

He tilts his head and takes a big, aggressive bite, chewing. Once he's swallowed, he asks, "Why would they think that?"

Throwing my hands in the air, I burst, "Gee, I don't know! Something about a video going around of you getting brutally fucked makes the guys around here think you're ready and willing for that kind of thing!"

His eyes catch something, mouth going suddenly still. It takes me until he darts out, grabbing my hand, to realize he's seeing my swollen wrist. His eyes go dark as he inspects it, turning it over to see the purpling skin against my bone. "Who did this?" he asks, voice low and dangerous.

I snatch my wrist away, scoffing at the flash of fury I'd just seen in his eyes. "Oh, this is rich. What's the problem, Heston? No one can hurt me but *you*?"

He doesn't let me get far, reaching out to take my hand back. "You like it when I hurt you. This?" Jaw clenched, he holds my hand up, showing me my wrist. "This is someone hurting you because you *didn't* want it. Maybe you're right—maybe I'm a psycho. But I'm not that kind of psycho." His eyes blaze into mine, full of something ominous. "Don't you ever fucking forget that."

It'd be stupid to call it possessiveness.

But that's what it feels like.

More gently than before, I pry my hand away. "Consider yourself understood."

Heston is no saint, but he's right. Out of all the heinous, unforgivable things he's done, none of them have ever been *that*.

Heston backs off a bit, even if he still looks angry. At Jase? At me? Who even knows? "You going to Dewey, or Collins, or what?"

"None of the above." My voice is quieter than I'd like. I don't want this man to think I'm weak. That he's broken me in some way. "I can take care of myself. That kid will have to ice his balls for a week."

He stares at me, realizing, "You're not going to turn him in." When I shake my head, he grins at me. It's not a kind grin. It's full of dark, incredulous hostility. "Wow, you are un-fucking-believable, you know that?"

"What?"

He tosses his burrito aside, not breaking my gaze. "You turn me in, but not this asshole? Seriously?"

Hotly, I insist, "It's completely different!"

"Yeah, it really fucking is!" he snaps, making me flinch. "Because you actually wanted to have sex with me, and here I am," he extends his arms, gesturing to the squat little living room, "living a like a goddamn felon while this kid gets to run around unchecked. Tell me what the *fuck* is fair about that?"

"You know what?" The adrenaline returns to me like a punch, making my voice shake. "I'm sick and tired of you all acting all innocent. It wasn't about the sex, Heston! How many times do I have to say it before it penetrates your thick skull?"

Red-faced, he explodes, "So I recorded it! Big fucking deal!"

"That's exactly what it was!" I advance on him, jabbing a finger into his chest. "You showed the whole fucking world a private part of me. A vulnerable part of me. A part of me I didn't even have a chance to understand yet! Can't you get that?" Quieter, I make the most shameful confession of all. "Sometimes, I think it would've been better if you *had* just ra—"

He grips my chin, cutting off my words with a sharp growl. "Don't you finish that fucking sentence."

My throat clicks with a loud, hollow gulp. "You don't know what it's like. Everyone seeing me like that—knowing that I liked it, *wanted* it?"

"You think it's easier to be a victim than a kinky slut?" If his sneer doesn't tell me exactly what he thinks about that, his words do. "That's fucking disgusting."

"I know it's not real," I say, trying to calm the rush of bitterness coursing through my veins as I put my hand on his arm. "I *know* that. But I also know what it's like to watch myself doing something that I can't comprehend."

"You want to comprehend it? You want to understand it?" He drops his hand, head shaking. "Maybe stop lying to yourself for five goddamn seconds. I know why you really turned me in. It was for *him*." His lip curls as he looks me up and down. "Everyone always does it for him. Precious little innocent Sebastian, with his adorable anger management issues. The kind of guy who'd hit someone because *he* liked it and damn the consequences."

Shrugging, I pick at the foil on the burrito. "That was a part of it," I admit, nodding. "You can't buy and sell and gamble on other people's lives. If you want to risk your own life—go for it—but betting on Bass', while he was hurt? That's not okay, but that was just the final straw. I did it because I was exhausted. That video has followed me around since the day you spread it. I wanted it to follow you around, too. I wanted you to know what it's like to feel this way."

He snorts. "Feel what way? So ashamed of liking it a little rough that I've lost all fucking perspective?"

"No." I raise my gaze to his, giving a heavy, tired shrug. "Like a joke."

"Yeah, well." He closes his eyes, rubbing his fingertips into them. "Mission accomplished. Because that's exactly what I am now."

"I don't regret it," I say, having no problem looking him in the eye when I do. "But I am sorry."

His face screws up. "How does that make any sense?"

It makes perfect sense to me. "It had to be done, Heston. I'm not saying you don't deserve it. But this feeling? I wouldn't wish it on anyone. Not even my worst enemy. Not even *you*."

"Not even the guy did that to you?" He gestures to my wrist, my sleeve, eyes brash.

Taking in a slow breath, I choose my words carefully. "It's been six months since I turned you in. What's it going to look like if I turn someone else in? Me, the school slut." Shaking my head, I explain, "You're a guy, so you wouldn't get it, but girls—especially girls with reputations—have to pick the battles we can win. Each accusation we make is a reflection on our credibility. It's fucked up and unfair, but that's the way it is. If I went to Dewey every time a guy touched me the wrong way, they'd stop caring. What you did? I had proof of that."

"I know all about needing proof." He pins me with those blue eyes. "You're a girl, so *you* don't get it, but if you bring a cute, sweet

Freshman to your room and fuck her hard enough to leave bruises, you better have some fucking evidence that she wanted it. I don't regret recording it. That was me being smart. If you're expecting an apology for that, then you'll be waiting a long time."

I don't know why I ever expected any different.

Before I make it even halfway to the door, he reaches out to stop me, hand curling around my waist. "Let me say my piece," he says, voice hard enough that it sends a shiver scattering up my spine. Despite the hardness in his voice, his eyes are full of something resigned and chaotic. "I shouldn't have shared it like that, though. Mostly because it was fucking stupid, but also…" He reaches up to tuck a lock of hair behind my ear, eyes tracking the motion as it lingers on my neck. "I didn't want to fuck with you like that, Little Red. Honestly, I wasn't thinking about you at all. For that—*just* that —I am sorry."

His eyes are too much, too intense, making it hard to think. To breathe. To stay standing. But when I look away, he grazes a knuckle beneath my chin, chasing my gaze.

"Look at me," he demands, waiting until I've met his stare to repeat, "I'm sorry, okay?"

I feel trapped in his eyes, frozen beneath the ice. Weakly, I ask, "You really didn't start that bet?"

His gaze drops to my mouth when he answers. "To be clear, the thought of someone touching you like I do makes me want to break fingers."

It feels like all the air gets sucked from my lungs when he dips down to kiss me, hand moving up to cradle my jaw, holding me close as he licks the seam of my lips. My mouth parts instantly, meeting his tongue with a hitched breath. It's not like the hard, biting kisses I'm used to from him. This one is testing, a question present in the way he dips and retreats, waiting for me to surge back before going deeper, harder.

He's asking if I want it.

My answer is the same as always.

I grab his shoulders, bunching the fabric of his shirt up his back until he breaks away to let me tear it over his head. He's back just as quick, a low, rough sound emerging from his chest when he shoves a hand up my shirt, grabbing my breast.

"What are we doing?" I ask, breathless as he walks me backward through the small room, into the hall, and then something I vaguely recognize as a bedroom.

"I have no fucking idea," he answers, pulling my shirt off. "But I'm pretty sure it ends in fantastic sex, so I'm going with it." He unhooks my bra mid-kiss—a skilled, practiced motion—and breaks away to watch as he palms my breasts in his big, warm hands. He groans, "Jesus, these fucking things kill me."

I arch into him when he bends down to mouth at one, squeezed tight in his hand, tongue flat against my peaked nipple. I know I've probably been hornier at some point in my *very horny* life, but currently, I'm hard pressed to think of one. His muscles shift as he pushes me back, guiding me toward the bed. It's unnecessary. As soon as the backs of my legs hit the mattress, I'm going down, already fumbling for the button on my pants.

Heston is two steps ahead of me, tearing the zipper down and yanking them off my legs. He looks fucking magnificent like this, laser-focused and hardened, a curt efficiency that could be mistaken for anger on anyone else. This isn't anger, though. The way he rips my panties down my legs and shoves his jeans down his hips is pure impatience.

But the way he kisses me after, dipping a hand between my legs to feel my wetness and want, is the act of someone who also wants to savor it.

God, do I know the feeling.

"How do you want it?" he asks, sinking two fingers into me.

I cry out, writhing against his hand. "Like this," I gasp, scrabbling at his arms for purchase. "Just like this." For a moment, I'm worried he thinks I'm asking for it face-to-face—something I know he won't do.

But the way he kisses me is perceptive, deep and unyielding, and I think he understands exactly what I want.

No pain.

Not tonight.

I go easy when he flips me over, rising onto my knees for him, eager and so full of the vibrations that it's a miracle my bones aren't rattling with how badly I need him inside of me.

I feel his hands on my hips, and I know what he's looking for. The bruises. But they're almost entirely faded now, just a shadow of a memory against my skin. Luckily, he doesn't make me wait, grabbing his dick and rubbing it against my folds, seeking, and then driving himself inside.

"Oh god, oh fuck." I push back into him, reveling in every slow, thick inch of his cock entering me. Most people would say the orgasm is the best part of sex, but this is mine; the long moment of being finally, gloriously filled, slotted together with someone warm who wants me.

I watch as his hands curl into fists on the mattress, bracketing my head. He grunts as he seats himself, mouthing at my shoulder. "Fuck, how are you this fucking *tight*?" It's an idle question, almost like he hadn't meant to say it out loud at all.

I tremble under the sensation of having him inside, so drunk on it that I don't even think to be offended at the implications of that tone—as if I should be loose or something. I'm also so drunk on it that I answer. "You're the only person I've fucked in months."

His lips still against my skin, a wash of warm breath tickling the spot. "No shit?"

I appreciate the rhetorical way it's phrased. For one, because I have no reason to lie. Why would I bother? To save my reputation? To stroke Heston Wilcox's ego? Any motivation seems pointless. For two, he doesn't even sound skeptical. He just sounds surprised, and a little intrigued. For three, even if I wanted to elaborate, I couldn't. He chooses that moment to drag away, surging instantly back into me.

God, it's so good. It's always so, *so* good. Each time he retreats, only to punch forward and fill me again, my breath gets a little shallower.

He shifts his weight to one arm so the other can sweep up my side, palming my breast as he fucks me. "It's that rubber band, you know," he rumbles, gently trapping my earlobe between his teeth.

I rock back into him, trying to stifle my cries. Who knows how thin these walls are. "What?"

"You wore it for a long time, didn't you?" He pinches my nipple, sending sparks exploding through my belly. "I remember it from that night. The rubber band around your wrist? It stood out like a sore thumb. It wasn't colorful like the one you wear now. It was just that regular boring beige kind. You weren't snapping it, though— not then."

"I have no fucking idea what you're talking about," I gasp, too lost in the motion of our bodies rocking together, the sweet drag of his cock inside of me, to make sense of it.

His palm runs around my shoulder, moving up to tangle in my hair, making a tight fist at the crown of my head. He doesn't pull it —doesn't even tug—just rests it there against me, like he wants me to know he could. "You'd snap it, wouldn't you? When you got like this, so horny and wet that you couldn't think of anything else? Probably thought you were forming some kind of negative association between the two. Then, as time went on, it'd get a little less effective. You'd have to hurt yourself in other ways. That pen you carry with you—you jab it into your thigh when you think no one's looking. Am I right, Little Red? Did you think you were controlling it?"

My brow screws up, half in confusion, half in senseless plea- sure. "What does that—"

He wrenches me against him, dragging us upright, and I settle into the cradle of his lap. For a moment, I forget he's said anything at all, taking another fat inch of his cock as I sink down.

"You were wrong." His thumb sweeps over my nipple, making my spine arch in response. He takes the opportunity to mouth at my neck, eyes watching over my shoulder as his hand palms my breast. "You thought you were connecting arousal with pain, but you were just connecting pain with arousal. Doesn't take a psych major to figure it out."

"What?" I ask, stilling my restless squirming, chest heaving as I turn to look at the sharp edge of his jaw. "What are you saying?"

"You wanted to understand it," he answers, dick twitching impatiently inside of me. He gives my hair a light tug, pulling my head back until our eyes meet. "Maybe your wires got a little crossed, but there's nothing wrong with you. So you like a little bit of pain. Who cares?"

Dazed, I stare into his eyes, trying to parse what he's saying. Could it really be so simple? Instead of forming a negative association between the two, have I formed a *positive* one?

"So I'm only going to ask you one more time." His fingers release my hair, dropping to curl around my neck. "How do you want it, Little Red?"

I bite my lip, thinking that this is enough. This right here, having him inside of me. I know without needing to ask that he'll do it—he'll keep fucking me like this, if that's what I want. Slow and deep, teetering at the edge of something darker and more enticing.

I meet his gaze. "Make it hurt."

He has me back on all fours before I can even blink, kneeing up close against me. His voice is low and rough when he says, "Right here," squeezing two greedy handfuls of my ass cheeks.

"Yeah," I agree, rocking back into him. "Yeah, just...*yes.*"

God, yes.

"Bite the pillow," he orders, massaging my cheeks. The second I bury my face into it, one of his hands disappears. He pulls his hips back, slamming forward just as his palms comes down in a hard, sharp slap on my ass.

My yelp into the pillow fades into a frantic moan. I don't know why I thought I could settle with fucking Heston like a normal person, all soft and boring. No, this is where he shines. The sting of his palm as it meets my tender skin again and again has me panting with lust, so strung out on it that my fingers scrabble at the sheets, twisting into anything they can find.

His slaps get progressively harder, like he's testing, trying to find my limit. "Fuck, look at you," he says, palm soothing the flesh after a particularly satisfying whack. He sucks in a hissed breath before grabbing my hips and fucking me in earnest. I don't need to glance over my shoulder to know he's staring at the marks he's made. If I close my eyes, I can imagine the look on his face—hard and full of wild abandon.

The orgasm I have moments later is almost an afterthought, everything lost; my breath, my equilibrium, my mind. I fall forward, but he holds me up as he continues to pound into me until he jolts to a stop, cock twitching inside of me. He groans, loud and tremulous, and then his body falls over mine, his chest rising and falling.

Our skin sticks against one another and even though he's warm, the feel of him against the swollen flesh on my backside feels cool and soothing. It's not exactly intimate, but there's no doubt that this is the closest we've ever been, our bodies glued together in the afterglow. I wait for him to move, but he doesn't, so I close my eyes and allow myself the peace of the moment.

It doesn't last.

"That was…" he says, searching for words.

"Fucking intense."

"That's one word for it," he says, slowly standing and pulling out.

The loss of him inside of me feels similar to ripping open a wound.

For one moment I felt satiated. Whole. The next, all the pain and loss is back.

He'd called me on using my rubber band, on how I inflict pain to hold back my demons. In a terrible twist of fate, the man who's caused me so much grief is the only one that understands how to make it better.

He can't know that. He can *never* know that. I suck up my emotions and face him, my expression schooled into something calm and disinterested. As far as Heston needs to know, he's no different from any other guy. He's just easy and fulfills a need.

Nothing more.

14

I watch, leaning against the headboard as she searches for her panties and bra, both lost during the frenzy of everything. She's sitting on the edge of the bed, but the second she bends over to check the floor, I can see the red handprint on her ass.

It's late. Past midnight. Way past her curfew.

Worth it.

"You don't have to do that," I say, rolling to my side and propping up on an elbow.

"Do what?" She looks over her shoulder, giving me a peek at the side of her tit. God, her tits are magnificent. I reach across the small bed and drag her back over, palming one in my hand.

"Get dressed," I say in her ear. I press my cock into her rosy-red ass cheek, feeling it twitch back to life, and she doesn't argue as my hand wanders down her belly, dipping between her legs. She's wet. Again. This girl really does want it all the time.

"Yeah," she says, suddenly squirming away, "I do." She spots her bra on the chair and grabs it, pushing her arms through the straps. "Trust me, there's nothing I'd rather do than fuck you all night, but

I have a roommate and classes in the morning, and two best friends that are nosy as hell. This was a huge risk."

Sighing, I flop back down, knowing she's right. Giving into this thing between us is one thing. The reality of our situation is something else entirely. We seem to have come to an unspoken agreement that we both like fucking like this, which is fine by me. Finding a girl who likes getting fucked the exact same way I *want* to fuck, and on a constant basis?

This is the jackpot.

But there's the issue of me being on probation, plus being an instructor—*her* instructor. I know I like to play the odds, but not getting busted here is a fool's bet.

She fights with the clasp and I climb out of the bed, gesturing for her to turn around. She turns, pulling her hair over her shoulder, giving me room to slide the little hooks together.

"Thank you," she mumbles. I run my finger over the Devil's Mark on her neck and she flinches. "Oh, there they are." She darts away, spotting her panties by the bedroom door.

Since it looks like we're not having another go, I grab my own shorts and tug them on. "You still not going to tell me who gave you that mark?"

"What?" She pulls her shirt over her head, the torn sleeve hanging limply. She fingers it, eyes rolling. "No. I can't."

I narrow my eyes, tracking her as she picks around the room. "You mean you won't."

She finds her jeans and steps into them. "Why does it matter?"

"I'm just curious."

"Well, don't be," she insists, avoiding my eyes. "It's nothing."

"See? That's the exact opposite of what a Devil's mark is. It means something. That's the whole point." I know from my tenure here that most Playthings get marked with a hickey. A Devil marking his girl with a tattoo is rare. They're too permanent, too visible, to put on some casual fling. Hickeys are gone so fast, people barely have a chance to gossip about it. "Someone cared about you enough to give you that mark. You belonged to someone. Is it so wrong to wonder who?"

She shoves her feet in her shoes, looking exasperated. "It's wrong for you to badger me about something I've already answered." She stands in front of me, giving me a firm look. "You need to drop it."

"Fine."

It's categorically not fine.

And it's not fine that it's *not fine*. I shouldn't even care. So some Devil was committed to her enough to brand her for life. Who cares? Only it doesn't make sense. Even if the guy graduated already, there'd still be some hints of him. You don't get someone's Devil mark tattooed on you without having some serious fucking attachment. But her phone's lock screen is just her and six other girls—the same girls Micha had told me were sitting at the Devils' table last year. The fuck does that even mean?

I like to think it's just about getting information for Collins, but I've never been good at lying to myself. The reality is that I need to know whose dick she's basically made Devil matrimony to.

From the depths of my brain comes a disturbing whisper: *Maybe it's Sebastian.*

I give her the blandest smile I can muster. "You're right. It's none of my business."

Sighing, she rests her hand on my chest, pushing up on her toes to kiss me. But I shift my head to the side at the last moment, letting her lips clumsily graze my cheek.

Yeah, I'm petty as fuck.

Who's surprised?

She stumbles back, and even worse than this completely unwelcome investment I've been saddled with, is the sudden burn in my stomach when her face falls.

"Well." She gnaws on her lip for a moment. "See you in class, I guess."

"Yeah," I say. "See you." She walks out, and I let her go, both satisfied that I've upset her and weirdly shitty for doing so.

For the first time in days, I go into my medicine cabinet for some of that sweet, chalky disappointment.

If there's one trait that every Wilcox man has, it's stubbornness.

Well, and also apparently stomach ulcers.

But mostly stubbornness. It's made my father millions. It's what drives Sebastian to win every fight and every race. And it's what makes me refuse to back down over this new little stand-off with Georgia.

It lasts for days.

I'd started it that night at my apartment, snubbing her when she tried to kiss me. She raises the stakes when she 'trips' by the faculty lunch table and spills mac' n' cheese all over Gina, the water polo coach. Things are chillier between us than they've been in a while, as though we'd let out all that heat and passion and desire, and now there's nothing but apprehension and animosity.

You know, like every other day.

I don't worry about it. Georgia needs dick almost as badly as she needs air, and we both know mine's the best. I'll outlast her. The sex is good, but I can live without it.

I think.

By the time I get to the club on Thursday night, all I want is a drink and to enjoy myself. Some little shit thought it'd be a fun prank to fill the equipment closet's lock with heavy-duty super glue. I'd spent my entire evening picking it out of the lock with a screwdriver and a bent fork, and it still wouldn't work.

Underworld is packed, which means it's making money, which means I'm one step closer to financial independence. It feels nice to enjoy a little success, even if I'm not the one getting the profits—yet. Big Gene really ass-fucks me by taking half of my gross. After paying the suppliers, the staff, and the other bills, I'm usually only left with enough to pay my car insurance, phone plan, daily necessities, and a few mediocre takeout meals. Not being rich is annoyingly expensive.

At least I finally got some new shoes—even if they are from some cheap, tacky department store.

I eye a couple girls from Saint Mary's, wondering if I should invite them to hang out in the VIP area with me. I decide I'm not feeling it, though.

So does Big Gene. "Not so fast," he says, dropping into the seat in front of me. "You're supposed to be a taken man, Wilcox. Better keep those eyes to yourself."

I stare at him. "Don't you ever have better things to do than be here every night?"

"No," he answers, lacing his fingers behind his dumb, half-balding head. "But you certainly do. Seems like you're barely around anymore. Boyfriend duties?" He's been trying to drag details out of me for days now.

"You'd have to be a boyfriend to have boyfriend duties."

He doesn't look amused. "You haven't locked the girl down yet?"

"How many times do I have to tell you," I say, head throbbing in annoyance. "She's not that type of girl."

He argues, "All girls are that type of girl."

"Not this one."

"Try harder," he stresses, eyes darkening. "I need something on that girl's family. Her father, her mother, her brother, her goddamn dog, I don't fucking care."

Grinding my teeth, I insist, "I'm getting there."

"How?"

"We're fucking," I say, crushing a napkin in my fist. "There's not much room for pillow talk when we're trying to not get caught, but trust me. Shit's happening. Chill the fuck out and let me work."

He leans forward, rapping one knobby knuckle against the table. "I think this little arrangement we have for paying off your debts has given you the misconception that I'm a patient man. I'm not going to give you forever. You just remember that."

I don't move when he leaves, slinking off to parts unknown. Gene and Collins are like two ends of a noose's rope that gets a little tighter by the day.

Tara's just refilled my drink when I see a familiar face come through the door. No, make that *two* faces. I see this for what it is—an opportunity to loosen that noose, just a little.

"Hey, you see those guys?" I point them out to Tara. "Send them up here and bring drinks. The Gene special." I give her a wink, knowing she'll understand just what I mean.

"Sure thing, honey." I nurse my drink and watch from above as she approaches them.

A moment later, Emory and Carlton push back the heavy curtain, a flicker of wariness crossing their faces.

Emory's expression graduates to full-on hostility the second our eyes meet. "What are you doing here?" he asks, sneering.

Fair enough. Our last couple of encounters haven't been the best, although Carlton and I have always circled the same activities. The latter just gives me a hesitant chin jerk.

"Welcome to Underworld," I say, gesturing to the dance floor. "This is my place."

Emory's face shutters. He looks at Carlton and says, "Seriously? You knew about this?"

Carlton shrugs, looking rueful. "Come on, it's business, bro. This place is killing it."

"But Georgia," Emory says to him, voice low. Not so low that I can't hear him add, "And Bass..."

Carl doesn't bother lowering his voice. "I texted Georgia, she's cool. And Bass isn't even in town right now. Chillax." To me, he says, "You mind?" and points at the chair.

After that Bass comment, I'm just annoyed. "I invited you up, didn't I?"

Carl takes a seat, but Emory spends a moment fuming silently at the curtain before he follows suit. As soon as he sits, Tara arrives with the drinks; two pitchers of cold beer and six shots. She'll keep them coming until these two are shit-faced.

"What brings you down here tonight?" I ask, throwing a shot back.

Carlton takes a glass, giving it a sniff before following suit. "I figured I'd come and check out the clientele. See if there's a demand that needs supplying." He takes in the place and I can tell from the twinkle in his eyes that he likes what he sees.

"You want to sell here?" That could be a problem. Too much heat around here wouldn't bode well for my probation.

He grins. "You know me. I'm an entrepreneur."

I give him a long, narrow-eyed look. "What are we talking? I can't let shit get too hot."

He's already nodding. "Right, no, I get it. I'm not only about the hard stuff, you know. I'm expanding into edibles. Here, check it out."

He reaches into his bag and pulls out a cellophane-wrapped cookie, handing it to me. The clear plastic is sealed with a big yellow smiley face sticker.

I raise an eyebrow at him. "You realize I can't eat this. I have to take a piss test every month." Carlton frowns, but when he goes to take it back, I yank it away. "I'll have one of my staff taste it."

Many people see Carlton as some goofy low-level stoner, but that's not the case at all. He's smart enough to play into that, to let people think he's harmless and shiftless and not at all responsible for supplying this town's most illicit substances. Now that I'm out of the game, he probably makes the most money at the fights and races, slinging his product hand over fist.

I let him talk about it for a few minutes, watching Emory in my periphery. It'll be easy to make Carlton talk. He wants something from me, and I want something from him. These things have a way of working themselves out.

But Emory's not so easy. "What about you? Going into business with Carl now?"

He stares at the shot I push toward him, but doesn't pick it up. "Nah, I just had a family thing I came home for. Thought I'd tag along and see the new club my sister's coming to." Emory holds my gaze, the threat clear.

"Only once, that I know of," I say, pouring myself a glass of beer from the pitcher. "Seemed like she had a good time, from what little I saw of her. Believe it or not, I actually have better things to do than fuck with your sister. Not that I'd want to. I got no beef with Vandy."

"That's never stopped you before," he mutters, finally picking up the shot and tossing it back. "How did you end up owning this old dump?" he asks, even though it's clear in his eyes that he knows this is no dump. Not anymore.

I lean back, looking around. "High friends in low places." Giving the booth a pat, I explain, "Won it in a bet, fair and square."

Emory scoffs. "Of course you did."

Realizing this is going to be harder than I thought, I throw back my second shot. As expected, Carlton takes my lead, grabbing his second, and then moments later, Emory too.

Carlton leans back on the leather seat. "It's pretty nice in here, dude. I'm impressed. Word's been on the street about it for weeks now."

"Thanks," I say, tilting back when Tara arrives with more shots. I'm halfway to handing her the plastic-wrapped cookie when I pause. For some fucked up reason, I get this flash of thought that Georgia would really like it. Isn't that what she'd demanded before? Chocolate after sex? It does look good; chocolate chip, chewy, nice and fresh.

I let Tara walk away.

I expect things to be a little strained, but as we tip back drinks, the better history between us starts seeping through. Devil bonds run deep. But there's more than one reason I'm playing nice tonight. There's information I want, and then there's information I need. Finding out who gave Georgia that mark falls somewhere confusingly between the two.

The small talk gets a little bigger. I ask what they're doing these days. It's school for Emory and dealing for Carlton. Somehow he talked his folks out of college.

"Eh, they're too busy getting divorced to worry about what I'm doing, you know?"

I shake my head, still nursing my first beer. I'm not the one who's supposed to be getting sloshed here. "Yeah, I know a thing or two about your parents not giving a shit about you." I swallow my drink, picking up another shot. "I can't even go home—not that it's my home anymore. My dad won't take my calls. He has my email blocked. *Email blocked.* I had to break into the club just to get a face-to-face with him, which ended in security chasing me out. Oh, and then there's the dry cleaner." I pitch forward, holding Carlton's confused stare.

"The dry cleaner?"

"They took away my fucking dry cleaning privileges. I just want you to let the pettiness of that sink in. I'm using a fucking fifties-era coin Laundromat like a goddamn bum." Okay, maybe I'm a *little* sloshed. My stomach is going to pay for this tomorrow. "But he's apparently the reason I'm currently working this Preston probation gig."

"Yeah, Vandy said you were coaching swim." I can tell Emory's getting sloshed too, going off how loose his shoulders have gotten, that arrogant tilt of his smile as he chuckles. "Two steps forward, three steps back?" He's still suspicious and bitter, though. Fucking quarterback metabolism. This asshole's probably going to drink me out of house and home before he gets properly shit-faced.

"Laugh it up," I mutter, pouring him another glass from the pitcher. "It's not so bad. Coach James has always been pretty cool, and it's not like it's hard. No one in this town swims better than me."

"Not since Hamilton left." Emory's voice is slurring on the consonants, which is the only thing that keeps me from biting back.

I slouch into my seat, ignoring the obvious jab. "Preston sucks without you guys around, though. The Devils were fucking legendary. I can't believe Collins shut us down."

"Collins? Please. Everyone knows you were the reason we got shut down. Picking on that kid was fucking dumb." Emory shakes his head. "God, what the hell were you thinking?"

"I was thinking that I wanted to raise some hell because Hamilton was fucking Gwen behind our backs." It was petty and dumb, but it was high school. If you can't be petty and dumb at seventeen, then when can you? "But I like this rewrite of history you've got going on, Em. Like you weren't up there with me, laughing your ass off about it. Like you didn't go into that room with Skylar and—" He bangs his glass down and I pause, fighting down a smirk.

Yeah, I know all the dirt on this self-righteous asshole.

"That was a mistake," he says, voice hard. "And if you know what's good for you, you'll keep your mouth shut about it."

I hold up my hands, palms out. "I'm just saying, we all made mistakes. It was a dick move to pull that on a little kid, I know that now." I shrug. "Honestly, I've gotten to know him a little. He's in one of my swim classes. He's a mouthy little shit and a total pain in my ass, but he's actually pretty cool. You know. For an Adams."

Carl throws his head back, laughing. "Right? Micha is hilarious. He has zero fucks to give. I mean, he took that prank and went fucking viral with it. He became a legend. You can't not love that kid. I'd throw fists for him." Carlton is no football player like Emory. He's already fast approaching three-sheets-to-the-wind status. Despite that, I can hear the warning in his voice, loud and clear.

"I just said I liked him, didn't I?" We drink for a long while, shooting the shit, things growing a little more lax. I watch as Emory's eyes glaze over, reminded that the drunker he gets, the louder he is. We take a stroll down memory lane, reminiscing about some of our less damaging pranks. "Remember that time we stole Collins' car—"

Emory snaps his fingers, bursting, "And parked it in the lobby! Holy shit, I'd almost forgotten about that."

This was before Carlton got drafted in, so I explain, "We had to take the doors off the admin building to get it to fit, then put them back."

"Which," Emory adds, voice way too loud, even over the music, "we didn't have the proper tools for."

"Or skills."

"Or time." Emory busts out laughing. "It took them for-fucking-ever to figure out how we did it. We had to donate all our athletic equipment to some Northridge alternative school as punishment."

"And Hamilton threw a tantrum," I add.

"The biggest fucking tantrum," Emory agrees, wheezing with laughter. "And he was just on swim, so he didn't even have to let go of much. Some fucking goggles and a Speedo? Jesus Christ. He was such a baby."

When the laughter dies down, I pour each of us another shot and innocently ask, "It must have sucked last year without the Devils. Weren't you supposed to be the next leader? All that seniority and you were just another Preston schmuck. Collins really won the war, didn't he?"

"Psssh." Emory waves a hand dismissively. "Not even."

Carlton throws him a look. "Hey, man—"

"Nah, nah, check this out." Emory leans forward, elbows on his knees, head swaying on his neck. Oh yeah, this guy is fucking wasted. "So last fall, I get this message. Some random alumni wanted to get the Devils back together, I guess. I didn't know who these guys were—still don't—but I know they're bigger than Collins. So they fuckin' made it happen."

I fake a surprised laugh. "What, seriously?"

He nods heavily. "The catch was that we had to go super old-school. I'm talking rituals, acquiring collateral on everyone, initiations, the whole shebang."

"That sounds...interesting."

He points his glass at me. "It was fuckin' epic, dude, you don't even know. Made the shit we used to do look like child's play"

"You had to find new members?"

"Oh, yeah," Emory says, elbowing Carlton. "We had to go through so much crazy shit together. You wouldn't believe the kind of stuff they threw at us. But we killed it."

"Made us tight," Carlton adds, seeming just as lubricated. "You know, like family."

Family. It's all I can do not roll my eyes. "Speaking of family, I assume Sebastian was initiated?" I've seen the tattoo on his chest, but I want confirmation.

Emory nods. "'Course. He's a legacy. We all agreed on him first off. I know you two have your differences, but him being your brother was the whole reason we brought him in."

"I see." I do the math. There were twelve chairs. That's a lot of dicks to narrow down. Maybe some of those are for the alumni running the show. I only know of the three who were already there; Emory, Carlton, Ben, and now, Bass. "You added McAllister?"

Emory almost looks offended that I'd need to ask. "Absolutely. He was already in before he left freshman year."

"Right."

"And we let in Tyson Riggins," Em adds.

I frown. The name is familiar. I realize I've seen it on the record wall at the pool. Micha mentioned him, but I figured he was just a hanger-on'er. "The diver. He transferred from Northridge, right?"

"Yep."

That one sits strangely with me. The Devils are about legacy and exclusivity. "So you let in a kid from Northridge? Just some random nobody?"

Carlton gives me a nasty look. "Fuck off, Ty's a good guy. The alumni wanted something different—"

Emory cuts him off. "No, not just different. They wanted us to go back to our roots. The Devils' roots. The way people like Hamilton ran the Devils? That's not how they used to be. Back in the day, things were less about popularity, money, and looks, and more about the quality of the potential Devil."

"Sure, sure." It sounds crazy to me, but if they want to water down their criteria, who am I to give a fuck? I narrow in on the information I want. "What about the Playthings? That didn't change, did it? You still take them up the Stairway? Give them the mark?"

It's not a tough question, but they exchange another long look before Emory says, "Well, that's probably the biggest change."

My eyebrows hike up my forehead. "The Playthings changed?"

"We still *have* Playthings, they're just..." Emory makes a vague gesture, but it's Carlton who interprets it.

"Members," he says.

I put my drink down. "Excuse me?"

Emory elaborates, "Yeah, we have female members. Devils. Equals all around. They get their own marks and everything."

"You're shitting me?"

Emory grins at me, lifting his glass. "Nope. It's kind of hot, too." His smile twists into a grimace. "Well, unless it's your sister."

"Your sister," I say, blinking in realization. "Vandy's a Devil." That thin slip of a girl. I'll be damned.

"Sure. She's a legacy, like Bass."

I blame my considerable buzz for how long it takes for the pieces to click together. All the stuff I found in the bunker. The other six seats. The photos of the tattoos that clearly belonged to girls. The way my brother was so overprotective of Vandy when I'd fucked with her that night at his fight. Why they'd all rallied around Georgia when she and Syd went to the police.

"So, if someone—a girl—has a Devil's mark tattoo, she's probably just...a Devil?"

"Definitely a Devil," Carlton says. "Why? Did you see one?"

Emory groans. "God, don't say Vandy's. Reyn will skin you alive if you got near that tattoo." The look of disgust on Em's face means that he's probably thinking that he'd help him.

"No, not your sister." I run my hand through my hair. "Haynes is in my swim class."

"Oh," Carlton says casually, then his expression darkens as the elephant in the room appears. "*Oh*."

"How's that going?" Emory asks.

I'm fucking her so hard, she'd scream if we didn't always have to be quiet. I send him a bland smile. "It's civil."

He puts his glass down, leaning over the table, and I know he's smashed. There's no way he would have just spilled all that if he weren't. But the way he's looking at me right now is alarmingly sober. "Heston, I know shit hit the fan and I know you blame her for it, but if you hurt her..." He stares at me, nostrils flaring wide. "If you hurt her *again*, I will fucking end you."

In a low, rigid voice, Carlton adds, "We all will. You got that?"

I look between them, finally understanding. Here I was worried about Georgia belonging to a Devil when she actually belongs to eleven.

I shift my shoulders against the fiery sting of my stomach. "Yeah, I got it."

15

Dr Ross' worried eyes hold mine. "It's unlike you to not turn in a paper." She brought me out into the hall to ask why my essay was late. I have no real excuse, other than not feeling like doing it.

"I can get it done by tomorrow," I assure her, feeling my stomach churn with anxiety. I really hadn't expected it to be due so soon. "I just had a bad week and got off my routine a bit."

Yeah. A bad week. There was the epic rush of sleeping with Heston, knowing that I had his dick on tap, and not being able to think about anything else. And then came the immediate tumble when he refused to kiss me because of this tattoo on my neck. And *then* came a very minor pit of depression, which I can't even decide is because of my hurt feelings over the whole thing, or that he can hurt my feelings at all.

No, the actual issue is this thrumming, crazy-making hunger.

It hasn't been this bad in a while. Heston was right about one thing—hurting myself doesn't work anymore. It doesn't temper the need, it just amplifies it. But for some reason, the second I feel my mind wandering, stomach dropping with that telltale tingle of lust,

I can't stop myself from doing it. Part of it is the muscle memory. Habit. Conditioning. But another part—a part that I'm afraid to cop to—is that I *want* to feel it amplified. The higher the climb, the bigger the drop. Even though it's not good for me, I can't stop myself from wanting to chase it.

She frowns at me, not looking very reassured. "Each day you're late, I have to take off ten percent from your total grade."

"I know." I give her a weak smile, feeling tired and wrung out. I'd been up until three in the morning riding my own hand, desperate and frustrated. "I'll have it finished by tomorrow, promise."

"I'll keep an eye out for it." She squeezes my arm. "And if you're struggling, go talk to your counselor. Or me. Or someone else, okay?"

"I will." It's a lie. No one can know why I'm so wound up. First, Heston would get in a boatload of trouble. Second, if people think I'm a slut now, what would they think about me screwing the guy who caused me so much grief? "Thanks, Dr. Ross. Definitely tomorrow."

Clutching my books to my chest, I beat a hasty retreat. All of my teachers are aware of my breakdown in the ninth grade. Because of this, they've granted me the privilege of special accommodations, just in case I'm experiencing anxiety attacks or depressive episodes. If I absolutely have to, I can request to turn in an assignment late or leave the class without asking. I try not to take advantage of it because it only brings more attention to the fact I'm a hot, crazy mess. If anyone saw my thigh right now—if they realized that I've been hurting myself—they'd take it the wrong way. They'd think I was suicidal or having a crisis, and I'm *not*. It's not like that at all. It's just a temporary means to an end.

But right now, I'm clutching onto any lifeline being tossed my way, no matter how guilty and nervous it makes me feel.

I gather up a believable facade and strut down the hall, head held high. The worst thing, of course, is to let these vultures see a weakness. I pass Josie, who's talking to several boys, fitting right in to Preston like she's always been here. I've avoided her as much as possible since I heard her talking to those guys about me outside the dining hall, but it's difficult since we live together. This is exactly what I was worried about when the term started. It's impossible to hide a manic or depressive episode from someone who sees me every single morning and night. Passing her, I see Fiona in her cheer uniform, alone at her locker, probably a little amiss without Sydney here to boss her around, and I sort of relate. I miss the rest of my Devils now more than ever.

As I near the end of the hall, I spot Ozzy leaning against the wall, scrolling down this phone.

He looks up at my approach, sending me a smile. "Hey, Georgia."

"Hi, Oz." I've given him some time. There's no way he hasn't heard the rumors about me yet. But his kindness doesn't seem attached to any obvious motive. He hasn't hit on me, hasn't tried to make a move, doesn't even flirt. If anything, he treats me just like he treats Caroline and Vandy. It's...nice. Kind of like being around one of my Devil brothers. Suddenly, it comes to me. This could solve at least one of my problems. I skid to a stop, doubling back to stand in front of him. "Hey."

He looks up at me, putting his phone away. "Hey. What's up?"

"I, uh, wanted to ask you something."

"Okay."

I tuck my thumb under the strap of my bag, fidgeting with it. "There's this thing...at the country club. A girl thing?" Well, that came out weird. I've never had to really ask a guy out before. Usually, I can flirt until they do the heavy lifting—that is, when they don't just come to me whether I like it or not. "It's this totally stupid Debutante Ball. My mom is making me do it."

He snorts a laugh. "Wait, you were serious that day at lunch? They still have those?"

"Unfortunately, yes." I shift to my other hip. "So the thing is, I need an escort, and I was sort of thinking if you didn't have anything better to do—and you probably do—that you might want to go with me? And while I can't promise it won't be super lame, I can definitely vouch for the after-party. Tons of good food. Probably booze, too. Someone always sneaks it in."

Ah, yes.

Food and booze.

I know the way to an eighteen-year-old man's heart.

He opens his mouth to reply and I blurt, "It's okay if you say no. It's a huge hassle and you'd have to wear a full tux, so no pressure, and it'd totally just be as friends—"

"Georgia," he says, interrupting. "It's cool, it sounds…" He pulls a face. "Well, not exactly *fun*, but tolerable. I don't mind taking you."

I don't mind. Be still my beating heart. Just what every girl wants to hear.

Regardless, I do feel relieved. "Yeah?"

"Sure."

Grinning, I say, "Awesome. Great. I'll get you all the details, okay?"

I walk away feeling a million times better. Energized. Maybe even a little motivated to get that paper written. See? I just needed to get out of my funk. Stop thinking about Heston and his petty bullshit. Even though I'm holding that pen in my hand, I don't even feel the urge to push the sharp point of it into my thigh.

Buoyed, I turn the corner, heading toward the staircase, which is when I feel a hand grip my arm, yanking me out of the hall and into a storage closet. The move is so quick, so fast, that my first worry is that Jase caught up to me. Panicking, I struggle against the grip, but I'm spun around, my lips suddenly captured by an insistent, unyielding kiss.

I continue to fight, but his hands hold me steadily in place. I figure out pretty quickly that it's not Jase. Too tall. Too strong. And as my fingertips skitter upward, I admit there's only one gene pool that produces a jaw this sharp.

With both hands, I shove him off.

"Jesus, what the fuck, Heston!" I exhale and then get a better look at him. His eyes are red and puffy, and his hair an absolute mess. He's lucky I didn't just slam this pen into his eye. "You look like shit."

"Thanks," he drawls, looking unamused. "It's just the agonizing pain I'm currently feeling. And you look..." his cold blue eyes sweep over me, "pretty hot, actually. That's annoying."

"Is there a reason you're mouth-raping me suddenly?" We've been avoiding each other for days now, locked in a standoff over the tattoo, but he's been downright chilly for all of it. "What's your fucking deal?"

He answers by ducking his head and pressing his mouth to my neck, fingers ghosting over my hip. "I drank too much last night. Now I sort of want to die, but I figured I'd do this first."

I swallow at the feel of his lips parting, his hot, wet tongue licking into the spot of skin below my ear. "So you're drunk?" I ask, voice weaker than it has any right to be.

"More like hungover." He hums when I tilt my head, giving him more access. He uses it to gently suck at the tendon below my jaw. "Ran into your boys at the club. Emory and Carlton."

"My what?" I'd like to say it's a convincing show of coyness, but the truth is that his fingers find their way to my lower back, sliding down over the curve of my ass, and my brain stops functioning. I only have access to a scant amount of brain cells, and I use them to remember the pen, stabbing it into my thigh.

Focus!

"Your boys." In a lower voice—almost a purr—he breathes into my ear, "Your Devils." He gathers the back of my skirt up, hand ducking beneath to grip an ass cheek in his palm. He makes a gruff sound into my throat, asking, "Why didn't you just tell me the mark wasn't from a guy?"

I try to blink through the sudden haze of *sex wet ripe want need*, but it's getting difficult. "Because it wasn't any of your goddamn business." My breath hitches when his fingers yank my panties aside, the increasingly warm air of the closet hitting the bare skin of my ass. I can tell from the way his fingers brush the skin that he's searching, but I take a longer moment to realize what he's searching for.

He's wondering if his handprints are still bruised into the flesh.

They're not—the marks faded a couple days ago—but I still make a sound. My gasp is small and pained and completely fucking fake.

It has the desired effect. He bucks into me, hardness pushing obscenely into my hip, fingers tangling into the hair at the base of my neck. "God, you're a mouthy bitch." He punctuates this with a hard, aggressive kiss, tongue digging forcibly between my parted lips.

I'm hit with a sharp burst of resentment. It's not fair, how easy I am. The way I want so badly to open to him, to let him in, to give him a part of me. He doesn't deserve it, not after rejecting me for days.

He grunts into the kiss, knocking me back against the wall, hand dropping to meet his other, still gripping a tight handful of my ass. But he bumps into my wrist before he gets there—the one jamming the pen into the soft flesh of my thigh. I hadn't realized it before, too distracted by how electrified my nerves feel when he kisses me like this, but suddenly the pain hits me. The sting is too distinct, far beyond the dull background ache I'm used to.

Something trickles down my leg.

Blood.

He goes eerily still, breaking away from the kiss. It all happens so fast, the flick of his eyes to my hand, the way he grabs my wrist, yanking it away, prying the pen from my white-knuckled grip. His face is so still and blank that it could have been carved from marble, except for the heat of his eyes when he pins me under his glare. He shows me the pen before he chucks it aside. I watch it bounce off the wall, but his hand captures my chin, fingers digging into my jaw as he wrenches my face up. "Look at me!" His voice grinds harshly through clenched teeth as he hems me in, "This shit stops now."

I shove him back. "Fuck you! You don't get to ignore me for days and just—"

He comes right back, towering over me. "You could have come to me any time, but you—"

"I'm not your fucking doormat, you arrogant—"

"You want someone to hurt you?" He catches my wrist before my fist meets his chest, eyes boiling. "That's for *me* to do. Not some stupid Freshman fuck, and not you. *Me.*"

"I'm not your punching bag, either," I snipe back, even though his words have my thighs pressing together, desperate for any sort of friction.

"This isn't about me wanting a punching bag," he snaps, eyes flashing. "I know how you like it, how to hide it, and when to stop. This?" He yanks my skirt up, revealing the wound I'd just made. "This is some crazy, unhinged bullshit. You obviously can't hold yourself back when you're like this. I can."

I tear my skirt out of his grip, covering my thigh. "Why do you even care?"

He holds my gaze for a suspended moment, the muscle in the back of his jaw ticking. Instead of answering, he says, "If I find you doing this shit again, that's it. I'm done fucking you."

My mouth parts, half in shock, but half in alarm, too. He's a jerk, and maybe I am ashamed of this thing we're doing—maybe it eats me up inside a little—but for all that conflict, he's right. Heston knows this fucked up, twisted thing controlling me. He understands it. He knows how to navigate it, how to bat it down to something manageable. No one else could ever get it. I'd never let them.

I look at him, knowing my lip is trembling with the tears welling up, unbidden. "I just wanted it to stop."

His forehead creases, but the moment of confusion is brief, wiped away almost instantly. "Jesus Christ," he mutters, eyes going to the door before landing back on mine. "I told you it doesn't work that way." His voice is tight with barely veiled frustration, but his lips are already back on mine, and this isn't like the kiss before. This one is slow, guided by the palm he cups my cheek with. He doesn't close his eyes, holding me there, watching me as his lips work against mine.

I hate the knowledge that I'd beg for it.

He doesn't make me. "It'll have to be quick," he says, reaching for the button on his pants. "And quiet."

I turn around so fast my head spins, reaching beneath my skirt to shove my panties over my hips. His hands are faster, though, fingers hooking in the waistband and dragging them down to my knees.

"Stop," he says when I squirm impatiently back into him, so full of some unholy mixture of need and anticipation that I'm shaking. He grabs my hip, stilling me. "Calm down. I've got you."

It's a miracle I don't scream when he slides inside me.

I sob at the way he enters me, slow and drawn out, hands holding my hips in place so I can't shove back into the hard, thick length of him. There's a puff of breath against my neck and then he shushes me, the sound far too gentle and soothing for the way he's holding me, fingertips bruising.

"You like that, huh?" He pulls his hips back, letting his dick slip out, and I bite back a perturbed whine. He shushes me again, lining himself back up and sliding inside once more. The sound he makes is gruff, almost as agonized as I feel. His fingers pull my hair away from my neck, making room for his hot, dirty mouth. "You want to be pissed at me? Fine. But when you need this—" He wraps my hair around his fist, tugging in opposition to the thrust of his hips. "—you come to me. Swallow your fucking pride and get some dick. You understand me?"

I nod, but I can barely focus on anything but the sweet drag of his cock and the way he feels, all curled around me like I'm some curiously precious project. "Fine, yes. *Okay.*"

He rewards me with a sharp punch of his hips, burying a soft, guttural sound into the increasingly damp skin of my neck. It feels like we're fucking right beside a boiler, a bead of sweat making an itchy track down the small of my back.

I can tell by the way he's breathing—these short little grunts of breath—that he's lost in the motion of our bodies. I take the opportunity to make some demands of mine. "Our agreement was that I'm entitled to kissing," I growl, shoving my hips back into him. "Never fucking do that again. Do you understand *me*?"

His response is to grab my chin and wrench it to the side, mouth clumsily meeting mine in something that's far too full of tongues and not nearly coordinated enough to be called a kiss. It doesn't matter. I reach back to lace my fingers into his messy hair, tugging him closer. It's sloppy and dirty, and I can't get him close enough, frustrated at the barriers between us, annoyed that I can't wrap my legs around him and kiss him properly, infuriated at this half-experience.

Nevertheless, it's enough.

My orgasm is bittersweet. If it were up to me, I'd have drawn this out, felt him inside of me for hours, gotten absolutely fucking stupid on the way his hand feels, shoving up my shirt, trying desperately to get a handful of my breast but unable to get anything more than the sweat-dampened fabric of my bra.

He comes with a short, bitten off rumble against the back of my neck—right over my tattoo.

Breathless and slick with sweat, I remember what all of this was about. "So that's why you wouldn't kiss me? Because you thought some other Devil had a claim to me?"

He's breathing hard against my neck, his spent dick still nestled inside of me. I can practically hear him rolling his eyes. "I don't share with other Devils," he says, bracing a hand on my hip as he slips free. "I hear the rules have changed, but I doubt that's ever going to be one of them."

"And now?" I ask, turning to watch him pilfer a roll of wrapped toilet paper from a shelf.

He rips it open, little bits of his hair plastered to his forehead with sweat. "I'm not sure about the Playthings being equals. That's weird as fuck and doesn't actually make much sense. But so long as I'm the only one you're fucking, I can deal with it."

My first instinct is to tell him to fuck off. Playthings being equal is weird? Doesn't make much sense? I should tell him to get his sexist, chauvinistic, self-entitled ass away from me. But when he breaks off a thick fistful of toilet paper, he doesn't use it to wipe the sweat from his eyes or the come from his dick.

He crouches down and cleans the blood from my leg. Softly, he says, "Stay still," and carefully dabs at the wound, forehead creased as he carefully assesses it. It's probably just to cover his ass—to make sure I can't blame it on him.

I couldn't move if I tried.

It's silent after that as we right ourselves, cleaning up and catching our breath. It was quick and quiet, just like he demanded, and it might not have been exactly what I wanted, but it was enough to quiet this thundercloud whipping me up on the inside.

Before we leave, I hear a loud crinkle, turning to watch Heston pull something from his pocket. He meets my eyes, raising an eyebrow. "Never let it be said that I'm not accommodating."

He hands me a cookie.

I turn it over in my hands, befuddled and lost. The sticker holding the cellophane closed is a big yellow smiley face. "You're giving me one of Carlton's weed cookies?"

He pauses, eyes pinging from mine to the cookie. "You've had them before?"

"Of course I've had them before." I rip it open, breaking off a piece to cram in my mouth. There's just something about chocolate after sex that wraps it all into a nice little bow. I sigh happily. "It's Vandy's recipe."

His eyebrows shoot up his forehead. "Little innocent Baby V is making *weed cookies*?"

Chewing, I correct, "The cookie, yes. Not so much the weed part. She's a really excellent baker."

"Well." He stares at me, wiping his wrist over the sweat covering his upper lip. "How is it?" And then, "Should you really be eating that right now? You still have class."

"What? You're going to act all 'teachery' all of a sudden?" I make air quotes over the word because it's still impossible for me to acknowledge he's an authority figure at the school. "You just fucked a student in the closet, Mr. Wilcox, and provided her with illegal substances."

"Which is why I don't need you high and blabbing about it later."

"I only have two classes left. These things take forever to kick in."

He hums skeptically, but the bell rings, cutting him off. Feeling lighter than I have in days, I push up on my toes and kiss him sweetly on the mouth.

"Thanks," I say.

"For the cookie?" He licks his lips, presumably tasting the sugary chocolate.

"For the cookie, and the amazing sex, and," I drop my eyes, feeling awkward, "for you know, cleaning up my leg."

"Just don't do it again," he says with a shrug, like it's not a big deal. But we both know it is. All of this is increasingly a big deal. He jerks his chin toward the door. "You go. Get to class."

"Yes, Mr. Wilcox," I tease.

He rolls his eyes. "Go. Before I give you detention."

"Is that a threat or a promise?"

Maybe I can blame it on the weed hitting me sooner than I expected.

He doesn't respond but opens the door while hiding behind it. I walk into the hall feeling a million times better than I had a short while before. I have a date to the ball, I'm sexually satiated, and on my way to a fantastic buzz. Now I'm definitely out of my funk.

"Don't touch anything."

It was a bad idea to bring him here. Heston slowly roams around the bunker under the tower—the Devil's Lair—taking in the group's history. A group he was part of, but didn't respect. Not that way he was meant to.

He points to a photo of one of the tattoos. "Are you going to tell me whose inner thigh this is? Because that's some next level kink."

I turn the photo of Vandy's tattoo over, shooting him a glare as I pass. "No. I'm not telling you anything. I told you, stop touching stuff."

He rolls his eyes and walks over to where I'm standing over the desk, running through the list of possible members we complied. I'm still not sure, which is actually why I brought him. Emory and

Carlton obviously saw fit to spill the beans about the Devils, so I might as well make use of it. There's a particular darkness needed to be a Devil and I know Heston can sniff it out.

He moves behind me, and I start when I feel the tip of his nose against my neck. "Fuck, you smell good."

"Everything smells good compared to the air down here," I reply, but his words act like a spark. I turn to face him, swallowing. "The girls are going to lose their shit when they see you here, so you're going to have to behave. Keep the assholery down, would you?"

There's this lock of hair hanging in his eyes that my fingers twitch to sweep away, the feeling only intensifying when he cages me in, palms planted on the desk beside each of my hips. "You think I can't act civil?"

I watch the corner of his mouth, fascinated at the way it pulls and tucks with his smirk. "Not really."

"If I'm too nice, they'll get suspicious, don't you think?" He tips forward to press his lips to mine, tongue peeking out to run along the seam of my lips. "We're enemies." He kisses down my jaw. "Can't stand each other." A nip at my throat. "Bad, bad blood." A lick at my overheated skin.

He doesn't feel like an enemy right now. He feels warm and good, and exactly like what I need. His hands grip my hips and he moves us toward the couch. I follow easily, letting him lead, because it's been hours since that closet and I'm ready for more—always ready for more, couldn't get enough if I tried. It can be just like then. Quiet. Fast. So hot that I can still feel him inside of me, even—

The hinges creak in the stairwell, and a moment later the big door opens with a loud moan.

I lurch away from him, spine rigid. "Fuck, shit."

Heston just rolls his eyes, slouching back over to the shelves.

"Hey!" I say as soon as the door opens, pretending like my hands aren't trembling. "There's been a *small* development you should be made aware of."

Vandy's frozen in the doorway, wide eyes pinging back and forth between us. "What the fuck," she breathes. And then, much louder, "What the fuck is *he* doing here?!"

Caroline openly gapes at Heston, just as frozen as Vandy. No words come out, but I see the judgment—the open contempt—blazing in her eyes.

"So your brother and Carlton told Heston about the Devils. Which, if you think about it, makes sense because he technically used to be one—"

"Not in good standing," Caroline finally speaks. "He was banned." I've known Caroline for a while now, but I've never seen her truly angry. It's a sight to behold. For someone always regarded as a scrawny little geek girl, she looks like she could throw down.

"Right, right," I agree, glancing back at Heston for a little help. He flops down on the couch and gives me a bored look. "Emory and Carlton—well, and me—we just thought maybe we could use another set of eyes on the new member list, and since he's here and everything..."

Heston looks annoyed at my blathering, finally speaking up. "I can make sure you get the right kind of Devil."

Nodding, I agree. "Yes! A unique perspective."

"Over my dead body," Vandy says, eyes narrowing. She jerks her head toward the door. "Georgia, could we have a word? *Alone?*"

"Sure." I glance back at Heston, stomach fluttering with nerves. "Don't touch *anything.*"

I follow the two of them back out the door and into the cramped hallway. I've barely got the door closed when Vandy says, "What the hell is going on? Why did you bring him here?" She lists off on her fingers, "He's a creep. A pervert. A criminal."

"You just listed half the characteristics of our pledge class, V, including your brother and boyfriend." Emory's confession was getting a blow job from Skylar Adams that terrible night all hell broke loose at a Northridge party. And Reyn...well, everyone knows Reynolds McAllister will steal anything not bolted down, and half the time he'll steal that, too.

Her arms cross. "It's not the same. Heston isn't a Devil. He's *Satan.*"

Caroline adds, "Georgia, he *hurt* you."

I point out, "He's at Preston to work that off. You know, make a change."

"And you believe that?" Caroline asks, eyebrow raised dubiously. "You think he really wants to change?"

No. Not in the slightest. "I think that we're struggling here and could use some help. Heston isn't who I'd pick either, but we don't have a lot of choices of people who are in the inner circle and know the students."

"I don't trust him," Vandy says. Caroline nods in agreement.

"Good." I give them both a firm look. "We're right not to trust him. That's something that's earned, Devil or not. But I do trust your brother, especially when it comes to our secret society, and with you. Those are the two things that mean the most to him. It means something that he let Heston in, and I'm not sure exactly what, but I owe it to him to find out."

Her lips set into a tight line, obviously thrown off by that one. Exhaling slowly, she says, "I agree Em wouldn't do anything to hurt me or the group, but my brother isn't exactly known for his decision-making skills, especially when it comes to his dumb high school idols. He worshiped Heston and Hamilton back in the day."

I know what she means. Emory and the other guys really looked up to Heston and Hamilton Bates. Both of them were atrocious assholes, but they're also a big part of why we're standing here right now, determined to do right by the Devils. "Hamilton changed, didn't he? Maybe we should give Heston a chance."

The look she gives me is incredulous, and all I want to do is cringe myself into some sort of cellular event horizon. Me, defending Heston Wilcox? I might as well hang a sign around my neck that says *'I'm fucking Satan, ask me how!'*

Thankfully, Caroline steps in. "I'm not sure I believe that, but whatever. He's here. He knows. We might as well get something useful out of it by implicating the *ever-loving shit* out of him."

"But if he's an ass, we're kicking him out," Vandy declares.

"I have no problem with that."

We file back in the room and I don't look at Heston, even

though I feel his eyes on me. I feel like I should take a shower. Rallying behind Heston isn't something that's natural or, like, even fucking sane.

I point to a seat in the circle. "Well, if you're going to join us, take a seat." He heaves himself off the couch and walks over, taking a chair on the far side of the circle. I grab my list. "So we have—"

"Hold up," Vandy says. We all look at her. "If he's going to sit in the circle, he needs to hand over some collateral."

"Collateral?" Heston says. "Like money? Property?" He barks a laugh, spreading his arms wide. "I'm wearing everything I own, blondie."

"No," Caroline says, glaring. "As Devils, we deal in secrets. You have to share your biggest sin."

"We all had to do it," Vandy says, giving him a mean smile. "It's the first initiation rite. If you want to be a part of this, that's the price."

"Here's a flaw in this awesome new Devil structure all of you are clearly too simple to see." He leans his head back, looking perfectly at ease as he peers down his nose at us. "I could tell you anything. I could say my biggest, deepest, darkest sin was cheating on a test in sixth grade. How would you know?" He gives a scoff, looking bored again. "I can't believe I thought this sounded interesting last night. I really must have been drunk."

Before V and Caroline can protest, I cut in, "You're right." Shrugging, I look at my girls, explaining, "It was different when we did it. All of us were here. We had to hear everyone's confessions, and after some of the stuff we heard, it was obvious that nothing but the worst would be accepted. Heston won't have that, though." I shift my gaze back to him, lifting my chin. "You're going to have something *far worse.*" I tick off on my fingers, "You shared that video of me. You shared the video of Sydney. You kicked Gwen Adams in the face. You sold drugs to Vandy, who you probably already knew was an addict. You pulled an appallingly transphobic prank on a middle schooler. You bullied your own little brother into fighting for you, tormented him for years, and almost got him killed, all for some money."

"Did I kick puppies?" he asks, faking a pout. "Am I responsible for global warming?"

"You're responsible for a lot of things," I say, crossing my legs. "And that's just what we know about."

Vandy catches on, adding, "So anything you say will have to be worse than all of those, because no one in this room believes for a second that's the worst you've ever done."

He holds my stare, completely unreadable. Just lounged back like he could take a nap doing this. So above it all. So fucking bored with it. "And you think I'd trust the three of you with an admission of guilt for something I haven't been caught doing? Do I look like an idiot?"

"You're free to leave." I gesture to the door. "But we're in the business of keeping secrets, not spreading them."

His eye-roll takes forever, going from the floor to the ceiling, back to his own shoes. It's the most ridiculous thing I've ever seen. "Alright then," he says, giving this little laugh that tells us just how seriously he's taking this. "I told my mom to kill herself."

Caroline scoffs. "Oh, come on."

His gaze flickers between the three of us, eventually landing on mine. There's something in his expression that suggests maybe he's trying to decide between two impossible notions. He must make a choice. "You know how people always say they don't have a favorite kid?" he asks, not breaking my gaze. When I nod, he goes on, "My parents—and I cannot stress this enough—aren't those people. My dad always liked me best. First born, and all that bullshit. He took me to all the special events, introduced me to all the important people, put me in all the best programs. He barely acknowledged Sebastian existed. Until I got arrested, that is." His smile is full of salt and razor blades, meant to cut, to *sting*. "But my mom? She only ever had eyes for Bass. He was her precious, untainted baby. When I got sick, our paid help would take care of me. When Sebastian got sick, my mom would sit by his bed for days, spoon-feeding his spoiled ass like the world was ending. Made me fucking sick."

"So what, you said something mean?" Vandy's lip curls up. "You're going to have to do better than that."

"You don't get it," he says, brow crouched low in a dark expression. "I don't know how much Bass has told you about her, but our mom has a shit-ton of issues. She has this whole major depressive disorder thing." He flicks a hand out in a wave that looks more dismissive than it feels. "Some days she's fine, but other days, she's a complete mess; won't come out of her room, won't eat, won't even talk. One time she went forty-seven days without saying a single word. She lost so much weight, she was hospitalized for a week." He inhales, shoulders shifting against the back of the chair.

This is discomfort. I realize, sort of alarmingly, that this isn't something he talks about—maybe ever. I shift uncomfortably in response, unable to help it.

"My point is, she's really fucking fragile. So yeah, I said something *mean*." He says the word derisively, as if he could spit it at Vandy's feet. "I told her the world would be better off without her in it, and a few hours later, we were all sitting in the emergency room while she had her stomach pumped." Looking at Vandy, his voice is perfectly measured as he adds, "Valium. Twenty-six of them."

I stare at him, unblinking, mapping the stony, unapologetic angles of his face. The silence is thick enough that my baffled, "Why?" comes out sounding choked and too harsh.

"Does it matter?" His gaze swings around to me, and suddenly his face isn't blank at all. It's twisted into a tight, ugly fury. "Is that what this stupid fucking rite of yours is all about? Did you sit around and tell your biggest sins and then rush to justify them as... what? Accidents? Stupid choices you made in the heat of the moment? Fuck that." More strongly, he repeats, "*Fuck that.* I told my mom to kill herself, and I knew there was a chance she would. There's no polishing that up into something shiny. I own my shit." He reaches up to push his hair from his face, jaw locking tight. "Are we done or what?"

I know from the way he's looking at me, all still and dead-eyed, that he's not asking about the Devils. Maybe he's wondering if it's too much to know this and still be touched by him, consumed with him.

Clearing my throat, I give him my answer.

"Not quite."

~

WE'RE BEST LIKE THIS. Caught in a rhythm, the sound of the groan caught in the back of his throat like it's desperate to claw its way out. I like it when he makes those sounds. It means he's close, and that only intensifies when his fingers twist in my hair, pulling at my scalp. Once I get the first salty taste of him on my tongue, his controlled movements grow erratic. What was it he'd called me before? Oh, right. *Unhinged.*

It's a grim look on me, but not on him. I like Heston best when he's losing it. When he lets go; jaw slack, eyes glazed, face red. Panting, rocking, thrusting deeper and deeper and deeper until—

"Holyfuckingshit," he grunts, hips bucking into me. I hold him there, deep against the back of my throat, until he slows, falling back against the bed like a sack of rocks. "Goddamn, Little Red. Fuck *me.*"

Because I'm not done with him, I get off my knees and kiss up his flat abdomen. Part of it is that I want him to know I meant what I said before. The confession he made down in the lair...I won't hold it against him. I have a much easier time holding everything else against him. He offered that confession up because he saw it for what it was. Something abominable. Something unforgivable. Perhaps even something that haunts him. He tried so hard to brush it away that I suspect it couldn't be anything else.

And if Heston can regret—if something can haunt him—then that means he's human.

He's something I can reach out and touch.

And that's exactly what I'm doing.

His chest heaves as I make my way up, kissing, licking, sucking. When I reach his mouth, he tucks my hair behind my ear and says, "I'm going to need a second to recover." His hand clenches around my thigh, running up until he feels the wet heat between my legs. His fingers move, brushing over my clit. I shiver but force myself to shift away.

He notices, raising an eyebrow. "Come on, I know you're not finished." I'm not. He gets that about me—that I'm never really *finished*. That's the reality of being a hypersexual, always ready to go, forever needing a little bit more. "My dick is just a little raw," he says, red cheeks expanding on an exhale.

We've been fucking in his apartment for the last two hours. I'd waited until long after dark to sneak through the trees to this little building on the edge of campus. Considering how distant he'd been during class, I expected him to turn me away. But he opened the door, took a long look at me, and then tugged me inside. He had two fingers buried inside of me before I even got my shoes off.

"I thought maybe we could try something different," I say, laying back on the bed, spreading myself open.

Instantly, his eyes jump to mine. "Anal?"

My knees clamp shut. "What? No!"

He sighs, looking distinctly disappointed. "What kind of different?"

My hand creeps down my bare belly, fingers dipping between my legs. "I want to feel your mouth on me."

He chuffs a laugh, even though he's not smiling. "I'd rather do the anal."

I glare at him. "I'm not letting you fuck me in the ass, Heston."

He shrugs, stretching his arms over his head. "Well, I don't eat pussy."

I'm so distracted by the shift of his toned muscles that I almost miss what he's saying. "Excuse me?"

"Pussy," he says, over-enunciating. "I don't lick it. It's not my thing."

Sitting up, I pull a pillow in front of me, gaping down at him. "Seriously? I just gave you an epic blow job. I've given you *several* blow jobs."

"And they were all fantastic. Good job. Top marks. Gold stars all around." He reaches over to pat me on the knee and I jerk away, standing.

"How is eating pussy not your thing exactly?"

He rakes his hair back, sliding me an exasperated look. "Are you going to turn this into a thing?"

"I just want to know."

"I don't like it," he says, shrugging against the bed. "Shit's gross."

My eyes practically bug out. "Oh, like sucking your dick is a walk in the park?"

His eyes narrow. "I didn't make you suck my dick, you know. You wanted to."

"First of all," I say, bending down to snatch my underwear from the floor, "that's not strictly accurate, seeing as how you basically coerced me into sucking you off that one time—"

"Coerced?" He lifts his head to watch me slide my panties up my hips. "Coerced you by putting my dick in your face and letting you have what you wanted."

"Second of all," I continue, ignoring him, "if you're not going to get me off, I may as well go back to my room and do it myself." I slip on my pants and reach for my shirt, his words screaming in my head all the while. *Shit's gross.* Gross?! My pussy is fucking rainbows and sunshine. "I should've known you'd be too selfish to actually please a woman. That's just one of the many ways you're different from your brother."

He sits up, eyes blazing. "The fuck did you just say?"

"Sebastian," I say, ignoring the chill that runs down my spine at the tone of his voice. "He gives fantastic head. So selfless and giving. Really takes his time to make sure he's making a girl feel good."

"Well, you know what they say," he replies, smile sharp and fake. "You are what you eat."

I snort, not even able to handle his juvenile bullshit. "You know what, Heston? You want to do anal so bad?" I extend my arms to him in a wide flourish. "Go fuck yourself. You're the biggest asshole here, after all."

He brings his palms together in a slow clap. "Real clever, Haynes."

Shaking my head, I cram my feet into my shoes without even bothering to tie them. "You're an actual piece of shit."

"And you're an actual fucking slut," he says, dropping back to the bed. "I'd rather lick the gym's urinal. It's probably seen less dick than that thing between your legs."

It's like a slap, and my body reacts like it, eyes blinking back hot tears. "Fuck you, Heston."

His gaze jerks to mine at whatever's in my voice, but he doesn't stop me as I storm out. The last thing I want him to see are the tears spilling over as I march back to my dorm. It's not like he hasn't said it before, but I thought it was different now. I thought he understood me.

Apparently not.

16

"Wilcox," Collins says, glancing up from the open folder on his desk. "Sit."

I spent a lot of time in the headmaster's office as a student. Many tedious disciplinary talks were had right here, in this very seat I'm about to take. It's weird being here again, settling into the leather, looking across the gaudy, intricately carved desk into the headmaster's disapproving face.

Not once have I felt as apprehensive about it as I do now.

I'm not afraid of Collins, but he holds way more of my future in his hands than I like, which is why I do as I'm told. It doesn't hurt too much, especially when I consider that I fingerbanged Georgia in this room a few weeks ago.

Take that, asshole.

The headmaster sighs and turns to the file cabinet next to the desk. As soon as he opens the drawer, a long row of paper files is visible, little meticulously labeled manila folder tabs peeking out of the stacks. Collins fingers through them and slides in the file he'd been looking at before shutting it with a smooth click, and opening a different drawer. A shiny silver key hangs from the lock, adorned with a dangling tassel—the kind you'd see on the end of a bookmark.

Headmaster Collins' still maintains his files on paper.

Son of a bitch.

The last time I came in here, before I called for Georgia to join me, I'd been trying to get into his computer in an attempt to find some dirt on the Haynes's. Improper donations, bribes, financial forms; I would have taken anything. But I'd obviously been looking in the wrong place. Collins is old-school. Fucker probably can't even remember his own email password. I should've guessed.

"I'm required by the court to turn in consistent reports on your progress. Coach James says you're doing an excellent job; getting along with students, fulfilling the curriculum, completing your tasks." He peers over his glasses. "Dean Dewey has nothing to report. Interestingly enough." The last part is muttered begrudgingly.

"Because there's nothing to report," I reply, propping my temple on my fist, so bored that it's actively painful to play along. "I know it's impossible to believe, but I don't want to be here anymore than you want me here."

I can see that the paper in front of him is from the Department of Corrections, Probation and Parole. He checks off a few boxes and then looks up. "Have you attended an addiction program?"

I hold his stare, unflinching. "I have a lot of problems, but addiction isn't one of them." Although lately, I can't seem to quit Georgia's pussy. I don't think they have recovery programs for men who can't stop fucking the girls who ruined their lives, though.

Collins poises his pen over the paper, shooting me a look. "Gambling counts as an addiction, and the judge made it clear you need to attend a program." He's right. The judge made that clear. I was just kind of hoping no one would remember.

"Whatever," I say, looking away. "I'll take care of it."

He makes another note on the form before hovering his pen over the signature line. Annoyingly, he stops short of signing it. "Have you made any progress on the extra assignment I gave you?"

"You mean your weird paranoia about the Devils still being functioning?"

He glares at me. "It's not paranoia."

He's right about that. The memory card is burning a hole in my pocket. I keep it with me because Collins' paranoia isn't exactly unfounded. If I left it sitting around in that piece of shit apartment, other people on campus would have access to it; Collins, Dewey, maintenance. I don't know what's on it yet, but after being forced to reveal my biggest sin to the group, I have my suspicions.

"We're in the business of keeping secrets, not spreading them."

All I'd have to do is hand it over and I'd get Collins off my back.

I lean forward and rest my elbows on my knees. "Have you ever considered that messing with a historical secret society may not be in your best interest?"

Collins pauses, eye twitching. "Is that a threat?"

I shake my head. "It's just reality. You may think you're chasing after students, but what if you're really just fucking with alumni? Isn't the point of a secret club like this to make powerful connections and lifelong bonds?"

"It's a nuisance," he snaps, setting the pen down. "I assume all this stalling is because you have nothing."

Holding his stare, I lift my hips, pulling a square piece of paper from my pocket. I toss it on the desk. "I found this."

Collins slowly unfolds the paper. On it is a list of names. I didn't take it from the room below the staircase. Well, not exactly. I caught a brief look at the list they've been building, so I plucked out a few of the lesser desirables—among them Gus and Jase Meyers—and decided to serve them up as temporary scapegoats.

Collins frowns at the list. "Where did you get this?"

I lean back in my seat, stretching out. "You asked for dirt, not my sources."

"How do I know this is real?" He studies the names again, mouth curving thoughtfully. Oh, yeah. This should keep him busy for a while.

"That's not my problem." I reach over the desk and point to the signature line on my probation form. "I have a class in fifteen minutes. Are you going to sign that, or what?"

He frowns but scribbles his name at the bottom of the page. It's fast and dismissive, like he just wants to get me out of his face. Fine by me. "I expect further proof before I can sign your final paperwork."

I jerk my chin in a nod, which is the only acquiescence I'm willing to give. I have everything I need to take down the entire club, right in my pocket.

But I won't.

Collins must be a special kind of stupid for not seeing the Devils for what they are: *my* territory. I don't care if they've rebranded. I don't care if they don't want me. I don't care about the new rules, or rituals, or the color of their stupid fucking robes. I've been kicked out of school, my circles, my family, and my own goddamn home.

I see the smug expression on Collins' face as he looks over that list, and I just want to laugh. You'd think after all this time, he'd understand.

A Devil never loses.

I only see Georgia once over the weekend.

I'm just about to head out to the club for a quick interview with a local DJ. Saturdays are always our biggest nights, usually enough to make even Gene back off a bit. It's got me in a better mood than I've seen in a while, and the fact that I'm coming off a solid six uninterrupted hours of sleep probably helps, too.

That must be why when I see her in the parking lot, back resting against the tire of my Escalade, the first thing I feel is a fierce spike of satisfaction.

She's spread a light sweater across the pavement to sit on and she's...*knitting*? These two metal rod things are bobbing around in her hands, up and down, side to side, a long line of yarn disappearing into a tote bag beside her. When her eyes rise at my approach, there's this split second where she looks relieved—shoulders dropping, chest expanding on an exhale.

It's gone just as fast, face shuttered, cheeks bursting with a sudden, vivid pink. Her mouth presses into a tight slant when she stands, tucking her things into her bag. We stare at each other as she loops it over a shoulder, fingers curled around the strap.

Clearly still pissed I wouldn't lick her pussy.

"I need it," she says, voice clipped as she looks away first.

But she's keeping her word.

I keep the smirk from my face, pressing my key fob to unlock the doors. "Get in."

Things are tense inside the car, but I don't really feel it, and I don't actually give a fuck. As soon as I back out, I press a palm to the back of her head and push her down toward the dash.

"Hey!" she says, shooting me a furious glare as she jerks away.

"Someone will see you," I explain, using the hand on the steering wheel to point at the campus up ahead.

She slaps my arm away. "Use your words, asshole! *God.*" Nevertheless, she ducks down low, turning her head just enough to show me the vicious expression on her red face. It only hardens at the sound of my chuckle. "Fuck you."

"Patience," is my wise reply, trundling through the lot and up to the gate. I have to roll down my window and stretch to swipe my staff parking card.

"You're in a good mood." It comes out sounding more like an accusation than anything. "It's annoying."

I don't argue either point, waiting until I'm past the intersection on the east side of campus, to give her head a tap. "All clear."

The fact that my dick's already hard is a bit of an issue. In no universe should I be this worked up at the mere prospect of getting some pussy. It only gets worse when she straightens, huffing as she smooths out her red hair. She's wearing this tight shirt, neckline scooping low enough to show her cleavage. I never understood how guys could find those school uniforms hot. *This* is hot, the pale, delicate tops of her tits peeking out of her top. She's wearing a necklace, and the little golden cross pendant that's hanging from it settles into the ridge of her cleavage, in serious danger of being smothered.

She flings a hand out at the road, sighing. "Seriously? You just ran a stop sign."

My eyes dart away from her tits, teeth clenching.

By the time we reach our destination—a patch of dirt overlooking the lake—my dick is throbbing and far too eager. The last time I was here, the girl in my passenger seat was Reagan. It was really annoying at the time. She flipped the fuck out on me, yelling about how she wasn't that kind of girl, refusing to be pawed at in a car like some cheap slut, demanding to be taken back to my house —my *mansion*—and treated like a 'goddamn lady'.

Georgia slaps a pack of wet wipes on the dashboard, climbs right into the backseat, and starts unbuttoning her pants. "Well?" she asks, spinning her hand. "Get your dick out and let's go. I don't have all day."

The contrast is stark.

Rolling my eyes, I climb out of the car and go around to get into the back, like a civilized individual. She's waiting for me, still looking surly and like maybe she resents having to do this at all. That's fine. When she lifts her hips to push her jeans down, I lean in for a kiss.

She turns her face away.

I pause, scoffing. Apparently it's only a shitty move when I do it. Well, I'm not some oversensitive little bitch. I grab her by the chin and force her mouth to mine, not at all deterred by the way her face screws up in protest. It doesn't last long, anyway. As soon as I reach into the top of her shirt, the fabric digging into my wrist as I wrench it down to get a nice handful of her tit, she stills, melting into the motion of my lips.

She tastes coffee-bitter when my tongue plunges into her mouth, but the sound she makes is sweet when she arches into me, her nipple pebbling against the pad of my thumb. I take my time, kissing down her jaw, licking into the hollow of her collarbone, finally tasting that plump curve of her cleavage. When I rise back to her mouth, she's turning away again. I don't let her, fisting the back of her hair and crashing our mouths together, making her take it. She gets her revenge in the form of teeth sinking into my bottom lip. I take it like a man, licking against her tongue. Fuck, I could do this for hours—fighting her, forcing her to feel it, making her hips buck into thin air, seeking me out, knowing that she's desperate for my dick and too proud to show it.

But she's right.

We don't have all day.

I yank her pants down, movements jerky and uncoordinated until I finally break away, dodging her knee when she kicks them off her ankles. My hand runs up her thigh, eyes narrow as I check for new marks, making sure her word's really being kept, that she isn't hurting herself.

The skin is smooth, and aside from the old mark, seemingly unblemished.

Satisfied, I push on her shoulder, but it's unnecessary. She's already turning, legs spreading, chest heaving as she braces herself against the door.

I don't bother checking if she's wet, grabbing my dick and sliding slowly inside. Her hand curls into a fist against the window, jaw going slack as she takes me inch by inch. She likes this part of it —that much, I know. One of these days, I'm going to tease her with it, sliding into her tight cunt and then taking it away, making her squirm and beg until I do it again.

Today, I decide to fuck her hard and fast.

Her forehead bumps the window with my first thrust, a loud gasp preceding the bang of her fist as she braces herself. "Oh, god," she breathes, bouncing back into me.

"Fuck that," I growl, grabbing a fistful of her hair as I pound into her. "I want to hear you fucking scream."

I can tell when it finally hits her that we're far away from anyone else. Until now, every time we've fucked, we've had to be quiet and careful. Even when we're at my apartment, there's still a cloud of worry. Someone could walk by, and that little glorified garden shed isn't exactly the pinnacle of insulation. Even if it were, I'm always in danger of getting one of Collins' spontaneous visits.

Still, it isn't until I ram my dick hard into her that her little squeaks bite off into sharp, loud cries. It makes my blood rush to my head, hearing the frantic, high-pitched whine being tugged from her throat. I press my mouth to her jugular just to feel the vibrations.

I get this intrusive and totally fucking unwelcome thought that maybe this is what Sebastian heard when he fucked her. Did he fuck her like this, rough and nasty, the way she likes it? Does he know the right way to hold her hips, to press marks into her flesh? Has he looked at them after, watching her all strung out after an orgasm, wearing his bruises? I wonder what it was like when he ate her pussy. When that big dumb head of his disappeared between her legs and brought her off.

Her next cry is a little too surprised, hand coming up to grab my wrist. "OW!" She shoots me a fiery glare, prying my hand off her tit. "The boobs are off limits for bruising, asshole!"

I pant into her shoulder, flexing my fingers like I'm just realizing they're attached to my hand. In a weird way, I kind of am. So I clamp onto her hips instead, squeezing tight, and it's not even about the bruises. It's an admonishment.

This is exactly the kind of fight I don't like having.

After, when I'm taking her back to the campus, it leaves a foul taste in my mouth. I roll the windows down to air out the smell of sex, but instead I'm just assaulted by the scent of her hair, whipping around us like a grumpy tempest. Neither of us says anything, and it's not until I park at the end of the road before the intersection that I even look her way.

I think I want to apologize.

I'd rather shove hot pokers under my fingernails.

She slams the door a little too hard when she steps out, making the whole car flinch, and doesn't look back as she walks away, chin held high.

∾

Since Collins isn't going to let up on the program requirement any time soon, I take Sunday to do a quick Google search on my phone for the closest meeting. There's one at a church eight miles away.

I firmly believe that forcing me into a meeting like this is more about torture than some ridiculous attempt at rehabilitation. I know all about what real 'help' looks like, and it's not something you get in some dank church basement. It's a three-hundred dollar an hour shrink in their penthouse office that overlooks downtown. It's medication—heaps upon heaps of brightly colored pills—red to get you up, blue to get you down, white to even it all out. It's schedules and home visits, hiding sharp objects, finding excuses to look in on someone so they don't feel babysat, even though that's exactly what's going down. It's my mother, being wheeled out of our mansion with her lifeless body strapped down to a gurney. "To keep her safe," they'd said.

Safe from falling off.

What a joke.

The church doesn't even look like a church. It's a sad little building all tucked away with other sad little buildings, and one of them is a Thai restaurant, so basically the instant I step into the place, my stomach rumbles hungrily—painfully.

The capper is when I see someone I recognize at the snack table, a sticker on his breast with his name written on it.

Warren Fucking McAllister.

I'm three steps back into the hallway when I hear my name, followed by, "The hardest part is walking through the door."

My eyes roll so hard that I can see a brain cell offing itself just to escape the coming interaction. I turn. "Wrong place," I tell him, "but good on you for dealing with," I eye him, "whatever it is you're dealing with."

"Sex addiction," he says bluntly. "I came to my first meeting two years ago. Now I run this one."

"Well, I'm not a sex addict," I say, warily watching people filter in. "At least, no more than any other regular guy. So like I said, wrong room."

"Our group encompasses all kinds of addictions. Drugs, food, sex," his eyebrow raises, "gambling?"

"I don't have addictions. I have ambitions." I pull a paper out of my back pocket. "But the judge is making me get this signed before my probation is over. How about, from one Devil to another, you sign this and let me get the fuck out of here?"

Warren looks down at the sheet and then back up at me. "This isn't something you can network your way out of, Heston. I know things have been hard for you lately, and I'm guessing that's not something you're used to. You can turn this around, but it's going to take a lot of hard work and reflection."

"Jesus." I look away to avoid laughing in his face. "Is this how you got Reynolds on the straight and narrow? Cliché platitudes about introspection?"

He's the one who laughs. "Afraid not. Reynolds' judge shipped him off, and I got worse. Destroyed my marriage, almost lost any chance of having a relationship with my own son. I let my compulsions take the lead. When he came home...well, that's when I realized I had to get it together. For him."

I give him an insincere smile. "Lucky for me, I'm not a dad."

"Yeah, you probably are lucky about that." He jerks his head to the circle. "Come on. I promise no one will bite."

It's obvious he's not going to do me a solid and sign the paper. Not much, this whole Devil solidarity lark. Uneasily, I follow him into the room and take a seat among the other attendees. Warren starts the meeting with a small opening and then asks for people to speak. Thankfully, a guy to my right jumps right in.

Once again. Hot pokers. Fingernails.

I only half listen as he talks about his cravings for booze. The stupid decisions. His shitty mother. Warren makes his way around the room, allowing each person to speak, and I couldn't care less, and I mean that literally. There doesn't exist within one human the capability to *not* care about something as much as I don't care about these peoples' problems. I tune halfway in only because it confirms what I already know: I'm nothing like them. I choose to gamble. I enjoy sex. I like to party. None of it controls my life. I was brought down by pettiness and jealousy, and my own rotten fucking luck.

In the recesses of my brain I can hear Georgia saying, "*You did this to yourself.*"

"Heston," Warren prompts, pulling me from my thoughts, "do you want to share?"

I let my head fall back, muttering, "Hot fucking pokers." There's a stain on the ceiling in the shape of a drooping eye. *What the hell.* I've got nothing to hide—not from these losers—and who knows. Maybe if I do the whole kumbaya shtick, Warren will sign my paper and let me fuck off. "I'm Heston. I'm here because the judge ordered it." I make that clear right up front. "I make bets—gamble —on fights, races, debts, women." Shrugging, I add, "I'm good at it."

"What do you feel when you gamble?" Warren asks.

I narrow my eyes. This is that introspection he was talking about. "I feel good when I win and pissed when I lose." I grin, lifting my chin. "Not that I lose very often."

"But what do you feel before the outcome? The 'why' behind your actions?"

I glare at McAllister. Is he fucking kidding me with this shit? He just raises his eyebrows and patiently waits for an answer. Walking out of here now would just make it seem like I *do* have a problem. Sighing, I push my hair out of my eyes and try, "What I'm feeling at the time is boredom. Believe it or not, there is such a thing as having too many options. I had cars, boats, credit cards, connections. My life has been set up for me since I was a kid. My father had it all laid out—zero risks. No matter how much shit I stirred up, he got me out of it because nothing was going to stop me from following his grand plan."

"Until now," Warren counters. "Hasn't he cut you off? Don't you think he's hoping you clean up your own messes for once?"

"Sure, that's my old man. A real paragon of virtue and parenting all of a sudden." I scoff, knee bouncing restlessly. "People are so fucking stupid. You really think any of this is about me? It's not. It's about him having a new golden child."

"Your brother."

"All hail Saint Sebastian, am I right?" A flicker of anger churns in my stomach and my heel taps the floor, a rapid rhythm against the cheap linoleum. "Everyone acts like I'm the bad guy here, but you know what Sebastian used to be? Jack shit. Just some scrawny little sophomore itching for a fight." I jab my finger into my chest. "*I* gave him the opportunity to shine. *I* carried all of our father's expectations on *my* back while he was getting coddled and pampered. I left him my goddamn *legacy*, and what did he do? He came in and took what was mine."

"That's just one of the many ways you're different from your brother. He gives fantastic head. So selfless and giving. Really takes his time to make sure he's making a girl feel good."

I jolt to my feet. "Is that enough introspection for you?"

"I think it's time we wrap up," Warren says, as though I'm a toddler having a tantrum in the middle of a group of adults. I'm halfway to the door when he calls, "Heston, if you want me to sign that form, bring it to me before you leave."

I stand out in the hallway for ten minutes, letting my anger burn itself out in my own head. That's the real way I'm different from my brother. He'd be punching something right now, completely unable to control himself. Me? I gather it all up and tuck it away, and by the time I walk back into the room, I mainly just feel bored again.

Bored and like my stomach is turning itself inside out.

Warren takes the form I hand him and walks over to the table by the entrance to grab a pen. "I know it may not seem like it," he says, "but talking about all that is a sign of progress."

I snort. "Unlikely."

"I know your issues go beyond gambling," he mutters, staring too hard at the paper. "I've heard about the videos."

"Watching underage porn, McAllister? That shit will get you in trouble. Trust me."

He gives me a look. "I haven't watched it, but I've heard about it. The way you treat those girls crosses a line, whether you want to admit it or not."

"Seriously? You're giving *me* sex advice?"

He shakes his head, tucking the form back into its envelope. "You're chasing a high, son. Sex, drugs, fighting. All of it leads to the same place. I'm just saying, maybe you should consider what a problem looks like. The things I've heard are worrying."

"I've never done anything to a girl that she didn't obviously fucking want." At his expression, I roll my eyes, "Fine, whatever, recording them. But that was just social insurance." The baffled look he gives me tells me the irony of this statement isn't lost on him. "My point *is*, don't project your shit onto me. I don't have any problems with sex." More bitterly, I add, "Depending on who you ask, of course."

"So there is a problem." He instantly sobers, looking more disappointed than is frankly necessary. "Heston, if you've forced yourself on someone, or—"

I shut that shit down immediately. "Fuck you, I'm not a rapist!" It comes out in an angry hiss, my eyes scanning to make sure no one's around. Incredulously, I explain, "My steady piece is just pissed that I don't eat pussy. Jesus."

"Oh." He looks unjustly relieved, giving me a double-take. "Wait, you mean you don't..."

Bluntly, I repeat, "Eat pussy."

His forehead creases. "Does she not... uh, do oral for you?"

"Sure she does." I snag a can of soda from the refreshment table, cracking the tab. "She sucks dick like it's a calling."

He gives me a wry look. "Isn't that a bit of a double standard?"

I point the can at him. "You know what's a double standard? If I browbeat some girl into sucking my dick, that'd be fucked up. Arguably criminal. So why is it she gets to pressure me about it? Tell me how that's fair, *Warren*."

He watches me take a sip of the soda, mouth pursing thought-fully. "Sometimes it's not what you say, but how you say it."

"I told her it was gross."

He barks a disbelieving laugh. "I'm sorry, you told a girl her pussy was gross? Did you ever want to sleep with her again?"

"No, I said *eating* pussy is gross."

"And what do you think she heard?" He gives me an expectant

look, even though it's clearly rhetorical. "You've got a lot to learn about women."

I look away, sniffing. "Whatever. Bitch just wants me on my knees." That's the clincher. Eating pussy is too intimate. Too self-less. Too goddamn submissive. I want a female under me, on her knees, bent over and *taking* it. I'm no one's fucking pussy-licker.

Warren rests his hand on my shoulder and leans in, "From one Devil to another, let me give you a little tip. There is *nothing* like feeling a woman come on your mouth, tasting her, smelling her, hearing her cry out your name as her fingers curl in your hair. Pleasing a woman is *true* power. Don't waste the opportunity."

He claps me on the back and walks over to a few of the other remaining members, leaving me with the impression that Warren is either a first-rate perv or a goddamn genius. I guess it's up to me to figure out which.

17

"I had this vision of what swim class would look like," Micha says, looking jaded as he surveys the natatorium. "There were supposed to be super hot guys in Speedos, really mature and competent divers, that kind of thing." He plucks a chip from the bag, cramming it into his mouth. "Instead, it's *this*."

My gaze follows the flick of his hand to where two Freshman are pretending to hump an inflatable giraffe on the pool deck. I get a chip and munch on it. "How do you think they got that in here?" Pool toys are strictly prohibited in the natatorium, probably because teenage boys can't be trusted to do stuff like not hump them.

"I don't know. It's not exactly low key." We both tilt our heads as one guy mounts the giraffe, pretending to ride it like a horse. "How am *I* the freak of the school?"

"Ooh," I say, jabbing an elbow into Micha's side. "Look."

Heston exits the office, walking right toward where the group of Freshmen are simulating a particularly baffling make-out session on the giraffe. I can feel Micha getting excited too, hand darting toward his mouth with another chip.

"What do you think he's going to do?"

I hum. "Knowing him? Possibly nothing."

Aside from the last couple classes, I haven't really spoken to Heston since we fucked in his car on Saturday—not that we did much speaking then, either. I can feel the need ramping up, but it's manageable. *For now.* It's going to take a lot more than low-level horniness to send me his way for relief. He still hasn't apologized for calling me a slut, although I don't know why I'd ever expect him to. It just serves as a reminder that this thing we're doing is so toxic that a canary could fly between us and instantly drop dead. I'll use him when I absolutely need him, and not a second sooner.

When he looks up from his clipboard and sees the giraffe shenanigans, Micha and I are glued to our seats, watching as he casually lopes past the group. He lifts the pen from the clipboard, curls his hand into a fist around it, and then expressionlessly buries it into the giraffe's ass.

The sound of a sad, hissing wheeze fills the room.

Micha and I burst into laughter at the crestfallen looks on their faces. The Freshman who was riding it deflates as much as the toy does, while the boy pretending to kiss it flinches back, staring wide-eyed at Heston, who doesn't even meet the boy's gaze. He just goes back to his clipboard, scribbling something down and stepping smoothly past the commotion.

"What's so funny?" a voice asks, drawing my attention to the two boys to my right.

Jase and his brother Gus stride up, pausing in front of us. I'm not surprised to see Jase here. The class right before the school day ends always has him in it. Lately, Micha and I wait until after dinner to show up, but today we're waiting for Coach James' performance report, and he's almost always gone by the time Heston's class with us starts.

I make a face at the way leans in, foot propped on the bench beside me, blocking my view of anything but his crotch. "Nothing," I tell him, shooting Micha a disgusted look.

Since Jase doesn't seem to be put off by anything less than

sledgehammer-levels of subtlety, he just shrugs it off. "I heard your roomie's going to be out tonight. Got the place all to yourself, eh?"

It's true. Josie's great aunt or whoever passed away a couple days ago, so she's flying out with her parents to a funeral out west. It's four glorious days and nights with no one else in the suite, and until about three seconds ago, I was really looking forward to it.

Before I can dwell too long on the reality of this rapey piece of shit knowing that I'm going to be alone for the next four nights, Gus pipes in to Micha, "What *are you* today?" He stares down at Micha with an expression that looks more appalled than genuinely confused.

"What 'am I' today?" Micha asks, using his fingers to quote. Unbothered, he kicks back, picking another chip from the bag. "Busy," he answers, expression pensive. "Kind of annoyed. Hungry. And surprised, honestly. I didn't think you cared so much about my general state of being, Gus."

Gus eyes him. "I don't. I was just curious what you were identifying as," he wrinkles his nose, "in all that *shit* you're wearing."

I bristle more than Micha seems to, back going rigid and straight. "It's makeup, idiot."

Micha has gone a little ambitious today; fake lashes, little whorls painted on the outside of his eyes, lids sporting a gradient of pink and turquoise. There's a silhouette of a flock of birds spreading out toward each temple.

It looks cool as fuck.

Jase laughs, nudging his brother. "He identifies as a gay bird."

Gus gives Micha more of his stink eye. "More like he identifies as a circus freak."

It isn't until I stand, pushing Jase back, with all intentions of getting into Gus' disgusting face, that I realize Heston is right behind them.

"Want to know what I identify as?" he asks, clamping a hand on Jase's shoulder. "Ten hours of detention." He gives Gus a hard look. "And whatever Dewey thinks will complement it best."

"What?" Gus gapes at him, eyes sparking. "Dude, what the—"

"It could be fifteen hours," Heston adds, shoving Jase away to stand between them and Micha. "Actually, now that I think about it, fifteen sounds really good. What do you think, Adams?"

Micha chirps, "Twenty."

Heston turns his head just enough for me to make out the flash of surprise in his eyes. "Spiteful, Adams." Nodding, he adds, "I respect that."

Micha munches another chip. "Thanks."

Jase looks like he wanted to argue, but Gus must realize that the more that happens, the more detention they'll get. He grabs his brother by the arm and drags him away, shooting Heston a threatening look as they skulk away.

"Class isn't until seven," he says, turning to us with narrowed eyes. "Is there some reason the two of you are loitering on my bench, getting crumbs everywhere?" His glare doesn't have any actual heat to it, so the barked words fall flat.

"We're waiting on Coach James," I tell him, not flinching at the way he watches me. "We get our first performance reports today,"

The thing is, I know he's waiting. Every day, there's a glance across the dining hall, a stare across the pool, quick flicks of his eyes in the hallways, like he's wondering if it's time—if I'm ready to go again. The way he's looking at me now, blue eyes pinning me, the scruffy edge of his jaw tightening, makes me wonder if he's not just waiting.

Maybe he's hoping.

"Coach James isn't doing your reports," he says, pulling two envelopes from his clipboard. "I am."

I only just manage to bite back my groan, and I can see Micha doing the same. He probably has to give his report to his mom, but mine's going to Mrs. Gilbert. If she's unhappy with my progress, then god only knows what she'll make me do.

He stands there for another suspended moment, expression indecipherable, before turning on his heel and striding away.

"Am I crazy or did Wilcox just kind of defend me?"

I look at Micha, dryly explaining, "Oh yeah, Heston has this whole thing. It's like when a cat catches a mouse, and instead of killing it, he just viciously plays with it for hours on end, and the second anyone or anything tries to take it away, the cat gets all possessive and pissy, and won't let anyone else touch it." Rolling my eyes, I conclude, "No one's allowed to bully us but him."

"What do you think it says," Micha wonders, holding the envelope up to the light and squinting.

"Probably that we suck," I answer distractedly, watching the way Heston walks around the pool deck. Those muscles, that swagger, the way his hair falls in his face when he looks down. *I could have that right now*, I think, completely unbidden. I snap out of it, grousing, "Which is true, but it's still going to be a total pain."

Micha is watching me, eyes searching. "I've been thinking of recruiting you."

My eyebrow raises. "For what?"

He puts the bag of chips away, turning to me, legs folded. "I'm currently the mastermind behind a diabolical plot to drive Wilcox insane."

"Huh?"

"Pranks," he says, voice low, leaning in close. "Every day, I do something new. Super glue in the door lock, stealing his clothes, soaking his office chair, all kinds of stuff. I'm working on some exponential severity. Today, wet socks. Tomorrow? Who knows? Maybe food coloring in his swim cap. I could use some fresh inspo, though. And who better to get it from than someone who hates him as much as I do?"

I stare at him for a moment before turning, mirroring his pose. I rest my chin on my fists, grinning. "Tell me more."

Micha smiles deviously.

∼

THE GLITTER BOMB should arrive in Heston's mailbox on Monday. *Perfect.* I shut my laptop, stretching out on my bed. It feels good to have the suite to myself. Quiet. Relaxing. I look around, thinking of how to best take advantage of this boon.

First, there's some dancing, my playlist jacked up as loud as I dare, considering the dorm adviser is just a couple floors away.

After that, I cook myself some quesadillas in the kitchenette, which I've not had nearly enough time alone with. Then I do a video call with Aubrey and Elena, for once not having to constantly watch what I say about the Devils just in case Josie is listening in. I carefully omit any mentions about Heston's dubious involvement. They'd completely freak out.

Hell, *I'm* completely freaking out.

It's just an inexplicable situation. Rationally, I know he's bad news, and it'd be downright stupid to give him any chance to ruin the Devils again. Micha looked at me today and saw someone who wanted to get revenge on an asshole. There's no denying that's true. But another part of me also needs to see if Heston Wilcox can be someone worth calling a Devil. If there's no sense of morality behind those cold blue eyes, is there at least a sense of loyalty?

Since thinking of Heston makes me think of Heston's dick, and since thinking of *that* makes me so horny that I can't even stand it, I spend the next hour making tender, sweet, battery-operated love to myself.

After fucking Heston for the last few weeks, it's a disappointment.

I take a shower next, deciding, *Screw it*, and not even bothering to get dressed after. I've never slept naked before, but I've always been curious about it. I hate waking up in the middle of the night to find my shirt all twisted, panties riding up my butt crack. This is freeing, though—the way I can slide right under the sheets without worrying about it.

That's precisely how I fall asleep.

Alarmingly, it's also how I wake up.

A hand clamps over my mouth before I can scream. The sleep is still thick in my head, blurring my sight even with the lamp that's still shining next to my bed. The person above me is a big, shadowed, blond-haired blob.

The second I hear, "Calm down, it's me," I strike out, fist catching him in the shoulder. "I said it's me!" he repeats, sounding aggravated.

I wrench my face to the side, dislodging the palm over my

mouth. "I heard you, you fucking lunatic! Ugh." My heart hammers away, still not convinced there isn't a danger here. It was that moment in the natatorium when Jase looked at me, making that comment about me being alone. The memory of his hand around my wrist and the way he so easily overpowered me. That glint of entitled want in his eyes.

I'm not convinced waking up to Heston is much better.

I flinch away, squinting at him. "What are you doing here?! How did you—"

Before I can fully voice the question, he exhales hard, raising his gaze from my bare chest to lock eyes with mine. "I've never done this before." It comes out strangely grim, mouth set into a tight line. "I'm not looking for constructive criticism. If it's not mine or God's name coming out of your mouth, then you can keep it fucking shut."

With that, he whips the blanket away and stares fixedly at the crux of my legs, palms sweeping up the tops of my thighs. I realize with a start that he's coaxing them open.

It hits me like a freight train, exactly what he's here to do. "I'd need two hands and both feet to count all the reasons you're fucked up for coming in here, in the middle of the night, like some psycho stalker creep. And I fully intend on letting you hear each one of them—loudly, and with feeling." Holding his gaze, I let my thighs fall open.

Tomorrow.

He doesn't reply, except for how he crouches down the bed, staring between my legs like my pussy holds the answer to some baffling riddle. I feel hot and too exposed, knowing that my face must be glowing red with each bit of coherence I slowly gain. Heston and I have had a lot of sex, but he's never really...looked. Not there. Not like this. I can still hear the sound of his voice, tired and aloof. "*Shit's gross.*" It makes me want to snap my knees closed and pull the blanket back over me.

Before I can, he touches the inside of my thigh and ducks down against it, tongue darting out to lick a hot stripe up my folds.

It's like a nuclear explosion that awakens all my senses. My head spins with the sudden rush of *wet hot sex sex sex*. The second flick of his tongue, positioned right on the apex of my clit, makes my breath hitch and my thighs open even more. "Oh, god," I breathe, melting into the bed.

He responds by sweeping his palm up my hip and settling there, tongue mapping my folds. The worst thing about it is how into it I am, letting my fingers tangle into his hair as he teases me. It's unskilled, as far as head goes. Hardly any technique. He vacillates between tonguing at my clit and my entrance, back and forth. Sometimes he approaches it like a particularly aggressive kiss, sucking on retreat. It's indecisive, lacking in any sort of purpose or goal.

And it might be the best I've ever had.

I keep my eyes trained on him because it's the only way I can really understand what's happening. That's Heston Wilcox. His head is between my legs. He's giving me clumsy cunnilingus and if he can manage to remain focused on my clit for five seconds, I just might come my goddamn brains out on his tongue.

The best part, by far, are the scant moments where he looks up my body at me with that half-lidded, cocky expression that's so infuriatingly *him*.

I chase his tongue with my hips when he strays, careful not to guide his head even though I'm dying to. He doesn't take it as gracefully as he could, letting out this annoyed punch of breath as he grips my thighs, holding me still in his sure grip.

By the time he brings his fingers into the mix, I'm already a complete mess of gasping breaths and sharp fricatives, lip trapped painfully between my teeth. My toes curl when he sinks two fingers into me, heels digging into the mattress.

"Please," I'm gasping, and I take too long to even realize what I'm babbling about. "Please fuck me, fuck me, please, *please*..." His ragged rumble against my clit makes me throw my head back, and then I figure out why his fingers leave me, the slick tip of a digit dipping lower and lower, until—

We both go still.

My chest is heaving and if I had the presence of mind to feel such a thing, I'd be embarrassed by the way my thighs are quaking around his ears. He meets my gaze and holds it, eyes boring into mine as his finger presses against my asshole.

There's this ridiculous rumor that I'm into anal. I'm not sure who started it, but at this point, there's no telling. The truth is that I've never done it. I've never even let another guy touch me there before. Heston's finger toys at my rim, like maybe he's waiting for me to argue about it. My belly explodes with anxious nerves, but beyond the mortification of someone touching me in such a private place is a spark of curiosity.

I sink my teeth into my lip and buck my hips.

Heston isn't a very expressive guy. I can tell when he's horny because he looks all pissed off and malignant. The other day, I could tell he was in a good mood because of the way he held himself—loose and obnoxiously brash. But I have no idea what to call this.

His jaw goes slack, and even in the low light I can tell his pupils are blown wide, the reflection from the lamp glittering around the edges of his irises. He holds my gaze as he pushes his fingertip past the resistance, breaths warm and shallow against my clit as he sinks his finger into my ass.

I fist a hand into the sheets and look away, unable to endure the intensity of it all. There's a burn that feels foreign, the sense of being invaded in a way that's not natural, and I know instantly that I'm into it.

So into it that I curl a fist into his hair, rock against his tongue, and come so hard that I see stars.

I'm boneless when he turns me over, only distantly aware of the sounds he's making—hard bursts of breath, shifting fabric, the short grunt he makes when he enters my pussy, hard and fast.

His mouth is right by my ear as he fucks me with short, commanding thrusts, making my headboard bang against the wall. "Fuck, that was hot," he growls, forcing a cry from my throat when he hits me at just the right angle. "I knew the rumors were true. You love it, don't you? Feeling me in your tight ass. *Fuck.*" He doesn't last long, grunting into my sweaty neck as he fills me, pulsing deep inside.

There's a moment when he's still inside of me, both of us breathing hard, that I feel his fingers on the side of my breast. I take a long moment to realize he's touching the bruise he made the other day in his car, when he squeezed too hard.

So softly that I might have missed it, he breathes, "My bad," and then gathers my breast into his soft palm, bending down to brush his lips over the bruise. If it can be called an apology at all, it feels like it's made more to my boob than to me.

I don't bother moving when he slips out. Everything feels slow and muddled, like maybe I never woke up at all. Maybe this is all some weird and very sexy lucid dream I'm having.

The next blip of any awareness I have is the sound of my alarm.

I look for Heston, but I'm in the bed alone. There's no sticky reminder between my legs, no sign that a man had been between them the night before, but as I wake, I notice the covers are straight and pulled to my chin. I prop up on my elbows and see the flash of something silver on the pillow next to mine.

I pick up the square and stare at it for a long moment, and the rush of truth comes back to me.

Heston had shown up under the cloak of night, not just for sex, but to give me what I'd asked for and a little bit of what I didn't know I wanted. It was surprising, and different.

It's way too early to think about what it means, so instead, I unwrap the foil, pop the chocolate in my mouth, and get ready for the day.

"Cheerleader," Heston observes from his spot on the couch. "Popular. She ditched the skank, so she must not be completely stupid." Caroline makes a face at him, which is fair. He's the one who dated Sydney—If you can call what they were doing 'dating'. He concludes, "She looks good on paper."

I avoid looking at him, afraid that I'll glimpse the way he's sitting, legs spread, lounged back, and become a slave to my baser impulses. It's been a couple days since Heston snuck into my room and ate me out, and with the way things are shaping up, I'll be seeking him out later for a repeat.

But for now, we need to choose the new Devils. This morning, someone had slipped another one of those black envelopes beneath my door. It was short and sweet; the initiation will begin in three weeks.

Since there hasn't been much headway being made, Caroline suggested a purely data-driven approach, which is why the three of us are huddled around her laptop, staring at a color-coded spreadsheet. It has a dozen rows with various attributes, some weighted more heavily than others.

Fiona seems to check all boxes.

"I'm good with Fiona," I say. Vandy gives me a begrudging nod, while Heston stares at his phone, looking bored as ever.

He's easier with the girls. "Josie is a bitch," he says when she's brought up, looking half distracted, "but she's got everything. Looks, money, attitude." He seems down with almost every girl suggested.

Aside from Micha, which had gotten a, "Yes, obviously, but you're going to need to invite his twin sister, because there's no way he can keep it from her," he's a lot harder on the guys.

Caroline skims the list. "How about Gus Meyers?"

"Pass," Heston says. I don't really like the way he says it—all obstinate, in a way the brooks no argument, as if he's the authority here.

Caroline turns to argue, "Gus is pretty popular. Smart. Rich. Athletic. He got a high score on the SAT."

"He's a douche." His eyes dart to mine and back to his phone, knee bouncing. "And his little brother is worse. You need to plan ahead for legacies."

Vandy shoots him a glare, but when she turns back to the screen, she mutters, "Something to consider."

"As much as I hate to say it, I agree with Heston." He fakes being shocked for the benefit of the girls. "Jase is pretty awful. I've had a run-in with him. In swim, I mean," I rush to elaborate, feeling twitchy under the weight of Heston's gaze. "Plus, him and Gus were mean to Micha. I'm a no."

"I trust your judgment," Vandy says, making sure she's looking at me when she says it. She's made it very clear she's not okay with Heston helping. "Who's next?"

Caroline grins at the sheet. "Ozzy Collins. He's nice. Funny. Smart. He doesn't play any sports, but I'm not holding that against him." She chews on her lip, forehead creased in thought. "The biggest drawback is being the headmaster's son. Do we think he'll rat us out?"

Vandy looks at the screen, head shaking. "It's risky."

I jump in, "Yeah, but what's the point of being a Devil if you're not going to take a few risks?" Since Vandy is looking unconvinced, I take a breath and turn to Heston. "What do you think?"

He's got his thumb on his bottom lip, sort of fidgeting with it as he reads something on his phone. When he looks up, blue eyes meeting mine, he drags it down, giving me a peek of his tongue. "I don't know him," he answers, shrugging like he didn't just soak my panties with that look of his. "But you've got to admit, there's something satisfyingly ironic about having the headmaster's kid in the society. Collins is a dumbass, he'll never figure it out."

I offer, "Well, he's escorting me to the ball in a few weeks. Maybe I can come up with some reason to spend time with him this weekend. Feel him out?"

Caroline's head whips around, eyes big through her glasses. "Ozzy asked you to the ball?"

"No." I snort a laugh. "I don't think he really believes they're a thing. But I asked him to take me and he said yes."

Heston looks at me, head tilted, mouth slanted into a grin. "How exactly do you plan on feeling him out? Or did you mean feeling him up?"

I shoot him a hard look. "I plan on asking questions, getting to know him better. Maybe get a better insight into his relationship with his father. Make sure he's not some kind of mole."

"Pretty pathetic mole," he replies, sliding his phone into his pocket. "I mean, if that's the case, maybe that's why he's going with you to the Debutart Ball. To get dirt on the Devils."

Vandy throws me an alarmed look, and I want to curse Heston for playing into her paranoia. She's taking this a lot more seriously than her brother probably did. "You'll have to be—"

Caroline jerks up from her seat, shutting the laptop in one swift motion. "I've got to go."

Vandy and I both gawk at her. "But our shortlist is still...you know. *Short.*"

If Caroline heard me, then she doesn't show it. She wraps her charging cord up and crams it into her bag. "I have some things to do," she coldly explains, not even meeting my gaze. If her chilly tone wasn't enough to clue me in, then the way she fumbles with her laptop, almost dropping it in her haste to shove it into her bag, definitely is. Caroline would hurt herself before she intentionally harmed digital electronics.

Vandy and I share a look, but it's me who reaches out to steady her. "Hey, what's wrong? If this is about the spreadsheet—"

Caroline jerks out of my grip, swinging a bitter glare at me. "You mean the spreadsheet of guys you haven't slept with yet? Yes, Georgia, it's *short.*"

My head snaps back in shock, but the reaction hits before the words even register. I've never seen Caroline angry like this before, and certainly never at me.

Vandy catches the words, though, jumping to my defense with a sharp, "Hey!"

Caroline angrily prods her glasses up her nose, holding my gaze. "I don't know why I'm even surprised. He's been here, what, a few weeks now? I guess the guy's gotta get the full Preston experience. Uniform, locker number, a notch beneath Georgia's name on the beam!"

Vandy cuts in with a loud, "Whoa!" but inside, I'm just a mess of panic and horror, convinced for a moment that she knows about me and Heston.

And then she says, "I guess that's what I get, thinking a guy like

Ozzy would notice anyone but you. Classic, really." She finally gets her laptop into the bag, hands shaking. "That's all guys ever want. And here you are, ready and willing. Perfect! I hope the sex is fantastic."

"Slow the fuck down!" I say, flinging my arms in front of me like I can stop the train wreck happening. "I'm not sleeping with Ozzy! And what the hell, Caroline? You had weeks to ask him to the ball! You kept going on and on about asking Em or George!"

"It doesn't matter now!" she yells, eyes ablaze. "But in the future, I'll be sure to stake my claim before the five-second 'Whorgia Haynes' grace period expires."

It feels like someone much larger than Caroline has just punched me in the stomach. I'm used to the names by now. The snide remarks. The way girls look at me like I'm trash. Never in a million years could I have been prepared for it to come from a friend.

Vandy steps in, holding her hands up. "Everyone, stop! You're not letting some stupid guy get in between you. Hoes over bros!"

Caroline's laugh comes out more like a sob. "Easy for you to say. You got Reynolds locked down before she could get to him—and she would have. She got Sebastian, didn't she? Probably Ben and Carl, too. Hell, maybe even Emory. After that revolving door between her legs, there's no one left for the rest of us, is there?"

I stare at her, my shock slowly giving way to a simmering rage. I've known her long enough to see the hurt beneath the fury. It's the only thing that stops me from lunging at her. The closest thing to a fight I've ever been in was fifth grade. Tillie Tipper, who stood behind me in chorus, put nail polish in my hair during practice. I didn't find out until lunch, but when I did, I hunted her down and took a swing. It was mostly just a bunch of hair pulling and a few scratches before the teachers separated us. I got a week suspension and a very, *very* brief reputation for being a bad girl. But here, feeling my fists tremble with how hard I'm clenching them, I think it'd go a hell of a lot different.

Taking a shaky breath, I say, "You're misreading the situation, so I'm going to give you a chance to walk out of here and cool off. But if you don't," I look her in the eye, voice low and composed, "I'm going to lay some fucking hands on you."

There's a low curse from the couch. When I whip around to glare at Heston, he just looks balefully up at me, wiggling his phone. "Not enough charge for video. Too bad, a cat fight would be epic."

By the time I turn back, Caroline's already marching out the door.

～

VANDY AND HESTON clear out of the bunker first, leaving me to lock up. I hang around for a while longer, though, stewing about the fight with Caroline. When I finally leave, it's already afternoon, so I'm careful to be quiet when closing the door and turning the key.

"Collins, huh?"

I whirl around, heart skipping a beat, to see Heston leaning against the stone wall, hands shoved into his pockets. "Shit. You scared me." I press a palm to my chest, willing the thudding to calm. "What are you talking about?"

"The date with Collins," he says, looking at me through heavy-lidded eyes. "When did all this happen?"

"A week or so ago." I hitch my bag higher on my shoulder, still in a crappy mood. "Actually, it was back when you were being petty little dickwad about my Devil's mark." His jaw tightens, then releases, and my stomach flutters anxiously. I'm not entirely sure why, but I need him to know, "It's not something I really want to do. It's completely lame and offensive. But my mom's been planning it since before I could walk, and I needed an escort, so I asked someone. Are you going to give me shit about it, too?" He stares at me, those icy eyes making tracks up and down my body, and I feel compelled to add, "It's not like I could ask you. My mom would have me committed."

His lips tip up, amusement dancing in his eyes. "Were you hoping I'd be jealous?"

"What?" I blink at him, feeling whiplashed. "No, I—"

262

"You think I want to put on a tux and dance like a clown? Make small talk with the Club's elite all night? Tuck your little hand into my elbow and present you to society in your virginal whites, like I didn't have my finger buried knuckle-deep in your ass two nights ago?"

"Oh my god," I hiss, reaching out to shove his shoulder. "Do you ever shut your damn mouth?!"

He smirks, raising an eyebrow at my crotch. "As I recall, you really seemed to enjoy it being open." Ignoring my groan, he shifts, adding, "So you're having cat fights over this guy now? Seems serious. Or as serious as you probably get."

"Great." I look away, laughing humorlessly. "Is this the part where you remind me I'm a slut again? Because it wasn't enough to just hear it from one of my best friends." My voice cracks embarrassingly and I clear my throat, hoping it went unnoticed.

There's a long stretch of silence before he answers, "This is the part where I remind you we have an agreement. No screwing other guys."

"What is with everyone!" I throw my hands up, at my wits end. "Contrary to what's apparently popular belief, I can go on a date with a guy and *not fuck him*!"

Heston's eyes slide to the archway leading to outside, jaw tightening. "Freak out a little louder, would you? I don't think the other half of the campus knows we're here yet." His only response to my glare is a jerk of his head toward the stairs leading up.

The only reason I follow him is because I *was* too loud. I should probably lie low for a few, make sure no one's standing around out there. When we reach the top, Heston leans against the stone wall, eyes tracking me as I slump onto the floor, tucking my knees up under my chin.

He sighs, long and obnoxious, like he's put-out by what he's about to say. "She's just jealous, you know. You're way hotter than her. She was right. What guy would notice her with you around? You've got huge tits and a reputation for being down to fuck. You're basically catnip for teenage boys."

I point up. "Look at that beam. How many Devils—how many

guys—have more than a dozen notches? Two dozen, even?" I don't give him a chance to answer. "No one cares when it's a guy. Hell, I bet you have tons, and no one's ever called you a whore."

"You think I never got any shit for the amount of notches I had?" He nods at the beam, eyes hard. "Take a look."

To prove my point, I do, scanning the initials for the 'HW'. When I find it, I pause, squinting. "That can't be right."

There are only four notches.

"One was just a blow job," he says, pointing to the first two slashes. "I've only ever fucked four girls, including you, so believe me when I say it's the opposite for a guy. If you aren't pulling tail on the reg like Hamilton, then you're going to hear shit about it."

I look at him, eyes wide in disbelief. "Four?!" It's not like there are rumors about Heston being a manwhore or anything, I just figured he's gotten around.

"Some girl sophomore year, you, Reagan, and then Sydney." He shrugs, looking amused by my reaction. "Why the surprise, Haynes? Quality over quantity."

"I just thought you were being an asshole," I say, head shaking as I compare our notches. "But I really am a slut compared to you."

I feel him behind me, chest nudging up against my back. His voice is soft in my ear when he says, "For whatever little it may be worth, I don't really think you're a slut." I shiver as he gathers up my hair, sweeping it off my neck. Into the skin beneath it, he whispers, "I think you're *my* slut."

Swallowing, I ask, "What are you doing?" It's a stupid question. His fingers are dipping beneath the waist of my jeans, teasing at the little dip between my hip and belly.

His lips are pulling the skin on my neck in these tiny little teasing pecks. "Adding a notch to my name," he replies, but before I can protest, his mouth opens, latching on in a forceful, marking suck.

I want to tell him it's a horrible idea. People will see it. They'll ask questions. It'll just be more fuel to the rumors going around about me. Whorgia Haynes, walking around with a hickey.

No.

A Devil's mark.

Heston's Devil mark.

The sound I make is nowhere even approaching negative, and when he shoves his hand down my unbuttoned pants, forcing it between my legs as he sucks his bruise into my skin, the only thing I do is rock into it.

"You were wrong," I say, eyes sliding closed as I ride his hand. "That night, when you snuck into my room."

I can practically feel his smirk against my neck. "Seemed like I was pretty right."

"I mean the rumor about me loving anal," I clarify, reaching back to lace my fingers into his hair. He obviously wants to do it, which is something that's been bothering me since he ate me out. I don't want him to have any illusions about what's on offer here. "It's complete bullshit. I've never done that before. Aside from you, I never even let a guy—" Maybe it's giving too much away to admit that Heston's the only person I've let do that to me, but when he slides two fingers inside of my pussy, I forget why. "I'm saving it."

"Saving it?" I feel his laugh more than I hear it. "For what, prom night? Your honeymoon?"

"If I ever do it, I just...I think I want it to be nice," I breathe, knees trembling from the way his hand is working me over. "I don't —I haven't been a virgin in a long time, so I want to—for the right person, who's not just in it for..." My breath hitches when he pushes his hardness into me, rocking with the motion of my hips. I try to focus. "I don't want it to hurt. I want it to be...nice. That's why I can't. Not with you."

To anyone else, that might have stung. Heston seems to take it as a challenge, fingering me harder—deeper—his forearm crushing me closer to him. "You don't think I can be gentle and romantic as I'm shoving my cock up your pretty virgin ass?"

Instantly, I respond, "No."

He just chuffs a laugh. "Fair enough." I whimper when he suddenly pulls his hand away, sliding it out of my pants. His voice is low and rough in my ear as he wagers, "Let me finger it again and I'll eat your pussy."

I freeze, my core aching with a release he'd been so close to giving me. "Here?"

I feel him shrug against me. "We're Devils, Little Red. I just gave you my mark." He hooks his fingers into my pants, tugging them down. "Might as well make the notches count."

Oh well, I think as I spin to capture his mouth in a hard, biting kiss.

What's another notch?

18

HESTON

In the dream, I'm looking at myself.

He looks like me, walks like me, talks like me. But he's younger. I don't know why he's here, but I instantly hate his fucking guts. This younger version of myself is a little too impetuous, a touch too transparent in the way he holds himself, all aggressive and arrogant. It's embarrassing. It also makes me flare with jealousy, the way people alternately cringe away and turn to him like the sun. They're afraid of him. They respect him.

Enjoy that shit while it lasts.

First, he's just walking around campus, getting fists bumps and obnoxious hoots. Oh yes, this Heston is still all the rage. He still has friends and family and purpose. He has...a girl? Beneath the arm tossed over her shoulder is a waterfall of bright red hair.

It's just a flash—more of an idea, really. I could have had her back then, easy. Not that I wanted to, but if I had? I get this clarity of thought that jolts me right out of it. It's some odd mixture of alarm and dread.

He would have torn that fucking girl apart.

Something seems off the instant I wake, and it's not just the weird dream.

"Uggghhhh."

I don't need to check my phone to know that I've slept too late. The sunlight coming into the window is too bright, stabbing me right in the temple, to mean anything else. I fumble for it anyway, realizing that my goddamn alarm didn't go off. Or didn't get set. Or whatever the hell. Slinging my legs over the bed, I wince, my morning wood painfully resisting the sudden move.

"Sorry, man." I give it a sympathetic squeeze. "Not right now." I search for my sweats, which is the only bonus of working at the pool; bottom barrel casual attire. Grabbing them off the floor, I pause, only vaguely remembering the flash of her in the dream. Well, I don't need Freud to figure that out. Our hasty and very messy exchange of oral up in the tower just fitzed with my head a little. It was the combination of the best of both timelines, being a Devil back then, and being Georgia's sexual lapdog right now.

Well, *that's* an uncomfortable realization.

"Except..." There are benefits to knowing a feisty nympho who's always down to fuck, and a blow job is exactly what I need to turn this day around.

My first class isn't until ten, which gives me a little time. There's no food in my kitchen, which is why I've taken to getting up early enough to hit breakfast on campus. My stomach is apparently quick to mutiny at even the hint of a delayed meal, so my plan had been to get breakfast and head to my office early.

I dress quickly, scowling in the mirror at a rogue piece of hair that refuses to lie flat. I bolt out of the apartment and start across to the dining hall, texting along the way.

H: Where are you?

G: Getting on the bus.

H: Are you joking?

G: Nope. Field trip to the battlefield. AP history.

My cock wilts in disappointment.

G: Why?

H: I require your cock-sucking acumen.

G: YOU require? That's not how this arrangement works.

H: Don't pretend you aren't down.

G: I'm not.

Frustrated, I try:

H: I'll eat you out again.

Why not? Fingering Georgia's ass has suddenly reached the top of my erotic itinerary. It's not just because I want to fuck her ass—although I really fucking do—it's just the way it drives her crazy. Makes her beg. Turns her all frantic and desperate, like a completely different person, stripped of all pride and awareness. Nothing has ever gotten my dick harder.

I stop outside the dining hall to finish the text and bound up the steps. Reaching for the door, I yank it back only to have it bang against the lock. I try again, confused why it's not opening, until I realize that it's four minutes past the closing time.

"Fucking seriously?" I bang a fist into the door, my stomach already beginning its song and dance of stabbing pain. I stare at the clock, trying to determine if there's enough time to run to The Nerd for an egg and bacon biscuit. It'll have to be the fastest fucking order in the history of bad diner fare.

My stomach does a somersault full of acid and agony, which leaves me fighting the urge to double over, hand pressed against a pillar in front of the courtyard. That's when I notice the black and red Preston bus. It's parked in the front drop-off cut, a cluster of students all standing around it, waiting to board. My eyes skim over the plaid skirts and black and white saddle oxfords, over the pimpled faces of teenage boys with their crooked ties and ill-fitting uniforms.

My gaze hones in on a familiar head of red hair. Without really meaning to, I watch her amongst her classmates. She looks different during swim class, always so wary around the pool, like it's some sentient being that could reach out and grab her at any moment. Here, in the harsh light of day, she fits in seamlessly, just another mindless Preston drone in the mass of uniformity.

It's not real.

From this vantage, an outsider would never know about the way she deflates when she thinks no one is looking, like she can relax for a moment. They'd never know the way she looks when she comes, face contorted with tortured relief. They'd never know what she looks like when she needs it—like really, colossally, fucked-up with this frantic, unhinged energy. They'd never see the fading marks on her thigh, the rubber band around her wrist, or the other ways she hurts herself that she thinks no one knows about. Hell, the ways *she* doesn't even know about yet.

That's what I am. I'm the snap of the rubber band. The stab of the pen. The five strands of hair she's yanking out when no one's looking.

I'm the blade she'll probably end up turning to.

I watch as her head tilts down to Vandy, and she says something in her ear, the corners of her mouth turned down. Those bright green eyes dart to Caroline, who has her nose in a book, a deep line slashes across her forehead. Guess they never smoothed over their little spat over the Collins kid.

Speak of the potential-Devil. He walks up to them, all dark hair and innocent smile. Oh look, good ole' Oswald showed up just in time for the field trip. I have this unwelcome thought that he'll make a good escort with all those boyish good looks, parading her around on his arm like a trophy. Collins, for all his father's prickishness, is pedigree. No doubt he'll be set up at a nice college next year, set on the path to greatness provided by his very accommodating father.

I remember having one of those.

Georgia's frown vanishes when she sees him, reshaping into a grin. He reaches out and teasingly tugs a strand of red hair. It's a quick flick, not drawn out enough to be overt, but too obvious to be missed. When she swings her hair back, his eyes go to the hickey on her neck, flicking away just as fast.

Yeah, he's feeling it out, alright.

They're right to be suspicious. I mean, who is this fucking kid? Suddenly he shows up and is best friends with the girl I happen to be fucking, embraced by the only three remaining Devils—the very group his father is obsessively trying to bury? Oh, and he also just happens to be available to take Georgia to the ball, at the very club I'm not allowed to step foot in.

How fucking convenient is all of that?

I'm considering how much fallout would happen with Collins if a sudden, haphazard, hand-breaking incident befell his son when I see Caroline glance up from her book. Her eyes narrow at Georgia and Ozzy, cheeks turning pink before she averts her gaze. Georgia doesn't miss this, a flash of something stiff and cheerless crossing her face. She takes a firm step back from Ozzy, and he lets her, pushing his hands into his pockets.

Ah yes, play it cool, Oswald. Respectful distance. Read her cues. No pressure.

You're never going to get into her pants like that.

Just then, Mr. Sward calls out, and the students file onto the bus. I turn my back and walk away before anyone sees me—or more likely, before I see Georgia and her *date* again.

"Fuck it," I determine, crossing campus toward the teacher's parking lot. If I'm late for class, then at least I'll have a full stomach. Before I even get off the sidewalk, I see the yellow swirl of flashing lights on the top of a tow truck. "Sucks to be you," I mutter, cutting between the cars.

And then I skid to a stop.

Dewey and Buster are standing next to the tow truck, and it's *my fucking Escalade* hitched up to the back.

"Hey!" I shout, zig-zagging through the vehicles. "What the hell are you doing? Get that shit off my car!"

Dewey throws up a palm, stopping me. "Your car is being repossessed, Wilcox. Don't cause a—"

I snatch the paper from his hand. "Repossessed?! It was a gift! A *graduation* gift. You can't repossess a gift!"

Dewey sighs, giving me a grave nod. "I know you're upset, but it's best if you just hand over the keys." He holds out his hand, waiting. Bile rises in my throat—fiery, cutting, rage-fueled bile.

I swallow it back and say, "I need to call my father."

The look of pity Dewey gives me makes me want to puke. Dewey pitying *me*? Turning my back on him, I whip out my phone and search the contacts, having to scroll up and down three times because my thumb's all fucking jerky. My dad's phone goes straight to voicemail, which is expected. I don't bother leaving him one, instead opting to call his office.

Dewey, Buster, and the repo guy are all standing around awkwardly, annoyed that I'm holding shit up, but too pussy to do anything about it.

"Jane!" I try to control my voice, taking a deep breath. "This is Heston. I really need to talk to my dad."

She hums. "I'm sorry, Heston. Mr. Wilcox isn't in right now. Would you like to leave a message?"

I crush the phone in my grip, biting back a curse. "Where is he?"

She smoothly replies, "He's in an urgent meeting. I can take a message."

Jane has been my father's secretary since the dawn of time. When I was a kid, she used to be responsible for buying my birthday presents. When I was a teenager, she helped me get my driver's license since my dad was out of town and my mom was having one of her episodes. She's known me long enough to understand what being cut off means.

And now she's talking to me like I'm a stranger.

"I don't want to leave a message, Jane. I want to speak to my dad. Right fucking now."

Click.

"Fuck." I take a tight, paced lap around an empty parking space. "Fuck!"

Dewey sighs behind me, a hand coming down on my shoulder. "Heston—just give the man the keys, okay? Don't make this harder than it has to be."

I laugh darkly. "Yeah, because that's something I'd do." I reach into my pocket and pull out my key ring with the fob. Turning, I dangle it in the air, letting them all see it, but when Dewey reaches for it, I yank it back and hurl it as hard as I can across the parking lot. It lands with a skittering clang three rows over. "If you want that key, go fucking get it."

"Mr. Wilcox!" Dewey admonishes, but I'm not a student anymore. I flip him off and walk away, head swarming with fury. It's the worst kind of anger—so goddamn futile and useless. Since there's no hope of actually talking to my old man, there's nowhere to put it.

Doesn't mean I don't try, though.

I call my mom next. It rings and rings, but I don't even get voicemail. The call just drops. Liesel, the head of housekeeping, actually does get a voicemail from me. "You tell my prick of a father to call me. Now!" There's one more person I can call, but I'm saving that shit for rock bottom.

My stomach is a raging mess by now, in a way that I know food isn't going to fix. I've got five minutes until my first class starts, so I book it back to my apartment, teeth gnashing harder with every step.

When I get there, I pat my pockets.

No keys.

"Goddamn it," I growl, remembering that I'd chucked them in the parking lot. "Motherfucking cock-sucking piece of fucking—" Bracing my hands on the jamb, I jerk my foot back and kick the door. Then I do it again. I keep doing it, right up until there's an ache in my ankle to join the tornado of anguish happening in my belly. "Fuck you!" I scream at the door, whipping around to sit on the stoop.

This is stupid.

This is some goddamn Hamilton Bates level of tantrum. I take a deep breath, knuckles digging into my temples, and try to compose myself. I just want my medicine out of the bathroom, but it's going to involve calling maintenance, and probably an alert to Collins who has probably already been alerted to the fact my Escalade has been professionally stolen.

Since I can't leave campus, my only hope is that, at some point, I left a bottle in the office.

So that's where I go next.

I don't know if it's my slight limp, my expression, or just a general aura of 'fuck off', but people give me a wider berth than usual, skirting around the pool deck as I storm past. I've only just opened the door to the office when the phone on the desk rings. I stand there and stare at it for a suspended moment. That phone has never rung before. If I were smart, I'd just ignore it.

"Hello." I'm an idiot.

"Heston, this is Ms. Hampton over in the front office."

"Okay."

"Coach James called out sick, so you'll be covering his classes for the day."

I take another deep breath. "Is there anyone else who can take it today? I'm actually not feeling that great. I was hoping to find someone to cover *my* classes."

"There's no one else," she says, completely unsympathetic. "Headmaster Collins said I should mention the agreement."

"The agreement," I bite out, fist shaking with how tightly I'm holding the phone. I have so many fucking agreements going that I can't keep track of them anymore. Georgia, the court, Collins, Gene. "Fine." I hang up the phone before she can respond, going quickly to my locker.

Finally.

Fucking *finally*, something's going right for me.

There's a bottle of Mylanta stuffed between a mildewy towel and a broken pair of goggles. It's only got one dose swirling in the bottom, but I throw it back like it's an elixir, hoping like hell it'll be enough to get me through until...

Until.

Until fucking what? Until my dad gives my car back? Until the school day ends and I can take a cab? Beg a ride off someone like a hobo? *Pathetic.*

Listlessly, I grab my whistle and head out on the deck, staring blankly at the mass of students. I take a deep breath and blow the whistle in a long, loud, screech. Twenty-five kids look up at me with wide-eyed expressions. Yeah, they know they're fucked. "Everyone in the pool! Four sets of fifties, one of each stroke." The class groans in unison, but I just march on by, throwing them glares. "No resting, no talking, and no whining."

No one argues, not even that little pussy, Jase Meyers, whose dive is shitty and formless. I lean back on the lifeguard stand and fist the whistle, white-knuckled, in my hand.

If my day is going to be miserable, then so is theirs.

~

Micha finds me just before lunch, icing my ankle on the pool deck as I bark at some sixth graders to stop wrestling in the deep end.

"I think we should have tonight off," he says, arms stiff at his sides.

I'm distracted, checking my phone yet again for a text from Liesel. I give him a quick, annoyed glare. "What are you on about?"

"Tonight," he stresses. I don't know Micha very well yet, but I can tell when he's ramping up to a truly ambitious rant. His nostrils get all big, and he keeps swinging his floppy bangs to the side. "Tomorrow is the assembly, and the rest of my class gets to skip class to attend. If I were in a normal intro class, I would too. Therefore, I deserve to miss class tonight." When I just stare at him, he narrows his eyes, flinging a hand out toward the pool. "Our performance reports were positive. We work hard to suck this badly at swimming! It's just one class!" Quieter, pleading, "I really want to go to Avery Nolan's Lakevale watch party with my sister."

I check my phone again, putting it down. "Fine."

"But!" He pauses, mouth clicking shut, eyes widening. "Wait, really?"

"I said fine!" I snap, grabbing my whistle. "Now fuck off." The whistle shrieks when I turn to blow it, loud and sharp, at a sixth grader who won't stop using the diving platform scaffolding as a monkey gym. "Cooper! Detention with Dewey! Hit the showers!"

Cooper's jaw drops, but he slumps off.

Taking a deep breath, I turn back around and reach for my phone.

It's gone.

I swing my neck around, searching the deck, but it's nowhere. It was right fucking *here*! I shoot to my feet, eyes pinging around all

275

the kids, knowing one of them took it. It takes too long for me to spot the black rectangle at the bottom of the pool.

"No no no," I chant, not even thinking. I take my shoes off before jumping into the pool, but nothing else—shirt, sweatpants, all of it. When I break the surface, phone clutched in my hand, water is leaking out of the buttons and speaker. I give it a shake, but nothing happens when I press the power button. "You can't be serious," I bark at it, incredulous.

What the *fuck* is this day?

Now I don't have a car, I don't have a phone, my clothes are soaked, and I can't get into my own goddamn apartment for something clean and dry to wear.

This is the mood I'm in at lunch when I trudge my way to the admin office, water squelching from my sweatpants with every step.

I tightly explain the situation to the receptionist, omitting exactly how the keys got lost.

"I'll give Buster a call," the receptionist says, giving me an understanding look. "Why don't you check your inbox? A package came in today. Maybe it'll lift your spirits!"

A package.

Huh.

Lifting the box in my hands, I don't recognize the return address. I get tons of deliveries at Underworld, but those are all from business suppliers. I don't remember ordering anything personal, not that I really could have.

"Looking for these, young man?" I turn to find Dewey behind me, lifting a pair of keys in his hand. He lifts an eyebrow. "Perhaps there's a lesson to be learned about impulsive tantrums and—"

I snatch the keys from his hand and storm away, cutting him off.

The first thing I do when I get inside is make a beeline for the medicine cabinet, chugging down three hard gulps of chalky awfulness. The second thing I do is peel my wet clothes off, slapping them angrily onto the floor. I take a quick shower, just to wash the chlorine off me, and emerge feeling marginally better. Clean, dry clothes, Mylanta, and ten dollars for lunch will go a long way to resetting this shitty day.

Before leaving, I look at the package, holding back.

Using the key, I slice through the packing tape on the top, anticipating something good—or at the very least interesting. Maybe Liesel or someone shipped me something from home, like my laptop, or clothes, or I don't know, a goddamn Escalade.

It's none of those things.

I'm hit with an explosion of dust—*glitter*, I quickly realize—right in the face. For a long moment, I just stand there rigidly, hands held out at my sides, watching the glitter flutter off my eyelashes with every slow blink. I release a hard breath, which sends a cascade of sparkly sliver to the floor.

The *floor*, which is absolutely fucking *covered* in it.

I carefully limp my way out the door, waiting until I'm off my stoop before shaking the glitter off. It barely works, of course. Even when I pull off my shirt and drag it down my face and arms, it's still stuck to me.

I have to choose between taking a second shower and making it to the dining hall in time for lunch. It's not really much of a choice, but I still spend a solid moment debating inside my head. It really says something that lumbering into the dining hall covered in silver sparkles is the least worst part of my day. Even putting the hood of my sweater up to hide my glitter-dusted hair does nothing to disguise the fact that I'm covered in the shit. I get my lunch to go, but not before the kitchen staff and half the students notice.

"Love the look, Mr. Wilcox," one particularly brave sophomore calls out as I pass by.

My shoulders tense and it takes everything I have, *everything*, not to unleash the pent up rage of the day on him, but I don't. I keep walking, focused on what I have to do next. I can't get my car back if I'm locked in a jail cell for assaulting a fifteen-year-old.

By the time the school day ends, I'm ready to jump off a fucking bridge.

One upside to losing my phone is that I have to use the office line to continue my quest to contact my dad.

For once, it doesn't go instantly to voicemail.

"Hello?" he answers, sounding wary.

This would be the perfect time to have a calm and mature discussion with my father about consequences and penalties and how I've learned my lesson. He'll want to hear that I'm going to be better, and that I understand the position I've put him in, and that I'm ready to step up and be the Wilcox he raised me to be.

I take in a deep breath. "You took my fucking car?! How the fuck am I supposed to get to my PO? My job? Do you fucking realize what you've—"

Click.

I slam the phone down hard enough to hear a crack, and then I rest there, forehead propped on the heels of my palms. I don't know how much time passes. I just stew in my own head for a bit, wondering how I'm supposed to make this work when everyone is so hell-bent on me failing.

I don't even look up when the door to the office opens.

"Okay," Georgia says, sounding out of breath as the door clicks shut behind her. "We have an hour before dinner starts and I just saw Jamison leaving campus with his little sister, so we won't have to worry about him needing the office." Jamison is the swim captain who shares my office. From the little sliver of space between my arms, I see her reach beneath her skirt and shimmy her panties down her legs. "I'm thinking we can start with some light oral and then a quick and dirty fuck, and be out of here in time for dinner, then class after that—"

"Class is cancelled tonight," I mutter.

"Oh. Really?" There's a pause, and then an excited, "Then our night's free! We can go back to your place and—"

"No." My teeth grind. "I don't feel like fucking right now."

She sucks a click with her teeth, pulling her underwear back up. "Like I said, that's not how this arrangement works. You're the one who said you always wanted it, because—and I quote—'I'm a guy'."

I finally look up at her, exploding, "I have no car, no phone, and a dozen different assholes breathing down my goddamn neck, so being your sentient dildo is pretty fucking far down the list of my priorities right now!"

Her head snaps back in surprise, eyes roaming over my face. "Oh. Shit." Her lips pull back in a cringe, voice small when she guesses, "Glitter bomb?"

Before I can answer, the door bursts open, and Micha skitters through, flapping a paper. "No time to explain! You have to sign this." He slaps it onto the desk—a class dismissal form from the front office. I get this hot spike of useless anxiety that he could have just walked in me with my face planted between Georgia's thighs, but it's brief. Mostly I'm honed in on his nail polish, all purple and full of glitter.

Glitter.

Micha, standing beside me earlier on the pool deck, watching me check my phone.

Micha, the day that my clothes and shoes went missing, roaming around the natatorium before lunch, even though he had no reason to be here.

Micha, bored, picking glue off the pads of his fingertips a couple weeks ago.

Springing out of the seat, I lunge over the desk, grabbing the front of his shirt in a tight fist. "This is all you!"

Micha's eyes go wide before instantly narrowing, jaw locking. "Get off me, asshole!" He tries to pry my hand away, but it only works because I let go, shoving him back.

"You threw my phone into the pool," I growl, vision going red as I round the desk, ticking off on my fingers. "You stole my clothes, my shoes, put the glue into all the locks, that fucking glitter—"

Micha smirks at me, eyes flashing maliciously as his arms cross. "Finally figured it out, huh? Took you long enough. I thought you were smart, but you haven't even listed half the things I've done." When I advance on him, he doesn't even look scared, unfolding his arms to splay them out, like a welcome. "What are you going to do? I'm a minor. *A student*. You can't touch me."

"Wanna fucking bet?"

"Whoa!" Georgia suddenly appears between us, palm flat on my tense, heaving chest. "Calm down, Heston! They were just some stupid pranks. And Micha is right. He's just a kid!"

"He's a dead fucking kid," I seethe. "Do you have any idea how much that shit costs? Of course you don't, because you're a spoiled, rich little shit!"

She looks between us, expression torn. Finally, she says, "Micha, go. Heston will turn in the form later, okay?"

"It's not like you don't deserve it," Micha says, brows crouched low as he picks up his bag from the floor.

Georgia shakes her head. "Not now, Micha."

He slips through the door and I start angrily collecting my things—not that there's much—hoping Georgia will leave.

Unfortunately, she has no idea how to do that.

"What the fuck do you think you're doing?" She says, ducking her head to catch my fiery gaze. "He's a kid! A student! You can't intimidate him like that. Do you want to go back to jail?"

I chew on a million responses, each one worse than the last. Running my hand through my hair, I argue, "I had a shitty day, and that asshole was a significant fucking part of it."

She gives me an exasperated look. "Shitty days don't mean you can abuse people."

"Days like this do. You have no fucking clue what I went through today. While you were off flirting with your new boy toy, I was here getting curb-stomped by the universe. Look at me." I hold my arms out. It's been hours since I received that package, but glitter's still falling off. "I look like a fucking joke."

"Micha didn't send the glitter bomb." She sighs, looking away. "I did."

I stare at her, frozen. "*You* did."

She winces. "It was just supposed to be a silly joke. Obviously, I didn't know what kind of mood you'd be in when you got it. I'm sorry, okay?"

Taking a deep breath, I grind out, "Follow your own advice, Haynes. Leave."

19

Georgia

I've never seen Heston like this before. He's always calm and collected, calculating and smug. For years, I've basically operated on the belief that nothing got to him. Even lately, with the way he often looks tired and a little frayed around the edges, he's still carried an air of composed arrogance that made it seem like a temporary inconvenience.

The wild, crazed look in his eyes—the way his shoulder twitches with a barely restrained motion that I can't even predict—is something I've seen before. Just never on him.

It's more like Sebastian.

"Hey," I say, trying to get him to look at me. There's a patch of glitter glued to the tip of his nose, and any other time, it'd be absolutely hilarious. Instead, it just makes my stomach clench with guilt. "Tell me what's going on." When he doesn't answer, just releasing this short chop of breath, I reach out to brush my fingers against his tightly curled fist. "You know how you told me to come to you when I'm down or feel like hurting myself? You can come to me, too."

"I already told you," he says, voice clipped as he flinches away from my gentle touch. Even though I've just begged him to let me help, I really feel like I should duck for cover. "I've had a shitty day."

I reach for the waist of his pants and inch him toward me. "Whatever is going on, we can work through it." I splay my hands on his flat stomach, feeling the taut muscles underneath the cotton. "If you're frustrated, you should take out on me. Not Micha or whoever else crosses your path."

I lift up on my toes and kiss his chin. He turns away slightly—not a full rejection, more of a warning—but he doesn't respond. I look up at him and see his jaw tight, eyes pinched at the edges. His hands come down on my wrists and he pushes me away. "Sex is what *you* use to feel better, Little Red. What I need help with requires pants."

I tilt my head, regarding him. Any other time, the words might have stung a bit. Right now, I take them as the sulky request they're meant to be. "Tell me."

He looks away, the tendon in his neck jumping out with a swallow. "My dad had my Escalade repo'ed."

"Wait. This whole conniption of yours is because of a car?" I blink. "Jesus, you really are a Wilcox, aren't you?"

His blue eyes whirl to me, flashing in scorn. "Don't you fucking compare me with Sebastian," he snaps. "His cars are toys. Stupid childhood fantasies he plays with because he's bored. Mine was...*is*..." His jaw ticks around an aborted response, hand coming up to irritably rake his glitter-dusted hair back. "I *need* it. Without a car, I can't get to my appointments. I can't get to work. I can't do anything."

In an effort to be understanding, I ask, "Did you call your dad?"

"Of course I called my dad." He huffs, some of the tension falling from his shoulders. "When he does accept my calls, he just hangs up on me."

Ouch. I'm aware things have been tense with the Wilcox family, but I know from little bits Heston has revealed that his dad went out of his way to get him probation, so I figured the cold shoulder was just a temporary thing.

Pushing my hair behind my ear, I start. "Okay," and stiffen my spine into something that's far more assured than I feel. "Okay, problem solving. We can handle this. What can I do? How can I help?"

He snorts, head shaking. "What, like you're going to give me money?" It's said dryly, but the second it comes out of his mouth, he looks at me, considering. "Your parents *are* loaded."

I raise an eyebrow. "To pay for your Escalade? I don't think so. They keep an eye on my expenses. I don't think a charge covering the car of my arch nemesis is going to pass muster."

He rolls his eyes. "Fair enough."

I lean against the closed door, thinking. "You don't have any money? Doesn't Underworld get a lot of business? Can't you just pull some out of that?"

"No." Annoyance flickers across his features. "Everything with the business is tied up."

"Oh." I deflate, feeling a bit lost. Heston is right. My family really is loaded. I don't think about it much—it's all I've ever known, after all—but I'm not totally ignorant. I know I live comfortably, far better than most.

Sighing, he flutters his fingers through his hair, sending glitter scattering. "Just...can I at least borrow your car or something?"

"What for?"

"I need to go down to the dealership so I can resolve this. There's got to be some kind of arrangement I can make." Smiling bitterly, he adds, "Apparently I'm good at collecting those."

I don't say the first thing that pops in my head, which is that there's no way I'm letting him just take my car. "I'll take you down there. You can meet me outside the gate, two blocks down." I toss him a Preston Swim baseball cap hanging behind the door. "Wear that. I can't be seen driving you around, any more than you could be seen driving me around."

Thirty minutes later we're at the Select Motorcars of Northridge dealership. It's pretty off the beaten path from Preston students and faculty, so I bite the bullet and go in with him.

The manager, Jerry, smiles when he sees us, although his eyes skim critically over my uniform and Heston's faded sweats. Once he establishes we're not here to buy a car, but for other business, he offers us a seat in his office and a drink before asking, "What can I do for you, today?"

Heston reaches into a basket on the desk filled with granola bars and rips off the packaging. "My father and I are having some… disagreements. He repossessed my car today, and the paperwork said it came here. I want to see about getting it back."

"Ah," Jerry says, circling his desk and flipping through some papers. "Wilcox. Here we are. Even with depreciation, that vehicle has a value of over ninety thousand dollars."

Heston takes a bite of the granola bar and chews before asking, "How much will that cost me if I can't pay for it all at once?"

"How much do you have for a down payment?"

Heston's jaw freezes, mid-chew. "At the moment? None."

Jerry stares at him, and I can tell from the way his brow twitches that he's struggling to keep a composed face. "I see. Well, if you have good credit, we can try a traditional loan, which will be…" he grabs a calculator and punches in some numbers, "about five grand a month."

That flare of wild anger, the one I'd seen back at the pool, flickers barely under the surface. Before it can fully emerge, I jump in. "Jerry," I say, grabbing Heston's hand. "Can you give us a minute?"

He gives us a pandering smile. "Of course. Take your time."

He walks out, shutting the door behind him. I look at the simmering man beside me. "Heston, look. You can't afford this car. You just can't. I know that sucks and I know you don't want to hear it, but you're going to have to look for something cheaper."

He balls up the granola bar wrapper and throws it at the trashcan. It misses. "I'm not getting another car," he insists, arms crossing over his chest. He looks like a petulant toddler. "I already have a car."

I force my eyes not to roll. "You need something to get you to your appointments and work. It doesn't have to be an Escalade. For five grand, you can buy something used and still—"

"You're not listening!" he snaps, bringing a palm down on the desk. "It doesn't have to be an Escalade, it has to be *that* Escalade. I don't care if I pay five grand a month. I don't care if I have to pay ten."

Now, I do let my eyes roll. "That's just ridiculous."

"Of course it's ridiculous!" he explodes, reaching up to jerkily adjust the hat beneath his hood. "Fuck, you think I don't know that? I'm not an idiot."

I watch him for a long moment, the tired circles around his eyes, the way his hand tenses when he pushes it into his stomach, jaw clenched with a hard swallow. "Then what is it? Why is that car so important?"

"You wouldn't get it." He shakes his head, looking away. "You've still got everything. The money. The nice, *loaded* family. People tripping over themselves to help you, to make sure you make it through. People who give a shit. People who like you. I don't have anything." He meets my gaze, and I almost flinch at the spark of vulnerability I see there. "That car is it. The nice life with the loaded family? Aside from my name—and trust me, he'd take that if he fucking could—it's all I have."

"That's not true," I argue, trying to get through to him. "You have a successful business."

He gives a low, dark laugh. "Trust me. Even that's not mine."

I have no idea what that's supposed to mean. "You're more than a car, Heston."

He presses his fingers into a temple, massaging it. "You can't really be this naïve, Little Red. It's about having the best. It's about upholding a reputation."

I reach for his hand, looking bluntly into his tired eyes as I give it a shake. "What are you doing? It doesn't matter what kind of car you drive. You could be driving around in a piece of shit beater or the newest flashy Lambo, and no one would care." For a split second, the crease in his brow fades away. And then I add, "People would still look down on you. Your reputation is a total dumpster fire."

I've known Heston long enough to understand what he appreciates and respects, and I've always held unapologetic frankness as being high on the list. But the instant the words leave my mouth, I know it was the wrong thing to say. His expression alters, shifting from annoyed to something different. Something new and eerily still. It lurks in the way he averts his eyes, the tightness around his mouth, the tired curve of his shoulders. His very essence is *screaming* it.

I'm struck with the startling realization that I just hurt his feelings.

I didn't even know Heston Wilcox *had* feelings.

"Heston, I didn't mean—"

He stands. "Let's go."

I fumble with my bag and follow him out of the dealership and into the parking lot. I can't decide what I'd regret more; the offer I'm about to make, or seeing that look on his face and not making any effort to wipe it away.

In the end, it's an easy choice to dig into my purse. "Listen, I have a credit card for emergencies. It has ten grand on there. I'm sure my parents won't notice right away if I use it. Let's go back in, okay? We can pay for a month of the car. I'm sure by then something will give—you and your dad, the club, whatever." I reach for him, but he shrugs me off.

"Forget it," he says when he reaches my car. "Just drop me off at the club."

I eye him suspiciously. In the past, Heston has done one thing in particular to raise money. Gamble. I can only assume that would violate his probation. "Heston..."

His eyes snap up to mine, glossy and lost. A piece of glitter flashes in this eyebrow. "Can you just take a break from looking down on me and *not argue*? For once?"

"I didn't mean—!"

"What did I say before? I take care of my own shit."

At his dark-eyed glower, I deflate, unlocking the car. This isn't something I can smooth over in the parking lot of a car dealership. "Fine. I'll drop you at the club."

The ride is silent. I feel bad, even though I know I shouldn't. None of this is my fault. All of this is the consequences of his own behavior, and yet...

Seeing him like this doesn't give me any satisfaction. It makes my skin feel like it's not right. If Heston is one thing, it's consistent. I don't like this rash, diminished side of him. Everything feels wrong and just a little tilted. It's giving me vertigo.

"Do you want me to come in with you?" I ask when I reach Underworld's parking lot.

"No." He gets out but then leans back down, not meeting my eyes as he taps the hood of my car. "Thanks for trying."

He slams the door and walks away. I wait for a moment, wondering if I should follow him anyway, but ultimately let him go. Heston is not my problem. He's a fuck-buddy. My nemesis. He doesn't need me to save him any more than I need him to save me.

THE FIRST THING I do the next morning is find Micha and drag him away from his sister. "The pranks are done," I tell him, brooking no argument.

Micha brooks one anyway. "So what if he found out? Like I said, he can't touch me. Plus, I'm just getting started." There's a glint of excitement in his eyes when he adds, "Your glitter bomb was amazing. Public humiliation? It's the perfect revenge, isn't it? So now I'm really liking the food dye in his swim cap idea, but I was thinking maybe something more permanent. Hot pink?"

"Micha," I snap, willing him to understand. "It's over. Let it go."

He looks me up and down. "What's your problem?"

"All this stuff you're doing—that *we're* doing—it's gone too far." Shaking my head, I voice a more rational worry than me not liking the sight of Heston so beaten down. "You're pushing him, and I don't like how close to the edge he is. He's going to do something stupid."

Micha argues, "Heston always does something stupid."

"Not like this." Heston is normally a very calculated sort of asshole, but right now, he's frayed and unpredictable. "Just cool it, okay? He gets the point. You wanted to make him miserable, and you did. Job done. Mission accomplished. Take a bow, you beautiful jerk."

Micha groans, crossing his arms in so sulky a gesture that, for a moment, lends me this flash of clarity that he and Heston are probably more alike than he'd admit. "It was getting so good!" He gives me a hopeful look. "You really think I made him miserable?"

"Oh, definitely. You had him on the ropes." I pat his arm. "And look, I know Heston is...well, *Heston*. But weren't you sort of getting along with him? Didn't he stand up for you to Jase and Gus? Maybe it's time to just..." I flap my hand in an anxious gesture. "Let him be the change we all want to see in the world. Give him a chance."

Micha looks offended at the implication. "Get along? We watched two episodes of Lakevale together, and that thing with Gus and Jase was just Heston doing the bare minimum of his job." He gives me a suspicious look. "I think you're blinded by all those good Wilcox genes."

"Oh, come on."

"No, *you* come on," he insists, huffing. "He's handsome and ripped, and yeah, maybe he can occasionally cosplay as someone who doesn't deserve to take a barefooted hike on miles of Legos, but that doesn't make him a good person, Georgia. Being a good person takes effort and empathy."

"Okay, so maybe he isn't putting in the work to become a good person," I say, unable to argue with that much. "But I am. And I think knowing when to let shit go might be a big part of that. So..." What happens in the space after that sentence is a big realization. "I think...I think that's what I'm going to do."

Micha's eyebrows climb his forehead. "You're, like...what? Forgiving him?"

"Yeah," I answer, confidence building. "That's what I want to do."

Micha shifts, giving me a dubious look. "You know I've heard the rumors, right? You're obviously the girl on that video he passed around. He did those *things* to you." Part of me dies inside at the possibility of Micha having seen that. He must see this on my face, because he's quick to add, "Ew, I didn't watch it! But from what people say, it was pretty bad."

I point out, "And he's paying the price for that. I don't need to heap anything else on him. It doesn't make me feel any better about it. I thought it would, but I was wrong." Not liking the way Micha's watching me, I roll my eyes. "I'm not some stupid, gullible girl. Trust me when I say I'm doing it more for myself than him. I don't want to carry the poison of hating someone around forever. If I can forgive him for...doing *that*, then maybe you should try it, too. Isn't that what the Adams do? Forgive and rebuild? You're better than all this petty bullshit, Micha Adams." It's not my most subtle guilt trip, but it gets the job done.

When I turn on my heel to leave, he's frowning in thought.

I DON'T SEE Heston in the morning, and I don't see him at lunch, either. My thumbnail gets gnawed down as I search the faculty table, and then the benches outside the dining hall. It's ridiculous to feel this anxiety over it all. I meant what I told Micha before. I don't want to see Heston suffer unnecessarily. That doesn't make me a doormat, it just makes me someone with a baseline amount of compassion for other humans.

But the worry is stupid.

I know it's stupid, and yet I can't get rid of it. Heston is a grown man. If he makes a bad decision under duress, then it's not my problem.

So why does it feel like my problem?

There's an assembly on something exhausting—body image issues or unrealistic beauty standards or whatever—happening all of fifth period. I only step into the gym long enough to verify that Heston isn't there.

Not in the mood to feel crammed in with all those people, I

decide to duck into the Devil's lair for some silence. Clear my head. Soak in the peace.

When I open the door, Caroline's head jerks up. I freeze, hand clenching on the knob, and she quickly looks away, wiping her tear-stained face.

"I didn't know anyone was down here," I say, turning to leave.

But she shoots up, crying, "Georgia, wait."

I reluctantly turn back to her, mouth pursed. "What?"

"I'm sorry." She sniffles, loud and wet, and if she didn't look so miserable, I probably would have left already. "I didn't mean all those things I said."

I finally close the door. "Yes, you did. Somewhere deep down, that's exactly what you think about me."

"That's not true! I just—" She exhales shakily, taking off her glasses to wipe her eyes. "You're my best friend."

Lifting a shoulder, I reply, "It doesn't feel like it."

"I think I just got so jealous, because you're..." She waves at me.

"A huge slut?"

"No!" she cries, shoulders slumping. "You're so much prettier than me, Georgia. More experienced. More popular. More *everything*."

Crossing my arms, I bite out, "I'm not prettier than you, Caroline."

"Yes, you are! And that's fine. It *should* be fine." She pauses, eyes brimming over once again. "But I really wanted him to like me."

"Ozzy?" I guess, feeling annoyed. "How do you even know he doesn't?"

She sniffles again, looking away. "He doesn't look at me the way he looks at you. I saw him yesterday, flirting with you. Tugging on your hair. He's never like that with me."

"So what?" I burst, throwing my hands up. "Guys are horn dogs. They flirt with me because they want under my skirt. Do you know how many dates I've been on? Like a proper date. Dinner and movies, holding hands, a sweet kiss goodnight. The answer is zero." I shake my head, willing her to understand. "It doesn't mean anything. Out of all the guys I've slept with, none of them have wanted to stick around."

"But isn't that what you want?" Before my anger can flare up again, she elaborates, "You're always saying how that stuff is dumb, and how you don't want a boyfriend."

"I know, and maybe it is. But lately I've been thinking..." Taking a breath, I articulate the very thing that's possibly been bothering me for longer than I'd like to admit. "I've been thinking maybe it'd be kind of nice, you know? To have someone who wants all of me— not just the part between my legs."

"But you do have a date." Caroline's voice isn't unkind when she says it, head tilted. "He's taking you to the ball, isn't he?"

It still pisses me off. "He's only taking me because I asked! You could have asked him, and he probably would have said yes. But you didn't. That's not my fault! You never even told me you were interested in him. If you had, I wouldn't have—" I let out a frustrated growl. "Jesus, Caroline, you're not the only one who's insecure and faking it. I'm used to hearing that kind of stuff from other people, but coming from the person who calls me her best friend? You have no idea how much that hurt."

Her face crumples. "God, Georgia, I'm so sorry. I don't know what came over me. All I could think about was the two of you—" She gulps, hands wringing. "I was such a bitch to you. I wish I could make you understand how terrible I've been feeling about it."

"I don't want you to feel terrible," I insist, thinking of Heston and his horrible, no good, very bad day. "I want you to be better than that. Guys come and go. Best friends are supposed to be stronger."

She nods, chin wobbling. "I know. I'm just not used to feeling this way."

"What way?"

She pulls in another sniffle, seeming to choose her words carefully. "Like my chest is caving in every time I look for him and he's not there? But then, also like it's caving in when he *is* there. Like I'd do anything to make him notice me. To see him smile. To see him smile *at me*." She falls back into her chair, shoulders curving dejectedly. "I know it doesn't make sense. If he wants you, and you want him, I should be happy, right? Because I like both of you, and I want you to have what you want. But instead, I just feel so...*betrayed*." She's quick to add, "I know it's not fair. You're right. I could have said something, and I didn't, because I'm a fucking coward. I'm sorry." Her lip trembles again. "I'm so, so sorry."

I watch her cry, stomach dropping in sympathy. "I'm not interested in Ozzy," I tell her, dropping onto the couch. "I'm actually kind of...seeing someone. Exclusively. He's the only person I've been with since last spring." It feels strange to describe Heston this way, but it's all true.

Her neck snaps back, mouth parted in surprise. "Wait, seriously?"

"It's not a big deal," I assert, knowing from the look on her face that she sees it differently. "We're keeping it really low key."

Her eyebrows furrow. "Why?"

Averting my gaze, I admit, "It's not someone you or Vandy would approve of."

"What do you mean?"

"He's..." I rub my forehead, trying to find something that could explain without actually giving anything away. I settle on, "Well, he's older."

After a long pause, she hesitantly asks, "Older, or like...*old*?"

My head snaps up. "No, this is not an Afton situation!" When her lips twitch, I follow my impulse to smile back. It falls just as quickly. "If you knew, you'd judge me."

That miserable expression folds her face again. "I wouldn't judge you. You can tell me anything." She deflates at the look I give her, fixing her gaze to a frayed sticker on her laptop. "It's going to take a lot of time, isn't it? For you to trust me with something like that, after..." I nod and she gives me a sad smile in response. "I understand."

After a long beat of heavy silence, I try, "If you asked me to, I'd find another escort. You know that, right?"

She gives a short laugh. "No, I'm not *that* pathetic." More solemnly, she adds, "Or at least I'm trying not to be."

"Caroline—"

She cuts me off, putting on a brave face. "It'd be a lousy first date, anyway. I still don't know how to walk in heels, and I'll probably spend the whole night feeling awkward and lost. Emory said he'd take me, and he'll make it fun. You know how he is."

I smile sadly. "Big brother to all."

Caroline's eyes go wistful. "He's really smart, you know." At first, I think she's talking about Emory, which is comically inaccurate. But then she explains, "We're in the programming club together and he can code circles around me. You wouldn't know it to look at him, but he's got some serious skills."

Well, that's something to consider for the Devil spreadsheet.

"What about your guy?"

"My guy?" I ask, startled. "What about him?"

She rolls her eyes, laughing. "What's he like? Is he nice? Cute?" She snorts. "Okay, he's obviously cute if you're with him. But is it, like, serious?"

I hold up my hands. "Whoa, no. No way. We are so not like that. This is a purely physical thing."

"Oh." She blinks, clearly having expected some kind of love story.

"It's just way too complicated for anything like that."

"Because he's older," she guesses.

I re-phrase, "*He's* complicated. Like a Rubik's cube that's also a grenade."

She studies me for a moment and then says, "Well, as long as he makes you happy, then I'm glad. I know you've had some shitty relationships in the past. You deserve someone that treats you well."

"As long as it's not Ozzy," I add.

She laughs uncomfortably. "Yeah."

Things feel lighter when I leave the lair, and I can't help but think about what she said, that I deserve someone who treats me well. How likely is it that I find someone that treats me well and gives me what I want? Zero percent from what I've seen.

But when I get to swim class, Coach James is there. "Heston is out for the day," he tells me and Micha, "so I'll be instructing you this evening."

I know I'm in trouble when I look for him and realize he's not here.

Because it feels like my chest is caving in.

20

HESTON

"No." I climb out of Georgia's car, but then lean back down, not meeting her eyes. "Thanks for trying."

I slam the door and walk away, desperate for a drink and anything else to dull how shitty I feel. That turns out to be a nap, which I take in my office, on the old sofa where I used to sleep, before the crappy apartment at Preston. It's a fitful, unproductive sort of doze, full of too many half-formed thoughts, nothing concrete enough to give me any sense of purpose. But that's the way it is always is now. Floating from problem to problem, grasping for anything solid and finding nothing but air.

I end up spending most of it staring up at the ceiling, replaying her words in my head, over and over. It's nothing I didn't already know. It's just different hearing it said aloud like that, like letting it free gives it form and substance—the only thing I can grasp.

I'm nothing.

Not to my family, my friends, the people at Preston, and certainly not to Georgia fucking Haynes.

Gene arrives earlier than I expect. I'm not even two thumbs

deep into my self-pity when he slides up to the bar, giving me that smarmy grin.

"Why so down, champ?"

This isn't a bush I feel like beating around. "I need an advance on that ten grand."

He laughs in my face, which isn't exactly unexpected, but still makes my teeth gnash. "An advance on what? You haven't given me a single thing, Wilcox. What kind of fool do you take me for?"

I push my glass away. My stomach passed agonizing pain hours ago. I can barely feel it anymore. It's just another shitty part of my shitty life. "I'm going to get what you want, Gene. It's only been a few weeks. I told you, her family's not around. But we're closer now, seriously."

"Seriously," he mocks, scoffing. "You owe me ninety grand and you're expecting an advance on—"

"It's fifty grand," I remind him, voice hard. "I won the bet. You cut my debt in half."

He nods, taking a drink from Tara. "Yes, I suppose you're right. The bet where you fucked the princess and caught it on video for proof. Compelling stuff."

I don't like the way he says it, like he knows something I don't. "You got something to say, then say it. I'm not in the mood to fuck around with you today."

"You still don't see what's right in front of you. Amazing." He laughs, but it sounds neither amazed nor amused. Setting his drink down, he leans in. "Let me spell it out for you. You could have had that ten grand and complete ownership of this club weeks ago." His eyebrows rise. "You've already got what I want."

My head is shaking before he even finishes his sentence. "No."

"A video of their sweet little princess getting grudge-fucked in her own high school is better than anything you could possibly dig up. Something tells me they'd pay a lot of money to keep that from getting out."

"I'll go to jail," is what I say, but deep down, there's a stronger argument churning in my gut. I couldn't care less about her goddamn family. Gene can take them down all he wants. But the thought of dragging Georgia into it doesn't feel right.

It doesn't feel like a win.

Gene shrugs at this, offering, "We'll blur your face."

"No one is that stupid. It happened in my office, during my probation." If I close my eyes, I can still vividly remember the shape of the bruises I pressed into her hips. The way she cried out when I slammed into her. The exact fan of her hair over the desk, jerking around as I fucked her. Most vividly, I can remember being unable to decide if I wanted to fuck her or kill her. I can remember it, but it's been a long time since I've been able to feel it. "I'll be in hand-cuffs again long before you see a goddamn dime."

He spreads his arms. "No proof, though, is there? Criminal court needs evidence beyond a reasonable doubt. No judge would convict you on circumstantial bullshit like an office."

"It's not happening," I snap, banging my glass onto the counter. "Drop it."

"You want your ten grand?" he hisses, close enough that I can smell his cheap, disgusting aftershave. "That's the only way you're getting it."

"I can still dig something up," I insist, feeling it in my bones. All I need to do is wait for Collins to duck out again.

"Maybe," Gene says, voice scornful. "Maybe not. Your choice, Wilcox."

Long after he's left, I sit there at the bar, staring into my drink. I don't really have the appetite for it, but I throw it back, anyway.

I need to be drunk for what I'm about to do.

~

I'm not totally convinced I have his number memorized, which is the only reason I don't hang up on the first ring. Chances are, a complete stranger will answer. I still have a way out of this.

True to the luck I'm having today, it's him who answers.

"Sup."

Sup? If I weren't calling to ask a favor, I'd tell him what a fucking tool he is. It's swimming around in my brain, kicking up a storm that makes my knuckles go white around the office's receiver.

Yep. This is rock fucking bottom.

"It's me," I start, and then a rushed, "Don't hang up."

There's a long pause on the other end, absent of static or shifting. The voice that answers is full of irate disbelief. "Heston?"

I'm almost the one who hangs up. Briefly, I think I'd rather go to jail than ask this asshat for a favor. My mind goes back to the hot pokers under my fingernails. That's definitely preferable.

I gather up my balls and begin, "I need a favor."

"You need a favor? From me?" Sebastian makes a sharp, cutting sound. "Go fuck yourself."

"Wait!" I've gotten pretty good at hearing when someone's about to hang up. "If you do this one simple thing for me, I'll never bother you again."

"You're not bothering me now," he volleys back, voice growing angrier. "Go ahead and threaten me, you prick. I fucking dare you. I'll drive my ass down there and—"

"I'm not going to threaten you," I growl, knowing it'd be easier if I could. But I've got nothing over this kid anymore. "I just want you to do it because I'm asking." Any other person could throw out some trite bullshit about brothers sticking together, being blood.

Sebastian *laughs.* "Are you on drugs now? Because you must be out of your goddamn mind if you think—"

I barrel over him. "I need you to call dad and tell him to listen to me. That's all I want." Bitterly, I explain, "He'll actually fucking talk to you."

"You want me to play middle-man between you and daddy?" He laughs again, voice mocking. "Oh, this is rich. The tables have sure turned, eh, brother? I don't recall you standing up for me with dad when I needed it."

"You were too busy kissing up to Mommy to notice," I bite,

before remembering I need his help. I exhale. "Will you just listen to me?"

"Oh, absolutely. I have to hear this. What's so urgent that you'd actually have the fucking nerve to ask me for help?"

At least Sebastian, of all people, will be somewhat sympathetic to this one. "He took my car away."

Or maybe not. "And?"

I grip the phone in my sweaty palm, head throbbing. "And I fucking need it! If I can't make it to my PO every month, then I'll go back to jail."

"Well, tough shit."

The fucked up thing is, I know the easiest way of handling him. Sebastian is reliable in his loyalties—his weak spots. He doesn't like people. He doesn't even see the people close to him as potentials for gain. Sebastian *loves*—fiercely, recklessly, obnoxiously. Always has. If I dangled the choice of him calling our father or having another video of Georgia floating around out there, he'd have the man on the phone in ten seconds flat.

The threat lingers on the tip of my tongue, and not only because it's the path of least resistance. A part of me wants him to know what she's doing with me. That he's not the only Wilcox that can please Georgia Haynes. He's not special. I do it better. When it comes to her, *I win.*

But I swallow it back, because the instant anyone finds out about us, all of this—my probation, my bet with Gene, my arrangement with Georgia—is all over. I'm not ready to fold my hand.

I'm not ready to give her up.

"Sebastian." I dig my fingers into my eyes, watching the fireworks of phosphenes. "Please."

Click.

I place the phone down on the receiver neatly.

Whatever compelled me to make that call, it's simple to turn it off. I flip it like a switch, gathering up what parts of myself haven't been beaten down yet. This isn't how I work. I'm not impulsive and hot-headed. I don't appeal to a better nature that I already know people lack. I'm an engineer. I add up the numbers, outsmart my enemies, and make my play.

And I always play to win.

~

"You're not Caroline."

Oswald Collins looks just as surprised to see me, standing stiffly in the doorway to the computer lab. "Should I be? Because pigtails aren't really my brand." He pauses, adding, "Although she does look pretty cute in them. I just don't think I could pull them off."

I suppose the administration aren't complete dicks, because they've given me the day off on account of taking Coach James' classes yesterday, despite feeling 'horribly unwell'. Okay, maybe I'd put it on a bit thick, but it's not like it's a lie. My stomach is still stabbing itself to death, I just don't have time to worry about. My day off has allowed me a late night to construct a solid plan, and the ability to sleep in.

Tapping my thigh, I ask, "Where is she?" I know that lately she's spending lunch in here, what with things between her and the other girls still being all catty.

"I don't know." Oswald turns back to the computer, screen filled with a bunch of indecipherable coding gibberish. "Though considering how she skitters away every time she sees me lately, your best bet would be to look elsewhere."

Jerking my chin at the screen, I ask, "Are you some kind of computer whiz, too?"

He snorts. "I don't know if I'd call myself a 'whiz'. Caroline's definitely better with software."

I hum, eyes narrowing. Initially, the plan was to ask Caroline for help, which was bound to include a lot of begging and-or bribing. She doesn't like me anymore than Vandy does. The other problem with that plan is making sure Caroline doesn't actually understand what she's encrypting.

But I see the advantage in this. Oswald giving a bro a hand. Not knowing me well enough to be suspicious and nosey. Becoming culpable...

"I need help encrypting a file."

He types something into the code he's looking at, quick and confident. "What kind of file?"

"A video."

He looks far more interested in whatever he's typing. "There are lots of programs that do that—set a password or a pin. Sometimes even puzzles."

I look around at all the lab bays, shifting. "I don't have a computer, and I don't have the time to learn a program. Plus, I need something a little more sophisticated than a simple password."

His forehead creases. "Sophisticated how?"

This had kept me up for a lot of the night. Without a phone or any access to the internet in my apartment, I hadn't been able to properly research. "Something that lets it open once without any kind of block, but after that, it's locked down."

He pulls a face. "Yeah, that's tough."

My jaw clenches as I watch him, barely paying me any attention. "Can you do it?"

Finally, he stops typing, turning to regard me. "You want me to encrypt a file for you."

I bite back a smart remark. "Yes."

Oswald watches me, head tilting. "I'll do it."

"Yeah?" Well, that was easy. I pause. "Why?"

He frowns. "Why? You asked me to do it. Now you want me to justify it?"

I shrug and drop into the seat next to him. "I forgot you're new. People around Preston don't usually do stuff without a catch."

"Oh." he laughs. "Well, here's a why. My father loathes you. Like, he probably has a five-hundred-page manifesto written about you and your friends and how you're the scourge of the earth. If he knew I was doing you a favor, he'd lose his shit."

That much I understand. I fish the USB out of my pocket. "I can guarantee that your father would go ballistic if he knew we were even breathing the same air."

Ozzy plucks the drive out of my fingers and slides it into the computer. I reach out and wrap my fingers around his wrist. "You can't watch it."

His eyebrow raises. "Okay."

"Or tell anyone you did this for me." He nods and I release my grip. "It's nothing illegal," I add hastily, "but it's personal."

"Gotcha." His fingers work quickly, typing in more of the gibberish. "It'll take an hour or so."

I bend over, open my bag and pulling out a bag of chips. Pinching the top together, I open it at the seam. "No problem." I pop a chip in my mouth. "I can wait, and if you need to go to class, I can give you a pass."

This teacher gig has its perks.

I eat while he works, opening my phone and scrolling through my social media. When my snack is gone, I trash the bag and say, "So I hear you're going to the Deb thing with Haynes."

His nose scrunches. "Yeah."

"You like her?"

"Georgia?" He throws me a quick look. "Uh, she's nice and I'm happy to go, but she's not really my type."

I snort. Georgia is every teenage boy's type. Unless... "Wait. Are you gay?"

"Huh?" The clickity-clack of the keys pause and he looks up at me in surprise. "No." He spots my arched eyebrow. "Seriously, no. I'm not gay."

"Then how is Haynes not your type?" Big tits, thick ass, puffy lips...

He continues working. "Don't get me wrong, she's sexy and fun, but...I don't know, there's no spark there."

I stare at him. "Spark."

"Yeah, you know. That chemistry that flickers between you and a girl you're really into."

"So you are gay."

"Jesus." He shakes his head. "Look, I've heard the rumors about Georgia, that she's...easy. But that's not my thing."

"You're telling me you're not tempted by a sure thing?"

"Not really." He shrugs and frowns at the screen, focusing for a moment. "There's something awesome about being with a girl you're really into—not just for sex."

I don't know where Oswald went to school before this, but he is clearly not Preston Made, and he obviously doesn't have the stomach to be a Devil. Not with this kind of mushy, romantic bullshit.

"Well, you'll be too busy with your escort duties to worry about getting up her crinoline, anyway. Trust me."

"You've been to one of these?"

"Oh, yeah."

"Any tips? I have no fucking clue what I'm getting myself into."

I dig into my bag again and pull out a pack of crackers. "First of all, do exactly what you're told. Wear the tux, show up on time, and comb your hair, or else some mother hen will harass your ass about it for an hour. Then, stay away from the bar." I shake my head at the memory. "You'd think that a drink to take the edge off would be encouraged, but it's not."

His upper lip quirks. "Okay. Anything else?"

"The girls wear these super virginal, ridiculous gowns that cover everything but their tits. Those are on full display." I shoot him a hard look. "It's a test or something, don't even think about going for it, or you'll get a knee to the balls." I tip my cracker toward him. "And that makes walking down the stage awkward and painful."

"Jesus Christ, Wilcox."

I shrug again, but add, "Haynes is going to look good. Really good, but..."

"But what?"

"But..." I think about the chemistry comment and what I heard between Caroline and Georgia down in the Devil's Lair. I don't know why I'm doing this, but I chalk it up to some kind of Devil loyalty. "Sometimes the girl you're really looking for is right under your nose. Someone you've skipped over for some reason. Too plain. Too quiet. Too shy."

He ejects the USB and holds it out. "You like shy girls?"

I snap the file in my fingertips. It's still warm. "Hell no. Shy girls are the worst. I don't have time for that shit. But I have a feeling one of the shy girls may like you." I stand and shove the file in my pocket. "Thanks, man. Good luck on Saturday."

He opens his mouth to speak, but I've already walked out the door. Good ole Oswald may be a bit of a mushy romantic, but he's okay. Maybe not okay enough to be a Devil, but probably pretty solid for Caroline if that's what she wants.

And if this file works, everything's going to be right in my world, too.

∾

I get to Underworld earlier than I have in weeks. Tara's surprised to see me here before the sun's even set, but she nods at the VIP area and I know Gene and his boys are already kicked back in there.

The look he gives me when I duck behind the curtain tells me he knows I'm caving. He flicks his hand at his guys. "Give us some quiet time, lads."

"Nah," I say, leaning against the table beside his. "I want everyone around to hear this deal."

Gene leans back into his seat, looking unaffected. "There's not really much to negotiate, is there?"

"This," I take the flash drive from my pocket, "isn't blackmail. It's my collateral. You give me ten grand, and if I haven't found better dirt on the Haynes's in one month, then..." I shrug, giving the drive a toss in my hand. "It's yours to do whatever with." It buys me time and a nice chunk of capital to grow into something useful. I already feel itchy and restless with the potential laid out before me. This could get me out of the hole. It could get me *ahead*.

Gene looks thoughtful as his eyes follow the flash drive. "Fine," he decides, and he must think I'm a total idiot for believing it could be that easy. "After you show me what's on it."

Shrugging, I take a seat. "Find me a laptop."

Twenty minutes and two beers later, Dirty ducks into the VIP booth with a laptop tucked under his arm. He sets it in front of me, and then sits directly to my right, looking a touch too eager.

I give him a disdainful look. "I'm not showing you, idiot. Gene only."

Dirty throws me a glare, but at Gene's nod, vacates the seat. While Gene makes himself comfortable there instead, I plug in the flash drive and make sure the screen isn't visible to anyone but the two of us.

I only let a minute of it play. It's the moment where I bend her over the desk, slamming her chest-first into the wood. "*Shut the fuck up*," I'm sneering at her, kicking at her ankles, spreading her open. My hand disappears from the frame, and I can easily remember why, dragging it down her pussy, feeling how wet she was for it. "*You like it rough—I know you do. Take it like the bitch you are.*"

"*Fuck you*," she spits, hips squirming.

"*Stay still*," I growl, lining myself up. I slam into her hard, tangling a fist in her hair and smashing her head down as I begin fucking her brutally. The screen goes blank when I close out the video, deciding that's enough.

"Goodness gracious, Wilcox," Gene says, tipping back his drink. He blinks at his reflection in the dark screen. "I knew it was a grudge-fuck, but that was excessive. You sure know how to woo a girl."

When he goes to stand up, I stop him. "That's not all."

He sits back down, raising an eyebrow. "I think I've seen enough of your bare ass for one lifetime, but thanks anyway."

Shaking my head, I click on the file again.

A timer pops up; 29 days, 23 hours, 45 minutes, 16 seconds.

Gene puts his glass down. "And what's this?" But he already knows. I can see it in the way his mouth flattens into an unhappy line.

"Encryption," I explain, taking a long draw from my bottle. "In a month, it'll unlock automatically."

He slides me a displeased look. "Bit unnecessary, don't you think?"

Sniffing, I close the laptop. "Like I'd really believe for a second you'd hold on to this for a month. You were wrong before when you said our arrangement has misguided me into thinking you're a patient man. You're not. None of us are."

There's a long moment of silence where I'm pretty sure Gene is inwardly fuming. The guy's been doing this for a long time, though. "So in one month, this thing unlocks." His poker face is impeccable.

"Yes." So is mine.

He smiles without actually looking happy about it. He knows I got him. "Ten grand, with the understanding that you're to keep digging. And if you don't?" With a nod at the laptop, he concludes. "I'm sending this to mommy and daddy."

I'm the first to hold out my hand to shake on it.

That's how I know I've won.

~

The money is fucking *beautiful*.

I sit in my office, counting it. Underworld can pull in five grand on a Saturday night, but knowing that every dollar of this is *mine* just makes it sparkle a little brighter. There's a smell to it, that soft scent of paper and possibility that I haven't been able to enjoy in a long fucking time.

It's eight in the evening and I'm a little buzzed—on both the beers and the fat stack of money. This could buy me two months of my Escalade. *Or*, the voice in my head says, *you can double it.*

Yeah, right.

I can fucking *triple it*.

I haven't been to a fight or street race since Sebastian left, but I still have contacts. Guys who'd be glad to let me in on a bet. People who'd be happy to inform me of the players and their odds. Sure, it's a little less certain without having control of my own ringer, but fuck it. Chance is chance.

I'm halfway to calling Carlton before a cloud of doubt smacks me right in the chest.

What the fuck are you doing?

I have ten grand in my pocket, guaranteed money, which could be lost instantly—just like that. There was a time when I'd have been completely convinced this was the smart move. An investment. A business deal. Now, with my luck being so shitty and not having access to more?

I just don't fucking know.

What I do know is that the thought of tripling this money is making my chest feel all fluttery and eager in a way it hasn't in a long damn time, and *goddamn*. I like it. If I feel this good about ten grand, I can only imagine what holding thirty grand is going to feel like. That's security. That's an adrenaline rush. That's a real fucking *win*.

It's embarrassing how long I sit there frozen, hand on the receiver, paralyzed by two opposing forces. One wants that thirty grand like fucking *burning*. The other remembers just how shitty it feels to have nothing.

The only reason I reach into my wallet and pull out the business card—cell number scribbled on the back—is because I just need a second opinion. I have no one else to ask. Everyone who might come to mind would just hang up on me. There's only one person who's made it perfectly clear they're willing to listen to what I have to say.

Warren answers on the second ring. "Yes?"

I'm taken aback by the quick response, stuttering out a quick, "Uh, hey."

There's a brief pause before Warren asks, "Who's this?" It's not unkind, spoken in that weird, too-optimistic way he has.

Momentarily, I consider hanging up. I don't. "It's Heston. Heston Wilcox."

If he's surprised to be getting a call from me, he does a damn good job of hiding it. "What can I do for you, Heston?"

"I had this..." I'm still getting used to being on the phone with a person who doesn't want to instantly hang up on me, so it takes me a second to collect my thoughts. "I have this opportunity."

"What kind of opportunity?" he asks.

"I came into some money," I answer, rolling my eyes at myself. What can I possibly get out of talking to this tool? "I have it in hand, but I'm thinking I should double it." Only, now that I've had the thought of tripling it, doubling it doesn't even seem satisfying. "That's not...stupid. Right?" I fucking hate the doubt in my voice—doubt that Warren himself had placed there. "That's smart. It's growing wealth."

"Hm," he says, and I know from the disapproving way it sounds that he disagrees. "It's not exactly guaranteed that you'll double it, is it?"

I know what he's asking; whether or not this is a gamble. "I'm good at what I do," I argue instead of answering. "Whatever you're thinking, it's not like that."

Warren seems to take a moment before saying, "Okay, say you doubled it. What would happen then?"

At least that's easy to answer. "I'd be fucking set."

"No," he says patiently. "I want you to close your eyes and really imagine that money in your hands. Imagine holding it, knowing it's yours. What goes through your head, son?"

Without really meaning to, I do what he asks, putting myself into a scenario of having twenty—thirty—grand. Fuck, that'd be sweet, having all that money.

You know what'd be sweeter, though?

Having forty, sixty...shit, maybe even over a hundred grand.

"It won't be enough, will it?" Warren sighs. "It'll never be enough. Not until you've gone through it all."

The worst part isn't even the realization that he's right. It's that twenty minutes ago, I'd looked at this stack of cash and felt *good*. Now it just looks pitiful. It's nothing compared to a hundred grand.

It feels like I've lost something—that ability to see ten grand and actually enjoy it. Looking at it now, all I can see is everything it isn't.

All I can see is a loss.

"Heston?"

I clear my throat, but find myself unable to speak. It feels like something just carved out my organs and left me hollowed out, because I'm looking at all this money and I can't feel it anymore. The optimism is gone. The sense of possibility. There's nothing but the dark cloud of disappointment.

Warren's voice is gentle when he asks, "Where are you, son?"

I clear my throat again, eyes fixed on the money. "I'm at work."

"I'll be there in ten minutes."

He lets me hang up first.

21

I must be legitimately crazy.

That's the only excuse I have for the fact I'm sitting on Heston Wilcox's front stoop at ten thirty at night, bags circled around my feet. Twice now, I've stood up to leave, only to catch sight of the sparkles littering the concrete, and then dropping heavily back down. To say I'm reluctant to be here is an understatement, but I've been waiting for two hours, and now it seems almost as stupid to give up and leave as it does to stay and wait. What's that thing I learned in Econ last year? Sunken cost fallacy?

So no, not crazy. Just stupid. At least it's a pretty pleasant night. The sky is clear, and the lights from campus don't really reach out here, so I'm able to look up and see a pretty spattering of stars, the crescent moon a soft glow rising higher above the horizon with every minute I stay here.

It isn't until almost eleven that I hear the distant rustle of footsteps. For a moment, this doesn't seem like such a pleasant night at all. It seems dark and isolated, ripe for an attack. Aside from that, I'm completely unprepared to explain to someone like Buster what I'm doing on this stoop at this time of night.

It's Heston, though.

He jerks to a stop when he finally looks up, spitting a low curse. "Jesus, make some noise." He doesn't sound mad, though, just tired and a little defeated. Looking over his shoulder, he sweeps his gaze up the path to campus. "How long have you been here?"

"Not long," I lie, doing my best to perk up.

He watches me, eyes narrowed. "You're lying."

"No, I'm not."

"Yes, you are," he insists, tapping his temple. "You always smile with half your mouth when you lie. Fucking awful tell, never play poker."

Rolling my eyes, I stand, lifting my bags as I do. "Fine, I've been here for a couple hours. Now open up so I can pee."

He gives me a baffled look, but digs his keys from his pocket, shouldering past me to unlock the door. I groan at what I see inside. The glitter. *Jesus Christ*. It's all over the floor in here—and half covering an ancient armchair.

Heston throws his keys on an end table, the motion careless and unconcerned. "I don't have a vacuum."

I make a mental note to bring my handheld over, possibly tomorrow. "I'll take care of it. Only seems fair."

"Whatever," he mutters, running his fingers through his hair as he looks at me, considering. "You need it?" He doesn't sound like he did yesterday when I went looking for it, tight and frustrated. Tonight, he sounds like he'd probably be down.

"No," I say, but at his raised eyebrow, concede, "I mean, yes, okay, I always need it, but..." I lock up, wondering what's worse; me being here for something other than sex, or expecting anything after the last couple days he's had. I settle on, "This isn't just a booty call. It's urgent self-care."

His forehead screws up. "The fuck does that mean?"

Undeterred, I unload my bags. "Since I didn't see you at breakfast, lunch, or dinner, I've got Chinese—which will need to be reheated—and extra egg rolls, because I noticed before that you *become* a vacuum when they're around. Plus," I add, taking out my laptop with a flourish, "essential Lakevale viewing equipment. I already have last night's episode queued up and ready to rock." I pull out two cans of soda, which I'd gotten at the vending machine. "Drinks, and then grapes for dessert, just to give us the illusion of nutrition." Quieter, I mutter, "Also, they were all I had in my fridge." There's something else in the bottom of my bag, but I rub my palms nervously on my thighs and decide to feel that out.

One of my group counselors used to say that whenever we were feeling out of sorts, we should try taking a nap, eating a filling meal, and taking some time off, which was much more sophisticated advice than Afton had once offered to the Playthings about dealing with their respective men.

"Feed him and fuck his brains out, and he'll be right as rain."

He gives me a slow blink before his eyes slide to the things I've unpacked. "You came all the way out here, in the dead of the night, to eat and watch Lakevale with me?"

I pointedly do not remind him that I'd arrived hours ago. "Is that okay?"

"Why?" he asks, looking at the grapes suspiciously.

Okay, I guess he's going to make me do this. I cross my arms over my chest and explain, "I think I put my foot in my mouth yesterday. I really didn't mean you should be looked down on or anything. I just—" Frustrated, I shift my feet, ignoring the dark look he's giving me. "There are some things money can't solve. That's all I was trying to say."

After a moment, he drawls, "Okay," in a way that seems like he doesn't believe me, but maybe doesn't feel like talking about it. His gaze goes to the cartons of food I laid on the rickety little coffee table. "I prefer my Chinese cold."

Some of the tension falls from my shoulders. "Grab some forks while I use the bathroom?" I don't wait for a response, strolling to the bathroom like this—being here for something other than sex— isn't incredibly weird. When I turn to shut the door, I can see him still standing there, unmoving, staring at the food.

Inside, I do my business and wash my hands, looking around the space. The bathroom is tidier than I might have expected Heston Wilcox to be capable of. No towels on the floor. No facial hair in the sink. Feeling nosey, I inch open the medicine cabinet and gawk at five bottles of Mylanta. Excessive. Maybe there was a sale or something.

When I emerge, he's sitting on the couch, holding two forks like they're mystifying instruments, forehead creased as he looks at them. The wrinkle in his brow smooths when he looks up to find me. "Ready?" he asks, voice wary.

I take off my shoes before joining him, setting up the laptop on the table and folding my feet beneath me when I sit back, carton in hand. "You have to get comfy," I demand, nodding at the way he's sitting, curled over with his forearms propped on his knees.

"Comfy?" He tosses me a derisive look. "What were you expecting? Boy shorts and bunny slippers? I'm not one of your Plaything buddies inviting you over for a slumber party."

I roll my eyes. "Take off your shoes and your sweater, and relax. That's the whole point of this self-care thing." Thinking, I add, "And you should be so lucky to know the comfiness of Plaything slumber parties. We do it up right."

As he's kicking off his shoes and looking really put out about it, he asks, "Any chance those slumber parties get erotic?"

"Nope." But as he's lifting his sweater over his head, shirt riding up to reveal the toned expanse of his abs, I add, "Although I have made out with Elena."

He rips the sweater off, eyebrows hiking up. "No shit?"

I wave a hand dismissively. "It was a drunken bonfire dare. We made Tyson kiss Ben, too."

He pulls a face. "Scratch that last one and give me details on the first."

Raising my nose in the air, I say, "I don't think I will," and reach over to start the episode.

Secretly, I've been binging Lakevale from the first episode for the last ten days. It's already on its fourth season, so I still have a way to go before I'm totally caught up, but I've developed a sick sort of affection for it. It's not a *good* show by any metric—Heston is crazy for thinking otherwise—but I must admit that it's confusingly addictive.

I don't tell Heston this.

Instead, when the theme plays, I dig into my food, pretending like I'm not watching him from my periphery. He looks exceedingly better than he had yesterday. His eyes still have that tired, hard cast about them, but without all the tumultuous energy to accompany it, he looks less like he's on the edge and more like he's just climbed down from it.

Still, when the show starts, he eases back, knees spreading in that way guys always do when they're comfortable. He splits his attention between the screen and his carton of food, shoveling it into his mouth in a way that's entirely without shame or insecurity. I get the sense that I've just done something really effective here.

He catches me looking during the first ad break, fork halfway to his mouth. "What?"

"Nothing," I say, gaze lurching away.

This episode is particularly stupid, but embarrassingly, I watch with almost as much intensity as Heston. When Vivian Slandarson uses her position as head cheerleader to infiltrate Lakevale's counterfeit money ring, he makes a soft sound, head shaking. "Classic Vivian. She never learns."

The characters' cheer uniforms are a truly unholy union of black and neon green, which I make it a point to mock every episode. Micha usually throws something at me for having the 'audacity', but Heston is even worse.

"Don't be stupid," he sneers, gesturing to the screen. "The black represents the persistent state of Lakevale being decayed and rotten to its very core. But the green represents growth and life. It perfectly encapsulates the struggle for power between the main characters and the Lakevale elite. It's an ode to the endless cycle of rebirth."

I gawk at him. "You take this way too seriously."

He shrugs, but doesn't argue.

The more I think about it, the more it makes sense. Not Lakevale—that will never make sense—but Heston's weirdly intense affection for it. If I squint, it's almost like Preston and the Devils. The struggle between the old and the new. It must be strange for

Heston, being caught somewhere in the middle, too old to be a Devil and too young to be our foil. The more I roll it around in my thoughts, the sadder it is. Maybe he doesn't love Lakevale so much because it's a 'contemporary masterpiece'. Maybe it just reminds him of better times. His golden years. Times where he was bigger and better, the star athlete, a king of the school.

Maybe he misses it.

He finishes his food right before the episode ends, leaning forward to place the empty cartons on the table. I don't miss his relieved sigh when he sits back, sighing, "Fuck, that feels better." When I look over, his hand is resting on his stomach and all the tension around his eyes has disappeared.

Jesus, maybe Afton and my hippie counselor were right.

When the credits roll, it makes the room feel darker, nothing but the soft glow of a lamp illuminating the room. The air feels suddenly charged, and I know without turning that he's watching me. There's always a strange weight that comes from being under his scrutiny, like a phantom hand resting on the back of my neck.

There's nothing phantom about the hand that finds my chin, turning me to face him. I blink at him, those blue eyes so close and intense. The kiss is completely foreign, soft and chaste and full of something that I don't really understand but also can't get enough of. It's me who deepens it, but he meets me like he's anticipating it —maybe even hoping for it—licking slow and dirty against my seeking tongue. His fingers weave into the hair at the base of my neck, tugging me closer, and I can feel him shift on the couch, thighs flexing.

When I move to climb into his lap, he curls an arm around my waist and yanks me the rest of the way in a swift, powerful move that briefly disorients me. As soon as I feel him, hard and eager beneath me, my body erupts in a rush of white-hot need. I grind down onto him, swallowing the rough sound he makes, and when he grabs my ass, I let him guide me into a sharp, hard rock against it.

He breaks away, smirking with his red, swollen lips. "So this is how you butter guys up, huh?" He bucks his hips, squeezing my ass, and I shudder at the way he sounds. Heston's voice always drops an octave when we're like this. Pressing a kiss below my jaw, he adds, "I'm a bit insulted you think I'm such a cheap date."

I rock against his hard cock, enjoying the way his jaw goes slack in response. "One, this isn't a date, and two, I'm insulted you think I *need* to butter guys up when I have *these*." I lift my shirt off, tossing it toward the other side of the couch.

I'd never admit it out loud, but I can't get enough of how much Heston likes my tits. He's instantly a little more alert, head snapping back to get an eyeful of them. "Good point," he says, hands sliding up my back to reach for the back of my bra. He has it unhooked so fast, I barely feel his fingers against my skin when he undoes the clasp. Once the bra is gone, he leans his head back against the couch, those blue eyes drinking me in.

There's a look he gets sometimes when we're close like this. It's all over his face when he reaches up to cup my tits in his hands. It's not just the way his eyelids get heavy, tongue peeking out to wet his bottom lip. It's a flash of unguarded wistfulness in his eyes, like he's touching something he thinks might get taken away. It's not careful or tentative. He still pinches my nipple a little too hard. Still gives me a devious grin when my breath hitches as a result.

No, it's not careful.

But it's reverent.

He pitches forward, tongue tracing a slow, lascivious loop around my stiff peak before drawing it into his mouth. As I wind my fingers into his hair, stomach swooping with the way his mouth feels on me, I consider that we don't get enough of this. Heston is usually behind me, and even though it's no less hot, there's still something missing from those moments. Until right now, I hadn't been able to put my finger on it.

It's the way he looks at me, eyes glazed and blazing, when he breathes, "Fuck, your body is perfect."

It's what makes me give in to the impulse that's been enticing me for days now. "Do you still want to do anal?"

His eyes jerk up to mine, thumb freezing halfway in its sweep across my nipple. "Huh?"

I fight back a smile at the dumb expression on his face. "*Anal.* You wanted to do it before. Are you still interested?"

His thumb finally moves, some of that shocked stupor fading away. "I thought you were saving it for someone *nice*." The edge of his lip hooks up when he says it, like 'nice' is the worst thing someone could possibly be. "Weren't you waiting for rose petals, candlelight, lavender-scented lube—real romance?"

"Oh my god," I say, laughing suddenly. I collapse against him to hide how red my face probably is. But not for long. I rear back and strain to the side to grab for my bag, shoving a hand inside until I finally fumble for the bottle I'd brought. Giving it a wiggle, I reason, "Fuck you. Lavender smells really good!"

"Jesus, you're so fucking predictable," he groans, snatching the bottle of lavender-scented lube from my hand. Dryly, he adds, "If you tell me you have rose petals and candles in there, then I'll..." He pauses, face blank. "Well, I'll still do it, because it's anal and I'm not an idiot, but I'd never let you live it down."

"Come on," I say, rolling my eyes as I rise from his lap. "I don't need rose petals, but a mattress might be nice. Something tells me you're going to want me on my knees." I'm saying it so he'll understand that I don't have any illusions about what it's going to be like, but a part of me is also reminding myself. Because Heston is right. I did want to wait. Not necessarily for romance, but for someone I wanted to give something special of myself to; this one thing that hasn't been owned by anyone else. I try not to think too hard about why I want to give it to him.

As we're walking to his room, he curls his arms around my middle, nipping at my ear. "Always," he says, voice low and impish.

～

"You need to relax," he says, kneading his thumbs into my shoulders.

"I am relaxed."

His thighs shift against mine when he knees in closer. His voice is wry when he observes, "Every time my dick touches your ass, you clench up."

I dig my face into his pillow, biting back a laugh. It's more from nerves than amusement. When he'd stretched me out, it felt good, but also a little weird. "Okay," I say, releasing a slow breath. "Try now."

He makes a small, dubious sound, but one of his hands disappears from my shoulders, and a moment later, I feel the head of his hard, slick cock prodding between my cheeks. I arch my back, spreading myself for him, and it's the sound he makes more than anything—this soft, surprised punch of air—that makes me feel ready.

I can feel the strength of his body as he presses the tip against me, forcing it past the resistance until it slots in. I gasp at the sudden invasion, even though I expected it. "Wait, wait, wait," I breathe, reaching back to touch his thigh.

The sound he makes in response is this hard, low-pitched rumble that shoots straight to my center. "Just push back," he says breathlessly, "when you're ready to take more."

I give a testing rock, feeling him slip deeper inside, and the hand that's holding my shoulder clamps down hard. I'm hit with a sudden moment of clarity that I've never been in a more vulnerable position. Heston could just shove his dick in there, and there'd be nothing I could do about it. For a moment, it makes me tremble, but it's not fear I'm feeling.

I trust him not to.

"You can take it slow," he says, even though the words are spoken so tightly, I know his teeth are gnashed. I rock back again, gasping at the stretch and burn, but the momentary discomfort just amplifies everything. "*Christ*," he growls, thumbing the inside of an ass cheek, spreading me open as I slowly sink onto him.

I'm breathing so hard that it's a miracle there's any oxygen left in the room for the way he's panting. I don't need to turn to know he's watching every inch of his cock disappearing inside my ass. He keeps telling me about it.

"It's halfway in," and, "So close, Little Red," and, "You're taking my dick so fucking good." The last one is said in a tortured sort of awe, which is what gives me the nerve to rock back one last time, finally clearing the space between us. His hands come down to my hips, fingers digging into the flesh as he holds me there, spitting a low curse. "Goddamn, that's tight."

It *feels* tight, like my body is cautiously willing to accommodate the size of him, but not a single atom more. More than that is how full I feel, like I'm not alone inside my own flesh anymore. It tears a small, agonized whimper from my throat. "Heston. *Move.*"

He makes a breathless sound and curls over my back, hands reaching up to brace around my wrists, pushing them into the mattress as he eases his hips back.

The slow, wet drag of his cock makes my fingers twist into the sheets, toes curling when he thrusts back inside. He's breathing hard and shallow, these damp little punches of exhalations against the back of my neck as he fucks me like that. Slow. Careful. Nothing like I'm used to from him.

The burn is less now, my body having made up its mind about whether this is good or bad. "Y-you can move faster," I stutter, chancing a rock back into his thrust.

He huffs against my neck, voice strained. "Trust me, I really fucking can't."

For a moment, I'm confused, wondering what the problem is. But then I feel him shudder and go still—just for a second—long enough that I realize what's going on. "Oh," I say, burying a laugh into the pillow.

He's about to come.

"Don't," he says, voice full of warning as I bounce with a silent chuckle. "It makes you...*clench up.*"

It's like that for a while—slow and cautious, nothing but the sounds of our hitched breaths and Heston's occasional, soft grunt. It's good. It is. But my clit keeps seeking a friction that isn't there.

Maybe Heston senses this, because he eventually stills, wrapping a muscular forearm around my chest. He sits back and takes me with him, and I'm not expecting the way it makes me sink deeper onto his cock, shooting out a hand to brace myself.

He catches me, clutching me tight to his chest as I rest in his lap. "Easy, easy. I've got you." And he does. He reaches around to dip a hand between my thighs, the move less fumbled and awkward than it has any right to be. He groans into my neck when his fingers slide through my folds. "Fuck, you're so wet for this. You actually like it, don't you?"

"Yes," I gasp, unable to feel shame when he touches me like this, so riveted and obliging as he rubs tight circles around my clit.

"Jesus, I can't believe you're—" His words bite off, lost to the motion of our bodies. It's so much hotter in here than it was mere minutes ago, the heat of his body feeding my own until we grow slick and flushed with it. He grasps me tighter, crushing me to his chest as his heaving breaths wash over my ear. "I don't care how many people you've fucked. But this?" He bucks his hips, making me cry out as he drives my ass onto his dick. "*This* is mine," he says, voice rough and guttural as his fingers work me over.

I feel drunk on it, so senseless that I'm babbling, "Yeah, it's yours, it's yours," and I just keep repeating myself. Probably because every time I say it, he rubs my clit a little closer—a little harder—until my thighs are quaking and I can't even move. I'm completely at his mercy, impaled on his dick as he rubs me off, grunting hard into my sweaty neck.

My orgasm rocks through me like an avalanche, starting deep inside and blooming out, making my back arch into the cradle of his body.

He growls a clipped, "Fuck," and then I can feel him surging inside of me—around me—filling me with his release. I'm still whimpering small, nonsensical things as I come down, breathless and burning up, but it doesn't matter that my limbs won't work. He lays us down gently, rolling us to our sides, and even when his dick slips free, he doesn't leave.

"Damn." He pants into my shoulder. His voice is grave, but when he props up on an elbow to look at me, I can see the spark of humor in his eyes. "Lavender is going to get my dick hard now."

I reach behind me to smack his arm, laughing breathlessly. "Oh my god, shut up."

"This is serious!" He dodges my hand, reaching out to snatch up my wrist. "What if Dr. Ross wears lavender perfume? You need to think about these things, Little Red."

It's then that I notice one of my bracelets is missing. "Oh no," I whine, but it doesn't take me long to find it wedged beneath my ribs. I dig it out, frowning. "I broke my tennis bracelet!"

It'd probably be more accurate to say that Heston broke my tennis bracelet, which must be why he heaves out this enormous sigh and says, "Give it here." Rolling to his back, his brow creases in thought as he lazily inspects it. "I think it can be fixed."

I turn toward him, resting my cheek on his shoulder to watch him fiddle with the clasp. "Good. Sebastian gave it to me."

He slides me a look, asking, "He did?"

I nod. "Last spring. It was a gift."

He hums as he turns it over in his hands, expression thoughtful.

And then he chucks it across the room.

"Hey!" I shoot up to catch it, but it's too late. It hits the wall and bounces off the dresser, disappearing somewhere behind it. "Heston!"

"It's garbage."

"It's pretty!" I snap, whirling around to glower at him.

He drags me back down, looking way too grumpy for a guy who just had sex. "You really want to wear something my brother bought just to get in your pants?"

Yes, is the answer to that. Sebastian has excellent taste in jewelry. Aloud, I say, "He wasn't trying to get into my pants. He'd already met Sugar by then. In fact, that's the reason he gave it to me. It was a 'thank you' for having his back." Sniffing, I rest back against his shoulder. "All the Playthings got one."

"Exorbitant overspending to make up for a lack of personality. Yep, sounds like my little brother." It's a bit ironic, since that's exactly how I might have described Heston a few months ago. He pulls me closer into his side, arm trapped under my waist. "Don't know why he'd need anyone to have his back with the trailer trash, anyway."

"Shut up." I shoot him a glare. "Sugar isn't *trash*, okay? She's had a really hard life, and she's strong as hell. She's *amazing*. You don't know anything about her."

"Whatever." He rolls his eyes, obviously deciding not to argue with me on this.

"We never had sex, you know. Sebastian and I? We fooled around, but...never *that*." I let my hand rest on the hard, flat planes of his stomach. "He and Sugar make a good couple." I say, hoping that he'll understand that I have no interest in Sebastian. He's a really great guy, but the chemistry was never there. For some reason, my words only serve to instill the silence with a heaviness that I don't really understand.

He clears his throat before tucking his hand behind his head. "My dad would have never let me date a girl like her."

I glance up at him, noting the tired lines around his eyes. "No?"

He shakes his head. "He would have wanted me to be with a girl like you, actually."

I snort, looking down to watch my fingers play in the hair below his navel. "There was a time my mom would have thrown a parade for me snagging a Wilcox. Before you besmirched your good name, that is." I worry for a moment that the comment might irk him, but when I chance a look up, he's just staring at the ceiling, eyes distant.

"That's why he really cut me off, you know. It wasn't the gambling or the videos. He wouldn't have given a shit if I'd done that to a girl like Sugar." His lips flatten into a tight, wry curve. "It was because you and Sydney were society girls."

I frown at him, feeling his stomach cave at the tickle of my fingers. "That seems a bit ungenerous."

"No," he instantly says, finally meeting my gaze. "That's what gets me. People think he's this upstanding moralist for putting his foot down and cutting me out. But it's all bullshit." He watches me, eyes searching mine. "When it came to girls, Sebastian and I had all these rules. Some of them were hard-coded into our trust funds, like that we needed to use birth control."

I give him a skeptical look. "You can't be serious."

He raises an eyebrow. "Oh, I'm serious. Do you have any idea how much our trust funds were—*are* worth? Imagine knocking up some random girl. She'd run roughshod over your bank account. It's easier to put on a rubber than bribe some girl into getting an abortion, so that's what we had to do."

I throw my leg over his, wondering, "Then why is it you *refuse* to ever wear a condom?"

"Because I love a good gamble?" He shifts his shoulders in a shrug. "I don't have to now. It's basically one of the only bonuses of this whole shitshow. Why shouldn't I take advantage of the finer things?"

"Well," I say, "I can see the logic in him not wanting you to have a child out of wedlock. I'm not sure how that makes him a bad person."

Shaking his head, he adds, "That was just the beginning. My brother always had it easy, but me? My dad was always on me to protect the family. He used to say that, with the way I treat girls, I'd need evidence. Insurance." He looks at me, eyes shuttered and blank. "Proof that they wanted it."

"You mean..." It finally dawns on me what he's saying. "Are you saying he wanted you to make those videos?"

"Wanted me to? Hell, he's the one who taught me how." He looks away, giving a slow, heavy blink. "Like I said. He's not the saint everyone thinks he is. He's not mad at me for doing it. He's mad at me for getting caught."

I think about that for a long time, tucked into Heston's side, the sweat drying from our skin. It'd be foolish to think that Heston's nature isn't his own.

But maybe nurture played a part, too.

22

Georgia looks peaceful when she's sleeping. Her red hair is fanned out over her shoulder, disappearing into the valley between her tits. I spend a long time looking at her body. I wasn't lying before when I called it perfect. That's exactly what it is. I've never had anyone as perfect as Georgia, with those full lips and shapely tits. Her skin is pale and smooth, but perfect for marking up. Her ass is round and ripe. Even her legs are great—soft thighs and dainty ankles.

For the millionth time, the thought crosses my mind: I can't believe she let me fuck her in the ass.

Maybe I should feel bad about it, because she might have played it off well enough, but she was clearly hoping to save it for something special, and I'm not stupid enough to think that's me. Maybe it was selfish for me to take it. Maybe a nicer guy—a guy like Oswald—would have been faced with the choice and made the one that was best for her.

I just really fucking wanted it.

Not only because anal is hot as hell, but also because of something else. I'm not great at explaining it to myself, but I think I wanted a piece of her. Something that was all mine. Ten years from now, she might be married and living the dream with some rich fucker who can buy her pretty jewelry, but he'll never be the first to fuck her in the ass. That's mine and mine alone.

It makes me toss and turn until I'm just laying here looking at her—this woman in my bed—feeling agitated and restless and so turned on that my dick is aching.

I move carefully when I slide out from under the leg she has tossed over mine, freezing when she stirs, only to clutch my vacated pillow and sigh, stilling once again. I move quietly across the room, unable to help myself from glancing back at the smooth curves of her bare ass as I pull on my shorts. I make a quick stop in the bathroom, and as I'm washing my hands, I look up at the medicine cabinet. It's a habit to reach for it, but I pause with my hand on the edge, thinking.

My stomach isn't hurting at all.

I leave without even opening it.

The laptop is still on my coffee table, empty cartons of food scattered around it. I'd had this plan since the moment she pulled it from her bag, wondering how best to get some time alone with it.

The memory card I'd found in the Devil bunker is still tucked into my wallet, so I pull it out, taking a moment to find the slot on the laptop before sliding it in.

Inside the folder that pops up are three videos. One is labeled 'Vandy Hall', another 'Caroline Richmond', and then 'Georgia Haynes'. I peer cautiously down the hall, listening for any sounds of wakefulness, before clicking the video file for Vandy.

"It started a few years ago," comes Vandy's voice, booming through the speakers. I dart forward, fumbling for the volume. *"I had a few surgeries that first year, and they had me on morphine for a while. Eventually, they put me on other painkillers. They were patches sometimes, but usually pills. I was almost always hurting, so I was almost always on them. It didn't seem like a big deal at the time. At some point, the pain stopped being so bad. Or, at least, it wasn't bad all the time. I could have stopped taking them."* She looks up into the camera. *"But I didn't."*

I realize what these videos are; the confessions they'd told me about. The ones that were a part of their initiation.

Vandy goes on about being addicted to the pills, but that's not news to me, so I close it out, glancing between the other two videos. Curiosity gets the best of me, and after listening for any movement from down the hall, I click on Caroline's.

"*My mom forged documents and paid someone to take the SATs for me. 'I' got a 1540.*" Caroline rolls her eyes, shrugging. "*She got a few wrong so it wouldn't look suspicious.*"

Boring.

I close it out, but I wait a few minutes before clicking on Georgia's. Fuck, this could be anything. This could be the dirt Gene's been looking for. This could be about her fucking someone sketchy. This could be something humiliating.

Reaching out, I rest my finger on the button and press down.

The screen changes to an image of Georgia in a badly lit room, nails picking at the seam of her jeans. "*I told everyone that I went on a six-month foreign exchange program to France during freshman year.*"

Her eyes are cast down, and she's younger here, different in the way she's curled in on herself. This is nothing like the woman currently sleeping in my bed, usually so fierce and assured. This Georgia looks nervous and reserved, voice quiet as she says, "*Really, I was in a psychiatric facility for what they called a major depressive event. But I was just... well, there was this video going around...*"

I click the button, stilling the image of her downcast eyes. "Shit," I mutter, dragging a hand down my face. That *fucking video*. Part of me is annoyed, because goddamn. I didn't tell anyone it was her. What's the big deal?

Another part of me remembers her saying that I'd showed the world a part of her she didn't understand yet.

Sighing, I start the video back up.

It's Carlton who speaks next. "*Oh shit! That was you!*"

Georgia's eyes go wide and hunted, and she turns them on Emory. "*This stays here, right?*"

Emory looks confused. "*Uh, yeah. That's the point.*"

She looks away, and everything about her looks limp. "*I broke up *with this guy, and he...well, you all know by now."* Her head comes up long enough for me to see a corner of her mouth pull up deprecatingly. *"He posted that video of us."*

My eyebrows shoot up in surprise. I don't need to see the tell to know that she's lying. We were never together, and she certainly never broke up with me. The way she avoids their gazes tells me exactly what's going down, though. She doesn't want them to judge her. Better to be a victim of some pissed-off, jilted asshole than the reality.

"I couldn't believe that he'd do that, and it's just always out there. It doesn't matter that you can't see my face, it's still—" She works her jaw, eyes growing wetter. *"It's such a violation. Most mornings, I couldn't even get out of bed, but when I did, I just wanted it all to end."* She adds in a rough whisper, *"So I tried to hang myself."*

I stare at the screen, missing whatever Elena says in response. Somewhere deep in my gut is a razor-sharp, excruciating twist, because I wasn't wrong before. Georgia is a shitty liar.

And she's telling the truth.

Through the muddled storm in my head, I hear her voice saying, *"I still see it sometimes, you know. All you guys share it around like it's this...fun thing. But every time I see it, I just hate myself."* My hand comes down heavy on the lid of the laptop, closing it with a quick click. I dig the memory card out of the slot and lean back into the couch, eyes sliding closed, jaw clenched.

"Fuck." I fist the card in my palm, feeling it dig into the flesh.

I've felt this before. The gnawing pain in my stomach. The swirl around my temples. The churning, angry, empty thing in my chest. I fucking hate it. It's the worst of the worst. Back then, when it was all about sitting in a sterile hospital lobby and waiting to hear whether or not my mom was breathing, I bitterly thought of it as disappointment. I thought my mom should be stronger and smarter, more resilient.

But when I put the memory card away and pad back into my bedroom, laying eyes on Georgia in my bed, all soft and fierce and full of life, I know that I was wrong. Because this thing I'm feeling right now isn't disappointment. Georgia's strong, smart, resilient.

Someone just came along and cut their way inside, poisoned her enough to make her doubt it.

It doesn't feel simple enough to put a single word to, but if I had to try, I'd call it guilt.

When I climb back into the bed, she wakes just enough to shift, curling into my side like she's seeking my warmth.

I've never felt colder.

∿

My first thought when my alarm goes off is that Georgia's gone, and that's a bummer. I could have used some morning sex for this morning wood that's digging into my mattress.

My second thought is the memory of that video last night.

It sits heavy and painful in my gut, forcing me to the medicine cabinet before I've even had my morning piss. I feel too much like I have a hangover for someone who didn't even drink yesterday.

When I get back out into the living room, the empty food cartons are gone. The laptop. The bra, the shirt, the shoes. Like she'd never even been here.

To think I'd been so disappointed in that ten grand last night after realizing it could have been a hundred. Now I lay it all out on my table, in the spot the laptop used to be, and stare at it, mouth resting on my knitted fists.

I sold that video of Georgia for this money. I lied about the countdown timer—just a little trick I talked Ozzy into adding so Gene would think the encryption was temporary—but it doesn't make it any less true. I sold that moment. *Her* moment. A moment of vulnerability, maybe full of something she still hasn't had a chance to understand. How could she, when even I don't?

And what the fuck did I sell it for? Two months of my goddamn Escalade?

Suddenly, this money doesn't look disappointingly small. It

looks really fucking big now. *Huge*. Important. Like something I need to make matter.

And I'm not sure that'll make it any better.

Warren picks me up at the gate early, a ride I'd arranged late last night over a bitter cup of coffee at The Nerd. He gives me a nod when I get in, slipping my seatbelt over my chest.

"Change of plans," I tell him, clearing my throat.

He looks fine with where I ask him to take me, although he shoots me a concerned look. "You still have the money, right?"

I take a second to realize what he's asking. I know I look tired and rumpled, probably sullen, so I'm quick to chew out a terse, "I didn't gamble it."

"Good. That's *good*, Heston." He nods, sending a small grin to the road. "For whatever it's worth, I'm proud of you."

I stare out at the passing scenery, face feeling barer than carved stone. "Don't be."

We have to wait in the car for ten minutes for the place to open, but for once, Warren doesn't try to make conversation. He lights a cigarette and rolls down his window, watching the passing traffic until a short little round man waddles up to the door and starts unlocking the door.

"You good?" Warren asks as I reach for the door.

"Yeah," I say, pausing before climbing out of the car. "Thanks."

It doesn't come out as easily as it had when I said it to Georgia, but Warren doesn't seem bothered by it. "Anytime."

The short little round man shows me around, and when he asks, "What's your budget," I look at a beaten-up Toyota and say, "I'm looking for something cheap. Three, maybe four grand."

He follows my gaze, nodding at the car. "Then that's out of your price range. Follow me."

I have to rush back to Preston for my first class, and the crappy Honda I'd settled on—thirty-five-hundred—doesn't really like it. Nevertheless, it drives. In another life, where my brother and I didn't fucking hate each other, I probably would have asked his opinion. As it is, I have to hope the weird grinding sound happening every time I accelerate is just a normal flaw in something this...*aged*. I pull a face at the dusty dash, knowing that it's a piece of shit—knowing people will *see it* as a piece of shit.

But at least it's *my* piece of shit.

It's ten minutes before his and Georgia's class starts and Micha's standing in the doorway of my office, waiting for me to acknowledge him.

"I'm not in the mood, Adams."

Huffing out a breath, he sweeps in like he owns the place. "Look, if I'm being honest? I don't regret most of the pranks I pulled—it was hilarious—but..." When I look up, he's glaring at his shoes, arms tightly folded over his chest. "Maybe dunking your phone was too far. It was nice, and probably expensive, and I know not everyone has money." He finally looks up, reaching into his bag. "So here."

I raise an eyebrow at the box he extends to me, a glossy photo of a phone embossed on the front. "You bought me a phone?"

"Not exactly." He shakes it, insistent, and I know from experience that going along with Micha is easier than arguing with him, which is the only reason I snatch it from his hand. He watches me inspect it, explaining, "We give these out at the library for our low-income food drive program. It's already got a plan and everything. It's not the best, but it'll get you by until you can get another one."

My face curdles. "You're giving me a *charity* phone?"

"Yeah." He props a fist on his cocked hip, looking haughty. "Got a problem with that?"

I look down at the phone, which is nowhere near as new or nice as my last one. On the other hand, it's better than nothing. "No," I decide, kicking back as I tear into the box.

Micha lingers annoyingly as I unbox it, straightening out the charging cord and powering it on for the first time. He's fidgeting with the zipper to his bookbag, and I don't miss the brief glances he sends me. "So," he starts, sounding tentative and quiet and weirdly hopeful. "Did you see Lakevale?"

I look up at him, nose flaring with my sigh. This little shit really pushed me too far. But watching him watch me back, eyes shrewd and bracing, like he's expecting me to strike out, all I feel is begrudgingly impressed. Micha Adams takes care of his own shit, and I respect the hell out of that, apparently even when that shit is *me*.

Shaking my head, I thumb my name into the phone's start-up screen. "Vivian, right?"

He exhales loudly, but then instantly bursts, "She never learns!"

"At least Mortimer and Nancy finally hooked up. Was getting sick of that whole plot line."

"Isn't it the best!" He pours himself into the chair, elbows resting on my desk. "Who do you think killed Mina?"

We lob theories back and forth until Georgia arrives, looking between us warily. "Everything cool?"

"Yup," Micha says, grabbing his bag and standing. "I'm going to get dressed out. See you in five."

She watches him go and then looks back at me, raising an eyebrow. "The two of you worked it out?"

I don't answer, because it's the first time I've seen her since last night, and it's this disturbing, violent clash of images that crosses my mind. Her, spread out on my bed, taking my dick. The wetness of her eyes as she told the Devils about the video. The soft part of her mouth as she sank down on my dick, teeth digging into her lip, against her feet swaying as she hangs, lips blue, eyes wide and lifeless.

I try to shake out of it, standing up to move to the door. I close it with my foot at the same moment I grab her by the arm, pushing her up against the wall and taking her lips in a hard, burning kiss. She makes a soft sound of surprise, but melts against me, arms winding around my neck as I lick into her mouth.

It's a dirty kiss, full of hard breaths and an urgency that I can't exactly explain, probably made all the weirder by the way I grab her chin, breaking away to look at her. Her eyes aren't green this close up. They're a whole palette of colors—browns, blues, hazels —all bleeding together to create this brilliant emerald that's shining back at me. I want to tell her not to be stupid. I want to say I'm sorry, and that I'll make this money count, and that what she admitted to in that video isn't worth it. *Nothing* is worth that. Death is never anything but a loss.

But staring into her emerald eyes, all I can afford to say is, "You have to win. Got it?"

She gives me a confused look. "Is this another lecture on my stroke? Because I already told you, it feels weird to—"

I silence her with another kiss, not missing the scent of the perfume she's wearing.

Lavender.

∼

The next two days are blissfully free of bullshit. After Monday, most of the kids in my classes are so terrified of getting sent to Dewey that they behave particularly well. After getting the video, Gene chills out hard enough that he actually doesn't bother coming to the club for a couple nights. Even my stomach seems to settle, giving me some respite from the usual background ache that's always there.

Georgia and I have become pros at finding places to fuck. If it's during school hours, there's the utility closet, good for some quick, hard, dirty fucking against a shelf, or the Stairway to Hell, when weather permits. If it's outside of school hours, she'll come to my apartment, but since I need to get to the club every evening, we make it just as fast.

Either way, it's always hot, frantic, quiet, and a little too rushed. I only really had it once, but I already miss the idea of her spread out naked on my bed, free to touch and taste at my leisure.

This is why I've been looking forward to the weekend, even if we're both too busy to commit to anything solid. I know she's got that stupid ball, which is going to take up all day tomorrow, and tonight I need to be at Underworld. That means if we want any time together, we're going to have to either take it now or wait until Sunday.

Fuck waiting.

I walk across campus, unabashedly seeking her out. At first I'm not sure why there are so many students still on campus. They usually clear out pretty fast on Friday afternoon. But then it hits me; there's an away football game and most of them are waiting around for the bus. Two of them are Vandy and Caroline, who are both waiting near Georgia's dorm. Biting back a groan, I pull back, ducking behind one of the massive oaks nearby. Neither of them saw me, which is good because they can't. We've been a little risky lately, lazy with the way we've been running around, but these girls? Devils or not, they'd throw me under the bus, even if it's just to protect their friend.

I peer around the tree, noticing that Vandy has a fancy camera hanging around her neck. I remember now that she works on the paper.

"Where is she?" Vandy asks, hands resting on her camera. "I need to get on the bus or Mr. Lee will throw a fit."

Caroline answers, "She said she'd be here."

"She probably forgot." Vandy pulls out her phone and checks the screen. "You know how she is. I love her like a sister, but she can be so flaky sometimes."

Caroline hums. "Maybe she's with that guy she was talking about."

Vandy's neck snaps up, eyes narrowing. "What guy?"

Exactly, Caroline. What guy?

"Um," Caroline rubs her neck. "Well, when we had that fight about Ozzy, she told me she was seeing someone. Nothing serious," she adds quickly, "but apparently it's exclusive."

"Why didn't she tell me?" Vandy sounds hurt. Maybe a little worried.

"She said we wouldn't approve." Caroline looks up at the dorm. "He's older and apparently 'he's complicated'." She uses air quotes. "You know she's not super open about her dating, or...well, *sex* life."

It clicks pretty quickly that I'm the guy her friends wouldn't approve of.

"Is she embarrassed of him or something?" Vandy asks, frowning. "If he makes her happy, then—"

"I told her that," she cuts in. "If I had to guess, I'd say the sex is good, but it's lacking in some of the other stuff."

"What stuff?" Vandy fidgets with the camera. "She's never been interested in much more than sex."

"I told her that too!" Caroline picks at her cuticle. "You know what she told me?" Vandy shakes her head. "She said she's never even been on a date. A real one with dinner and a kiss goodnight."

"Aw, that's the good, cheesy stuff," Vandy says, eyes lighting up with her sigh. "Sitting through a movie, leaning your head against a guy's shoulder, holding his hand."

"Reyn does all that?" Caroline asks.

"Oh, yeah." She grins wickedly. "I reward him handsomely, too."

Caroline's nose wrinkles, even though her eyes flash wistfully. "Well, this guy must be pretty crappy if he doesn't even take her on dates."

Snorting, Vandy agrees, "Definitely."

The dormitory door swings open and Georgia walks out, Josie at her side. The girls told me they'd make an effort to get to know her a little better since she was on the Devil short list.

I walk off, knowing a hook-up isn't going to happen.

The next morning, as soon as I wake up, I thumb through my phone, trying not to cringe at the fact I only have four contacts; the Preston admin office, the club, Warren, and Georgia.

H: Coming over today?

While I wait for her response, I use the bathroom—skipping the Mylanta—and hop into a quick shower. By the time I get out, she's answered.

G: Nope. Important 'lady' duties today.

I scratch my head, taking a guess.

H: You're on your rag?

I'm ruffling a towel through my hair, glaring down at my phone when her response comes in the form of a photo.

It's her. She's standing in front of a mirror, phone held close to her stomach, giving its reflection a wry grin. She's wearing a long white dress, two delicate straps over her shoulders, waist flared out into something vaguely resembling a crinoline cupcake.

G: Me and the girls are getting ready for a full day of torture.

G: Hair and makeup. Nails and flowers.

G: Oh and pretending our mothers aren't the actual worst. FML.

I roll my eyes, falling onto the couch. Christ, the ball is like seven hours away. So much for a morning quickie. I look down at the photo, realizing this is how she's going to look tonight. In that dress. Face glowing. Dancing with Ozzy. I can picture it now, her mother simpering over the two of them, telling them to move closer together for the professional photographer she's probably paid to make Georgia look nice and normal and *money*. No one knows better than me, that's how rich people roll. Debutante balls are just glorified people-husbandry.

H: You look like an erotic marshmallow

G: Ha. Yeah I guess I look pretty stupid

The pause before her response is a little too long not to read into. Georgia's getting ready for an actual fucking ball. Maybe she thinks it's dumb, and maybe she doesn't belong there, but she's still a girl. Of course she wants to look pretty.

"Shit," I mutter, dragging a hand down my face. I type out a lightning-quick reply, and then immediately shove the phone in my pocket, glaring up at my ceiling. I expect the burn in my stomach, but not the one in my chest. The text told the truth. It doesn't mean anything. I still dig my phone out of my pocket, looking for a confirmation it's been read.

There's a little check next to the message.

H: You're beautiful, Georgia. I told you before. Perfect.

23

H: You're beautiful, Georgia. I told you before. Perfect.

I can't help the smile that breaks out as I read Heston's text, trapping my lip between my teeth as I struggle for something to type back.

"Who's that?" Vandy asks, neck craning to get a look at my phone.

I quickly stow it back into my purse. "No one."

She gives me a skeptical look. "Then why is your face all red?"

Caroline turns to look at us, eyes brightening. "Oooh, was it your new fella?"

"Caroline," I hiss, but Vandy flaps a hand.

"She already told me." Vandy pats some more concealer on her chin. Even though we're having our makeup professionally done later, she's been stressing about a blemish all morning. "I don't see what the big deal is. I think it's cool you're seeing someone."

"Even if he doesn't take you on dates," Caroline points out, sounding disapproving.

I'd groan into my hands if it wouldn't just make my face redder. "This is exactly why I didn't tell you two. You have this idea of how relationships should be, and if that works for you, *great*. But maybe other people do it different."

What I don't say is that if I had a choice of being taken to a fancy dinner or Heston bending me over his couch and fucking the daylights out of me, I'd choose Heston every time, and *wow*. That's a weird realization to have.

Vandy frowns at her pimple. "You make us sound like judgmental jerks."

"You just sounded like you might be interested in that," Caroline says, shrugging. "As long as you're getting what you want, we're happy for you."

"Super happy," Vandy agrees.

It nags at me while we're having our nails done, this question of what I want. Maybe I had sounded a little wistful when I talked to Caroline about dates and dinners and sweet goodnight kisses. But none of it could possibly be better than that night in Heston's bed, curled into his side as his fingertips skated over my naked hip.

That's what I want.

Later, my mom stands behind me to oversee the hairdresser, making unhappy noises. "The tiara won't work well with it that high."

I pull a face when the stylist tugs a lock a bit more aggressive than necessary. "Maybe I don't need the tiara," I wager, sending her a look.

She sends a look right back. "You're wearing that tiara, missy. It's *special*. I wore it to my first ball, and your daughter will wear it to her first ball."

The stylist tries it on, making sure the curls frame it just-so. It's over-the-top, with dozens of tiny, gaudy crystals. Even though it sparkles like new, it looks old and ill-suited for me, like I've just pilfered it from a dead widow's jewelry chest.

"I think we'll go with the bouquet of lilies for the pictures," Mom says, fingering one of my curls. The look on her face is full of excitement. "Oh, I wish you'd chosen the other dress. It was so much more regal than this one."

I grumble, "I'm not royalty, Mom. And besides, I like this dress more." I adjust the fabric in my lap, still enjoying the way it sways when I kick my feet. This thing is going to be *fucking awesome* to spin in, and I wouldn't admit it to anyone here, but I can't wait. It's probably the only reason she let me choose it. She wants all the pomp and circumstance, but deep down I get the feeling she also wants me to enjoy it. Gushing over tiaras and taffeta is what normal, well-adjusted rich girls do. This dress is as close as I come.

Plus, Heston *had* called me beautiful in it.

Right before we're set to take pictures, Caroline has an utter breakdown about contact lenses. Her mom doesn't want her wearing glasses, and apparently Caroline has a deep phobia of touching her eyeball.

Emory sweeps into the room, shielding his eyes. "I'm here to touch some eyeballs and save the day! Cover yourselves, future ladies of society!"

Vandy laughs. "Em, we've all been dressed since noon!"

He peeks through his fingers, verifying this. "Oh, good. I've been informed that—" His words die off when he finally gets a good look at his sister. Vandy's wearing a sleek satin dress, structured at the bodice and flaring out into something that's also going to look awesome to spin in. Her hair's been pinned up into a soft waterfall of golden ringlets. In what's apparently tradition for these things, she's wearing something of their mother's; a strand of petite, layered pearls around her neck. She looks like the perfect marriage of modern and traditional. "Wow, you look like..." He gawks at her for a long moment, finally settling on, "a *woman*."

I have to look away when he gathers her into a hug she clearly isn't expecting. The two of them have been through a lot together, and hearing them laugh—Emory bending down to whisper something private in her ear—it makes me wish I had that.

George is probably in the kitchen trying to score extra dessert to make this whole thing feel worth it.

When Emory releases his sister, he turns to me, doing a double-take. "Georgia Porgia! Look at *you*! You sure clean up well."

"Thanks," I say, giving him a mockingly coy curtsey. When I'm back to my full height, I point to the tiara. "Like my horcrux?"

"That is some massively intimidating bling," he agrees, pulling me into a hug next. Into my ear, he whispers, "You're going to slay it." After me comes Caroline, and this is a double-take I understand. Without the pigtails, sweaters, and glasses, she's like a totally different girl. "Caro-*fine*, what have you done with my sweet, nerdy goth babe?"

She doesn't look flattered. "Contacts are bullshit!"

He catches her wrist before she throws the box. "Calm down, I do this every morning. Have a seat. I'll teach you my secrets."

Once that crisis is averted and the organizers announce that it's time, we're directed to our separate areas. The presentation of the debutants has two parts. The one where we're initially presented by our fathers, and then the one where we're handed over to our escorts. There's some archaic symbology going on here, one man giving his daughter, dressed in virginal white, over to a younger man. Gross. Whatever. It's almost over.

We're shuttled to the side of the stage where we meet up with our fathers, or stepfathers, or whoever the stand-in is for the night. I see my dad and he smiles, beaming at the sight of me.

"You look beautiful, honey," he says, kissing me on the cheek.

"Thanks, Daddy."

My dad is a good guy. A busy guy. He's running for office because he wants to make a difference and yeah, a little bit because of the power that comes with it. Our money is old, but he's determined to do something with it, and he and my mom make a good team. He tempers her need for perfection in a way I've never been able to.

He clasps his hand over mine when I hook our arms together and leans in. "I got your scarf. It'll be great for when the weather cools off."

I grin. "The colors are okay? I didn't want to go too bright, but I know yellow is your favorite."

"It's perfect." His eyes skim over me, like he's searching for something. I know what it is, he's always wanting to make sure I'm okay. He pays for my school, my therapy, medication and any other treatment. He's awesome, but in the end there's still only so much he can do. Once he's satisfied, his gaze darts up to the tiara. "Guess your mother won that fight."

I touch the crown. "God, do I look like an idiot?"

"You look gorgeous." He squeezes my hand, and we take a step forward as the line diminishes. "Thank you for appeasing her. This is very important to her."

I sigh. "I know. I don't want to fight with her. It's just so hard to be what I'm not."

"It's okay to compromise as long as you're true to yourself. You're strong, honey. Stronger than anyone I've ever met." He chuckles. "Including your mother."

His statement makes me feel better, even though there are so many days when I don't feel strong at all. The days when it's like all I do is cave to my compulsions, but knowing my dad believes in me helps. It doesn't hurt that when we walk out on the stage, I do feel a little bit like a princess in my amazing dress.

I'm met on the other side by Ozzy, where we pause for the photographer. I send him a raised eyebrow. "My, my, Oswald. So dapper."

He folds my hand into the crook of his arm. "Not so shabby yourself, Haynes. That dress looks like some prime twirling material."

"Right?" I twist my hips, giving it a wave. "It makes up for the lame elbow-length gloves."

He shares my grimace, adjusting his own gloves. "I've never been to one of these before, so you'll have to tell me if I mess something up."

I wave a hand dismissively. "Just look pretty and rich, that's all they ever want."

He nods. "Got it."

Ozzy escorts me across the stage, to the middle where, this time, I walk down the center section, and pause as I've been instructed. I spot my father in the crowd and he smiles proudly. Everyone claps politely, like they've done for every other debutante, but as I do my spin, I can't help but see heads tilted together and mouths moving in whispers. I want to chalk it up to paranoia, but I know better. I have a reputation—one that, to a certain degree, I've earned.

I do what I always do, smile bigger, push my tits out further and give them the best goddamn twirl I have in me.

Fuckers.

When the formalities are over, Ozzy and I are sitting at our table, sipping punch and picking at slices of cake. Well, I'm picking at mine. Ozzy shovels a forkful into his mouth and enthusiastically offers, "Damn, this is good!"

I chuckle, looking around to find Caroline and Vandy.

Vandy's easy to spot. She's out on the dance floor with Reyn, smiling up at him as he leads her in a waltz that's far less clumsy than I'd think him capable of. Caroline's standing near the grand staircase, hands folded in front of her as she watches the dancers. I know Emory and his dad are checking the Vanderbilt score on their phone, and she looks so alone standing there, watching the other couples. I look at Ozzy and am hit with a spark of selfless genius.

I nudge him with my elbow, jerking my chin at her. "Hey. Doesn't Caroline look pretty tonight?"

"Definitely," he says feelingly. "All of you do."

"Yeah, but I mean...Caroline especially." I give him a smile that lets him know he doesn't need to be an equal opportunity flatterer. "What do you think of her?"

He actually puts down his fork to turn and look at her. "Caroline? She's cool. *Hilarious.* Really good with software."

Nodding, I squint at him. "But do you *like* her?"

He gives her a more considering look. "Well, sure. It's just..." Just then, Caroline looks our way and sees him staring. She quickly jerks her gaze away and Ozzy's head tilts. "I'm not sure she likes *me.*"

I roll my eyes. *Boys.* So clueless. "You should ask her to dance."

His forehead creases. "I don't think she'd like that. She always seems to avoid me."

"Trust me," I insist, pushing his plate of cake away. "If you asked her to dance right now, you'd make her night. Her *month.* Hell, possibly her year."

He looks at me, eyebrows hiking up his forehead. "Seriously?" Swinging his gaze back to her, he still looks doubtful. "If I get rejected, you owe me a dance to soothe my shattered ego."

"Sure thing!" I slap him on the shoulder, pushing him from his seat.

"I'm going, I'm going!"

I watch, glued to my seat as he approaches her, and I have to give him credit. For someone I know is a bit unsure about being welcome, he still strides up to her with confidence and swagger. Caroline notices him coming her way. I can tell because she goes rigid, eyes looking a little panicked. Thankfully, she doesn't run away, acting surprised to see him in front of her. Since his back is to me, I don't see him ask, but I see her reaction.

She freezes, gaze pinging to mine from across the room.

I give her a toothy grin and two thumbs up, nodding encouragingly.

At least one of us should find some happiness tonight, although I reconsider ditching my date when my mother finds me a few minutes later.

"You shouldn't be sitting all alone," she says, reaching out to fussily adjust my tiara. "Please find someone to dance with. The Collins boy is perfectly fine, but..." The face she pulls is probably too subtle to be caught by anyone else, but I know her well enough to understand the slight pucker in her brow. His dad works in education. Ozzy might be pedigree, but he's not elite enough for a Haynes. "The VanCarrow boy doesn't seem too attached to the girl he's escorting. Perhaps you can get a dance from him, strike up a conversation." In a lower voice, she leans in to add, "A conversation with your voices and nothing more, hm?"

My face explodes in a furious blush. "Mother!"

She looks unbothered by my offended tone, tucking her clutch under her arm. "I know how these after-parties unfold. You're out in society now, sweetheart. It's time to consider these things. No one wants to buy a cow who's giving the milk away for free."

That doesn't make me any less irate. "I'm not a cow, I'm a person!"

"You're a Haynes," she corrects, voice hard, "and I've coddled you and your brother about it for too long. Your responsibility to this family is to one day forge a strong, lasting partnership with someone of appropriate standing, just like me you and your father did. You can't do that if you keep up this...*loose image* of yours. Don't be upset." She fakes a smile for a passing couple before once again meeting my gaze. "I want you to be happy, Georgia. I've seen women who've fallen out of society's favor, and trust me, it's miserable. I don't want that for you." Her eyes soften when she sweeps one of my curls back. "The VanCarrow boy is so nice. Please try, for me?"

Feeling rankled and insulted, I flinch away from her touch, but do as she asks. Ferguson VanCarrow is standing stiffly by the chocolate fountain, easy to find as the result of his freakishly tall height. I know he used to get teased about it, back when we attended the same summer camp, but high school is different from seventh grade. Women love tall men. He looks far more comfortable in his own skin as a result. Perfect posture, impeccably tailored tux, tidy hair.

I hope my smile doesn't emerge looking like a grimace. "Hey, Fergie."

Ferguson was briefly the target of some of my more intense fantasies. I went through a very serious 'tall guy' phase in eighth grade, and he was basically my number one. I never got the opportunity to feel him out, but now that I do, I find that he just looks kind of boring. Too stiff. Too clean. I can't imagine those soft hands pressing bruises into my hips, or lying next to him in his bed, sweaty and fucked out and desperate for him to keep touching me.

He looks surprised to see me. "Oh, hey."

"Hey." I give him another smile, idly looking for something to dip into the chocolate. I don't really have the appetite for it, though, so I turn to him. "Would you maybe want to dance?"

His head whips to the side to gape at me. "Huh?"

It's not really the 'done thing' for a girl to do the asking, but his reaction still confuses me. "I just...I mean, my escort came as a favor—a friend, you know? And he's dancing with someone else, so I thought…"

Fergie looks away, eyes locking on something across the room. "Uh…" His head dips, voice quiet when he says, "Look, Georgia, you're really hot and all, but my mom's here tonight."

My confusion only grows. "What?"

When he finally meets my gaze again, he gives me a rueful look. "Come on, you know what tonight is about. She'd kill me if everyone saw me dancing with you."

I follow his eyes across the room to where a stern-looking, elegantly dressed woman is sitting. She's sipping on a flute of champagne and shooting daggers at me over the rim. I glance away, face heating. "Oh."

"Yeah." At least Ferguson sounds a bit bummed about it, and for a moment, it's almost like I've found an ally. Here, like this, we're just two kids being unfairly herded by our snobby, overbearing parents. Then he whispers, "But hey, if you wanted to find me after," giving me this quick, leering glance that has my insides shriveling up. "I've been dying to take your pussy for a ride, Haynes."

My spine snaps so straight that it's a miracle it doesn't fracture. "Excuse me?"

At least he has the sense to look abashed, eyebrows furrowing. "I just meant…everyone talks about it. I'm the only guy in my group of friends who hasn't gotten some yet, so I thought—"

"You thought that I'm worth *fucking*, but not sharing a public dance with?"

"Well…" He reaches up to scratch the back of his neck. "…*yeah*."

The worst part about it is the way he says it, all baffled and small. There isn't an ounce of unkindness in his tone. It's like someone just asked him if the sky is blue and he thinks it might be a trick, but facts are facts.

The sky is blue.

Georgia Haynes is for fucking and nothing more.

I look back at his mother. No doubt the rumors have reached her, which is exactly why she can't have her fine, upstanding, misogynist son seen with the likes of me. Any other day, I might have walked away, stowed myself in some nook and blinked back my tears.

Today, I shimmy up against him, resting my hand on his chest as I gaze up longingly into his eyes. He gawks at me, body going so stiff that his lips barely move when he asks, "What are you doing?"

I give his chest a little rub, pouting. "But Fergie, didn't you like it?"

He flinches at how loud my voice is, hands reaching up to grasp my shoulders. "What the hell? Get off me!"

"You said last night was special!" I cry, noting the small audience we're drawing to our left. "I've thought about it, and I don't care if it's small. We can work around it. Don't you want to be with me again?"

He shoves me off hard enough that I stumble back, twisting my ankle in my heels. Ferguson doesn't look troubled at the pained sound I make, sneering down at me as he straightens his jacket. "No one wants you, you trashy bitch." He strolls off like nothing just happened, but I can see his mother across the room, looking apoplectic.

That's what you get.

Unfortunately, my mother was watching, too. "What on earth was that about?" she asks, pulling me aside.

I shrug, trying to ignore the pang in my ankle. "He wasn't interested."

"You practically threw yourself at him!" Huffing, she gives a sharp shake of her head. "Until you've learned how to properly approach a man, I suppose I'll have to supervise."

This apparently means personally taking me around the room to appropriate suitors. It should feel incredibly demeaning, being paraded around like a bauble at auction. I don't actually get a chance to feel it, though.

"Devon is here with Alicia," Mrs. Monroe says, sniffing haughtily as she drags her son away. Devon gives me a second hopeful glance, however. Probably eager for another round, seeing as how I fucked him last year on the tennis courts during the Memorial Day fireworks.

Mrs. Bellam gives me the stink-eye and says to my mother, "Terribly sorry, but William can't dance. He has a medical condition." Brazen of her, given that he was just dancing ten minutes ago. Plus, I don't remember there being any medical condition when he was doing me doggy-style at that party sophomore year.

Mr. and Mrs. Lawlor don't even let us come near their dear, sweet Cameron. As soon as we get close, they scamper away, shoving him along.

By her sixth attempt at approaching a family, my mother is fuming. "This is humiliating. Why are you laughing?"

Because if I don't, I'll cry.

I take a sip from my flute of sparkling grape juice. "Maybe if my tiara was bigger? You know, since all of those boys have gotten the milk, we should probably show them that the cow is coming with a nice chunk of jewels."

That was the wrong thing to say. Her mouth gathers up into a tight, pursed scowl. "That's it. We're leaving."

"No," I growl, yanking my elbow from her grasp and spilling juice down my glove in the process.

"Georgia!" she hisses.

"It's enough that they treat me like a piece of meat," I tell her, feeling those tears start to finally well up. "I don't need you doing it, too."

"Then maybe you should stop acting like one," she snaps.

I stare at her for a long moment—this woman I've tried so hard to please all day—and suddenly I wonder why. I don't want to be here. I don't want to dance with Fergie or Devon or whatever other rich boy she thinks would make a 'suitable' future partner. I don't want to see her looking at me like that, all resentful and scandalized.

The only thing I've felt all night is *awful.*

Even after all the therapy and counseling sessions and medication, my mother still doesn't understand that this isn't something I have control over. Sure, I've made some terrible choices, but what's the alternative? More drugs? More therapy?

As much as I hate it, this is who I am.

The tiara takes some of my hair with it when I rip it off, shoving it at her. "If I ever have a daughter, I'm never forcing her to wear that. She'll never be paraded around one of these stupid balls like a glorified hooker, and she'll certainly never be shamed for making decisions about her own body."

My mom takes a deep breath. "Georgia—"

"You're not mad that I've had sex with guys, mother." I rip off my gloves, shoving them in the purse I snatch from the back of my chair. "You're just mad that your family legacy didn't get anything out of it."

I'm shaking as I storm out of the ballroom, and it's a good thing no one chases me. This rock in my throat is so eager to escape that my chest keeps hitching with the restraint of holding it in. I swallow thickly around it, willing it to wait. I won't let these people see me broken and ashamed. I'd rather jump in front of traffic.

I wait until I'm in the lobby to pull out my phone, and it hurts to see the last text there, knowing how radiant I'd felt when I read his words. *Beautiful. Perfect.* Now I feel alone and discarded, and I'm not sure how much longer I can hold it in.

G: Come get me

G: Please

G: Please

G: Please

I don't wait for a response. Regardless of how badly my ankle aches, I'll walk my ass back to campus, I don't even care. The first thing I do when I step outside into the crisp night air is bend down to pluck off my shoes, but then I find I can't stand up.

I crouch there and almost lose it. The wounded, raw thing roiling around in my chest claws up my throat, unrelenting to break free. It takes a while, but I wrestle it back, even if it's only temporary.

When I stand, I see him.

He's across the street, parked under a streetlamp, wearing a leather jacket and worn jeans. The thing in my chest squirms at the sight of him, resting nonchalantly against the door of his car, watching me with those heavy eyes. He holds my gaze when I cross the distance, crushing my purse into my stomach as I approach him. Heston is so good at being still—nothing like Sebastian at all. He's perfectly unreadable when he wants to be, and that's exactly what he is when I stop in front of him. Something about the way the light from the streetlamp hits his face has hollowed out his eyes, making them blots of shadow.

"Where's your date?"

"I don't know." Shrugging, I add, "I don't care."

He looks toward the entrance and the light brushes new bruises onto his eyes. "What happened?"

"Why are you here?" is what I say, folding my arms around my middle. "I thought you didn't belong here anymore."

He looks at me for a long moment. When he pulls a hand from his pocket, reaching up to brush a warm knuckle beneath my chin, the first tear finally falls, making a hot, wet track down my cheek.

Roughly, he whispers, "Neither do you."

~

When we get back to Preston, I follow him to his apartment without asking. I stare at the lines of his back as he walks, the way his shoulders move beneath his jacket, the glint of the moonlight catching the silhouette of his fair hair. Heston moves silently, almost lazily, but the way he holds himself is so assertive and sure that when he turns his head, tossing me a quick glance over his shoulder, it doesn't even shatter it.

The outside of his apartment is dark, my heels digging into the dirt before his stoop. I watch quietly as he pulls out a set of keys, unlocking the door and giving it a soft shove. It's no brighter inside, and for a moment, we stand there in the dark, breathing it in.

"No one would dance with me." I shoot for a sardonic tone, like

I'm making fun of myself, but it emerges more maudlin than intended. In truth, I don't know why I say it at all. There's something about being alone with him that always makes my tongue a little too loose. Sometimes he calls me a bad liar, but I'm not. I'm good at lying.

Just not to him.

I hear the shift of feet, and then the room is bathed in the soft light of the overhead lamp. Heston's shrugged out of his jacket, back turned, and I watch the curve of his broad shoulders as he takes his phone from his pocket, head bowed as he thumbs at the screen. When music starts playing, he sets it down, turning to me.

"I haven't done this in a while," he starts, pushing the coffee table aside.

"Oh, I-I didn't mean..." I'm struck speechless by the way he looks at me, his blue eyes somehow both hardened and gentle. He holds my stare as he rolls up his sleeves, and I'm powerless to do anything but set down my purse.

I'd unpinned my hair on the drive, and when I reluctantly step up to him, he reaches out to brush it back, revealing my bare shoulder. His eyes fix on the skin there, even as his hand rests on my waist, the other raised to fold my palm into his. I peer up at him, expecting to find something awkward or unpleasant when our gazes finally meet.

But I should have known better.

Heston straightens his shoulders and smoothly leads me in a tight, expert waltz.

I try to keep the smile off my face, but it breaks free, causing me to slightly misstep. "You're way too good at this."

There's a mirth in his eyes that takes me aback to see. "Better than you," he says, turning us in a swift move to avoid the armchair.

"Uh huh." I give him a conspiratorial smirk. "How are you at twirling?"

He answers by pushing me out on the next step, sending me spinning. I feel the dress flare out as I whirl, a laugh escaping my chest as I turn. He lets me indulge myself, spinning me until my laughter grows breathless. Maybe it's not under the bright lights of crystal chandeliers, or on the marble expanse of a ballroom floor, or done for all to see, but I find it doesn't matter.

It's exactly what I wanted.

That's what I want to tell him when I finally stop, but the words get caught in my throat. The dizzying feeling is only half from the twirling. The rest is from the way he's looking at me, eyes bright and hungry. Without putting any words to it, I reach behind me, fumbling for the zipper on my dress. His eyes darken at the sound of it lowering, and then follow as I push the straps off my shoulders, letting it fall to the floor.

His mouth parts only enough that I can see the pink hint of his tongue prodding at the seam. "You need it?" he asks, voice gravelly and quiet.

"No." I step out of the dress, bringing me right to his front, and peer up into his heavy eyes. Pushing my hand up the hem of his shirt, I say, "I just want it."

His jaw goes tense and releases right before he ducks down to take my mouth in a hard, scorching kiss. I revel in the sound he makes, something desperate and pleased, as I wind my arms around his neck. His hands find the small of my back, and this time he spins me in the hall's direction, walking me back.

When I land on the bed, the first thing I reach for is the button on his jeans. Heston's with me, tugging his shirt over his head and pushing me back, curling over me as he licks into my mouth. Somewhere between there and my back meeting the mattress, he manages to get my bra unhooked. His hands find my breasts a split second before his lips do, and I arch my back into his mouth, gasping at the way he sucks the swell above my nipple, marking his bruise into my flesh.

I still remember the way he looked those first times we did this —wild and hard, like he wanted to hurt me—but that's not the way he looks at me now. He rears back to yank my panties off, shoving his pants down in an eager jolt, and he looks at me like I'm a prize he's won. It's just as cocky as I'd expect from Heston winning anything, but I don't miss the brief flash of unease when he pauses, staring down at me.

My chest is already heaving when I ask, "What?"

He hangs there for a moment, a lock of blonde hair swaying in his eyes. It isn't until I reach up, sweeping it away, that he finally answers, voice quiet and sure. "Nothing."

He hooks a hand beneath my knee and lifts it, spreading me open.

And then he enters me in a quick thrust.

I grab at his shoulders, jaw falling open in a stunned sort of rapture. "Heston," I gasp, unthinkingly rising to meet his hips.

There's a wildness in his eyes now, but it's different. Through the thick fog of pleasure at having him between my legs, I remember that he's never done it like this before—face to face with someone. What was it he said to me before?

"I don't like people looking at me. It makes my dick soft. End of story."

His dick feels anything but soft right now as he drops to a forearm to fuck me in a hard, unhurried rhythm. I briefly consider closing my eyes to make it better for him, but find that I can't possibly do it. He looks so fucking fierce and determined that all I can do is hold his stare and wind my fingers into the back of his hair, breathing fast and too loud into the space between us. He fucks me with short, powerful punches into the cradle of my thighs, and each one features a low, guttural sound that makes me clench around him.

When I come, he digs his fingertips into my thigh, spitting a frenzied, "Fuck," and doesn't stop. Not when the tremors abate, and not when I cry out at the friction against my clit, shivery and over-sensitive.

A part of that may be the way I'm chanting, "Don't stop, don't stop, don't—"

When he bends to whisper a harsh, "Not fucking stopping," into my ear, all I can see is the shift of his taut, toned muscles as he fucks into me.

My heels scrabble for purchase as I wrap my legs around his hips, unable to help a weakly panted comment. "Told you this was better."

"Jesus," he grunts, rising to say, "Shut up." And then he kisses me.

It's even better than I thought it'd be, watching how red his face gets as he fucks me. The corners of his eyes are tight, the line of his jaw sharp and tense, but his kisses are slow and filthy, just like I always knew they'd be.

In the scant moments where he opens his eyes to watch me cry out, it still feels like I'm spinning.

24

This time, Georgia isn't gone when I wake up.

I can smell her lavender perfume, feel the warm weight of her curled into my side, the tickle of her hair, hear her measured breaths against my shoulder.

Also, I can feel her hand on my cock.

I make an encouraging noise, flexing my hips up in reaction. The breaths on my shoulder turn to lips, a soft kiss pressed into the skin. I'm not expecting it when she rolls on top of me, even though I should. One of the best things about Georgia is that she's so unashamed here, rocking down into my hardness, seeking, testing, asking.

My answer comes in the form of cracking an eyelid, squinting up at her as my hands find her hips. There's a blazing ray of light coming in from the window that slashes the curve of her pale shoulder, catching on her long tumble of curls. She looks like a blaze of hair and naked skin, and it almost hurts to look at her.

Too good.

Her green eyes are sleepy and soft, and her lips are still puffy and well abused. I can't help lowering my gaze to the column of her throat, her collarbones, and most importantly, her exquisite tits. They're perky and peaked, adorned with the hickey I'd left there last night. It looks so fucking good on her skin, a perfect harmony of blue and purple. I can see the broken capillaries fanning out in the shape of my mouth, still red at the edges.

"Mm," is all I'm able to muster, sweeping her tits up into my palms. When I thumb at her nipples, she sighs, eyes sliding closed as she rocks against me once more. I can feel that she's wet—probably woke up that way. We fucked long enough last night that my thigh muscles twinge when I flex my legs. But even though she came three times, she probably could have kept going.

Now she rests her hands on my chest and swirls her hips, bucking, lining everything up. And then she sinks down.

I don't know how I ever fucking deprived myself of this.

The way she looks when she takes my dick is the sweetest torture. Her jaw goes slack, eyebrows knitting together as her eyes fall closed. She takes it slower than I'm used to giving it, savoring every inch as it slides into her pussy. That look on her face is the only reason I don't drive my hips up and slam it into her.

When she settles onto me, pulling in a shallow, hitched breath, her teeth dig into her lip, eyes finally blinking open.

That look makes me want to squirm away. It's too early, too close, too good to hide what needs hidden—and god fucking knows there's a lot to hide. But it's easy to forget when she starts to ride me, tits bobbing with the gentle, grinding motion of her hips.

I mutter a low, "Fucking *Christ*, Georgia," because I've never seen anything hotter in my life. Those tits, those eyes, that swaying red hair, my bruises on her hips and thighs, the way she looks sleepy-soft but so goddamn eager. It's better than I thought it'd be, watching her take what she wants from me. When she leans down to kiss me, I fist my hand in her hair and decide I've shown enough restraint.

I wrap an arm around her waist to hold her steady, plant my feet on the mattress, and then drive my dick into her. The sound she makes isn't urgent or surprised. It's a gentle hum, like she'd been expecting this, hoping for it.

My thighs are going to hate me later, but for now, I don't care. I fuck her relentlessly and she takes it, panting soft and pleased into our stilted, wet kisses. It's dirty and sloppy and just what I always hoped morning sex might be.

After, when we're both breathless and boneless once again, she turns to me, temple propped on her fist.

"No one's ever fucked me as good as you do."

I lift the forearm I've slung over my eyes to send her a smirk. "Naturally."

She rolls her eyes, flopping back. "I should know better than to stroke any part of your ego by now." Despite the words, she's still all flushed and glowing, a soft delight held in her eyes.

I'm the one to roll over now, brushing my knuckles over the side of her tit. "Give me an hour," I say, nosing into the delicate skin below her ear, "and you can stroke any part of me you want."

She snorts, tilting her head to give me access. "Would that hour include you going to The Nerd to pick up breakfast?"

I reach for her chin, turning her to face me for another long kiss. "Will you still be naked when I get back?"

"Will you spank me again?" Even though she raises a haughty eyebrow, the apples of her chin bloom a bashful pink.

My dick twitches feebly. "Deal."

Georgia and I fuck for that entire morning, and I might stick around to make it an all-day thing, except I get a call from Tara that Underworld is having electrical issues.

Although 'electrical issues' is a bit of an understatement.

I spend the entire afternoon and night there, trying to work through circuit board diagrams and getting absolutely fucking nowhere. One of my bartenders briefly apprenticed with an uncle, so we try our best to double-team it.

By Friday, half our lights still aren't working and I haven't gotten a spare moment with Georgia since Sunday morning. It doesn't help that it's homecoming week at Preston and the whole place is filled with a manic energy. I'd be lying if I said it didn't fill me with a strange mixture of nostalgia and cheerlessness. Back in the day, homecoming had been a highlight of my school years, but now it's just another reminder that my life is standing still.

"Pep rally starts in ten," Coach James says, popping his head into my office on Friday. He holds up a folder. "Could you drop these by the headmaster's office? I'm on crowd control."

I grunt my agreement and stand, taking the folder. The last thing I want to do is sit in a smelly gym with eight hundred students cheering about how our football team is going to kick Thistle Cove's ass tonight. Thistle Cove has won state three years in a row, and with Emory and Reynolds gone, the team's gone to shit. Even with their old head coach in jail, they're going to wipe the floor with us.

"Just take this to his office?" I ask.

"Yeah, leave it in the box if he's already gone."

"Gotcha."

Like a fish swimming upstream, I cut through the students headed to the gym while I go the opposite way, toward the main building. The kids are decked out in Devil pride; the cheerleaders in their short skirts and the dance teams sparkly uniforms. Briefly, I think of Sydney Prescott and how stupid it was to chase after her. It'd be easy to blame that on her being a hot cheerleader, but mostly I just saw something my brother had conquered and I wanted to take it away, prove that he wasn't special. Even after it was clear he didn't want her, it was still obvious she wanted him. The whole thing was sloppy and obvious. Thank fucking god he's gone now, nice and comfy in Hartford, too far away to feel anything but a garden variety contempt for.

When I reach the admin offices, the lobby is empty, and I call out, "Hello?"

I spy a note on the secretary's desk.

At the Pep Rally. Be Back at 3:00. Go Devils!

I roll my eyes. Jesus, this place never changes. It's fucking surreal. Banners all over school announce the football game tonight and fireworks after the dance tomorrow. I'm wondering if anyone will notice if I skip the pep rally when another idea pops in my head.

Collins should be at the rally too, which means no one will be in here for at least an hour. Once again, I call out, making sure none of the other admins are around, but the place is a ghost town. Although I already gave Gene the encrypted file, if I can get substantial dirt on Georgia's family, maybe I can finally get it back and ease some of this weight on my conscience.

There's a whisper in the back of my mind—a reminder that it'll never be enough. That there's a chance it'll always be one more gamble, one slightly riskier bet, a higher price and a better win.

I try to tune it out.

No way he left the door open, I think. *Way too easy.*

If I've learned anything lately, it's that shit doesn't come easy to Heston Wilcox, but I'm a glutton for punishment and try the door, anyway. To my surprise, the knob turns, opening without resistance.

Well, maybe it's my lucky day after all.

I enter quickly and go straight to where I suspect he hides his key. I noticed the tassel on the end of his key ring when I was in here last time. It was distinctive enough, black and red and silver. So I search his rows of shelved books. I pull a few out to check for the tassel, but I don't find anything—not on the shelves.

There's an antique student roster fanned out in a display case near the window. The tassel is hanging from the bottom, nestled between the pages.

"Bingo," I mutter, fishing it out.

I slide it into the lock and spring it, pulling it open to 'H' and quickly find Georgia's file. Sitting in Collins' chair, I drop the file on the desk. It lands with a slight thud. It's not massive, but there's some weight to it. There's dirt in there, I have no doubt. The kind of dirt a potential politician might not want out in the open. I reach to flip open the cover, but find myself pausing.

"It won't be enough, will it? It'll never be enough. Not until you've gone through it all."

Goddam Warren, getting in my goddamn head.

But as I stare at the folder, the edge slightly bent, it's not really Warren I'm thinking about. It's Georgia.

I'm thinking of her, so perfect in that dress, looking miserable and sad.

How she felt in my arms while we were dancing.

The sound of her delighted laughter when I twirled her.

How good it was to be inside her, watching her, feeling and being with her.

I scrub my face. *Fuck.* That's what won't ever be enough. I can stop the gambling. I know I can. But I'm starting to think it'll be a hell of a lot harder to quit Georgia.

My stomach twinges, followed by a jolt of pain and the old, familiar taste of bile in my throat. I've felt better all week. In fact, I haven't had to take any medicine for a while. But now it's churning away in there, eating at my insides.

I don't want to consider the correlation, but I do know that toying with Georgia and her family isn't something I'm interested in. Not anymore.

Gene will have to be dealt with another way.

I push Collins' fancy chair back and catch a glance at the two locked drawers in his desk. Pausing to consider them, I put Georgia's file away, lock the cabinet, and insert the keys into the desk lock instead.

I may not be willing to sell out Georgia any more, but Collins?

That bastard is fair game.

"Shouldn't you be getting ready to make memories tonight?" I ask, propping up on an elbow. Georgia and I have been in bed all day, fucking and napping and eating delivery. "Picking out some slutty little dress and teasing all the boys with those weapons on your chest?"

"Shut up," she says. "Why can't you ever stop talking?" The words don't have any bite to them, though. Her words never have any bite when she's like this, soft and fucked out.

"I can think of a few things that make me speechless." I kiss her shoulder. "Seriously though, aren't you going?"

Her eyebrow raises. "Why? You trying to get rid of me?"

It's the opposite, actually. I don't want her to leave. There's something addictive about Georgia that I can't get enough of. It'd be easy to say it's her pussy, but I know it's more than just the tug in my balls. Sometimes when she's not here, I'll roll over and smell her on my pillow, and then wonder where she is and why the answer to that isn't 'in my fucking bed'. I can't admit that, so I arrange my expression into something aloof and shrug. "Just thought it'd be something you'd be into."

"I just had a ball last weekend. I think I've reached my limit on formal wear and pretense." Rolling her eyes, she adds, "You think I want to sit around and watch V and Reyn achieve epic couple goals, or witness the blooming new love of Caroline and Ozzy while I avoid freshman rapists and bitchy, coked-up, rich girls in the bathroom?" She makes a gagging face. "No, thanks."

"You truly have a way with words, Haynes."

"Thank you," she grins. "I try." She shifts, attempting to tug the sheet over her tits and pretty much failing. God, they're big and glorious. "What about you? What are you doing tonight? Chaperoning?"

"Hell no." I laugh. "Like Collins' would let me supervise a room full of teenagers. He'd probably accuse me of spiking the punch and defiling the coked-up bitches." I tuck a lock of her hair behind her ear, letting my fingers wander down to push away the little bit of sheet she managed to drag over her chest. "I'll probably go to Underworld. We've been dealing with a bunch of shit there all week."

She stretches like a cat, back arching into my hand when I brush the side of her tit. "I'll probably just hang out in my room."

She doesn't look sad when she says it—just resigned. Much like the ball, it's not like I could take her to the Homecoming dance, even if either of us wanted it. Plus, I've already made those memories. These are hers to make or squander.

So why does it feel like I'm depriving her of something?

I don't need to look too deep. It was all that bullshit I overheard between Vandy and Caroline about Georgia never having been on a date. She's never made any hints about wanting that, but I'm not dense. She's an eighteen-year-old woman. Of course she wants it.

But she can't possibly want it from me.

Nevertheless, the idea doesn't leave me—not when we dress, or after I've kissed her goodbye. Not even later, when I'm at Underworld, trying to come up with a way to pay an electrician. It nags at me, and once the night is in full swing and Tara has it under control, I send Georgia a text.

H: meet me at the lookout. 10pm

G: K

There are a lot of things I can't be, like a good guy with no criminal record, or the second richest Wilcox, or a business owner with capital and working soundboards. But I can be the kind of guy who takes Georgia out. Why the fuck not? What do idiots like Oswald Collins and Reynolds McAllister have that I don't?

I grab a bottle of champagne from behind the bar and thirty bucks from the till.

"Hey!" Tara says, batting away my hand. I grin and shove the money in my pocket, heading toward the door. Annoyed, she calls, "Where are you going?"

"I've got a date."

~

Blanket: Check.

Booze: Check.

Fancy Dessert: Check.

Fully charged phone with sexy music: Check.

Once I'm all set up, I glance at the time. *10:03*. She's either late, or she's just not coming. The longer I wait, the more sweat pebbles on the back of my neck. This looks fucking ridiculous. Georgia and I don't date—we fuck. We fight. Then we fuck some more. And the thing is, we're good at it. The chemistry between the sheets is scorching hot. But dating? Talking without the goal of getting naked and horizontal? That's outside of our wheelhouse. Why am I messing with a good thing?

She'll probably get here, take one look at everything, and laugh in my fucking face. How many dates have I been on, anyway? A grand total of none.

I know exactly what I was thinking; Caroline and her annoying little nerd voice.

"This guy must be pretty crappy if he doesn't even take her on dates."

Since when do I give a fuck whether or not I'm crappy?

I bend over to pick everything back up, hoping to stash it in my car before anyone comes up here and finds me looking like an idiot.

That's when I hear the sound of a car crunching up the gravel road, causing my insides to twist unhappily. Her little convertible pulls into a parking spot and she turns off the lights.

Too late to pull out now.

"Hey," she says, hopping out of the car. "What's going on?"

How do I even begin to explain this? "Well," I run my hand through my hair, scowling at the blanket I've spread over the ground. "I thought—"

"Did you set all this up?" She looks from the blanket out over the overlook. Recognition clicks into place. "To watch the fireworks?"

It's easy to exhale at the hopeful joy in her voice. "I thought maybe we could." Lamely, I add, "I got snacks."

It isn't totally without precedent. Every Monday evening, I watch Lakevale with her and Micha in the deserted natatorium. We long ago gave up pretending anything productive was going to happen on those nights. Lately, we each bring a bag of chips and something to drink and huddle around Micha's tablet, booing Vivian when she does something incredibly fucking stupid. They aren't *dates*, though.

She brings her hands together, looking happily surprised. "Did you bring chocolate?"

"Who am I?" I bend and pick up the box I got at the grocery store bakery. "Candy, cookies, a doughnut, three macaroons, a cupcake..." The randomness is the result of low stock, but only because of a pleasant discovery; the bakery lowers prices at the end of the day.

She peers inside, eyes lighting up at what's inside. Without waiting, she plucks out a macaroon, popping it in her mouth. "Oh god, it's melting on my tongue. So good."

I snake my arm around her waist and pull her in for a kiss, tasting the sweet chocolate for myself. Her tits press into my side and it'd be so easy to get her down on the blanket and bury myself inside her sweet cunt.

Not yet.

She pulls away, batting her lashes. "Is this how *you* butter girls up?"

I get this flash of memory from the night we did anal; her in my lap, tits in my face. I reach down to adjust myself. "Give me some credit." I pick up the champagne, raising an eyebrow. "It's much easier to get you drunk."

She immediately takes the bottle, eyes flashing in delight. "Damn, so fancy. You realize I'm a sure thing, right?"

"Well, I know you're a lady and all, but I didn't actually bring glasses," I offer, snorting when she lifts the bottle to take a drink.

Across the lake, the first zing of a firework sputters against the dark.

"Oooh," she breathes, dropping to sit on the blanket, giving it a pat. "Come on. Get comfy."

"What's with you and this 'comfy' thing?" I mutter, even though I obey, taking the bottle of champagne when she passes it to me.

We're quiet for a while, passing the bottle back and forth as we watch the flowers of pyrotechnics in the sky. I have no way of knowing if she realizes this was meant to be a date, but it doesn't seem so bad. Slowly, I find myself unwinding.

She lets out a soft, "Hey," eyes sparkling with the reflection of the fireworks when I meet her gaze. "Thanks." She isn't smiling when she says it, and it comes out sounding weirdly serious. I touch the side of her neck, drawing her close to press a kiss to her mouth.

"Any time."

Over the lake, the sky explodes in a flash of vivid colors—dozens of them, maybe even hundreds.

But all I see is the green of her eyes.

25

"So we're all decided?" I look around the bunker, waiting for everyone's nod before sealing the black envelope with our Devil nominees.

Vandy and Caroline are on the desk, clearing out the spreadsheet—best not to leave evidence—while Heston leans against the wall by the door, hooded eyes tracking me. I really wish he wouldn't look at me like that here. It makes it nearly impossible to ignore him, which is exactly what the girls think I *should* be doing. Instead, I'm antsy for later, fully intending to show up at his apartment so I can finally climb him like a tree.

There's one more order of business, though.

I pull another black envelope from my bag, drawing their attention. "This came last night."

Vandy's eyebrows climb her forehead. "The rites? Already?"

I shake my head, passing her the card. "Not exactly."

A Devil's allegiance cannot be allowed to decay.

The time will come for the new to prove themselves, but not before you renew your flame.

"I think the devil will not have me damned, lest the oil that's in me should set hell on fire."

Elvatio Infernum

Vandy reads it, passing it to Caroline, who reluctantly passes it to Heston.

"Fire, huh?" Vandy asks, sounding unbothered.

I nod. "We need to make an effigy and burn it in the middle of the lake."

Heston rolls his eyes so hard that it looks like he's having a stroke. "This is brainless. When I was a Devil—"

Vandy and Caroline both burst with frustrated groans, mocking, "When I was a Devil!"

Caroline fake-whines, "We just bullied up underclassmen, and it was so easy!"

"We humiliated girls for sport!" Vandy goes along.

"No one cares what you did when you were a Devil," Caroline says, glaring at him. "The Devils belong to *us* now. Deal with it."

Already sick of playing mediator between the three of them, I cut in, "Actually, this isn't just a test for us." I jerk my chin at Heston. "The old Devils are going to be invited, too."

Vandy frowns. "Like Sebastian and Em and everyone?"

"Yes," I answer, adding, "Plus people like Hamilton, Xavier, Ansel…all of them."

Caroline's face screws up. "But why?"

"If I had to guess?" All I can do is shrug. "Devil connections are an earned privilege? Since it's happening around Thanksgiving break, I assume some of them will be in town."

"Don't look at me," Heston says, looking rankled at the daggers Caroline and Vandy are glaring at him. "You think I want to burn some glorified doll out on the lake? Please. I actually have better things to do than piss off Collins and whatever rival school is the flavor of the year."

He might actually be telling the truth about that. I know Underworld has had a lot of problems lately. It seems like he's always over there dealing with them, instead of being here. With me. In his bed.

Naked. We had that really nice night watching fireworks, but not much ever since.

It's super annoying.

After the girls and I decide to go effigy craft shopping this weekend, Vandy tries to get me to come with her and Caroline to The Nerd. "Come on, it'll be fun! We're going through the Homecoming pictures."

I just barely stop myself from pulling a face. "I have to do a paper for History. Maybe next time?"

She pouts, but she and Caroline leave.

I stop Heston before he can follow. "Hey, you doing anything today?" There was a time I'd feel embarrassed at how hopeful I sound, but the way he winds an arm around my waist, bending to kiss me, makes me feel anything but.

"Plans today, Little Red."

"You've had plans all week." Now it's my turn to pout. "More problems at Underworld?"

He looks away, letting his arm slide from my waist. "Nah, just... stuff." It's unavoidably vague, and the way he shifts his gaze to the side, mouth tight, makes me think that's intentional.

"Oh." I'd ask for details, but something tells me it wouldn't be welcome. "Well, maybe next time."

Either it's the tone, or the fact I'm referencing *my* blow off to Vandy, but he reaches out to grab me under the chin, forcing my gaze to his. "Come on, don't be like that. It's just..." He rolls his eyes to the side, looking more annoyed at himself than me. "Personal shit."

"Yeah?" I tilt my head, wondering, "Would that have anything to do with that bartender who keeps blowing up your phone? Tara?"

He gives me a slow, wry grin. "So we're doing jealousy now?"

I shove his wrist away, instantly linking our fingers together to soften the blow. "I'm not jealous, I'm just curious."

He holds my gaze, and looking at him now, I can see how tired he looks. "Tara isn't personal. She's work." Tugging me closer, he adds, "And nowhere near as hot as you. I don't trade down. Plus, you and I have a deal about straying, right?"

I begrudgingly wind my arms around his neck, feeling a little better at the obvious bulge pressing into my belly. "So you'll be around later?"

"How about this?" He takes his keys out of his pocket, twisting one from the ring. "I probably won't be back until late, but you can go to my place tonight. Write your paper, take a nap," He leans in to gruffly suggest, "get naked, lube your ass up for me. You know, a proper welcome." I know from the sly smirk curving his lips that this is his way of asking. Truthfully, I'm surprised he's waited this long.

I snatch the key, scoffing. "If you want anal, then you have to show up and put in the work."

"Fine," he sighs, spinning me toward the door, obviously in a rush. Before it opens, he whispers into my ear, "Just leave the lube out and I'll do it myself."

A shiver runs down my spine.

It's still there even hours later as I'm leaving the library, laptop tucked under my arm. History research is probably the worst genre of school work, but at least I'm not as distracted by Mr. Francis as I used to be. In fact, I haven't gotten lost in hours of fantasizing in weeks. Part of it that the object of all my fantasies is usually up for, like, *fulfilling* them. But another part is that I don't really want to know what it's like with anyone else. Heston is so fucking good—everything about the way he moves, the way he fucks, the way he is after, always touching me, pressing his lips to any available patch of naked skin—especially my boobs.

I'm just thinking about heading over to his apartment when I run into Ozzy.

"Oh, hey!" I'm breathless, realizing now that I'd basically been power-walking. *Impatient much?* "How are you? Oh! I heard about Homecoming." I give him a friendly punch on the shoulder. "Way to go, slugger."

He'd asked Caroline the day before the dance, which would usually be a huge faux pas in the world of teen dance etiquette, but Caroline didn't seem anything but thrilled. I'd lent her one of my more modest dresses and spent way too much of the morning doing hair and makeup for someone who didn't even attend.

Ozzy gives me a stiff smile. "Yeah, yeah, it was great. Well, you know. As far as dances go." He gives me a look that says a ball and Homecoming have met his formalwear quota for the year.

"I'm glad the two of you are..." I make a gesture that's indecipherable, because I'm not sure if they've put a name to it yet. "Whatever you are."

"Yeah, thanks." He nods, giving me a strange look. "Could I, like, talk to you for a second?"

I blink at his grim tone. "Sure."

He looks around, adding, "Not here, though."

"Uh..." I follow his gaze down the hall. "Okay? Lead the way."

He directs me to the computer lab a corridor away from the library, silent the whole way. Just seeing the high, tense curve of his shoulders makes my stomach fill with a sense of doom.

"Is this about Caroline?" I ask when he shuts the door behind us. "Because look, she really likes you, and if—"

"No," he cuts me off, swiping a hand through the air. "Caroline is great. Amazing, even. And for what it's worth, I'm really into her, too. I was actually hoping you wouldn't tell her about this."

I give him a puzzled look. "About what?"

He takes a deep breath, lacing his fingers together in front of his chest. "First of all, I need you to know that I had no idea what I was doing."

"Ozzy," I urge, rolling my hand, "give me something here."

"Heston came to see me a while back," he blurts, looking nervous. "He said he was looking for Caroline, but she wasn't here. I was." He pauses, like he's waiting for a reaction. When he gets nothing but a nod, he explains, "He wanted me to encrypt a file for him."

"Oh." After a moment, my brows knit together in confusion. "Okay?"

"He told me not to open it—not to even look at it. Which, for the record, is kind of hard when you're encrypting a file." Ozzy reaches up to rub the back of his neck, wincing. "Especially when my encryption program caches a thumbnail of the video."

My blood runs cold, something odd and bitter bubbling at the back of my throat. "Video?"

There's a flash of guilt in his eyes that I'm hoping is really unnecessary. "Look, I've...heard things. You know, rumors? About you, and Heston, and a video." In a lower voice, he elaborates, "I'm pretty sure I saw you in this thumbnail."

I cross my arms, shifting uncomfortably. "Okay, yes, there was a video of us going around, a long time ago. Maybe he was just—"

"Georgia," he says, voice slow and confusingly gentle. "I don't think it was the same video."

I stand there for a long moment, staring at him, trying to fit his words into something that's easier to parse. "I-I don't—" Shaking my head, I try to swallow around the dark, panicked thing wedged in my throat. "Can you show me?"

He gives a heavy nod, but looks reluctant to move. "I only took a picture of this in case you needed it for..." he trails off, pulling his phone from his pocket. "I deleted the cache as soon as I realized what it was."

I don't care about that. All I can focus on is the phone is in his hand, the way he's thumbing it to life, swiping through a gallery of photos, and then turning it to face me. I only watched the video from that night in his room once. It was the catalyst to a month-long streak of self-destruction that would have even made Sebastian Wilcox flinch. I still remember how everything looked slightly blue, but I remember the small, pointless details most of all. The way the blanket on the bed rode up halfway through, blocking out my shoulder. The poster in the background. The hitch in my voice when I cried out, right before coming. The way his fingers looked, digging divots into my hips.

There's nothing blue about the thumbnail.

There's no poster in the background.

There are no sheets, no bed, no faceless side-shot that can be shrugged off.

It's an indistinct snapshot of a computer screen, pixilated with the angle and light of the monitor, but I'd know Heston's office anywhere. The flesh-colored mesh of naked skin is just as obvious, as well as my hair, darkened by dampness and tangled around a tight fist.

I'm not sure what's holding me up. It feels like my bones have vaporized, spine melting away to bond with my dull, aching organs. Maybe it's years of my mother's training, always having it beat into my head that girls must pretend. Through the crisp pang of silence in my head, I can hear myself suck in a breath, but I don't feel my lungs expand with it.

Ozzy sighs. "There's more."

My head snaps back, eyes widening in horror. "There's more?!"

He rushes to say, "Not videos! I mean, not that I know of. It's about the encryption." There's a sudden slump to his features. "I tried to tell him! I'm not good with software. He wanted me to do some weird, fancy shit, and I tried my best, but..."

My voice feels dry and squawk-like. "But *what*?"

"I'm not sure it's secure." He lifts his arms in a wide shrug. "He wanted this fake timer countdown to it unlocking, which is why I had to get this other program I'm not fluent in, because the timed encryption was a native feature, which should have been..." He shakes his head. "Never mind. The point is, the timer may be functional, which means—"

Since I don't understand any of this, I turn on my heel and reach for the door, walking out of the room.

I'm not sure how I get from there to the courtyard. It's like I just jump space and time, too caught up in this enormous boulder of nothingness inside of me to realize that it's aimlessly rolling me forward. I stand there for a suspended moment, looking around me at all these people. All these eyes on me. All these ears listening. All these solitary souls that'll consume a part of me.

I wonder how long it'll be before they see it.

I let the boulder roll me forward because staying still makes the panic swell thick in my veins, and I don't think I can handle it. That suddenly becomes the biggest of my worries, the memory of the last time throbbing painfully near my temples. I know what this path looks like. I can recognize the numbness, the pulling away, the escape from the sharp brightness of it all. I'd fight against it, but I'm not sure the alternative is any better.

I let the boulder roll me past the dining hall, past the athletic field, to the old, worn walkway that leads to the tree line behind campus.

That's how I find myself at Heston's door.

Mechanically, I pull his key from my pocket and push it into the lock. My mother's never going to speak to me again. I turn the knob and shove the door open, stepping inside. No one's ever going to want me. I drop my bag on the floor and leave the key on the table, in the same spot he always leaves it. I'll have to move away to avoid the looks; I already know I can't do it again.

This is how it goes.

The boulder rolls me forward while my thoughts churn through what's to come. I see it for what it is. Self-preservation. Survival. An attempt to shield myself by preparing for each terrible, degrading, invasive thing. I've spent years alongside it, running from it, getting behind it. I know every angle of feeling used and too exposed. I'm not the weak, confused girl I used to be. Because *this*, I know.

It's all the other parts that are horrifically new.

This time, there were promises, agreements, *trust*. If I thought I hated myself last time, then I don't even know what to call this sick, toxic, revolted thing that's turning inward right now. Could I have been so *fucking stupid* to believe that he's changed? That he might care about me? That all those times laying in his bed, feeling his fingers run through my hair, his lips brushing over my temple, could have been *tenderness*?

I empty my lunch into his toilet, fingers curled around the bowl as I retch, as if I could purge myself of the gullibility that led me here. It took me two years to forgive myself for going up those stairs with him. For enjoying it. For not realizing what was happening.

For not speaking up sooner. But as I walk robotically into the hall, catching sight of the bed I'd been so eager to crawl into, it feels like this self-hatred is tattooing itself on my soul, and I know what's different.

Last time, I didn't love him.

26

The meetings haven't gotten any better.

Warren sits across from me, looking appropriately interested in whatever the guy to my right is saying, although I can't see how he could be. Just about everyone has something to say, except for me. Sometimes Warren will let me get away with just sitting here, but other meetings, he'll make me spout off about whatever twisted thing my mind is dying to latch onto, like some sick sacrifice to the addict gods.

But Warren himself rarely talks about his own shit.

It's bugging the hell out of me, mostly because it doesn't seem fair that he knows so much about my problems and I know fuck-all about his.

I do have other reasons for wondering, though.

I wait until just about everyone's left to approach him about it, sidling up to him at the coffeepot. "Heard Reynolds took Vandy to Homecoming," I start, already bored with the pretense. In a few hours, Georgia will be waiting for me, in my bed. The thought of her naked body between my sheets is making it really fucking difficult to be patient.

Warren gives me a nod. "Making up for last year, when he didn't get to actually take her, I suppose."

I take out my form for him to sign, shifting impatiently as he checks off the boxes and scribbles his name on the bottom. "Can I ask you a personal question? One Devil to another."

He hums, folding the form back up and handing it to me. "Of course."

I put it back into my pocket and decide I only know one way to exist. Bluntly, I ask, "What's the deal with this whole sex addiction thing?"

His forehead wrinkles. "What about it?" The absolute last thing I want to know about is Warren McAllister's unfathomable levels of horniness, and yet...

I fold my arms, jaw working around my question. "I guess I don't get it. Why's it so bad if you like to fuck a lot? Are you trying to cure it? Do you just never fuck anyone now? Is that the answer? Do you just quit cold turkey?"

"Heston, slow down." He looks taken aback, eyes growing wide at the avalanche of questions. "My god, when you say 'personal', you really just go for it, don't you?"

I shrug, not caring. "You know more about my gambling habits than most people. I don't see what the issue is."

His mouth slants into a droll expression. "I care about your problems. Something tells me you don't care about mine."

"That's not—" I start, but find that I don't have the energy to keep it up. "Okay, yeah, that's true."

He doesn't look insulted. "So why the sudden interest?"

I watch him pour a cup of coffee into a Styrofoam cup. "I'm kind of seeing someone."

Warren pauses, giving me a curious look. "Really? Is this the girl you wouldn't go down on before?"

I hold up a finger. "First of all, I ate this girl's pussy like it was fine dining. She has zero complaints in that department, trust me. Second of all, it's not...like, *serious*." Only that doesn't seem entirely honest. Whatever this is with Georgia, it doesn't feel *not* serious.

He must sense this, because he insists, "It must be *something* for you to be bringing her up like this. Which is good," he rushes to say. "The opposite of addiction isn't sobriety. It's connection."

Pulling a face at the platitude, I wonder, "And what's the outlook on two addicts getting connected?" I grapple for a second on how to approach this without giving too much away. "I think she might be like you. A nympho, you know?"

Warren holds up a hand. "Why would you think that?"

"I don't 'think' it," I say, giving him a look. "She doesn't just like sex. She *needs* it. She has this whole reputation because of it. Something tells me she'd get rid of it if she could." Narrowing my eyes, I'm quick to add, "Despite the fact I satisfy her in *every fucking way* possible. I just want to make that clear."

Warren scratches his forehead, looking as though he's choosing his words carefully. "Look, no two addicts are alike, but if you follow the breadcrumbs, we're all chasing the same chemical high. Oxytocin, dopamine, endorphins. To go back to your earlier questions, there's no 'cure' for addiction. And you just gave an example of how it can be so destructive. The social implications of—"

"Yeah, yeah, yeah," I wave a hand impatiently. "But say you were with someone and you just fucked them a lot. What's so bad about that?"

"Realistically?" he wagers, raising an eyebrow. "It doesn't always pan out, because some sex addicts get that chemical high from seeking new sexual experiences. New partners. New places. New risks."

Deadpan, I ask, "You're saying she'll fuck around on me."

"No," he answers, sighing. "I'm saying that's a possible way that a sex addiction can be destructive."

"Hm." I look at him, guessing, "Cheated on your wife, huh?" Before he can answer—not that he needs to, I've got this guy pegged—I continue, "I don't think that's her preferred type of self-destructive behavior, and trust me when I say she has one. God, she used to do this thing. She'd wear a rubber band around her wrist and snap it every time she—"

The color suddenly drains out of his face, and when he says, "Stop!" I unthinkingly go silent. Warren reaches up to pinch the bridge of his nose, nostrils flaring with his inhale. "Please tell me you're not talking about who I think we're talking about."

I go still, mouth parted on a denial that I can't voice. Is she really that obvious to everyone else?

Guess so.

When he drops his hand, his expression is tight with displeasure. "Jesus Christ, Heston, what the fuck are you thinking?"

My limbs feel a little too stiff to pull off nonchalance, but I try anyway. "I don't see how it's any of your business."

"You just made it my business!" He slams his cup of coffee down too hard, sloshing it all over the plastic tablecloth. "You listen to me. I don't care about her reputation. That girl has a chance of making it! The last thing she needs is another witless, dick-brained boy to come along and take advantage of it." Pointedly, he adds, "*Again*." Before I can even think to argue, the fury in his eyes stops me. "I know what you did to her. She might seem strong and tempting, but she's too fragile to keep toying with!"

"Why the hell do you think I'm here?" I snap, giving up on seeming casual about this. "You think you know me, just because I sit in some stupid sharing circle once a week? Fuck you."

His eyes bug out. "Aside from a few choice comments I'd rather scrub from my brain, the only thing you've said about her is that it's not serious."

"Of course it's fucking serious!" I explode, feeling my face go hot. The truth spilling out of me before I have a chance to filter it. "Why else would I walk in here and make an ass out of myself? Because I'm trying to find out whether or not this can actually fucking work!"

Warren shakes his head. "And if leaving her alone is what's best for her, would you do it?"

"It's not." It comes out as strong and certain as it feels. "She comes to you, doesn't she? When shit gets hard and she needs someone to talk to—that person is *you*, isn't it?" And fuck if that doesn't make my hands want to ball into fists. "So tell me, when's the last time she called you, *Warren*?"

"It's been a while," he starts, looking like he's ramping up to a lecture.

I don't let him. "That's because of *me*. Because *I've* made her better. Because I can be *good* for her—I know I can. I just need someone to fucking tell me how!"

"For Pete's sake," he says, face screwing up. "You're as bad as Reyn. You can't get it up for girls you haven't already put through the wringers? What is it with you kids and not leaving well enough alone?"

"Oh, I don't know." Belligerent, I pretend to think. "Our absent fathers are megalomaniacs and sex addicts who never taught us the value of meaningful connections?"

The look he gives me tells me that was a low blow. "Blaming your upbringing will only get you so many second chances, Heston. You're twenty-one now. At some point, you're going to have to put in the work and become someone worth giving that second chance to."

Raking my fingers through my hair, I look around the room, eyes landing on the circle of chairs. When I look back at Warren, I make sure there's nothing flippant about my next words.

"So tell me how."

∼

I get back to campus late enough that even Buster is probably passed out somewhere. Since I'm coming from Underworld, I'm tired and annoyed with the universe, but not so much that I don't feel a spark of anticipation at what awaits me.

The talk with Warren had gone on for longer than I'd admit to anyone who asked and was mostly just about how much I apparently fucking suck. Which is great. A real ass-pat to the ego. I've never cared if anyone thought I was an asshole before, and I'm not sure I like it now. I don't want to be Hamilton Bates, going around building houses for the less fortunate, rebranding myself into the perfect Stepford man. Fuck that. I don't care about being a good person.

I just want to be a good person *for her*.

When I get to the apartment, the soft light shining through the window makes my shoulders ease. I already know the first thing I'm going to do the moment I step through the door is get my clothes off and make a beeline for my bed.

What I find inside stops me short.

"What the fuck," I breathe, bending down to pick up the overturned lamp. I go to place it on the table, but that's been knocked over too. It takes me three tries to right it with one hand, finally setting the lamp down and turning to the room.

It looks like a fucking hurricane came through here.

There are papers on the floor, the coffee table turned upside down. From here, I can see the little kitchen is no better—all the cabinets and drawers pulled open and emptied, counter littered with junk. Everything is askew and rummaged through.

And among the chaos is Georgia, knees pulled up to her chest, staring sightlessly at the door I just came through.

Lifting a hand into the air, I repeat. "What the fuck?!" When I get nothing but a slow blink, all the worst thoughts cross my mind. Someone came in here—maybe that Freshman from before—and did something to her. Maybe Gene was here. Maybe Collins finally got fed up with waiting. It could be anything.

And she's not fucking *talking*.

I kick an old takeout container out of the way as I approach her. "Who did this?"

The closer I get, the more I realize how red the tip of her nose is, eyes dark and heavy and full of exhaustion. If that wasn't enough evidence that she's been crying, the hoarse sound of her voice when she croaks drives it home.

"I did."

"*You*?" I look around the room, completely fucking lost. "Why?"

She finally looks up, but it doesn't connect. It feels more like she's staring through me. "I was looking for the cameras."

My spine turns to steel at the icy contempt in her voice,

stomach doing a somersault of dread. "The fuck are you talking about?"

"It seemed kind of silly at first," she says in lieu of answering. "I mean, you barely have a phone, so how would you have cameras? But I figure if you had one in the office..." My blood runs cold at the look she gives me. "Then maybe I should check."

I stand, completely frozen, for far too long to play this off. There's a long moment of tense silence where I could come clean. But I don't. "What are you talking about?"

She gives me a slow, bland smile that's dripping with disdain. "You're really going to play dumb?" She tilts her head, those empty eyes searching my face. "Strange. I thought you had more guts than this. I must be even stupider than I thought. And trust me, that's saying a lot."

I'd flinch at the coldness in her eyes if I could move. Instead, I'm held under her gaze, mind racing with something to say. In the end, I find I don't want to lie. "It's not what you think."

"So you didn't record us fucking?" she asks, eyes still dim and lifeless. "Because the thumbnail Ozzy showed me was pretty convincing."

Well, I'm right about one thing. It *isn't* what she thinks.

It's so much fucking worse.

My stomach explodes in a fiery storm of razors at what I'm about to say, but all I can hear is Warren's voice, from six hours ago.

You'll need to be honest—first with yourself, and then with her.

"I took the video because I needed proof," I tell her, voice falling flat. "I kept it for a while, and then I sold it for ten grand to a Northridge loan shark who wants to blackmail your family with it."

Aside from glossing over the initial bet, it's as non-sugar-coated as I can possibly make it. It's one of those tactics my dad taught me; make something seem worse than it is, and then people will be relieved when they get the whole story.

I would have thought it'd make it easier.

Instead, the way the life drains from her face just makes my chest feel like it's being carved out. She presses her fists to her stomach, eyes wide and full of stunned agony. "Oh, my god."

"Georgia," I start, dropping my bag and keys, "just let me—"

"Oh my god," she gasps, sounding out of breath, looking lost. "I can't believe I let you do this to me again." The tears start in earnest then, rolling down her pale cheeks. "I can't believe I let you. What is *wrong with me?*"

Suddenly, I'm hit with the memory of her confession in that video. The imagined flash of her swaying feet as she hangs. The way her eyes looked when she lied about the reason for it being leaked. I'm struck by the realization that Georgia will never hate me as much as she hates herself.

"Fuck that!" I snap, voice hard and fervent. "This was *me*. You want to know what I did? Someone bet me I couldn't fuck you. He said you'd never go for it, but I knew he was wrong. I knew how to manipulate you. I knew what buttons to push. I knew about that fucking rubber band, even then." Feeling emboldened when she finally meets my gaze again, I explain, "That's why I recorded it. It was proof, so I could win. Because that's all I cared about."

I tell her because I'd rather see that spark of disgusted hatred in her eyes turned on me then herself.

And that's exactly what I get.

In a flash, she's cleared the space between us, face red and contorted, and it doesn't even matter when she strikes out, hitting me in the nose. I plant my feet, set my jaw, and I fucking take it, because this is better, *so much better* when it's aimed at me.

"You bastard!" she cries, bouncing her fists off my cheek, my shoulder, my chin. "I fucking hate you! You're evil, you piece of shit!" One of her punches lands right between my eyes, snapping my head back momentarily, but I recover just in time for another blow to land right on the ridge of my eyebrow. I can feel the sharp sting, skin splitting, but not before she catches me in the mouth, rattling my teeth. I can feel when she's burned through it, her fists barely fazing me until she eventually stops trying, shoving weakly at my chest instead.

She staggers back, exhausted and flushed as she releases a tight, pained sob. "It was all a lie," she cries, folding onto the floor in a heap of wild hair and limp limbs.

I take a second to get my bearings, pins of panic dotting the edges of my vision—or maybe that's just from her knuckles slamming into my temple. When everything sharpens, I suck my teeth, tasting blood, and crouch down to cradle her head in my palms.

"Georgia, look at me." She doesn't, eyes fixed somewhere on the floor as a sob wracks her body. I sweep her hair back anyway, ducking my head in an attempt to catch her gaze. "He can't use it. It's as good as deleted. Yes, I sold it for the money, but not without making sure it was useless to him." My bones feel heavy but oddly hollow as I thumb away the wetness on her cheeks. "And the bet was stupid, but that was a long time ago. I didn't understand then about the gambling addiction, and I was so fucking mad at you. Back then, I wanted to hurt you and I wanted to *win*, and I think..." I sigh, shoulders slumping. "I think I got manipulated, too. I know it doesn't make it any better, but—"

"I defended you," she gasps, pulling in a wet sniffle. "I told you things I've never even told—" She sounds so sick and disgusted with herself that it makes my stomach explode in a storm of fire. "I actually *cared* about you."

"You aren't listening to me," I realize, trying to shake some sense into her. "He can't use it, I made sure. Georgia, *I made sure*."

She stills, the sobs fading into hitched gasps, and then slowly into shallow breaths. When she finally looks up at me, her eyes are wet and terrifyingly vacant. "I thought I loved you," she croaks, chin wobbling. "How much did you get for that?"

"No," I say, cradling her cheeks in my hands. "Hey, don't—it's not like that. It wasn't a lie. Georgia, I..."

A better man could say it back. A stronger man could have heard her say those words and felt something other than the sickening churn of regret. I'm neither of those men. I'm the man who realizes I've lost it before I ever had to chance to grasp it. It sits heavy in my chest, a gnarled sense of failure. A casualty of my own doing.

Darting forward, I kiss her. It's a frantic, desperate move, made all the more painful by her lack of response. But this is how we work. We've never talked with words. I pull back long enough to say, "I'll fuck you, okay?" and reach for the button of my pants. That's what she always wants, my only value. Her lips are pliant and warm when I return, parted more in shock than anything. I lick into the seam of her mouth anyway, easing her to the floor. "I'll eat your pussy," I promise, hiking up her skirt. "Whatever you want. Just don't—" When I realize she's motionless, staring listlessly up at my chin, I pause, hand going still between her thighs. I look into her tired eyes, chest twisting with the knowledge that it's over.

I've lost.

I rest my forehead against hers, inhaling the soft scent of her perfume. What comes next is a plaintive, desperate confession that I might come to regret later.

"I need you."

She pushes me away, and I go without fighting, rolling to collapse at her side. I don't move when she rises to her feet, her motions slow and achingly deliberate. She smooths down her skirt and reaches for her bag, slinging it carefully over a shoulder.

She stops when her hand touches the knob of the door, turning only enough to give me a glimpse of her bland expression. "Ozzy thinks the video isn't secure," she says, voice rough and lifeless.

Long after she's gone, I still stare at the door, breathing in the acute awareness of all the empty space she's left behind.

Finding Big Gene at three in the morning is easier said than done, but I sure as fuck try. Driving around the derelict side of Northridge is an exercise in futility, so I hit all the obvious places first; the fights, the races, the poker games in the back of a bar that has no visible business name. Everywhere I turn up, I draw an audience. People excited at the prospect of my money, eager to take a bet, egging me on when I just walk away.

It'd be beyond difficult even without the money burning a hole in my pocket. I almost think of calling Warren, but I don't think I can handle looking him in the eye, considering the shit's that gone down.

I find Gene at a dice game going down at a dealer's warehouse. The space is smoky and dimly lit, hard to make out faces. But I'd know that big, round, balding head anywhere. He's standing in the back, watching with his shark eyes as he sucks on a cheap cigar.

The cigar bobs between his lips with a laugh when he sees me. "Off the wagon, Wilcox?" His attention is only half on me, the other half laser focused on the game going down. If I had the presence of mind to care about anything else, I'd wonder what he's got riding on it.

As it is, I lean against the wall at his side and pitch my voice low. "I need to buy the flash drive back."

He laughs again, although I don't miss the way his eyes go tight. "Sure thing. How much you got?"

I shove my hand into my pocket, fingering the stack of money. "Six."

"Six *what*?" He throws me an amused look. "Unless the words 'gold bullion' are about to come out of your mouth, then you can fuck off. You're distracting me."

"Cut the shit," I say, running out of patience. "Name your price."

He hums, watching as a skinny guy rolls a pair of dice. "It'll cost you seven hundred."

"*Grand*?!" I growl, turning to him. "That's bullshit!"

"That's business," he says, cutting me a hard look.

I fume silently for a long moment, already knowing how this song and dance goes. That's the issue with Gene. It's just like Warren said. It'll never be enough. To get out of debt, I'll just go into even more debt. On and on, tried and true.

You need to break the cycle.

Crossing my arms, I nod to the frenzy happening. "Maybe I'll just call the cops and get this whole thing busted up. After that, I can tip them off to the races. The fights. The poker games." My voice is low and full of warning when I conclude, "I can make 'business' very fucking difficult for you."

"You're trying to extort me?" Gene actually takes the cigar out of his mouth to laugh at that one. "You're bringing a knife to an H-bomb fight, sonny. Ah, god, it slays me." He grabs his side, wheezing with laughter. "I can't wait to tell Dirty about this. He'll piss himself."

I scowl at him, feeling ragged and wrung out and *not in the fucking mood*. "Gene, I swear to fucking god—"

"Swear to whatever you want," he replies, popping the cigar back between his lips. He gives it to strong puffs. "The flash drive's in your possession. You just don't know it yet."

"What the hell is that supposed to mean?"

"It means that you're not the only one who can make calls." He looks away from the game long enough to give me a stony-faced smirk. "For instance, I can call the cops and tell them this pal of mine—good fellow, but currently on probation—has been sharing around this video. Grotesque thing. Absolutely unconscionable, poor girl. And the flash drive with that video is currently hidden on the premises of this pal's very own business." He pulls his mouth back in a wide-eyed grimace. "You're good, Wilcox, but sloppy. You thought you covered your ass with the shitty encryption job? I'm not a fool. Your fingerprints are all over this. Not mine."

It feels like my strings have been cut, leaving me swaying and formless. For a moment, I'm completely fucking unable to find my next move, too muddled with my panic to calculate what should come next. Turning Underworld upside-down and inside-out, searching for it. That's obvious. I have time.

Don't I?

"Maybe it's time for you to accept that you're just not that good at gambling." Gene clasps me on the shoulder, giving me a loose shake. "But so what, Wilty Cock? In a few days, that file unlocks, which means I'm going to come into some massive stacks of money and *you're* going to get your club back. It's a win."

My eyes are drawn to his at the words, "A win." In the back of my mind, a plan is forming.

I don't need to win.

I just need Georgia to win.

27

"I don't understand," Mr. Francis says, frowning. "You've been doing so well lately, Miss Haynes. Frankly, you've become among the top of my class. I'm surprised."

I duck my head, trying not to meet his gaze. I already know what I look like today, all frayed and puffy-eyed and exhausted. "I meant to do it yesterday," I say of my History paper, "but something just came up. It's...incomplete." I wince at the hoarseness in my voice. Usually, I'm a lot better at hiding.

But right now, I can't.

I hear him sigh, setting down the stack of everyone else's papers. "You need to go see Mrs. Gilbert."

My head snaps up, eyes growing wide. "No, it's not—I'm just not feeling well. That's all. It's a..." I struggle for an excuse, eventually landing on, "...girl problem."

Not technically a lie.

Mr. Francis almost manages to hide his grimace. "Do you need to see the nurse?"

I know if I decline, he'll get suspicious, so I take the pass he gives me without argument, ducking into the girl's room to splash

385

some water on my face. This won't do—walking around like this, numb and visibly defeated. Maybe some people could get away with it, but not me. Not with my history.

Story of my life.

Looking in the mirror, I take a deep breath and pull out my makeup bag. The tears dried up sometime last night, but the evidence remains. I dab concealer onto the puffy circles beneath my eyes, rubbing it in methodically. Liner. Shadow. Mascara. A little blush for my pale cheeks. A slight tint for my lips.

I gather my hair at the top of my head and tie into a bouncing ponytail, trying a smile in the mirror. It looks stiff and disused. It'd be a passing imitation of someone who hasn't had their heart carved out with a rusty melon baller if it weren't for the lack of spark in my expression. My fake smile melts away, and it isn't fair. Isn't it enough that I'm walking? That I've managed to get out of bed and go through the motions? That I've gone four hours without thinking about—

I fumble in my bag for something—*anything*—but I can't find the old pen. The sharp one. The one that's good for jabbing. It doesn't matter. I'm resourceful. I grab my compact and open it, holding it in my palm as I smash it against the porcelain sink. There's a *crunch*, glass raining to the floor, but when I pull it back, there are multiple usable shards. I dig one out, blowing it clean before pulling up my sleeve and hastily pressing it into the tender flesh of my forearm.

My gasp is loud enough to surprise me, eyes falling closed as I sink to the floor. *Holy shit.* "Oh, *god.*"

I'm instantly hit with the realization that I'm never going back to rubber bands, pens, and pulling my hair out. This is the real deal —the immediate rush of endorphins, the swell of my chest as it fills with *something*. I stare at the wall as I push the jagged glass into my skin, shaking with the sudden, unavoidable presence of my heartbeat.

I'm not expecting the blood.

"No, no, no." My chest clenches and I lurch up, snagging a handful of paper towels from the dispenser above me. It doesn't sting when I press them to my arm in a rush to wipe it away, but I panic, worried that I've cut it too deep. "Shit," I hiss, peeling the paper away. Blood bubbles up, the dark red stark against my fair skin, but a few more pats and the surge begins to slow a little.

The experience offered enough adrenaline that I can see a flush of color in my reflected face when I stand. I pause as I look at myself, and it's not the same—it's not the rush of being filled, the quickening of my pulse as I'm touched, the explosive release of an orgasm. But this is safer. I rinse the shard of glass in the sink before stowing it away in my pocket.

I'll just have to be more careful next time.

I avoid the dining hall for lunch and dinner, afraid of seeing his face and thinking about it again. It's futile in the end, because I still have class with him at the end of the day, but I can give myself time to prepare. That's how, when I walk into the natatorium that evening, I'm armed with a dismissal form.

It doesn't put me at ease, though. I still spend too long out on the pool deck, stomach swirling with dread at the thought of walking back into that office. It takes me forever to take the steps into the corridor leading to it, throat locking up with each footfall, until I finally find myself standing there, staring numbly at the knob.

Wrapping myself in whatever armor I can find, I push the door open.

He's right there, behind the desk, jotting something onto the paper secured on his clipboard. He looks up at the sound of the door opening, though, those blue eyes locking instantly on mine.

It takes me a long time to realize the bruises and cuts on his face were made by me. At the time, it'd all seemed so ineffectual, my feeble fists knocking into whatever was closest. I'm surprised to see the split in his lip, the cut on his eyebrow, the bruise blooming over his temple, his jaw. It's a shock to think I'd made any mark at all.

I don't notice the slumped, dejected curve of his shoulders until he snaps upright, demeanor changing.

He clears his throat, pushing himself to his feet. "Good. You came."

My pulse rushes hot and frantic in my ears, and before he can say anything else, I toss the dismissal sheet on his desk and take two steps back. "Sign it."

He doesn't break my gaze as he reaches for the paper, sparing it only the barest glance before looking back up. "Your test is coming up soon. You still haven't—"

"I don't care." Without meaning to, my eyes go to the shelves above the lockers. That's where it must have been that night, all nestled away, watching me. My skin crawls under the weight of phantom eyes.

"It's not there anymore," he says, drawing my attention back to the intensity of his gaze. "I took it from Underworld. It was one of our security cams for behind the bar."

"Fascinating," I drawl, hand tightening painfully around the strap of my bag. "Sign it."

He drops the paper, eyes fixed to mine as he rounds the desk. "I'm going to get the flash drive back."

I take another step back. "Would you just—"

"It's at the club," he says, cutting me off as he comes closer. He only stops when I bump into the open door, something gentle and disappointed in his eyes. "All I need to do is find it, and then I'll give it to you. You can smash it, burn it, do whatever you want with it." Closer like this, I realize how frayed he looks, the dark circles beneath his eyes looking more like the result of sleeplessness than bruising from my fists. "I just need a couple days." Softer, he begs, "*Please*, just give me a couple days."

"Take all the time you want," I say, voice tight. "It won't matter."

His brows knit together, head tilting. "Why?" The words are laced with a tight desperation that nearly makes me flinch to hear. "Don't you get it? This will undo everything."

I wish I could see the plea in his eyes and not feel compelled to grant it. I wish I could see the cut of his jaw without remembering how it feels to press my mouth to it. I wish I hadn't laid in bed last night and tucked a pillow against my back, just to feel the weight of something tangible against me.

When his words register, I give a short, incredulous laugh that feels like razor blades in the back of my throat. "Are you really that deluded?" I ask, chest twisting at the way he's watching me. *Too much*. I always give away too much when I'm with him. "You can't undo what you did!"

"Because I recorded it?" He flings a hand toward those shelves, eyes flashing as he steps forward. "Georgia, that was months ago. You would have buried me if given half a chance. Because shit was different then, and you know it."

I inch back, heedless of the edge of the door. "I know that you're the same pathetic, selfish bully you always were, only now you're older and the stakes are higher." Even back then, I never would have thought Heston might get to my family through me. It's beyond sick. It's beyond betrayal. I've been fucked by a lot of guys who wanted nothing to do with me afterward, but it's never made me feel the way I do now.

Used.

"You're wrong." The muscle in the back of his jaw tightens. "That's what I'm trying to show you. I'll get the video back and then you'll see."

"And then what?!" I cry, throwing my hands up. "You think I'm going to run back to your bed and give you the opportunity to do it again? How stupid do you think I am?"

His eyes zero in on something at my outburst, eyes darkening. He darts forward too fast for me to react, slamming the door and snatching my wrist in one swift, violent move. He wrenches my sleeve up, nose flaring at the wound on my forearm. "What the fuck is this?" he asks, pinning me beneath his stormy gaze.

"None of your business," I snap, trying to yank my wrist free. "Get off me!"

He clamps on tighter, raising my arm between us. His voice is low and dangerous when he says, "You're cutting yourself now? What's the endgame with this, Georgia?"

I tug harder, insisting, "You don't know anything about it!"

"I know that it's going to escalate," he explodes, eyes full of a fire that burns too hot to hold. "I know that you're keeping whatever you did this with, in case you want to do it again." He instantly goes for my pocket and I curl back, struggling to duck away.

But not before he digs a hand inside and pulls the shard of glass from it.

I freeze, chest heaving only partly from the skirmish. It looks so much worse like this; him holding the glass in one hand and my wounded arm in the other. It makes me want to lash out again, hit him in the face. He should know what this is. He should understand that it's not *like that*.

"You want to be mad at me?" he asks, lips pressed into a bleak line. He puts the shard in my hand, yanking up his own sleeve. "Fine. Take your shot. Hurt *me*."

"I don't get off on hurting people. I'm not like you." I finally free myself from his grip, biting back a pained noise at the pull of the skin, the sting of the scab re-opening. I hastily cover it up, growling, "You don't get a say in how I—"

"If you think I'm going to sit by and let you do this, you're wrong." His expression is severe, unyielding, and when he goes to take the shard from my palm, I'm too busy fuming to stop him.

I cross my arms instead, hands fisting into my sweater. "Like you can do anything."

"I'm a teacher," he says, tossing the glass on the desk. "I can report it."

Raising my chin, I respond. "Go ahead. I fucking dare you. I'll tell Collins you've been fucking a student."

He's silent for a long moment, watching me. "I'll tell the Devils."

That pulls me up short, jaw going slack. "*What*?"

"I'll tell Vandy, Caroline, Emory. Warren, too." Shrugging, he adds, "Whatever. I'll even call my brother." He braces a palm against the door, caging me in. "If you won't listen to me, maybe you'll listen to them."

Shaking my head, I slide away, resenting that he's got me trapped in here. "If you think that'll make anything better, then you're wrong."

He slams his palm—hard, loud—into the door. "Then tell me what *the fuck* will make you stop doing this!"

Thrusting a finger at the desk, I wail, "Sign the goddamn form, Heston!"

He gives me a slow blink, like maybe he wasn't expecting the way my voice cracks, or how badly I'm shaking. Slowly, he pushes away from the door, reaching for the paper on the desk. Giving a flippant sniff, he snatches a pen from the desk and uses it to jot his name on the line. I watch, stupefied as he goes through the motions, deliberate and too stiff.

I yank it from his hand the second he extends it.

But before I can reach for the knob, he says, "If I see you doing it again..." Roughly, he shoves his fingers through his hair, eyes wild. "Then fuck it. I'll just go to Mrs. Gilbert. You can turn me in to Collins. I'll accept that."

I stare at him, unblinking. "You're bluffing."

The smile he gives me is crooked and all wrong. "I have it on pretty good authority that I'm shit at gambling. So believe me when I say I'm not doing it now."

"Why?" I wilt inside at the agonized tone it escapes in. "Why do you even care?"

His answer is worse than anything I might have imagined.

"Because I love you."

I stare in stunned disbelief, lifting my hands to give a slow clap. "Amazing. Every time I think you can't possibly stoop any lower, you—"

"Don't," he snaps, brows crouched low and angry. "I've only said those words to one other person, and she's the woman who gave birth to me. You're pissed at me, I get it. But don't fucking mock me because you can't handle the truth. I love you." He says it with far more conviction than he had the last time, and it just grows when it says it again. "And I'd rather go back to jail and have to start all over again than see you slit your wrists over some total fucking *bullshit*!"

I do flinch then, startled by the crash of the clipboard smashing against the wall. He'd hurled it so quickly that I didn't even see it sailing through the air. The office falls into a thick, tense silence, and for a long moment I find I can't move, frozen with my hand halfway to turning the doorknob.

He sighs, dragging a palm down his face. When it reaches his throat, he meets my gaze and releases a measured breath. "I'm sorry."

I don't even know what he's apologizing for. Making the video? Selling it? Trapping me in here? Threatening me?

Is he apologizing for loving me?

I don't find out.

I wrench the door open and run as fast as my unsteady legs will take me.

∿

"The horns aren't big enough," Caroline says, shoving her glasses up the bridge of her nose. "I think we should make them spikier."

Vandy taps her chin as she inspects the effigy we're building. "And curvier, right? Wait, let me see the picture again."

The two of them huddle around Caroline's laptop, pointing out the various details on Thistle Cove's Viking mascot. I keep layering newspaper onto the helmet, plopping on more glue before adding another. It's almost as easy to get lost in as knitting. Paper, glue, paper, glue.

Caroline groans. "This is hard! Aren't we supposed to have a fourth Devil to help us?"

I flinch at the mention of Heston, trying harder to tune them out.

Vandy scoffs. "Of course, he comes in to give his opinion, but sticks us with all the actual work."

The torso is already completed, composed of three different sections. Down here in the Devil's bunker, the ceiling is far too low to construct it at full height. The helmet itself is almost as wide as my car, and we'd had to move everything to the walls to have sufficient space. But it's a dank basement, and the ventilation is poor, which means that we keep having to take breaks up in the tower.

"What do you think, Georgia?" Vandy asks, turning to me.

My chief contribution so far has been to nestle the memory card with our confessions within the gluey, paper layers of the helmet, which was honestly more productive than I feel strictly capable of. Listlessly, I paint another glob of glue onto the newspaper. "Sounds good."

"That's it." Caroline snaps the laptop closed, whirling on me. "You need to talk."

"About what?"

Vandy props her fists on her hips. "About whatever's got you acting like this! You've been a total space cadet the last couple days —that is, whenever you're not crying and thinking we don't notice. Something is clearly going on."

Caroline sighs. "We thought we'd wait for you to come to us on your own terms, but you're not doing that."

Vandy sits down at my side, resting a hand on my back. She ducks down to ask, "Please tell us what happened? It might feel better to talk it out."

Shoulders slumping, I run the tip of my finger down the gluey bristles of the brush. "I can't."

"Why not?" Caroline asks, sitting down on my other side. "Is this because...I mean, I know I was a bitch before, but I really meant it when I said you can tell us anything."

"*Anything*," Vandy stresses.

I shake my head. "Not this."

We all go silent for a moment, which I spend pressing my fingertips together, fixated on the tacky sensation of press and pull.

"This is about that guy, isn't it?" Caroline guesses, gently bumping our arms together. "Because we wouldn't approve."

I finally drop the brush, inhaling sharply. "I just can't hear it right now."

The confusion is apparent in Vandy's voice. "Hear what?"

I finally turn to look at her, and I don't know what my face is doing, but whatever it is, it makes her face fall. "That I should have known better." It's strange. I'm not sure how I can possibly have any tears left, but they come anyway, flooding my eyes in a deluge of shame and wasted grief.

"Hey," Vandy soothes, quick and solemn. "No, don't do that." She curls her arm around me and pulls me into her side, hand cradling my head. "Whatever it is, I'm sure it's not your fault."

"Yes, it is." I sob into her shoulder, knowing that she's wrong. "I'm so fucking stupid, V."

"You are not!" Caroline says, sharp and insistent.

"I am," I cry, wiping my cheeks. Once I've got myself under control, I take a deep, calming breath. That's the clincher. Heston has a nature, and I knew it. All along, I knew exactly what he was capable of. Maybe he's lying about the flash drive. Maybe it's already out there and my father's about to get a call. Maybe there are more videos. Maybe it's all been a trick to maneuver me into this exact position.

But even if he's telling the truth, it doesn't make it better. If he's changed, and has grown to care about me, and really intended to keep that video locked, then it still means I failed. I let him in. I let myself love him, despite knowing who he was.

The biggest problem isn't that I can't trust him.

It's that I can't trust myself.

Weary, I rest my head in Vandy's lap, staring sightlessly at the paper maché. "Do you think it's possible to love someone and keep hurting them?"

Caroline hums in thought. "What do you mean?"

"If someone hurt you—like, really bad—but then they told you they loved you, you wouldn't believe them, right?"

Vandy's fingers run through my hair, smoothing it from root to tip. "I believe Reyn when he says he loves me."

Closing my eyes, I sigh. "That's different. That car wreck was an accident. He didn't mean to hurt you."

"No," she agrees, twirling my hair around a forefinger. "But he meant to steal that car. He meant to manipulate me into coming along. He just didn't realize how bad it'd be."

"What if he did it again?" I wonder, already knowing this is comparing apples to baguettes.

Vandy confirms this. "Reynolds would never put me in a position like that again. He'd give up his life before he let that happen."

"See?" I bolt up to look at her, pointing a finger. "*That's* love! It's not something that happens suddenly after you've fucked someone over. Reynolds probably loved you since you were little kids."

Vandy frowns in thought, but it's Caroline who speaks. "I don't know if that's fair, G. I think everyone loves in their own way, at their own pace."

"Great," I mutter sourly. "Vandy gets Saks Fifth Avenue 'love' and I get the counterfeit, street corner knock-off?" Laughing humorlessly, I admit, "Yeah, that seems about what I'm capable of getting."

"So this guy must have done something messed up," Caroline observes, "and now he's trying to get you back?"

Shaking my head, I admit, "I don't know. He says he wants to 'undo it'. Like he can just wave a wand and erase the fact that he—" My words bite off before I can give too much away. I wasn't lying before. I wouldn't be able to stand hearing that I should have seen this coming. It's bad enough coming from my own thoughts. I don't need my best friends to beat me over the head with what I already know. "It doesn't matter. It's probably all a lie, anyway. I doubt he even knows how to love anyone but himself."

"I don't know who this guy is," Vandy says, tucking my hair behind my shoulder to catch my gaze. "But I know *you*, and sometimes..." She sighs, head shaking sadly. "It's almost like you're convinced that's not an option for you."

"You're really hard on yourself, Georgia," Caroline agrees, taking my hand in hers. "When I said those things to you...they were awful. They would have been awful if I'd said them to someone else. But I think it was worse, because at some point I realized you might really believe them. You give out such a tough, strong vibe that it's easy to believe you can take everything thrown at you." She swallows. "But that's not fair. Strength doesn't mean you don't have feelings."

Vandy seems to choose her words carefully. "If this guy really did something unforgivable, then you deserve better. And it's really getting to me that I haven't heard you say that yet. You *do* deserve to be loved. You know that, right?" She gently knocks our shoulders together. "You deserve to be happy."

"What if he did?" I ask, sniffling wetly. "What does it say about me that the worst person in the world made me feel better than I ever have before?" I don't give either of them a chance to answer. "It says that I'm a weak, gullible slut."

"No," Vandy says, voice hard. "It says that people aren't just one thing or another. Reyn is more than just a criminal. I'm more than the sheltered, crippled girl. Emory is more than an overprotective meathead. Caroline is more than a nerd." She grabs my shoulder, giving it a fervent shake. "And you're more than the guys you've slept with, Georgia Haynes."

"If this guy is really that terrible, and you managed to find the parts of him worth loving? I don't think that makes you gullible or weak." Caroline gives me a soft smile. "I think that makes you amazing."

Is Heston Wilcox more than an abusive, manipulative, entitled asshole? I can't ask them, because then all of their words will be taken back. If Heston's plan had been to shame me, make me question myself, make me loathe who I am, then he did it expertly.

These girls need to believe in love and redemption, but I know better.

For some of us, there's only pain.

⌇

Every time I close my eyes, I'm filled with the oppressive sense of dread. Since I can't sleep, I'm finishing up Micha's scarf, which has been particularly fussy due to the nature of the metallic-weaved yarn. It was the closest I could get to glitter, and with the rainbow of colors I used, I think it may be my best one yet. The sense of pride I feel when I look at it is the only time I've felt something other than horrible in days.

The letters 'HWC' popping up on my phone instantly wipe it away.

H: Come to Underworld

H: It's about the video

That sense of dread pulls me under, heart hammering wildly against my ribcage. It's just after three in the morning, which means Underworld closed long ago. It'd be beyond foolish to get out of bed, sneak off campus, and meet Heston in some dark, deserted night club.

This is what I tell myself as I pull on a pair of jeans and a sweater, grabbing my jacket. My hands are shaking as I grab for the warmest things I can find; thick, wool socks and the nearest completed scarf from my pile of gifts.

It's foolish, yes. But I've got enough things to regret without adding the possibility of letting the flash drive go to the list.

It's dark and cold, and as I sneak around the tower to the parking lot, white plumes of breath act as my wake. The campus is dead, though. The athletic field is tipped with frosty dew that disappears under my footsteps, and when I get into my car, I have to wait for it to warm up enough to clear my windshield of the fine layer of foggy condensation. On the drive across town, I wish I'd told Vandy and Caroline everything. Maybe then, I could have texted one of them where I was going, just in case.

I haven't felt this alone in a very long time.

It sits heavily in my chest as I approach the building. Nothing but a couple streetlights and the eerie glow of Northridge's skyline light distance between Underworld and where I park. I sit there for a long moment, willing myself to breathe, but my lungs feel constricted and far too small. It's then, as I'm curling my chin to my chest, struggling for air, that I realize what scarf I'm wearing.

It pulls a startled, disbelieving laugh from my throat.

It's the scarf I knitted for Heston.

I started it on a whim, that day I was trying to make him feel better. We'd watched that episode of Lakevale together over cold

Chinese food. After his whole rant about the school colors, I got the idea to make one just for him; black and neon green.

Black, to represent the persistent state of decay.

Green, to represent growth and life.

It'd all felt so stupidly cerebral at the time, like I was making some grand statement in the form of yarn. I'd crawled out of his bed later that night and gone straight back to my dorm to start it. Of course, once I'd finished it, I realized it looked hideous.

In short, it was perfect for him.

Now, I wish I'd burned it.

The cold slaps me in the face when I step out of the car, squinting in the direction of Underworld's entrance through the dense fog. It looks dark and empty, no signs of life. It isn't until I turn to cross the intersection that I see him.

Heston's car is parked across the road, his silhouette perched on the hood, tipping back a large bottle to his mouth. I cross my arms tight around my middle, ducking my head against the wind as I warily approach him, eyes scanning the surrounding lot.

When I get close enough, I can make out the details. Despite the biting cold, he's wearing nothing but jeans and an old, faded hoodie. When he sees me, throat bobbing with a swallow of whatever he's drinking, he looks just as exhausted as he had before, only now his eyes are red and a little glazed.

We stare at each other for a long moment, something sharp and bad-smelling burning my nostrils.

His face is unreadable, marked with tired lines and tense edges, but his eyes say enough. "I couldn't find it."

I say nothing, watching as he drops his gaze to the bottle in his hand. Inside, my stomach turns over on itself, knowing that it's over.

"I looked—I swear I looked everywhere, and it's just..." He pushes his hair back, shoulders curved into a defeated line. "It's a big fucking building. It'd take me weeks to go through everything. But I don't have weeks." His smile is sharp, laced with bitterness. "Gene's going to come tonight to get it, and I can't do anything to stop him."

My mouth works around my dry, paralyzed tongue. "Who's Gene?"

Heston licks his lips, a distant streetlight catching on the flat press of them. "Doesn't matter. It's not about him. It's about me." A gust of wind cuts through the lot, making his hair sway lifelessly in front of his eyes. "I just needed you to know, because you're the only good thing in my life. Everything else has been a constant avalanche of shit. My family. Collins. Gene. Everything just always fucking sucks now. But you? You're the one thing here that's worth half a damn. And I fucked it up." He finally looks up, meeting my gaze. My blood runs cold at the deadness there. "I fucked up, Georgia."

"Heston..." I try to inhale, lungs burning from either the cold or the panic clutching my chest at the defeat in his eyes. "There's still time. I can help look. We can get the Devils to come, we can all—"

It's like he doesn't hear me, raising his eyes to the building behind me. "I fucked it up, because aside from swimming and fucking, that's apparently all I'm good at. I see that now." He spreads his arms wide. "It's my superpower. I can ruin anything I touch." He raises his bottle of whisky to something over my shoulder, looking weirdly proud. "Case in point..."

I turn, feeling completely lost, deciding he must be too drunk to make sense.

My eyes grow wide when it hits me.

The eerie glow in the sky isn't the distant skyline of Northridge.

My lungs aren't burning from the cold.

It's not foggy out here.

Above the arch of Underworld's entrance, flames lick at the sky. Thick, black smoke billows like a rolling cloud above the roof. My arms drop limp to my sides as I look on, wide-eyed and slack-jawed.

"Thank god for shitty wiring."

"What the hell—"

"I know what you're thinking. Don't worry." At some point, he's sidled up to me. Unable to peel my eyes away from the flames slowly rising out of the roof, I watch from my periphery as he takes another slow draw from the bottle. "My dad made me go with him to this fundraiser a couple years back. Some dumb law enforcement banquet. It was supposed to be a good opportunity to build connections—you know, collect a couple 'get out of jail free' cards." His laugh is a sharp, gnarled thing. "I recently discovered that those connections will *not* get you out of sex offenses." He gestures to the building. "But hey, turns out, it does get you access to the six dispatchers working the night shift, and they'll gladly ignore any call you want for a cool grand each."

My mouth parts, but nothing comes out. Something inside the club jostles, followed by the muffled sound of a distant crash that would make me flinch if my muscles were working. When Heston wordlessly extends the bottle to me, I mechanically reach out to take it, wondering for a moment what he expects me to do with it.

I look at the mouth of the bottle and then throw it back for a thick gulp of whiskey that burns as hot as the flames slowly engulfing Underworld.

Maybe I fell asleep hours ago, and this is all a very weird and concerning dream.

"How long?" I ask, voice emerging rusty and cracked. "How long until someone comes?"

His eyes reflect the glow of the flames when he takes the bottle back. "Three hours maybe."

I don't have to ask to know that he's going to stay here, watching. "Oh." I'm silent for a long while, trying to wrap my head around what's happening. "Arson is a felony." I aim for shocked disgust, because that's exactly how I should feel. Instead, it comes out in a flat, awed sort of disbelief. "Even without your probation, that's like...a fucking million years in prison."

When I turn to him, he's gazing up at the club—*his* club—as it blazes away. "Yeah." He swings his eyes to mine, raising the bottle. "To my very last gamble, huh?" He drinks to it, throat jumping with two hard swallows before he passes it back to me.

I pause before following suit, taking one last drink. And then I tuck it into my jacket, securing it tight within the zipper. "This was all you had."

"Not all." His words are heavy with meaning.

The fire pops, and something cracks and falls inside. I take a reflexive step back. "I can't thank you for fixing a problem you created."

There's a heaviness to his nod, resignation swimming in his weary eyes. "I know."

Reaching up, I unwind the scarf and step in front of him. His blue eyes settling on my face feels just as intense as it always has, making my stomach twist. Sniffing against the cold and smoke, I feel just as choked by the knurled, hard thing in my throat when I stand on the tips of my toes. He remains silent, perfectly motionless as I wrap it around his exposed neck. I smooth the ends down with my palms, combing out the black and green fringe.

...an ode to the endless cycle of rebirth.

Behind me, Underworld burns, and somewhere in the storm of flames and cinder are Heston's past and future. I can't thank him.

But I can make sure it counts for something.

"I won't hurt myself anymore."

The way he looks at me then—searching and achingly soft— tells me what I already suspected: this promise means more to him than any thanks ever could.

When I walk away, he lets me go.

The enormous, unavoidable presence of him becomes branded into my brain, and it doesn't matter how much time will pass. I know that I'll always remember the way he looked right then, standing so tenaciously as he burned his life to the ground.

It's the moment I realized Heston Wilcox loves me.

28

Warren is waiting for me when I come out of the doors, papers clutched in my hand. He stands up when he sees me, setting an issue of Good Housekeeping down on the table at his side.

"All good?" he asks, and I can see that he's worried, although I'm not sure why. Who am I? Just some fucker who went to the same school he attended a couple decades ago.

I hold up the paper, voice hoarse when I speak. "Need to get these filled."

He nods, looking like he expected this much, and says, "I've got a pharmacy."

Before leaving, I pay the receptionist two of the five hundred dollars I have left. God only fucking knows how much the three prescriptions are going to cost, and then that'll be everything I've got. But when I went to the meeting this afternoon and ended up vomiting up blood in the parking lot, Warren wouldn't take no for an answer. He drove me straight to the clinic.

It's odd, but I just stopped noticing the pain after so long. For the last week, it's become a part of me, like the color of my hair or my double-jointed fingers. I'm blonde, and good at fingerbangs, and suffering from agonizing stomach pain every second of the day.

On the way out of the clinic, Warren holds the door open for me and I toss him a glare. "What the fuck am I, a terminal cancer patient?" I stubbornly barrel past. "It's a stomach ulcer, not a tumor."

He's been weird as fuck all day, throwing me pensive looks and acting like I'm about to keel over. "Looked pretty serious from where I was standing."

"I already apologized for your shoes," I mutter. It wasn't the first time I've thrown up blood this week, it was just the first time I had someone around to notice it and mention that maybe that's not fucking normal.

It's not all about Georgia. A lot of it is. Like how I see her around campus but can't get her to look at me. Or how she always has her head down, shoulders pulled tight around her ears. Or how, when she does look up, her eyes are somehow both distant and too alert, watching everyone suspiciously. Try as I might, I can't remember if she was like this when the first video leaked. I really hadn't cared then—certainly not enough to watch her cross the courtyard or dining hall.

Yeah, a lot of it is about the way I have to see her every day and act like it's not ripping apart something inside of me to know that I blew it.

But more of it is about the fire.

Underworld is nothing but a pile of charred rubble now. I'll say this for me: I can really burn a building down to ground. I've spent the last week waiting for that knock on my door. The ring of my phone. The drop of the axe. Georgia had been right. Arson isn't just sharing some sex video when you were sixteen and stupid. Just because I'm willing to go to prison to make sure that flash drive never sees the light of day doesn't mean I want to. I did my best to cover my tracks. I have hundreds of witnesses to attest to the fact that Underworld's electrical issues have been obvious and pressing. Still, I couldn't give a believable alibi if my life depended on it.

I got the call this morning, though, just past seven.

The fire has officially been ruled accidental.

It's good news, but far from being the end of the tunnel. There's still Gene to deal with. Now that I'm not spending every night at the club, and I've been avoiding the scene for months, he has less access to me. Nevertheless, I know it's coming.

I'll be ready when it does.

We've just pulled onto the highway when Warren says, "Georgia called me yesterday."

The prescription crinkles when I curl my fingers into a fist. I force my hand open and smooth the paper out over my knee. "Okay."

I'm not stupid. Georgia has needs. But she's not mine, and now that she's not mine, she'll get those needs met elsewhere. I can't even hold it against her. I know how it gets for her when she doesn't have it. She'll find someone to fuck because she has to, just to stay sane. It's been almost two weeks since we were last together, and even I'm about to lose my mind. I'm sure she's about to crawl out of her skin.

"We met for coffee," he adds, sounding deceptively uninterested. "She seemed kind of down."

"Hm." I turn to the window, also able to act disinterested. "I wouldn't know."

He lets out this long sigh that makes me want to jump out of the car, moving or not. "What happened?"

Shaking my head, I reach up to scratch my jaw, fingernails rasping on the stubble. "It was just like you said. I fucked it up. Whatever." Frustrated, I repeat, "It's whatever."

There's a beat of silence before he replies, "I wish you'd told me something was wrong. Maybe then, I could have been there for—"

"Jesus Christ. You're mad because you had to wait ten days for her to cry on your shoulder about what a piece of shit I am?" Shaking my head, I mutter, "Fuck you."

He gives me a quick look, eyebrows high on his forehead. "Georgia has a lot of problems, Heston." I can't fucking stand the way he says it. Like he knows more about her than I do. "But she also has a lot of friends, caring parents, attentive faculty, counselors, therapists. She has a strong support system, when she actually chooses to use them." Pointedly, he adds, "You don't have anybody."

I turn to glare at him. "Gee, thanks for reminding me."

His forehead wrinkles with a frown. "You're emotionally volatile right now. You're adrift. You're quite clearly suffering—physically and emotionally—and you've just lost your business and your...er, friend." Arching an eyebrow, he observes, "One might conclude that you don't have anything to lose, and I've got to tell you, that's a risky place for an addict to be."

I finally catch on to what he's saying. "You're worried I'm going to start gambling again?" My bark of laughter sounds just as rough as it feels in my sore throat. "I don't know if anyone's ever told you this before, but you need money to gamble. I've got three hundred dollars to my name and no paying job."

"You really haven't listened to a word anyone's said in those meetings, have you?" Warren smiles wryly. "Addicts find a way."

Sniffing, I look out at the passing trees. "This addict doesn't."

I meant what I said to Georgia about the fire being my last gamble. Somehow, despite everything, I managed to win.

For once, I'm quitting while I'm ahead.

When I get back to campus, I loiter for a while in my car. I've been avoiding my apartment, determined to spend as little time there as possible. It's still a wreck, trashed from the night Georgia found out about the video. The whole place reminds me of her. Smells like her. I can't even go near the bed, having recently been sleeping on the couch or in my office at the pool. I haven't even been back in twenty-four hours.

But school is out for Thanksgiving break, and although I don't have to leave my apartment, I do have to leave the natatorium, which has been scheduled for a deep cleaning over the holidays.

With nowhere else to go, I force myself back to the apartment, and that's when I see the black envelope tucked under the mat. It's damp and warped from sitting out for the last day or so in the cold sprinkle we've been having. I have to wonder who the hell is still sending me invites. Obviously, someone who doesn't realize I'm neither welcome by any of the members nor personally amused by their idiotic ideas of pranks and rituals and initiations.

Straightening up is like pulling teeth. My mind wants to be doing literally anything else. Still, I don't let myself look at my phone until I've gotten the front room at least mostly in order. After that, I allow myself to slump on the couch and bring up ChattySnap.

Georgia has three new photos.

One is of her and Vandy in what I'll have to assume is Vandy's bedroom, making bitchy faces at the camera. The second is of what must have been her lunch; a tortilla filled with shredded meat and avocado. The third is of her and my brother.

My stomach plummets.

Georgia has her arm around his neck, pulling him close like she's got him in a headlock. There's nothing sexual about it—even if his cheek is right by her tits—but she's wearing this happy, playful grin that makes me want to hurl my phone at the goddamn wall.

The caption reads: '*Reunited and it feels so good! Can I trade in my brother for this one? #JustKiddingGeorge #Mostly #TotallyJoking #Probably*'

I stare at it for too long, letting my stomach churn in anger and resentment, before reaching for the black envelope that was left on my front stoop. At first, it's just a reminder that Sebastian isn't special. That I was invited, too. That I belong to this world just as much as he does. But then I open it and read the card.

"*Soon they reached the fields of asphodel where the dead, the burnt-out wraiths of mortals, make their home.*"

Go, Heston.

Elvatio Infernum

Well, if they want to set a goddamn effigy on fire in the middle of the lake, there's two things I can definitely add to the mix.

Recent experience and some gasoline to pour on it.

∿

The lake is quiet, other than the occasional fishing boat zipping across the clear water. Well, that, and the sound of the party on the shore. Preston's swimming platform is a hundred and fifty yards out from the campus' shore, but from this side of the lake, it must be a thousand, and even squinting, I can't see it. I know it well, though. Coach James used to send us down there to race each other during varsity season. I know the stinging chill of that water. I know what the surface is like when it's too windy. I know what it's like when it's still.

Two years ago, I would have strolled in like I owned the damn place. Now, I hang back and observe the scene first. It takes me three tries to count all the heads.

There are twenty of them.

Hamilton showed up—alone. I don't see Gwen anywhere, although I know they're still dating. Micha feels the need to update me on the Adams Family details. My former best friend looks just as moody and arrogant as ever, tipping back a longneck as he watches Xavier tell a story, animated and loud enough that I know he's had a few, as well. Ansel is sitting between them, strumming on his ukulele, and from the hat and cardigan, I guess he's still playing up the hipster thing. Rounding out the old guard is Emory, sitting with his arm slung around Aubrey's shoulders, tucking her into his side against the chill.

There are all the kids Micha had told me about earlier in the year—the ones who sat at the Devil's table. The diver, Tyson. Afton. Elena. Carlton. Ben. Reynolds has his long legs sprawled toward the fire, and Vandy has parked herself right between, lounging against his chest as they laugh at whatever Xavier just said.

There are younger people—new pledges, like Micha and Michaela, along with older pledges like Josie and Collins—that I'm surprised to see. I know their moronic initiation is still a couple weeks away, but I wasn't expecting them pulled into all this so soon. I haven't decided how I'm going to handle Collins selling me out like that. As pissed as I am, he was looking out for Georgia's best interest. I can't hate him for that.

Caroline is off to the side, head ducked down as she speaks into Georgia's ear. I watch as her mouth slowly spreads into a grin, something gentle and carefree about the way she looks, despite having chosen a spot outside of the crowd. Regardless of the chill, Georgia looks like warmth personified, her red hair glowing in the fire's light. Her cheeks and the tip of her nose are flushed from the cold, but she looks loose and comfortable as she turns to her friend, saying something back.

The only reason I don't turn on my heel and walk away is because Caroline stands and walks off, leaving Georgia sitting there all alone. Warren was right. She has a support system full of people ready and willing to help her. Better people than me. More qualified. I'd wager most of them actually have their shit together, and I doubt any of them have hurt her as much as I have. All of them are more deserving of her attention than me.

But none of them want her as much.

Silence falls around the fire in stages when I emerge. First the laughter dies off, and then the chatter, one by one, all of them turning to look at what's got everyone so quiet all of a sudden.

There's a collective groan that makes my face turn to stone.

"Who invited this asshole?" Hamilton mutters, sounding annoyed and disappointed, like I just ruined something really good.

Well, that *is* my superpower.

"Yo, look who showed up," Carlton calls out, exhaling a cloud of smoke. "The prodigal son returns."

"Hey, I'm the one still stuck in this hellhole," I say, still discretely searching the area. Some of the pledges are lugging what I assume are pieces of the effigy down to the dock. My eyes lock with Georgia's over the fire, but she doesn't hold it. I casually look back at the guys. "You all made it out of here."

The silence that follows is the epitome of discomfort. But even sober, Carlton has never been good at reading the room, and it looks like he's well into his blunt stash, so when he nods to the cooler and offers, "Grab a cold one," he doesn't even notice the glares everyone shoots him.

"Nah, I'm good," I reply, digging my fists into my pockets. "Can't drink anymore."

Carl's eyes widen. "Shit, are they piss testing for that, too?"

I blink at him. "No, you idiot. It's a medical thing."

He doesn't look offended, shrugging it off. That's the best thing about Carl. Everything is water off his back. "More for us."

I don't ask where Sebastian is, but I can't stop myself from looking for him, knowing my knuckles must be white from how hard I'm balling them in my pockets. Much like Hamilton, the last time I saw him, I was doing an excellent job of fucking his fists up with my face. My jaw still clicks in a weird way when I chew.

"Heston!" Everyone whips around, probably to wonder who would say my name like that—like they're actually not miserable to see me. Micha bounds up the dock, arms spread wide as he approaches me. "Dude, we are doing *crime!*"

I bump the fist he holds out, snorting. "Sure, setting paper mâché on fire will be a story for the ages. And the fifteen-foot bonfire, visible from every inch of shore, is just covert enough that no one will ever suspect us of being involved."

Morons.

If he catches my sarcasm, he doesn't let it damper his enthusiasm, glancing back to peek at his sister. "Our parents think we're at the movies with Hamilton."

Suddenly, I don't like the way he looks, eyes a bit too wild, voice a touch breathless. "Hey!" I grab his shoulder to steady him, ducking down to inspect his eyes. "Did someone give you something?"

"Huh?" He looks confused. "Like what?"

When I'm satisfied that the spark of exhilaration in his eyes is purely organic, I breathe a sigh of relief. "Never mind."

"It's the *crime!*" he says, looking far too full of energy. *Jesus*, to be fifteen again. "It's just like last week's episode! Right? Vivian and Gerald?"

"I don't know." Pushing my fist back into my pocket, I admit, "Haven't seen it yet."

Micha's head pulls back on his neck. "You *what*?"

"Micha," Hamilton barks, pushing to his feet. "Go sit."

Micha gives him a miffed look. "Fuck you, I'm not a dog." This is, of course, in direct opposition to that way he was just running around here like an overeager crime puppy.

He throws out a tight, "*Micha*," but I'm the one Hamilton's glaring daggers at, shoulders tight, chest puffed out. Oh yeah, he's a *big man*, with his fucking douchebro haircut and nine hundred dollar loafers.

Rolling my eyes, I explain to Micha, "I don't think you're supposed to talk to me."

He pulls a face, looking between us. "But we talk like *every day*." I shrug to tell him this makes just as little sense to me, but he ultimately slumps off to the log where Michaela watches the whole scene. When he passes Hamilton, he mumbles, "Thought you were cooler than this."

That pretty much sets the tone.

I don't sit. I just stand there and watch, pretending like I'm not glancing at Georgia every ten seconds. The couple of times I do catch her looking back, her gaze is just fixed on the scarf around my neck.

So is Vandy's.

I feel my shoulders go tense, annoyed that I'm second guessing my decision to wear it. She gave it to me. It's cold as a witch's tit, and I'm not exactly working with a full wardrobe these days. Why shouldn't I wear it? It's *mine*. Before I can dwell on it, the sound of a motor approaches the dock, a boat easing up from the darkness. Georgia lurches up, looking nervous suddenly.

A few seconds later, I realize why.

My brother comes marching up the dock, shucking off a pair of gloves. "Okay, the chest is done. All that's left is the head. You're up, Georgia. Elvatio infernum or whatever."

Her eyes dart anxiously between us. "Why don't you come with me?" She grabs his arm, clearly trying to turn him around before he sees me.

It doesn't work.

He freezes, not budging an inch at her tug. "What the fuck is he doing here?"

She gives up, sighing tiredly. "He was invited, Bass."

"Invited?" He sneers at me, lip curling. "To do what? Stand here and bring us all down?"

"Yeah, because you're such a fucking prize." I raise my chin, asking, "Accidentally assaulted anyone today?"

"*Intentionally* assaulted anyone today?"

I spread my arms. "The night's still young."

Sebastian gives me a sharp smile, eyes thinned into slits. "How's your life, Heston? Happy with your choices? Is shit looking good from where you are?"

"You made it perfectly clear you weren't interested in my life, baby brother."

He pushes past Georgia to come closer. "So I shouldn't expect any more calls from you begging for my help? Too bad. That shit kept us laughing for days." Stopping in front of me, he pitches his voice mockingly. "*Sebastian, daddy won't talk to me. I need a car to make my court-appointed meetings. Boo hoo.*"

"Fuck you," I spit, feeling my blood boil. "If you'd put your fucking grudge aside for one second, then I wouldn't have had to —" My jaw locks, eyes pinging to Georgia. I finish, "People think you're such a great guy. You're no better than me."

Hamilton stands up. "Sebastian never kicked my girlfriend in the face."

"I wasn't trying to kick her, I was trying to..." I reach up to scratch at the stubble covering my jaw. "Well, I was trying to shove her with my foot, but—"

Hamilton barks a disbelieving laugh. "Oh, my bad. You accidentally kicked the fucking daylights out of my girlfriend in the process of pushing her face with your foot. You're right! That makes it so much better."

"Why are you even here?" Sebastian asks, and I can tell that he's close to bursting. He's so goddamn easy, it'd take almost nothing. "Look around! No one likes you, Heston. No one fucking wants you here!"

He's not wrong. I wonder again who sent me that invite. Who sends any of the invites?

I'm beginning to have my suspicions.

"I do," Micha pipes in, and when everyone cranes around to look at him, he shrugs. "Heston's not so bad, you guys. He's got good taste and can occasionally be pretty hilarious. I mean, he's a jerk and all, but he's also kind of too pitiful to hate." He tilts his head, considering. "It's like when you see a mean, mangy dog on a street corner. Sure, the dog might bite a little, but it looks so sad that you just want to take it home and address all of its unresolved trauma."

"Micha," I snap, "get off my side."

He gives me a toothy grin. "I'm stickier than glitter, Coach. Deal with it."

Sebastian gestures to him. "Great, you've managed to fuck with the kid's head. Nice job. But other than that, no one—" He must catch the flick of my eyes to Georgia, because he darts in front of her, blocking my view. "Don't fucking look at her. No one wants you here less than she does. After what you did to her, you should be in prison!"

"Hey!" Georgia snaps, shoving between us. "Don't you dare bring that into this. My life is more than a yardstick to measure your dicks with! That's for *me* to throw in his face, not you. And since no one seems to want to actually fucking ask me," she says to Sebastian, eyes flashing, "I *do* want him here."

I stare at the back of her head, dread filling my stomach at her words. The last thing she wants is for people to know about us. Fuck, I don't want these people to know about us, either. They're out for my blood enough as it is. Quietly, I try to tell her, "You don't have to..." but can't take all the eyes already on us. "I'll go. He's right, this was a bad idea."

"No." I watch her hair sway with the sharp shake of her head. "Heston is a Devil, whether you all like it or not. He got an invitation like everyone else, right?"

I nod, wondering why she's sticking up for me. Pity, probably. Like Micha said, everyone here hates me or pities me. One sucks just as much as the other.

"No one knows better than me that he's done some really messed up things, so I'm not going to act like everyone needs to give him a chance." She pauses, shoulders tightening with an indrawn breath. "But I have."

"You *what*?!" my brother says, looking at her like she's lost her mind.

"Oh, my god." Vandy says slow and drawn out. She's looking between us, face pulled into a horrified gape. "It's *him*, isn't it? *He's the guy.*"

"What guy?" Bass asks.

"The guy. The one who..." She looks at Caroline, who for being a brainiac catches on a little slower.

The comprehension that crosses her face a moment later makes my spine go rigid. It doesn't get any better when she breathes, "Oh, Georgia..." It's pitying and patronizing, and from the way Georgia stiffens, she's already picked out every thread.

From over on his log, Micha snorts. "The two of you are just now figuring all this out? I've been watching the unbearable mating dance of Hestia for *months*. For the record, that office you use isn't nearly as insulated as you seem to think it is."

"Wait, who's Hestia?" Ansel asks, looking lost.

Most everyone else has already caught on.

Georgia groans. "I could do with approximately twenty less Devils in my business!"

But Sebastian is looking straight at me, those wild eyes of his filling with rage. "You seriously have the fucking nerve...with *her*?"

Georgia goes instantly to grab his arm, tugging him back.

"Bass," she warns, throwing me a helpless look. "Don't, okay? Let's just—"

It's not that I don't see that way his face hardens, or how he's suddenly hurtling toward me. It's that the only thing I can focus on is the way he jerks violently out of her grip, wrenching her forward into a stumble that sends her crashing gracelessly to her knees. I see it coming, though. This is the thing about Sebastian. He's all heat, no head, uncaring of who he hurts in the process. He's the living manifestation of the saying 'when you're a hammer, everything looks like a nail'.

I've watched my brother hit a lot of people. Hell, I've been some of those people. For all that he's an impulsive meathead, he's good at it. He's always made it look easy, effortless.

Tonight, I discover that it actually hurts like a bitch.

Sebastian's jaw is like pure steel, and that's exactly what it feels like when I slam my fist into it.

"Don't you fucking touch her!" Despite the pain shooting up my arm, I find it almost impossible to stop. But there are a lot of edgy Devils hanging around, and they're there in a flash, ripping us apart before my brother can even get a hit in. I try to break out of someone's grip, but it's like iron.

Ben's grip, I find out. "Whoa there," he grunts into my ear. "Come on, everyone chill. Georgia's fine, look! Everyone chill!"

It takes Reynolds and Emory to push Sebastian back, but once it's clear he's not getting through, he lurches away, not breaking my gaze.

"I will bury your ass, Heston! So help me fucking god, I'll—"

"Enough!" Georgia howls, clambering to her feet. I only get a moment to verify that he didn't hurt her before she throws us both a tight, red-faced scowl. "We're down here to pull off this prank, not re-enact the last episode of Lakevale! If the two of you want to wrestle like fucking children, then be my guest. I'm finishing the job."

With that, she marches off to the dock, ignoring Vandy's pointed look when she storms past. Caroline calls her name and chases after her.

"You good?" Ben asks, giving me a slap on the back that's a little too firm to be called friendly.

"Sure," I answer, jaw tight as I flex my fist. Behind me I hear the motor crank and turn to look, but I feel a sharp tug on my shirt. Looking down, I see Vandy below me, eyes bright with anger. I grimace. "I don't want to hear it."

"I don't think I care." She gives me a long, baffled look. "You know I defended you? Well, not you, but 'the guy' I told her might be worth another chance. The guy I mentioned might have some good in him."

I look over her shoulder. McAllister is only a few feet away, waiting to pick up where my brother left off. "Guess you want to take that back now that you know it's me?"

"I don't know what I want, and I suspect she doesn't, either."

Caroline walks back up and shoots me a glare. "She'd already left by the time I got to the dock."

"All she has to do is put the head on and toss the match," Vandy says, looking exasperated. "She should have just let Bass do all of it, but she was insistent about doing the head herself."

I turn, staring out into the blackness of the lake. The only light comes from a lantern someone left on the platform and a small light on the boat. This prank is so overly complicated and ridiculous.

I keep waiting for the flames in the distance, the chill cutting through my jacket as I stand there, watching. There's the sound of a boat zipping by in the distance, but it's going parallel to the shore—not Georgia.

The longer I wait, the more my eyes adjust to the darkness. I can see the lights of Preston, way out there above the trees. Houses on the south shore. Boat lights to the east. Suddenly, I'm thinking the bonfire was necessary. With nothing to light the way, she'll need the point of reference to steer.

As I'm mulling it over, I see it. There's a boat about a hundred yards to our left, rushing toward the shore. It's a small boat, engine running, too far away to make out any details.

But not too far away to see that there's nobody on it.

Over by the fire, someone laughs. Ansel strums out a chord and Emory releases an obnoxious burp. Someone jangles keys, opens a can of soda, sneezes, yelps against the cold of someone's nose on their neck.

"Shut up," I say, too quiet as I scan the distance. When Xavier barks out a laugh, I whirl around, roaring, "Everyone, shut the fuck up!" Mostly, they fall silent, even if they are all glaring at me. I turn back to the lake and strain my ears, the hairs on the back of my neck standing on end.

"What is it?" Micha asks, standing to approach.

I shush him, but I can't hear anything. The wind is too loud. The traffic, just across the trees, muddles everything up. I watch as the abandoned boat clumsily collides with the shore and sputters there, motionless.

"She's in the water," I realize.

"Who?" Micha asks, and then, louder, "Georgia's in the water?!"

Hearing it said like that kicks me into motion.

I toe off my shoes and reach for my scarf, ripping it from my neck. Everyone's standing up to come over and see what the fuss is about, but I'm already pounding down the dock, shedding my jacket and shirt as I go. I drop them at my feet, uncaring of where they land.

"Hey!" An arm grabs me, spinning me around, and I find myself face to face with my brother. "What do you mean she's in the water?" Despite the bitten-off, hostile way he asks, his own eyes start scanning distance. I can see the moment he recognizes the empty boat, a football field's length away, because his face pales. "What the fuck?"

I wrench my arm from his grasp, reaching for the button on my pants. "Go get the boat. Meet me out there."

He looks lost for a moment in his shock and panic, but at my words, his face firms up into a fierce scowl. "Fuck that!" He rips the zipper of his jacket down and shakes it from his arms. "You go get the boat."

The dock vibrates with the thunderous pound of everyone

running toward us, faces tight with varying degrees of shock and worry.

"Get the boat!" I repeat, shoving my pants down my hips. When he opens his mouth to argue, already half-slipped out of his shirt, I snap, "Goddamn it, Sebastian! Do you really think you're going to swim faster than me?!"

Something in Sebastian's face cracks and he freezes, chest expanded on an aborted exhale. "Fuck," he grinds out, elbowing back into his shirt. "Find her!" He's already running back when he says it, turning on his heel to race back to shore.

By then, I'm out of my pants and springing to the end of the dock, leaping into the water with a quick, expert dive.

29

Turns out, a piddly little johnboat is nothing like a yacht. This is made obvious when I have to circle around the effigy three times, struggling to find out how to cut the motor. When I do, I come up short, having to rock the boat to inch it close enough to reach the pole Emory and Hamilton had set up. The head is light but awkward and unwieldy. Straining up to reach high enough to place it, I curse myself for not claiming the bottom piece.

Once it's secured, I breathe a sigh of relief. There's a total clusterfuck waiting for me back on the shore, but out here, everything seems quiet and simple, all the pieces having clicked together for once. I take a moment to gaze up at the Viking, knowing that the memory card with mine and Caroline's confessions is trapped within that helmet. That's why *we* had to be the ones to do this—place it and set it alight.

I'm done trusting videos in the hands of anyone else.

Without the enormous head, the balance of the boat is different and takes some adjusting to. Since I'll need to speed off as soon as the fire catches, I reach for the cord to start the motor and pull. But it's harder than it seemed before. Out on the dock, my anxious energy and the drive to run away must have fueled the force of my pulls. Out here, it takes me more than a dozen tries.

When it finally catches, motor sputtering to life, everything happens too fast.

I realize too late that I'd cut the motor wrong. The throttle was never taken off, which means that the boat jerks instantly to life, hitching up as it races away. I fall forward, hip crashing against the side as I struggle to find my bearings.

I never do.

Stupidly, my first thought as I tumble over the edge is that I haven't lit the fire yet. It's a strange sense of inward-pointed annoyance—so inconsequential in the grand scheme—that it's almost a relief to have it wiped away by my crash into the water.

The lake, I find, is nothing like the pool at Preston.

This water seeps through my layers of clothing in a shock of icy blades that I'm not prepared for. It makes my muscles lock up tight, and the weight of my clothes is just as unhelpful as I flail, trying to rise to the surface. I still remember that day in the pool when I sank to the bottom. The odd, ethereal way it felt to be suspended in its weightlessness. The glow of the blue. The quiet and calm. At the time, I hadn't let myself find a foothold on the notion, but now I understand what was so fascinating about it.

It's exactly how I'd wished death would be.

That day in my dorm, freshman year, when I'd put that rope around my neck and planned to end it all, it hadn't been anything like that moment in the pool. It'd been full of panic and grief, a hopelessness so thick that I'd been desperate to break free, even at the cost of succumbing to it. It'd been, in the end, horrifyingly simple. But there was no serenity in it. No solace. No sense of peace.

There's no peace here, either.

This murky, frigid water clutches me like an icy fist and I thrash against it, kicking violently. It takes me too long to see it for the useless, ineffectual sort of reflex that is. Somewhere through the blinding fog of panic, I try to call up Heston's voice.

Get to the surface, Haynes. Head back, tits up.

I reach above my head and wrestle against the water, forcing myself to the surface. The air is almost as cold as the water and it feels sharp when I suck in a gasp, sputtering out a wet, hacking cough.

You want to know what wearing wet clothes does? It weighs you down. It tangles you up. For someone who can't swim, it wants to see you fucking dead.

I sink three times while I struggle out of my jacket, my sweater, my shirt. With each layer lost, the cold bites into me with stinging teeth. By the time I've shed them, barely managing a frantic tread above water, my body is screaming with exhaustion.

If you're ever in trouble in the water, you'll need to be able to float on your back. It saves a lot of energy.

My body feels frozen solid, tense and shivering, but I try. I never really mastered the float, but I know I can do it for a while, if I just...

Get on your back. Relax your shoulders. Head all the way back. Take a deep breath and relax.

My chest hitches with painful, shuddered breaths as I float, teeth chattering. I just need to get my energy back, and then I can try swimming. The sky is a sheet of black, and the longer I stare at it, cutting my arms through the water, the less relaxed I feel. I wait, floating there in the dark, cold water, and nothing happens. I *keep waiting* and I never feel more capable of doing what needs to be done. This isn't renewing my energy, I realize. It's just saving the scant amount I have left.

There's no way I'll be able to swim all the way back to shore.

After what feels like hours, my skin feels numb from the cold, but everything else aches agonizingly with it. It's hard to relax when you're vibrating with shivers and slowly giving in to the panic that you can't save yourself.

Doesn't mean I don't try.

Finally, I let my ass sink and clumsily spin, trying to find the effigy. I can cling to the pole and hope that someone notices I haven't returned. Right?

But the Viking isn't as close as I'd hoped, jutting out of the water far enough away that my stomach plummets at the thought of clearing the distance.

I'm losing to the black hole of hopelessness when I hear it.

A voice.

Frantically, I spin, keeping my head above water just long enough to howl out, "Help!" I sink back into the water, but force myself to fight against the stinging and exhaustion, breaking the surface again. "Help!"

The voice that answers isn't just a barely comprehensible garble of sound anymore.

It's *him*. "Georgia!"

"Heston!" I get so excited that I forget to reserve any of my energy, flapping wildly in the direction of his voice.

Take a deep breath and relax.

Heston will come to me. He *will*. But he can't do that if I end up sinking to the bottom, too wrung out and tired to fight anymore.

It takes everything I have to make myself go still, tipping up to float on my back again. I can't hear him anymore when I'm like this, the world cut off to me once the water covers my ears. But I still call for him.

"I'm over here!" I yell, hoping like hell he can hear me.

At some point, my chattering lip wobbles. All of this is so fucking stupid. I hate this goddamn lake. I regret not forcing Bass to come with me. The effigy was dumb. I could have just burned the memory card in the bonfire. Now I'm facing a watery grave because of some idiotic sense of theater.

The tears have just begun warming my cheeks when I feel a surge of water nearby. I jerk up to look, paddling frantically at the sight of Heston swimming toward me. "Heston!"

"Hold on!" His long arms chop through the water, bringing him closer and closer, until we finally collide. The first thing I do is latch desperately onto his neck, and I'm surprised to find the water rise over our heads. I feel his grunt, legs bringing us to the surface with a strong, powerful kick. "Let go," he gasps, prying my arms away. "You're panicking, you'll take us both under. Let go and relax."

It hurts to slip away from him, back into the icy water, but it hurts more to hear the breathlessness in his voice, to know that he's probably almost as exhausted as I am. So I do it, peeling my arms from his neck and sinking.

He's there in a flash, grabbing me around the chest and dragging me with his kicks toward the shore. I reach up to grab his arm, but otherwise let myself go limp, lost to the chilled embrace of the lake.

For a second, it doesn't even feel cold anymore. It just feels like nothing, only Heston's jostles and grunts serving to remind me I'm not suspended in space. I only rise to awareness when he stops suddenly, panting silver plumes of breath above my head.

"The boat's coming." He sounds relieved, adjusting his grip on me. "Just hold on, okay? Georgia?" The only response I can give is a weak nod, my jaw completely locked. He spits a curse and starts moving us toward the distant sound of a motor.

The motor moves closer though—that godforsaken fucking motor—and then a light is shining on us and Bass is calling out, "We've got you!"

"Take her," Heston tells him, arm hooked over the side of the boat. It's only then that I notice how hard he's shaking, struggling to keep me clutched to his chest.

Sebastian reaches for me, pulling me out of the water and over the lip of the boat. It should be a relief—a moment of victory—but I don't allow myself to feel anything but worried until Heston heaves himself into the boat with me. I watch as Bass grabs his leg, helping him over, and then Heston collapses, panting.

"Get us back to that fire."

But Sebastian takes his coat off first, throwing it around my shoulders, and it's only then that I notice Caroline is with him, staring at me with enormous eyes.

"Are you okay?" she asks, looking stunned and frightened.

I'd answer, but the motor roars to life, and then we're zooming across the surface of the lake toward the fiery glow in the distance. I reach out to clumsily tug on the sleeve of her coat instead, hoping that she understands what I'm asking.

She sort of does.

Caroline hurries out of her coat and sweeps it in the air, tucking it over my shoulders. Jerkily, I pluck it away, trying to turn to cover Heston with it. "Oh!" she says, bounding forward to take it from me.

Heston finally moves then, accepting the jacket only to place it back over my shoulders. *Idiot.* "Give me your hands," he demands, even though he just snatches them up himself. He takes my fists into his palms and then brings them to his mouth, huffing warm, chattering air over them before rubbing. "Fuck, *say something*, Little Red."

My jaw still feels tight and rusty, but I manage to eke out a weak, "Sorry."

He gives a tense, shuddering laugh, those blue eyes flashing in relief. "I bet you are."

I spend the ride to the shore curled against his chest, cheek pressed into his neck against the whip of the wind. This close, I can feel the shivers that wrack him, and it might be useless, but I hope he's getting some warmth from my body when his arms crush me closer.

Everyone's waiting at the dock when we arrive, Heston and Bass lifting me onto the platform.

They part for us like the red sea when Heston barks out, "Move!" all but dragging me in the bonfire's direction. He thrusts me in front of it, breaths coming in choppy. "Hold your hands out, get them warm." Everyone's returning to the fire now, looking relieved and harried, so I'm hesitant to obey. The jackets are the only thing covering me.

Heston grabs the sides of my face and forces my eyes to his. "Look at me! This is important. Did you take your clothes off because they were heavy, or because you were hot?"

Hot? Nothing about that lake was anything but freezing-ass cold. Hitching in a painful breath, I chatter out, "H-heavy," and watch as the tension falls from his shoulders.

"Jesus Christ." He sweeps my hair back, frantically wringing the water from it. "Good, that was smart."

I tip closer, body shuddering with a shiver. "I-I-I floated, like you said. S-save energy."

"I saw," he says, giving me a tight smile. "You did good. Didn't drown. Gold star."

When the warmth finally hits me, it's like a barrage of needles. The only thing that makes it bearable is Heston hysterically rubbing feeling into my back and arms.

Micha steps in to say, "Here," and hands Heston a pile of clothes. Instead of pulling them on, he just digs into the pocket of what I now realize are his pants. He emerges with a jangle of keys.

He looks around, eyes landing on Sebastian, and hurls the keys at him. "Go start my car and crank the heat," he orders, throwing his discarded jacket over my shoulders. "There's a gym bag in my trunk. Bring it to me." Sebastian snatches the keys out of the air and stares at them, lip curling up when he levels his brother with a glare. Heston's jaw goes tight at the look, and when he bites out a tense, "*Please*," Sebastian looks away.

"I don't know which car is yours."

"Silver Honda," he replies, dragging me close. "It's the shittiest car out there, you can't miss it."

Sebastian runs off, while the others collect their things. With a start, I realize people are leaving. Ansel, Xavier, Afton, Josie, and Tyson are already trudging into the trees. Most of the pledges are with them.

"The effigy," I say, pushing away from Heston. "We have to...the fire."

He looks at me like I'm crazy. "Fuck the effigy!"

From across the fire, Emory agrees, "I think we've risked enough for the prank tonight."

Frowning, Reynolds adds, "It's not that important."

I swing a panicked look at the girls and they shift uncomfortably.

It's Vandy who explains, "The memory card with our initiation confessions is in the helmet."

Heston's hand stills on my back. "You can't be fucking serious."

Caroline grimaces. "It seemed like a good idea at the time?"

Heston turns to wipe his chin on his shoulder, looking annoyed.

"Any volunteers to go back out on the boat and set that fucker on fire?"

Micha gushes, "I'll do it!"

Heston and Hamilton give the same answer in a perfect, snapped unison. "No!"

Heston adds, "Anyone with actual boating experience?"

"I'll do it." This time, it's Ozzy who steps up. "I go fishing with my uncle all the time. The boat's no problem."

"I'll go with him," Caroline says, giving me a resolute nod. "I'll make sure it gets done." I know it's stupid. This whole night has taught me that much. But Caroline and I agreed it should be one of us, and I feel better knowing that we're going to keep it.

Sebastian returns just as they leave, huffing as he drops the gym bag at Heston's side. "Your car's a piece of shit."

Heston haphazardly unzips the bag, muttering, "Yeah, well, it's what I've got." He pulls out a towel and since it's getting really annoying that he keeps piling things onto my shoulders, I shove his hands away.

"Dry off and get dressed first. I'm okay." It's not a lie. The fire is warming me and I'm cocooned in everyone else's winter wear, but Heston's just sitting here in his shorts.

He must know that arguing is pointless, because he rolls his eyes and starts pulling on his pants, scrubbing the towel through his hair. When he's pulled on his shirt, I make him take his jacket back, but all he'll accept is a trade for the towel.

Still, I pause.

Damp hair all flopped into his face, he watches me, those blue eyes passing a message to mine. Then, he stands up, steps in front of me, and demands, "Everyone turn around."

Aubrey's eyes narrow. "What?"

"She needs to change," he says, voice a touch hostile as he pulls a shirt and a pair of sweats from his bag. "So turn the fuck around. Watch the lake for the fire to catch."

Aubrey leans around to look at me, ultimately nodding. "Okay, give the girl some privacy. You too, asshole." Sebastian flinches at the smack she lobs to the back of his head, but reluctantly does as he's told, allowing me to finally shed the jackets.

It's warmer by the fire, but the wind still makes my skin prick up. I don't get very far into clumsily patting my chest with the towel before Heston takes it from me, gently drying my arms. He runs it over my shoulders and belly, crouching down to get my thighs and legs. His eyes follow methodically, aiming his attention at every inch of skin that passes, until I realize why.

He's checking for cuts.

Probably, he thinks he's being subtle about it, but I catch the way he lingers on my forearm—the old cut from my compact mirror that's only recently lost its scab. There's nothing to find.

When he rises, he shoves the hair from his eyes, gaze sweeping down my body one last time. They pause on my breasts, but quickly flick away, lips pressing into a flat line. "This first," he says, pushing the shirt over my head. It smells like deodorant and chlorine, but it's dry and soft. When he instructs me to step into the sweatpants, I use his shoulder to balance myself.

And when he stands back up, looking down at me, his eyes are glued to my lips.

Unconsciously, I dart my tongue out to wet them, belly clenching at the way his eyes darken. "Thank you," I say, teeth still chattering. The gratitude isn't just for the clothes, and not even for risking his life to save mine. But I'm not sure how else to say it. Not with words.

I've never had to thank anyone for loving me before.

"I'm good," I tell everyone, expecting that I'll need to put some distance between us. But just then, there's a flash of light across the lake, the effigy going up in a column of flames.

They let loose a loud, jubilant cheer.

Heston pulls me back into his chest, head shaking. "This is still the dumbest fucking thing I've ever heard of."

I tuck myself against him, watching his face as the fire casts it in a warm glow. "Yeah, well, you light your fires and I light mine."

I ride with Heston to the rendezvous.

Unfortunately, so does Bass.

"What are you *doing* to this thing?" he asks from the back seat, fingers pulling at his hair. "It sounds like it hasn't had an oil change since the Bush administration." Eyes narrowing, he elaborates, "The *first* one."

Heston accelerates, looking less bothered by the weird grindy noise than the bitchy brother in his back seat. He growls, "It's running, isn't it?"

"Not for much longer," Bass mutters, double-checking his seatbelt again.

"You could have ridden with someone else," I point out, not for the first time. Apparently he'd gone to the lake with Emory, who was acting as a designated driver for those who wanted to drink or smoke during the bonfire.

Predictably, that ended up being far too many people for his single truck.

Sebastian scoffs. "And leave you to the mercies of the shit mobile? I don't fucking think so."

I release a weary sigh, because it doesn't take a genius to realize that it's not really about the car. "I've ridden in this car before, Bass." I stop just short of adding, *I've ridden the man driving the car before, too.* But the admission still hangs heavy in the air, a pointed acknowledgement that Heston and I have been together outside of academic obligations.

When we reach the abandoned parking lot, Heston rolls his eyes. "This is the elusive 'secret' society that's been working under Collins' nose for a year?" Flinging a hand toward the scene, he adds, "Gee, I sure hope no one notices the twelve cars hanging around an empty parking lot."

"You could always make it eleven by fucking off," Bass says, wrenching the back door open with an awful creak.

I don't follow him as he crosses the parking lot to where Sugar waits in her Mustang. Even in the dark, I can sense the moment she realizes I'm in the car with Heston. I'm sure Bass will give her all the sordid details and I'll have even more explaining to do.

Just not tonight.

The car is warm and my legs are Jell-O. Plus, I don't feel up to the conversations I know my friends are itching to have. I can see Vandy perched on the hood of Reynolds Jeep, sipping from a coffee, and her eyes are trained right at us.

"Are you okay?" Heston's voice is quiet, uncertain in a way I'm not used to hearing from him.

"Just tired, I think." Turning to him, I give a small smile. "You?"

"Fucking wiped," he admits, tipping his head back against the seat. "I haven't gone that hard since I swam against Hamilton freshman year."

I watch his hooded eyes as he stares out at the parking lot. "You're always saving me from drowning."

"Not always." He lolls his head against the seat to meet my gaze, eyes full of a dark weight that makes my chest twinge. "Sometimes I'm the one pushing you under."

"Sometimes," I agree, reaching for the hand he has resting on the steering wheel. "But I believe you don't want to be."

He looks down at our hands, watching as his thumb makes a slow, gentle circuit against my skin. "Georgia, there's something I need to tell you." Everything slows down as I wait, fearing the worst. Another video. Another bet. Instead, he says, "I got a call yesterday from the investigators. They ruled the fire an accident. Electrical."

I release the breath I've been holding, giving his hand a squeeze. "That's good, right?"

"Yeah, it's just…" He looks at me, mouth tilting into an unhappy line. "The club was insured."

I blink at him. "Oh."

"I didn't want you to think that's why I did it. Insurance money never even crossed my mind, and I wasn't—"

"I get it." I squeeze his hand again, offering a grin. "That'll help you, right?"

"I don't know." He shakes his head, looking out the windshield. In the distance, Micha, Elena, and Afton are performing one of the dance squad's old moves. "Honestly, I'm not sure having money is very good for me right now."

"Because of the gambling?" I ask, forehead creasing with a frown. "Is it...hard?" Aside from a couple throwaway comments, Heston's never really talked about it much. I'd always gotten the sense that it wasn't something he took very seriously.

Now, however, he looks anything but flippant. "It can be." Beneath the weariness in his eyes, there's the ghost of something frustrated and pained. "Sometimes, something just seems like the best idea. Like you've got it all figured out, because..."

"Because you've rationalized it," I guess, giving a wry laugh. "I happen to know a thing or two about that."

"That's why I needed you to know." He turns to me, gaze turning to steel. "I might fuck up, because I think...whatever this is —addiction, impulse, whatever—maybe it's not an easy thing to kick. Maybe I'm not strong enough. Maybe it's just a part of who I am." Before I can argue, he pins me under his gaze. "But I swear to fucking god, I'll lose everything before I make you a part of that again."

I swallow thickly, stomach flipping. "Heston..."

"I'm not asking you to trust me," he says, cutting me off. "I'd be pretty fucking worried if you did."

Knowing that there's a chance I won't be able to give it, I ask, "Then what are you asking for?"

His eyes flick down, landing on my mouth, and suddenly it's like two weeks of dormant lust springs to the surface all at once, settling liquid-hot at the base of my spine. He reaches over to touch my chin, thumb dragging heavy and warm against my bottom lip. "Please don't go to someone else."

My breath hitches as I'm pulled into his gravity, tipping forward in anticipation of the kiss. Despite everything, this is where we've always shined, and I can feel the heat of it now, thawing out my insides, suspended in dwindling breaths between us.

And then Sebastian bangs on the window.

We both jump, Heston whirling around to glare murderously at him. "What the fuck!"

Bass scowls into the window, yelling, "Pop your hood, asshole!"

"Why?!"

Bass bangs the glass again. "Just fucking do it!"

Heston watches as his brother rounds the front of the car, waiting. "Goddamn it," he growls, hunching down to look for the hood's release.

I take the opportunity to finally step out of the car, suddenly needing the crisp air. It's not running if I walk, and that's exactly what I tell myself as I amble toward the girls, legs protesting against the movement.

Vandy doesn't wait for me to reach her, limping over the distance to grab me in a big, suffocating hug. "You scared the crap out of me!"

Laughing weakly, I hug her back. "Imagine how I felt."

I'm startled to feel another pair of arms wrap around me, engulfing the both of us.

Caroline squeezes. "No more boats."

Vandy and I agree, "No more boats!"

Pulling back, Vandy takes a deep breath, stilling me with a look. "Heston."

I look away, already knowing what she's going to say. "I said you wouldn't approve."

"You deserve better," Vandy says, sounding sad. "I stand by that. Even if he saved your life and looked pretty convincingly worried about you while he was doing it."

I arch an eyebrow. "I thought I deserve to be happy, too."

Vandy looks over my shoulder, brow puckering dubiously. "Can Heston really make you happy?"

I follow her gaze. He's still in the driver's seat, but he has his door open, leg kicked out. His hand is covering his eyes, like he's just praying for the strength to endure. Sebastian is beneath the hood of his car, tinkering around with something.

"It's...complicated," I answer, rolling my eyes. "I don't blame you for not getting it. Sometimes, even I still—"

"Get the fuck away from that!" I hear Heston snap.

Sebastian barks back, "Or what?! You'll hit me again? You punch like a fucking girl, by the way. *Worse* than a girl, actually. Elena actually bruises me."

"Oh, Jesus," I groan, turning to find them squaring off again.

Caroline sighs. "I'll get Em and Ben."

"Don't bother." I walk back to the car, feeling weary down to my bones, and shove myself between them. "What the hell, you guys?"

Heston's got this muscle in the back of his jaw that always sort of fascinates me. It always balls up tight when he comes. Right now, it's twitching. "He's fucking with my car!"

"I'm *fixing* your piece of shit car! It sounds like a pterodactyl eating a box of rusty bolts."

I put my hand on Heston's chest, looking up into his eyes. "Just let him fix it." To Sebastian, I say, "And you, stop being such a dick about it."

"Fuck that." Heston's chest tenses under my palm. "I don't need his help. He'll probably just cut my brake line or something."

Bass' eyes bug out. "The brake line is under the car, you smooth-brained moron! I'm looking at the engine!"

"I don't want you looking at my engine!"

Sebastian fists the wrench in his hand, shoulders snapping back as he takes a step forward. Instantly, Heston grabs my arm and pushes me behind him, body coiled tight. Bass doesn't miss it, eyes zeroing in on the motion in an offended snap of his head. "I wouldn't hurt her, she's one of my best friends. I love her!"

Through gritted teeth, Heston says, "Well, so do I, so let's not test it."

Sebastian's eyebrows lurch up his forehead. "You *love* her?" He gives a sharp, skeptical laugh. "You don't know how to love anything."

"Stop!" I jump between them again, heart hammering in my throat. "No one is hurting me, and everything is *fine*. Just fix the car, Bass." When he's stormed back to his cursing and banging beneath the hood, I turn to Heston. "What's the big deal?"

He's still fuming, jaw clenched tight. "I don't want anything from him. Especially not at the risk my only fucking possession."

"He's really good at this stuff," I insist. "He'd cut off his own hand before he hurt a car."

His eyes flash angrily. "That's exactly what he's going to get if he—"

His words cut off sharply when I strain up to press my mouth to his. Heston's lips go pliant in an instant, hands coming up to frame my face. The kiss is mostly chaste, unhurried, even though I can feel the weight of eyes on us. I twist my hands into his jacket and welcome the wash of his eager breath as the tension slides from his body.

When I pull away, his eyes are lidded and dark, thumbs rubbing warmly against my cheeks. "Let him fix it," I say, giving his jacket a soft tug, "and you'll be the only one I go to."

"Oh." He gives me a slow, dazed blink. "Okay."

I don't last long in my dorm room.

Part of it is that my hair is wet from my shower and I'm still shivering, even buried under a pile of blankets. Every time I close my eyes, it feels like I'm back in that lake, thrashing around through a gaping maw that's ready to swallow me whole.

Another part is the way Heston had looked at me when we separated at the Devil's tower an hour ago, expression carefully void of anything but a polite scrunch of his mouth.

Josie isn't back from the celebration yet, so it's easy to sneak out, hefting my bag over my shoulder. I'd think I'd be immune to the chill in the air by now, but I'm not. It feels like I've taken a bit of that lake back with me and it'll always be nestled inside my bones, my marrow turned forever to ice. Briefly, I wonder if he feels the same, worries that he'll never feel completely warm again.

When I get to his stoop, I consider asking him, but the sight of him when he opens the door steals the words from my throat.

He looks exactly the same as when I'd left him—jacket and shoes and all. The only difference is the way his eyes take me in, pupils blown wide.

I adjust the weight of my bag, still shivering into the wind. "I was just…" Taking a walk? Wandered off and found myself here? Wanting to see if your bed makes me feel any less like I'm drowning?

Luckily, he doesn't make me finish, taking a step back so I can shuffle past him.

The inside of his apartment is somehow colder.

My eyes take in the space, fingers tightening around the strap of my bag as I'm hit with the memory of tearing everything apart. The living room looks like it's been tidied hastily, everything from the floor piled onto the nearest flat surface. But the kitchen looks exactly as it had that night, cabinets pulled open and torn apart.

Heston follows my gaze, reaching up to push his hair back. "I haven't come here much," he says, rough voice shattering the silence.

"You live here." It's a pointless comment, made more apparent by the slow, tired blink he gives me.

His movements are stiff and mechanical as he finally slips out of his jacket. "I guess."

It doesn't answer the question I can't bring myself to ask. I don't have the right, and god only knows I'm the one more likely to have a dissatisfying answer.

My eyes stutter on the orange bottles of pills on the coffee table. It's rude of me—invasive and unfair—but I find myself drawn to them, bending to pluck one up and inspect the label.

Heston clears his throat. "It's nothing. I have this dumb stomach ulcer." When I put it down, only to pick up another, he explains, "Just some antibiotics and acid blockers."

Gently, I place the bottle down, asking, "Is it helping?"

He lifts a shoulder, looking bored. "Maybe. It's only been a few days."

Nodding, I look around, feeling awkward and out of sorts. This isn't how it's ever worked with us. Usually, things unfold easily—

naturally—in a way that I may have taken for granted. For a moment, I consider asking if it's okay for me to be here.

But his voice stops me. "Do you need it?"

I turn to him slowly, hoping that I'll have an answer by the time I meet his gaze. In the end, I find it difficult to be anything but honest. "Yes." My answer comes out solemn and quiet; a confession that makes my shoulders tense to hear said aloud.

There's a spark of relief in his eyes, and I realize what he wants to know even before he reaches up to ruffle the back of his hair, eyes sliding away. "How long have you...uh..."

"Needed it?" It's not often Heston beats around the bush. I'm not sure I like it. "Since that night I left Underworld, I guess." Up late into the nights, seeking relief from my own hand. Sitting in class, thinking of his body and the way it used to move against me. At lunch and dinner, distracted by the shape of him in the distance, curled over a tray of food. Squirming and restless after, forcing myself to get distracted with some*thing* instead of some*one*. "I've knitted so many fucking scarves, I should open an Etsy shop."

If I thought it might bring some levity to his eyes, then I'm mistaken. His face is shuttered, hardened into an unreadable mask when he asks, "Do I need to go get some condoms?"

Well, that's one way of asking it. "I don't know. Do you?"

His mouth presses into a grim line. "Not on account of me."

There's a tension in my back that slowly releases, allowing me to breathe. "Me, either."

Heston probably deserves an Oscar because there isn't a hint of surprise on his face. He just nods, the unhappy lines around his mouth disappearing.

Before that flash of heat in his eyes can grow, I say, "I'm just really beat right now, though. Do you think we could..." I pivot to the hallway, unsure how to ask. I've been antsy with the temptation of sex for a long time now, but I've spent longer fantasizing about being in his bed, feeling the weight of his arm around me, than anything else. Suddenly, the thought strikes me as embarrassing. "...sleep?"

I know Heston must be just as tired, if not more so. I've seen him around campus these past couple weeks, and he's looked harried and exhausted for most of it.

He toes off his shoes, saying, "Yeah," and when he brushes past me, he reaches out to touch my hip as he goes. Just a small little thing. A physical 'hello' that makes my body burst with awareness. "Let me get cleaned up real quick," he says, not waiting for a response.

When he disappears into the bathroom, I let out a breath, padding into the bedroom. I was at my worst in here, tearing through everything in my attempt to find a camera. His curtains are torn down, the dresser drawers still halfway ajar, clothes spilling out of them like a gruesome reminder. I swallow thickly as I turn away, dropping my bag to tend to the bed.

I know from experience that Heston owns one pair of sheets. I also know from experience what's been done on them. They're already ripped halfway off, so I finish the job, balling them up and throwing them aside. I pull a clean pair from my bag, losing myself in the motions of making the bed, putting on new pillowcases, reorienting myself with the pull I feel to slip between them.

I finish it off with the two thick blankets I'd brought with me, folding them down.

I wait until I'm under them to undress.

Heston finds me like this when he wanders in from the bathroom, towel wrapped around his hips, skin scrubbed pink. He pauses in the doorway when he sees me, curled on my side, waiting for him. There's a beat where his eyes fall down to my bare shoulders and I think he might say something, but when I let loose a hard shiver, he looks away, shamelessly dropping his towel.

Even when he's turned the light off, I look my fill as he crosses the room, his thick cock heavy between his strong thighs. Heston's never been shy about his body, and was always content to wander around like this in between our goes at each other, allowing me to appreciate the taut, shifting lines of his muscle.

When he finally slides under the blankets, blasting me with a brief chill, he mutters out a soft, "Come here," and lifts his arm, making a space for me.

I take it instantly, luxuriating in the expanse of his skin. He's still warm from his shower and I greedily steal it away, pressing my peaked nipples against his side, shivering thigh thrown over his hips. One of his arms comes around my shoulders, fingers tangling in my hair, but the other reaches down to grab my thigh, kneading slowly into my sore muscle, holding me close.

The chest beneath my ear vibrates with a soft, satisfied rumble.

I close my eyes, finally feeling warm again.

~

It's not a dream—not exactly.

There are no images or real thoughts. When I get like this, sometimes it's just a feeling. The pull of something deep and fundamental. Primal, like an instinct. I chase it mindlessly, just like I always do, body clenching with an orgasm that's too fast and ephemeral to be satisfying.

I've had a lot of wet dreams in my life.

This is just the first time I wake up next to someone in the middle of it.

"Shh," Heston's saying into my ear, his warm palm smoothing the hair back from my sweat-dampened forehead. He presses a gentle kiss to my jaw, voice thick with sleep. "You need it?"

I nod into the pillow, sprawled on my back, thighs clenching together for any bit of friction. I can feel his hand grazing against my hip as he slowly strokes himself, and I wonder how long I've been like this, writhing and desperate. My hand descends, wedging itself between my thighs.

The bed dips when he shifts, lifting to pluck a lingering kiss from my lips. "Do you want it?" It's said so quietly that I have to rely on the shape of it being spoken against my lips.

My mouth parts and I lick out to taste the seam of his lips, moaning when I meet the responding point of his tongue. I'd almost forgotten what this was like, the warmth of his breath, the eager presence of him as he tastes me.

"No," I insist, wanting to tell the truth, despite how scary it is. "I don't want it. I want *you*."

His only response is a harsh breath, bed jostling as he works a knee between my legs. His hand follows my arm down to my wrist, catching it, prying it away from where my hips are bucking into my palm. "Shh, I've got you," he says when I whine, head digging back into the pillow.

Despite his soothing words, I can feel a tremor work through him when he touches me, fingers sliding through my wetness. He makes a noise—something tight and borderline pained—and then rolls to settle between my legs, wrenching one of my thighs up.

He enters me slowly, forehead resting against mine as my jaw goes slack, fingers weaving into his hair. "That feel good?"

Any other time, I'd rib him for the self-indulgence of wanting his ego stroked. But regardless of the cocky tilt of his mouth, I can hear the thread of hesitation in it, the need for a reassurance that I'm happy to give.

"Yes," I gasp, fingers fisting in his hair. "Don't stop."

His arms flex when he pulls back to fuck me, hips moving in a deliciously deliberate pace. It doesn't waver, even when he ducks down to mouth at the peak of my breast, tongue darting out to taste me. He shifts his weight so his hand can join in, gathering the weight of my breast in a wide palm. "So fucking perfect," he breathes, taking my mouth in a hard, bruising kiss.

I wrap my legs around him, knees clutching him too hard, trying to get him closer. I know I pull his hair too hard, but he just grunts in response, surging into me. His skin is beyond warm now. The blankets are too much—too hot—but neither of us pushes them off, content to sweat and pass our panting breaths from one neck to another. It's just like it was in my dream. Primal. Instinctual. Clutching hands and muffled cries. This is the best language we know.

I come in the middle of a long, filthy kiss, the arch of my back shattering it. He follows, though, pushing his quick punches of breath into my neck as a hand shoots out, clamping hard around the top of the headboard. He slams into the cradle of my thighs, muscles coiling as he fills me, thick cock swelling with his release.

It ends with his forehead pressed to the center of my chest. I watch, transfixed as his back bellows with his breaths, and when I sink my fingers into his hair, he pushes into the touch.

"I love you, too, you know." It's hard to say, coming out stilted and breathless. His back goes still for a moment, contracting with an inhale that goes on long enough to look painful. "But I made a promise not to hurt myself anymore, and I meant it. Not just for you. For myself."

His thumb rubs into the space below my breast. "Good."

Nodding, I stroke his hair, looking up at the ceiling. "So I won't let you be my next weapon against myself. If you hurt me again, that's it." Realizing what that sounds like, I struggle to clarify, "I mean, outside of this, like—"

"I know what you mean." When he raises his eyes to mine, I know he understands. Pain with sex is different. When it's him doing it. Being careful. Making sure that I'm safe and feel good. Wearing his marks in my skin.

He wraps his arms around me, cloaking me with his warmth, and maybe this is a mistake. Maybe it'll all end horribly. Maybe he'll break my heart again. But as we drift back into sleep, his fingertips grazing soothing circuits into my naked skin, I feel happy.

And I don't think I could ever come to regret that.

30

HESTON

When he gets into the car, I'm already annoyed.

It doesn't help when he wrinkles his nose at the interior. "Your car sucks."

"So I've heard," I say, just as unimpressed with the scrawny man sitting in the passenger seat.

The drive to Northridge is mostly spent ignoring him, which is easy enough. I've got Georgia and Micha's swim exam coming up, which takes up more of my mental energy than is probably necessary. The fact of the matter of is, I've been kind of dragging ass as far as teaching goes. Bigger fish to fry, drama at every turn. Which sort of pisses me off, because when I can focus and actually get a rhythm going, I suspect I'm not actually bad at it.

I just don't have any proof to attest to that fact.

I park outside the dimly lit no-name bar, already knowing that Gene's going to be here. "Remember what we talked about," I start, turning to the man in my passenger seat.

He flaps a hand, looking unbothered. "Yeah, yeah, I know my lines. Just show me where this asshole is." His forehead is pulled into a tight, unhappy pucker.

I take a moment to reflect on my choices first. This is probably the worst idea I've had in a while, and considering recent events, that's saying a lot. But it's the only one I could come up with that didn't feature some form of gambling or debt shuffling.

Acknowledging the dread already pooling in my stomach—but without pain this time, thankfully—I wrench the car door open and step out, grabbing the small bag from the floorboard. "Pull your beanie on," I tell him, annoyed that I have to.

Looking just as annoyed at me, he tugs it over his head, making sure all his hair is tucked inside. "Happy?"

"Elated," I growl, shoving past him to approach the building.

Dirty is the one who answers the door, giving me a onceover that ends in a razor-sharp smirk. "You got some real brass balls, Wilcox." Sniffing, he steps aside. "I respect that." He doesn't look like he respects me. He looks like he's excited at the prospect of the coming entertainment.

Inside, it smells like Satan's armpit. Doesn't look much better, either. I'm at least relieved to see that the only people sitting around the table are Gene and his usual flunkies. I wasn't ready to deal with any external factors.

"Wilty Cock," Gene greets me, leaning back in his chair. "I thought I might need to send some of my boys out looking for you." The vicious gleam in his eyes makes it clear that I wouldn't have wanted him to find me. "Who's this?" he asks, raising an eyebrow at the man standing behind me.

"Him?" I turn just enough to see him through my periphery. "Nobody. I'm here to square up."

Gene puts his cards down, pushing his chair out to stand. "There's only one thing I want," he says, face set into hard, cheerless lines. "So unless you're carrying a copy of what's currently sitting in the Northridge ash heap known as Underworld, then I'm afraid we won't be square."

"Oh, that," I say, sounding bored. "Yeah, that was a shame. Pesky electrical problems, huh? What can you do?"

"You think I'm an idiot?" Gene's eyes flash in fury, and a couple of his flunkies stand with him. "I can make a call to those investigators any time I feel like it. So here's what you're going to do." He rounds the table with deliberate movements. "You're going to get me a copy of that video. Make a new one if you have to. I don't give a shit! I want Georgia Haynes on video, swallowing your cock through whatever hole you see fit to stick it in." He stops in front of me, punching the tip of his forefinger into my forehead. "And I think I'll take half of the insurance payout, too. Unless you want to go down for arson and insurance fraud, that is."

"I don't know what you're talking about." I push his hand away is a smooth, measured movement. "There's already a video of us out there. Use that, if you want it so bad."

"You really are dumb as a sack of rocks, aren't you?" Gene's eyes bug out. "Her family already knows about that video, you imbecile! How am I supposed to blackmail them with something that's already as good as public? It's called *leverage*, Wilcox!"

 Pulling a face, I reach up to flick at a bit of spittle that's landed on my nose. "I don't know. Why don't I ask one of them?" I turn to my accomplice, arching an eyebrow. "Thoughts, George?"

He gives a nod down at his phone. "Yep, got it." He raises the screen, giving it a wiggle. "That whole thing is floating around the cloud, as we speak."

Clouds.

So much better than hard-copies.

George would be scared if he had half the sense to realize Gene has kneecapped men for less. As it is, he just looks irritated. "My dad could bring a lot of attention down here, you know."

"He could," I agree, turning to Gene. "Or you could just let me walk away." I toss the bag on the table, giving it a nod. "There's your fifty large. Half the insurance payout. That's as square as I'm ever going to get." The insurance money had actually been a bit higher, but Gene doesn't need to know that.

George raises his chin. "And you better leave my fucking sister alone. The second I hear of anything fishy, this recording is going straight to my father's people."

Gene takes a break from glaring murderously at George to bark at me, "Have you forgotten the part where I have all the dirt on you?"

"I haven't." Shrugging, I gesture to George. "But I don't think he cares."

George sweeps a long, disdainful look over me. "Yeah, I can't fucking stand this guy. I don't care if he gets busted for anything. Be my guest or whatever."

"You're bluffing," Gene scoffs, taking a step back.

"Him?" I point at George, giving him a skeptical look. "Look at him. He's a pampered little pissant. This kid's never had to bluff a day in his life."

"Hey!"

"Am I wrong?"

George huffs, reaching up to scratch beneath his beanie. Some of his bright orange hair falls out. "Not really, I guess."

Turning to Gene, I say, "Find someone else to leech off of. I'm out."

I'm coiled up tight as we leave, half expecting one of his minions to stop us. I don't breathe until we're in the car, and even then, my hands are slightly less than steady when I jam the key into the ignition and speed away.

There's no way of knowing if it'll actually work, but even if it doesn't, at least now I know.

Gene really had left that flash drive in Underworld.

Collins' office is really swank.

For the right headmaster, someone could really do this place up nice. Replace the curtains. Bring in a mini-fridge and a wide screen. The little devil head on his desk is pretty cool, though. I pick it up, testing the weight in my hand. It's crystal, I think. Heavy.

Kicking my feet up on his desk, I toss it from hand-to-hand, waiting.

It's been three days since I dumped my fifty grand on Gene and skedaddled. I've been lucky not to hear anything from him, but maybe he's smarter than he looks. I might be a complete fucking mess, but I'm young. I can go rounds with him, if that's what he wants.

I doubt he does, though. That's the thing with people like Collins and Gene. They act all high and mighty, but at the end of the day, they're aging out of their gigs. Neither of them can match me for stamina.

Collins' face when he walks is priceless. He looks at me, face going red. "Get out of my chair!"

I toss the devil into the air, effortlessly catching it. "Not before we have a little chat."

Nose flaring with an inhale, he reaches behind him to slam the door. "How did you get in here?"

"Your receptionist fucking loves me." Leaning back, I luxuriate in the plush leather upholstery. The chair has a really smooth swivel to it, too. "I figured, since today is your deadline, I'd show some initiative. Come to you with everything I've found out."

At this, he looks a little less inclined to jump over the desk and throttle me. He places his briefcase on the floor, takes a seat, and orders, "Talk."

"It's kind of funny, actually." The devil bobs from hand to hand and his eyes follow it, narrowing as his gaze pings back and forth. "Considering that, statistically speaking, eight percent of Devils are pretty significant aspects of your personal life, you might have picked up on something. I mean, if you were smarter."

His forehead creases with a scowl. "What are you talking about?"

"Your son, for one." I shake my head, snatching the devil out of the air with an aggressive slap. "Going through a rebellious phase, I'm guessing."

Collins gives me a look that says I'm stupid. "Oswald wasn't here last year."

"He's here now." I raise an eyebrow, wondering, "Did you really think they weren't going to recruit anyone else?"

There's a long pause as he looks away, the vein in his temple jumping. "Son of a bitch."

I roll my eyes. "Come on, the headmaster's son? He's had a target on his back since the second he stepped foot into here. You should be grateful it's the Devils instead of relentless bullying. He *is* a bit of a geek."

"I'm going to wring his goddamn neck." He's halfway out of his chair before I raise a hand, pointing back at his seat.

"I'm not done."

Collins scowls at me, dropping back into the chair. "I only have one son, Heston."

"Sure," I agree, setting the crystal devil back onto his desk. "But you have a sweet little side piece, too."

He scoffs, even though I can see the color draining from his face. "I don't know what you're talking about."

I hold his gaze, lifting an eyebrow. "You spent most of last year fucking a student."

"I did not!" He lurches from his seat, eyes wide. "You can't just come in here and throw around—" I thumb my phone to life while he rants, turning to show him the screen. He goes silent, face falling a strange ashen color. "Where did you get that?"

It's a screen capture from a video—Jesus, there's always a video—featuring him being ridden by a blonde-haired girl.

My eyes go to his locked drawer, mouth curing into a smirk. "Keeping your jack off material in your office desk is a bit of a cliché. Although, I'm going to be real with you. I'm super fucking impressed." I give him a considering look. "Landing a sweet piece like Afton Cross? That's inspirational for stuffy old fuckers everywhere."

He lands heavily in the chair. "You don't understand."

"Oh, I definitely do." I thumb my phone off, tucking it back into my pocket. "Relax, Collins. You look like your asshole just sucked in the entire visible universe. I don't care who you're fucking. Trust me, I'm in no position to lecture you on fucking a student." Sighing, I sink back into the chair, resting my hands behind my head. "I'm just saying. Your little plaything is... well, a Plaything. Devil, to be exact." Drolly, I explain, "There's this whole new structure where the guys and girls are equals, yadda yadda. It's all very feminist, I'm told."

"No." He shakes his head, still looking peaked. "She would have told me."

I snort. "Why? Because you were her daddy's best friend and she was into jumping up and down on your dick? Maybe she was into you, but when it comes to secrets," borrowing something Georgia once told me, "Devils are in the business of keeping them."

It's probably cruel not to tell him the truth, which is that having an affair with him was Afton's initiation confession. Meaning, by telling him, she'd be putting him in the position to get shit-canned or worse.

I don't actually care.

"So this is what you're going to do," he guesses, giving me a scathing look. "Blackmail me into signing off on your community service?"

He's right. That would be highly characteristic of me. However...

"Nah," I say, dragging my feet off the desk to lean forward. "I'm finishing out this bullshit gig, and when you sign that paper, it's going to be completely legit."

His nose scrunches up in bafflement. "Why?"

I jerk a shoulder, tapping the little devil head. "I did the crime, so fuck it. I'll do my time, I don't have a problem with that." *Not anymore.* Looking across the desk at him, I make sure he understands how serious I am. "But you're going to leave the Devils alone. You're going to let them do their stupid, inane little pranks. You're going to sit back and act peeved when they undermine you. You're going to put up the pertinent amount of fuss, and then you're going to do *nothing.*" I roll my eyes at the look of barely suppressed furor on his face. "I mean, what's the big deal, anyway? The last prank they pulled could barely be called property damage. What's at stake? Your pride?"

"You know better than anyone exactly what's at stake," he says, fingers digging into the arms of his chair. "Do you know what it feels like to teach some jackass that it's okay to run rampant over this school, making other kids miserable? Knowing that he's going to get into a good college, where he'll spend four to eight years harassing—maybe even assaulting—as many people as he sees fit, only to get a job at his daddy's company, where he'll do nothing all day but bully the people who have been put underneath him?" His lip curls up as he looks at me. "You exemplify my reasoning for not allowing the Devils on this campus."

Nodding, I put the crystal devil back where I got it, adjusting him just-so. "I wasn't a very good representation of the Devils' ambitions. I was a bitter, fucked-up, entitled little shit. Sometimes, I still am. But that was just me."

"Oh, good," he wryly replies. "Because our upper-class prep school will never see another one of those."

"Not in the Devils, you won't." Standing up, I assure him, "It has oversight now."

He narrows his eyes. "Oversight from whom?"

"Nope." I stroll to the door, tossing him a wave. "I'm done digging up dirt for sad old fucks. I've got my own life to live."

"I can't."

I swivel the chair and see Georgia in the doorway of my office. Her hair is pulled back, the straps of her bathing suit peeking out from under her t-shirt. Behind her, Micha is out by the pool, dipping a toe in the water. I raise an eyebrow. "Can't what?"

She wrings her hands, shoulders inching up. "The test. Swim. Get in the pool. Any of it."

"Is there a reason you aren't speaking in complete sentences?" But I don't need to ask. Her test is in fifteen minutes and there's a lot riding on it. She has to pass it to graduate, for one. And I need her and Micha to both pass so that I can keep my promise to myself. When Collins signs off on that paper, it's going to be the real deal. That means I'm going to have to seriously impress Coach James for him to give his approval.

"Heston," she says, face pale, "it's not that I don't want to. I know we both need me to pass, but after the lake, I just don't think I can get into that water."

I don't need to see the dread in her eyes to understand. We don't get the luxury very often, but the few times we have, I've been the one waking her up from nightmares about it.

"You'll fail," I point out.

I'll fail.

She gives a tight nod, pacing in front of my desk. "Who needs a diploma anyway, right? College was always a long-shot for someone like me. I can get a job working on Daddy's campaign. Field experience means more than academics, everyone knows that."

I stand and cross the small space, easing the door to a scant crack. Georgia and I have been taking things slow since that night after the lake. She knows how I feel, and after fucking up so many things in my life, I don't want to ruin the little progress we've made. She still needs sex, and I still want to be the one who gives it to her, but even though we don't talk about it much, we're both aware that this is more than just fucking. More than hooking up. More than having feelings.

I haven't put a name to it, and I wouldn't ask her to. But I know that it's not something that's going to arrive overnight. Whatever we're doing, it's a marathon, and fucking on campus all the time is a surefire way to ruin it before it even begins. Like Micha said, screwing in the office was a sloppy move.

That doesn't mean I can't meet other needs.

I tug her into my chest, palm running over the back of her head. "I'll be there. If anything happens, I'll jump in and drag your ass out right out of that pool. You know that, right?"

She sighs, nodding against me. "I know. It's kind of our thing."

I know it's a joke, but it still feels good to hear this knowledge that I'm more than just some guy who keeps sinking her lower. It doesn't last long. "I'm sorry I couldn't show you."

"Show me what?"

"How good it can be out there. In the water." I stroke her hair, thinking of what it feels like every time I dive into the pool, cutting across the water. "For me, it's like…"

When I trail off, she looks up, asking, "What's it like?"

I did my first lap when I was seven. It was the first time I really worked hard at something and had someone tell me it was good. Not because of my name, but just because of this *thing* I could do with my body. I struggle to find the words. "It's like my own world. I control it. Harness it. When I'm in the water, I know I'm good at something. I know I can win. No matter how high I go or how low I fall, it'll always be the same. That's what it's like for me. A guaranteed win, every time I jump in."

Her breath comes out shaky. "That sounds nice."

"I realize it's not the same for you, but you've got this, Little Red. I know it's going to be hard, but you did it when you had to, and you'll do it again. People like us? We survive, because there's no other option. You're stronger than you think." I cup her cheek with my hand, tipping her face up to search her eyes. "But hey, if you really can't? I'll deal."

I mean it. I've put Georgia through enough already. I'm not going to force her to do anything she's not comfortable with, even if it means setting me back to zero on my service hours and getting a new sentence.

She lets out a soft breath, eyes falling closed. "Well, it's hard to say no when you're being all nice about it."

I tip down to push a kiss into her hair. "I can be a dick, if you want. It *is* my factory setting."

"No," she says, pressing her nose into my chest. "I like the nice."

"Then how's this?" I sweep her hair away from her neck, kissing a slow wager into her neck. "If you do it—pass or fail—I'll take you out tonight." Hesitantly, I tack on, "If you'll let me."

It'd be a stretch to call what we do *dating*. I'm still her teacher, which means we can't exactly waltz into The Nerd and make out in the corner booth. But ever since that night, I've made it a goal to ask her every few days, even if it is something painfully lame, like dessert at the overlook, or watching the newest episode of Lakevale on my couch. She's only said no once, and only because she had a paper to write.

Her breath stutters, head tilting to the side. "Yeah?"

I hum into her skin. "Wherever you want."

"The Yarn Barn?" she says, voice hopeful.

I pause, hoping that she can't feel my grimace. "Sure."

"I felt that face you made." She laughs, nudging me back. "I still have to make four scarves!"

A knock interrupts us, followed by Micha's fake whisper. "Put your clothes on. It's time for the test." I yank the door open and he stumbles in, pretending to shield his eyes.

Georgia pushes his face away. "Don't be gross, Micha."

He rolls his eyes. "Don't worry, I won't tell anyone. If they drag Heston out of here in handcuffs, I'll have to take the class all over again." He flashes me a smirk. "And without you here to torture, what's the point?"

Georgia pushes him out the door, and I grab my clipboard, following after her. I'm looping my whistle over my neck when I realize that it's not just Coach James waiting by the end of the pool. Collins stands next to him, looking like a proper asshole in his uptight brown suit.

"The headmaster wanted to see the results himself," Coach explains when I reach them. He's obviously miffed about it, but either Collins is too laser-focused on the pool to notice or he just doesn't care.

"Whatever," I say, noting that he's not the only one here. Ms. Gilbert is sitting in the stands. Vandy, Caroline, and Michaela are a few rows back, holding up obnoxiously decorated posters that cheer on both swimmers. It's all a bit much, if you ask me.

Of course, then the back door opens, and another person enters, stopping by the edge of the stands.

Warren.

"I invited Mr. McAllister as well," Collins says, nodding at Warren, "that way we can all handle your paperwork at once and turn it in efficiently to the judge." He gives me a look that's more malicious than I think him capable of. It's clear that even though I have his balls in a vice when it comes to the Devils, he's going to go out of his way to compensate in other areas.

I watch Warren climb the stands and greet Vandy and the others, taking a seat at their side. He throws me a wave and I scowl back, squaring my shoulders.

Georgia's standing by the side of the pool, hands balled into fists at her side. To everyone else, she probably just looks intent on the task at hand, but I can see her tells. There's a fine tremor running through the muscle in her outer thigh. She keeps rhythmically clenching her hands. There's a subtle shadow beneath her eyes, evidence that she hadn't slept well last night.

I get this flash of terror that this is one of those moments she'd be most inclined to reach for something sharp.

Coach James leans toward Collins, whispering. "Georgia Haynes, senior. As I understand it, there may be a bit of a phobia. She couldn't even go into the deep end..."

I'm doing the math in my head—wondering what I'd need to call the whole thing off, just let her off the hook—when her focus shifts to Collins. The apprehension hardens into a grim resolve, shoulders pushed back, chin lifting.

"Can we get started?" she asks.

"You'll each have to swim a full length and back," Coach James says, reading out the list of requirements. "It's the stroke of your choice, although I need to see that you can float on your backs. You may not touch the bottom, and you have to tread water for twenty-seconds in the deep end before turning back. Your entire face must go underwater." He looks between them. "Understood?"

"Yep," Micha says, looking warily out at the water. "You said twenty-seconds?"

"Yes."

Georgia's eyes are traveling the distance of the pool, and even though she's still wearing that brave mask, the color has seeped from her face.

"Sir," I say, stepping forward, "Ms. Haynes is still struggling with—"

"No. I'm ready," she says, pulling off her sweatshirt. "I can do it. No struggling."

I will her to meet my gaze, mouth pressing into a tense line once she does. I promise her, "I've got you, Haynes," and am relieved to see a little of the tension falling from her frame.

"Go, Georgia!" the girls shout, the cheer echoing off the metal roof.

Some of the color comes back to her face at the ruckus and she flaps a hand at them, visibly battling a smile as she toes up to the edge of the pool.

Coach James hands me the stopwatch and I ask, "Are you ready?" She nods and stares out at the water, all game face. I hold my thumb over the timer button. "Ready, set, go!"

I start the time.

She jumps in artlessly, splashing water across the deck. Micha bends over and cheers her on, "You've got this! Get it, girl!" Her movements are messy and spastic, more like a dog-paddle than a formal stroke, but she hits each beat, submerging her head and getting to the marker at the middle of the pool. She stops and takes a breath before sinking all the way under. I drop to a crouch at the edge, heart pounding as I search the water, prepared to jump in after her.

She bobs back up with a loud gasp, eyes wide and panicked, searching the deck. They stop on me, and I can't read the question there, but I answer it with a dip of my head.

"Tread water! Twenty-seconds!"

She nods, thrusting her chin into the air. Her arms flail and I'm not sure how much her legs are moving, but the time ticks by. My eyes ping back and forth from the watch to her bobbing head, forcing myself not to freak out at the way she's gasping for air. Sweat beads on my forehead as the time ticks away, until finally, it ends.

"Back float!"

At least this one, she has more than the usual experience in. She tips up onto her back, body looking stiff as a board as she stares up at the ceiling, puffing these small, anxious breaths.

"That's it! You're done. Swim back!"

The little group of spectators cheer like they're watching the goddamn Olympics. Frantically, she paddles over, panting, with those wide, terrified eyes, and I'm there to meet her, reaching out across the water. Her hand slaps against mine, clutching on tight, and I yank her out in one swift move.

"Did I do it?" she breathlessly asks, checking over her shoulder like she's afraid the pool is coming for her.

"You did it." I feel as breathless as she looks, and in that moment, all I want to do is grab her face in my hands and plant a hot, bruising kiss to her mouth, because holy shit. I'm proud that she made it. I'm proud that I taught her. It may be the first real thing I've ever taught someone to do.

Micha brings her a towel and wraps her in it. "Your doggy paddle is on point, sis!"

She laughs tiredly, pulling the towel around her shoulders. "Now you get to look stupid, too." I don't miss that she's still inching away from the pool.

"Okay Micha, you're up," Coach James confirms, waving me over. I get there just in time to hear him whisper to Collins, "Micha Adams. Sophomore. This kid didn't even want to go in the *shallow* end."

I get this strange feeling that Coach James is trying to talk me up, although I'm not sure why. We've worked well together these past few months, but I wouldn't necessarily call him a friend. Still, he shoots me a confident grin and faces the pool. Maybe he just hates Collins' too.

Micha tugs on his swim cap and goggles, pulling each arm across his chest in an exaggerated stretch. I stop just short of rolling my eyes. If the exam were on *acting* like a skilled swimmer, he'd be getting a trophy. The girls stand up to cheer for him just as jubilantly, chanting, "Mi-cha! Mi-cha!" and Georgia joins in, clapping with them.

I pull out the stopwatch, beginning, "Are you ready?" At his very precise nod, I hold my thumb over the timer button. "Ready, set, go!"

What happens next must be the result of some reality-altering hallucinogen.

Micha takes his dive start with a form that can only be described as flawless, puncturing the surface with a graceful dolphin kick. It leads him into a perfect freestyle, his arms slicing cleanly through the water. I watch, eerily still as he stops to touch the edge, turning to swim back. It's not formal enough to be competitive, but it's not sloppy enough to be amateur, either.

I lead him through the drills while the girls go wild, flapping around their posters and looking excited for him. Georgia's hugging the towel to her chest, chin ducked as she watches, and I don't miss the way her face falls.

Micha does his float and then swims to the edge of the pool, jumping out like it's barely even fazed him. "Did I do okay?" he asks, batting his eyelashes like he's the most innocent thing to step into this natatorium.

I click the stopwatch, tightly announcing, "Sufficient."

He looks unbothered by my tone, accepting the towel Georgia passes to him.

"That was..." she trails off, looking momentarily speechless. "Like, *wow*."

He preens. "You're not just saying that?"

"You were like a real swimmer," she says, that frown returning. "Why couldn't I—"

"He already knew how to swim," I snap, looking to make sure Collins and Coach James are too caught up in whatever they're bickering about to notice. "This whole time, he's been playing us!"

"Yeah," Micha admits, looking unabashed as he peels off his cap. "Come on. My sister is a swim star. She taught me to swim before I even knew what eyeliner was."

Georgia's jaw drops. "Seriously?" At his shrug, she asks, "Then why were you here? You said you didn't—"

"My mom took me swimming when I was like four or something and I hated it, so she just assumed I never learned." He rolls his eyes, snapping off his goggles. "I figured it'd be an easy way to check off her whole 'life skills' requirement. And then, once I found out Heston was teaching…" He looks at me, grinning with all his teeth. "I thought, what better opportunity to fuck with him all semester, right?"

Before storming away, I point a finger at him, seething. "You are such a dick."

"You're welcome!" he calls to my back.

Collins gives me a bland, unimpressed look when I enter the office, followed by Coach James and Warren. "It seems congratulations are in order. You managed to teach two mature human beings how to not drown."

Warren looks taken aback at the tone, but it's Coach James who cuts in.

"Heston has done more than teach those two students. He's been a competent assistant coach this whole semester. He's taught the middle-schoolers proper form. He's wrangled the high-schoolers into submission. He's been an enormous help." He puts his hands on his hips, shaking his head. "I know Heston's history here. I'm not a fan of it. But I'm glad to see him turning over a new leaf, and if I'm being quite honest, I'd be happy to see him take up the post in a more official capacity."

Collins looks completely galled at the suggestion. "I beg your pardon?"

"We both know Columbia has been after me for the past couple years," Coach explains, looking rueful. "I'd like to have someone to train up to take over for when I inevitably give in to their offers. Heston here would be my first choice." After a beat, he adds, "And my second, and my third."

"Well…" Collins gapes belligerently. "Who's your *fourth*?"

"Headmaster," Coach says, leveling him with a look. "Someone very wise once told me you can't raise a child when you're acting like one." He holds up a hand at Collins' visible desire to argue. "I realize that sounds excessively insolent. I only mean that we can't teach maturity if we don't demonstrate it. This is a teaching moment."

"I agree," Warren says, clapping me on the shoulder. "As a board alumnus, I think Heston's earned his second chance here."

Collins' jaw locks and he whips out the paperwork. "One thing at a time, gentlemen."

I watch as they each jot down their signature, verifying that I've put in the complete number of service hours. It all goes too quickly for me to really grasp, but when I walk out of the office forty minutes later, I'm carrying the papers for my release along with a job offer.

I accept both.

31

For the first nineteen years of my life, Christmas was always a whirr of parties. There were the Chisholms, the patriarch having long been my father's partner. Then the Nguyens, because anyone who was anyone went to the Nguyens' Christmas party. There was always something going down at the Club. Most of it was networking, the tedious amassing social capital, and handing someone's wife a gift without even knowing whether or not it was wine or some useless gadget she'd never touch, because someone else did the shopping and gift-wrapping.

Despite that, I always really liked Christmas at my house. For all the parties we ended up attending, the Wilcox tradition was to never throw one of our own. Fourth of July, sure. Halloween? Why not? But Christmas in our house was always spent with us in our separate worlds, barely passing one another by. For my mom, it was probably lonely—at least until Sebastian went to her. But the rest of us liked it that way—an evening carved out for nothing but ourselves. No obligations. No pretense.

Georgia shifts in her seat, letting loose a soft sigh. "Either we go in or we leave, but I'm not sitting in the car all night."

I peer up at the McAllisters' sleek condo, feeling my stomach fill with dismay. There's a Christmas tree in the window and a big star hanging over the front door. Reynolds is having a Secret Santa party. Well, that's not entirely accurate. *Vandy* is having a Secret Santa party, and Reyn and Warren agreed to host.

"You should go by yourself," I tell her again. "I'm just going to fuck up everyone's mood."

Her fingers are cold on the back of my neck, but the way she's looking at me when I turn is pure warmth. "We were invited."

"*You* were invited."

She rolls her eyes, elaborating, "It was heavily implied that you would be with me. Vandy knows. Reyn knows. Even your brother knows you'll be there. *With me.*" Sighing, she adds, "Warren will be there. The two of you get along."

It's been a month since that night out on the lake, and things might be a little less murderously hostile between me and the Devils, but there's no ignoring reality. None of them can stand me. Frankly, I can barely tolerate most of them myself.

It's just this problem.

This problem where I'm hopelessly, stupidly, recklessly in love with their friend.

Lately, it's been pushing me into more and more of these situations, and it's the complete fucking opposite of fun. I'm used to not caring that people hate me. I don't need friends. But now I'm spending all this time thinking about how they could drive Georgia away from me. Talk her into seeing sense. The only way to prove that I'm not out to hurt her is by doing shit like this.

Showing them.

Nevertheless, it's a slog. I'm Heston fucking Wilcox, and even I have my limits on sitting around with people who hate my guts. At some point, it does shit to a person. Seeing as how I had brunch with my brother and my mom yesterday, I'm feeling a little less tolerant than usual. That was uncomfortable enough.

"We could always just go back to my place," I suggest, letting my palm fall on her leg. When I sweep it up and inward, wedging it between her soft, warm thighs, she pulls in a breath, teeth sinking into her lip. Huskily, in that way I know she likes, I add, "I can unwrap you like a present."

It's a dirty play, and the look she gives me tells me she knows it. There was a time this would have gotten her in my backseat, legs spread, tits out. But there are just some things she refuses to cast aside for sex. Schoolwork. Friends. Family.

She doesn't fuck me because she needs it. Not anymore.

She only fucks me when she wants it.

Georgia sighs, turning to glance into the back seat. I don't need to follow her gaze. There's a box of gift bags sitting back there that she'd probably protect with her life. "I need to hand all those out."

My girl's been knitting up a goddamn storm, keeping her hands busy when I can't be there for her. It's a pretty good coping mechanism, and she's getting really good at it. I still wear mine, uncaring when people rib me for the fluorescent green. These are things Georgia has made with her hands. I've watched her do it, seen the concentration and care she puts into them. Hours upon hours of not just labor, but thought, too. Colors and designs. Gradients. Fiber types based on allergies.

I might not be the most social person anymore, but I'm smart enough to understand that this—giving them to people, showing them off, seeing their reactions—is the payoff to that. And she deserves to see it.

In a decisive move, I open the car door. "Okay, let's do it."

She seems surprised for a moment, lagging behind while I duck into the back seat, pulling out the box. When she catches up, she's wearing a bright, cheerful grin that I just can't bring myself to tarnish. A minute later, we're on the front step, stopping in front of the door. The star over our head makes her hair shine like a halo of fire, which seems appropriate.

Georgia is the Devils' angel.

And maybe, if I keep doing stuff like this, she'll be mine.

She rings the doorbell, stepping back to clasp her hands in front of her. "I love you," she says, ducking her head to hide her smile.

Something catches in my throat to hear it said like that—so

casually, like she's losing nothing to give it away. I plaster over it with a suspicious look. "Are you just saying that because I'm totally pussy-whipped and you know I'll do anything you ask me to?"

She cocks her head to look at me from the corner of her eye. "I'm saying that because it's true." Quietly, she adds, "And because I like the way your face gets when you hear it."

I shift the box, shoulders feeling tight. "How does my face get?"

She looks at me, mouth pushed into a sideways pucker as she thinks. "Happy," she decides.

I'm still staring at her when Vandy swings the door open, grabbing her friend in a hug.

Huh.

So that's what that is.

～

I was right.

No one wants me here.

Luckily, Georgia was also right about everyone expecting me. It's always a little better that way, able to sit tucked away in the corner armchair while they all gush over their presents. If I'm lucky, they ignore me.

If I'm not...

"This is the alternator," Sebastian shows me his phone, swiping through the pictures of something round and silver and weird looking. He neither looks nor sounds happy about it, jaw tight as he explains, "I think this is the problem. That grinding noise...probably the bearings."

I flex my shoulders, brows crouching low. "And?" Brunch yesterday had been one unkindness shy of seeing actual violence. The only good thing about it was that my mom looked normal. Clear-eyed. Nervous and wary, but not unwilling to sit at the same table as me. That's something.

Sebastian is something else. "And I've got it in my trunk. So I'm going to change it." He says it forcefully, in much the same way an irritated parent would send their child to bed without dinner.

I can't stop myself from bristling. "I don't want you banging around in my engine again. It still doesn't steer right from the last time!"

Across the room, Georgia and Sugar turn, faces falling in exasperation at our standoff.

"It steers fine!" my brother demands, looking affronted. "It's not my fault you haven't had an alignment since—"

"Why do you even care?" I burst, glaring up at him. "My car is shit. So what?"

He responds by puffing up his chest and snapping, "So let me change your fucking alternator!"

"Fine!" I snap back, tossing a hand toward the door. "Be my guest!"

Fuming, he stomps out the door, stopping just shy of slamming it behind him. Sugar doesn't follow him, even though it looks like she wants to.

Instead, she diverts her path until she's standing in front of me. She juts her chin out, that delicate-looking face of hers hardened into a scowl. "He's trying, you know. Might be nice if you put your dick away for a few minutes and met him halfway."

I look at the door incredulously. "Halfway to *where*? We hate each other. Always have. Suddenly, he wants to do something nice for me? Excuse the fuck out of me for having two brain cells to rub together, but I seriously doubt it."

"Did it ever cross your mind that this might not be about doing something nice for *you*?" She raises her eyebrows, giving me a brash look. "Maybe it's about Georgia and your mom wanting to see something better in you. Maybe he wants them to know that if it doesn't work out, it won't be because of him. Maybe he just wants to make them happy and this is the best way he knows how."

With that, she spins on her heel and finally follows him, closing the door behind her.

I'm rubbing circuits into my temples when Georgia eases

herself into my lap, gently pulling my wrists away. She replaces my fingers with her lips, planting a soft kiss on my temple.

"You look unhappy." She sounds unhappy saying it, like I'm draining the cheer from her.

Which I probably am.

I wind my arms around her waist, pulling her close. "Only with myself."

She frowns, holding my tired gaze. "Want to leave?"

"No." It's not a lie. "I just need a little time to talk myself into what I'm about to do."

"What are you going to do?"

"Apologize," I say, and inside something bucks angrily against the very idea. I tamp it down. "To my brother."

Her eyes light up, mouth lifting into a surprised grin. "Really?"

I'm quick to temper that enthusiasm. "Don't get your hopes up. We're never going to get along."

That's what I remind myself as I step outside into the chilly air. Sebastian hates me. I bullied him for the majority of our childhood. That's just the way it has to be. And Sebastian took my life from me. My status. My future. My family.

Only nowadays, it feels less like a loss.

"Hiding from the squealing?" Warren's sitting on a bench, nestled into the darkness of a finely manicured garden that he probably has fuck-all to do with.

I glance out to the driveway, making out the shape of my brother curled beneath my hood.

Well, the apology isn't going anywhere.

I take a seat at Warren's side. "Nah, I just came out here to eat some crow."

"Ah." He nods, taking a drag from a cigarette. "That's always fun."

Sourly, I reply, "With as much as I'm chowing down, maybe I'll acquire a taste for it."

"But not tonight," he guesses, tipping his head toward the Honda. I shake my head, already dreading it. "Are you doing it for you, or are you doing it for her?" Jesus. This guy knows me too well.

Laughing, he adds, "I'm not a shrink, Heston. There's no wrong answer. I was just curious."

"Both," I say, cramming my hands in my pockets as I watch Sebastian dig into a toolbox. "But more for her, I guess." Turning to him, I confess, "You know Georgia's family. They wouldn't want her slumming it with some socially disgraced assistant swim coach. It's not enough." *I'm* not enough.

"But they might accept a Wilcox," he guesses, even if he does shake his head. "I don't think you're giving her enough credit. Georgia's her own person. She'd like their approval, but she doesn't need it."

I point out, "But she would like it."

He nods. "Sure. Just so long as you're doing it a little bit for you."

We sit for a while, watching as Sugar hands Sebastian things from the toolbox. It's always easiest with Warren. He doesn't push. He doesn't make me say I'm sorry when I lash out. He doesn't tell me I'm not good enough, or that I have to try harder. Idly, it strikes me that for whatever his earlier flaws in the ways of parenting, Warren is probably a good dad. The kind of dad that might have pushed Bass and me closer together instead of farther apart.

"Family is important," he says, almost like he's read my thoughts. "It took me a long time to figure that out. Too long, if I'm being honest. Long enough that a lot of bridges couldn't be salvaged." Looking pensive, he dabs out his cigarette, scraping it against the dirt. "But I think family might be a bit like love. It's not something you just wake up one day and suddenly find. It's something you build. It doesn't need to be blood. I believe that."

I groan. "If you're about to give me some corny line about us being family, I'm going to have to take so many cool points from you."

Warren barks a surprised laugh, but doesn't look offended. "I guess I do sort of think of you as family now. Don't tell Reynolds, though. He's got terrible only child syndrome. The kid could never share for shit."

"Don't worry," I assure him. "The last thing I need is another brother."

"That wasn't exactly the kind of brotherhood I had in mind." He shoves his hands in his pockets. "Our little Devils need a mentor. Someone on campus. Someone they can go to." The look he gives me is heavy with significance.

"Our..." I start, but then everything clicks together. I'd suspected it that night at the lake, and now I know. "You're the one who sent me the key to the Devil's Lair. And the invitation."

He nods. "After you got the Devils shut down, a few of us alumni got together, shared a few drinks, and made a new plan. I know it probably seems silly, but the Devils meant a lot to us. There's a history that runs deep—a history that had been forgotten over the years. So we decided to start it back up again, just a little differently." He stares out at the street, something troubled crossing his features. "When Reyn came back from military school, he was... well, a lot like you've been since last summer, actually. Alone. At risk of re-offending. In need of something structured." Turning, he meets my eyes to say, "I didn't want my son to fall back into the same kind of toxic environment it was when he got sent away."

"You mean the kind of environment I helped create."

Warren doesn't feed me some bullshit about not being at fault. He just gives me a single dip of his head. "Do you remember what I told you at the meeting, that day I found out about you and Georgia?" Pausing, he adds, "I mean, before I realized it was Georgia. I said something very wise and catchy about having connections."

I think back, searching my memories. "The opposite of addiction isn't sobriety. It's connection."

"Exactly." He looks satisfied as he stands, giving me a nod of acknowledgment. "You really helped them out this year, picking the new pledges, stepping up when Georgia got in trouble during the prank, pointing out the weak spots. People think leadership is all about being kind and wise, but sometimes it's about having the balls to say what people don't want to hear." Lifting an eyebrow, he tips his head at me. "I know you protected the group from Collins, Heston."

I freeze, wondering if this is one of those secrets I should be keeping. "How?"

"A Devil has his ways," is his answer, finger tapping his temple. "None of the others would have had it in them to throw Afton under that bus. They would have protected her at the expense of the whole group. But you put the Devils above any one person, and that," he stresses, "*that* is what leadership looks like."

The moment feels awkward—heavy with a meaning that I struggle to put words to—but before I can, the sound of metal clanking on asphalt shatters it, followed by a string of growled curses.

"I can probably keep an eye on them," I agree, rising from the bench. Giving Warren a long-suffering look, I admit, "God knows I may be the only one with any control over Micha. And even that's questionable."

He laughs and shoots me a wave before heading back into the house, leaving me to take a halting step toward the road. Sugar's holding his flashlight, looking cold and bored as he tinkers around loudly. Pulling in a steeling breath, I set out to do what I came out here to accomplish.

Bass is neck deep in the car when I amble up, ducking my chin into my scarf. There's a greasy smear of a palm print on the thigh of his pants already, and his shoulders go stiff when I stop, lingering by the hood. I suck up all the anger and bad blood, and try to remember what Sugar said. He's trying. For Georgia. For my mom.

That much I can understand.

"So you think that'll make it run smoother?" I ask, propping my elbows on the frame.

He tightens something with a wrench, only faltering briefly. His voice sounds resigned, but not harsh. "It should. I mean, the whole car needs a complete overhaul." He shakes his head at something lurking beneath a hose, looking annoyed at it. "But, the bones are good. Fixed up right, these things go for about twice their blue book value."

I give him a second look, surprised. "What? Really?"

"Oh yeah," he says, nodding eagerly. "People love fixing up these old cars. They're lightweight and great for racing."

Sugar rounds the car just then, ignoring Sebastian's sound of protest as the light disappears. She hands the flashlight to me, giving me a warning look before marching back toward the house.

Sighing, I point the light to where Sebastian's hands are connecting something. "I thought you weren't doing that anymore. The racing."

"Not competitively," he confirms. "But I still show off my wheels. Jasmine is too pretty not to be admired."

It's a tacky throwaway comment, full of that pompous arrogance that always makes me flare up around him. For the first time, I don't give into it. "Listen," I start, shoving a hand through my hair. "I've got something I need to say."

He peeks up from his task, throwing me a sharp frown. "What?"

"I'm...sorry," I tell him. I have to force the word out over the rock of resistance in my throat. "About the fights and races. About using you to help me fix my gambling debts. Things were really out of control for a while." Shifting uncomfortably, I confess, "*I* was really out of control for a while."

He gives a humorless laugh, body jumping when he yanks a big round thing from the engine. "Is this the part where you blame everything on your 'addiction'?" He tosses what I can only assume is the old alternator aside, running a rag around where he pulled it. "Like you've done the twelve steps and now you're all born again, so everyone has to give you a chance?"

I bristle at the contempt in his voice, even though he probably has every right. "No. It's the part where I own up to my shit and tell you I'm trying." Shaking my head, I aim the light into the vacancy left by the old part. "I'm not a new person, Bass. I'm just trying to be a better version of the regular one." Wryly, I add, "I'm shooting for twice my blue book value."

"And why is that?" he wonders, sounding less than generous as he fits the new part. "Because you blew your life up and you want it back? How long will this last?"

"I don't want it back," I say easily. "The trust fund, dad's money, the privileges and connections, the expectations...you can keep it. Money can probably solve a lot of problems for most people, but for me, I think it just creates them. I'm better off with nothing but Preston wages."

Sometimes even those are tempting. Even the insurance money is unreachable. Briefly, I'd considered investing it by playing the market, but then I had to force myself to face the truth.

That's just gambling with more steps.

Instead, I had Warren help me put it into a secure account. I do my best to just act like it doesn't exist. Most days I barely think about it.

"Well, for the sake of everyone around you, I hope it sticks." It's the closest I'll ever get to a voice of support from my brother. "And if it doesn't? You can bet your ass I'll be here." The look he gives me is hard, dark, full of warning. "If you hurt her, I'm going to come for you."

I don't need to ask who he's talking about. "Good," is my only response, and I mean it. There's a sense of relief in having someone other than Warren holding me accountable. Sebastian gives me a baffled look, tightening down a bolt, which is when the girls emerge from the house again.

Both of us turn to glance at them—Georgia and Sugar, standing beneath the glow of the star.

Without really meaning to, I muse, "She's kind of like mom, isn't she?" Realizing how that sounds, I rush to say, "Not in a gross, Oedipal way."

"Because she's more fragile than she looks," he says, understanding.

Neither of us specify which girl we're talking about.

The front door slams and the pair of them tentatively walk down the steps, eyeing the two of us. "Everything okay here?"

Bass taps the newly installed alternator with the head of his wrench. "We're good." He could be talking about the car, but when he tosses the wrench in the toolbox, closing the hood with a thud, he turns to me. "Bring it by the garage this week and I'll give it a tune-up. Merle hates it when I have extra cars in there. It's hilarious."

I blink at him, feeling caught off guard. "Yeah?"

"Sure." He shrugs, bumping his shoulder into mine when he passes. "You can hold my flashlight."

I roll my eyes at his retreat, lugging that toolbox back to his trunk as Sugar follows. "Douchebag."

Georgia wraps her arms around me, nestling against my side in a way that makes it impossible not to pull her close. "Well, that seemed...civil."

I push my nose into her hair, inhaling her scent. "It was."

"I guess there are Christmas miracles, after all." Despite the joke, her voice grows quiet and serious. "Thank you. For trying."

Everyone filters out of the house just then, Devils and their ilk, birds of a feather. I watch as their eyes find us, skittering to a stop like they're trying to do the long division of this thing we've got going on. Probably, they're all asking themselves how long we can possibly last, because they don't understand how we fit.

I tip her face up, staring down into her pretty green eyes. "Sometimes you save me from drowning, too."

She tilts her head like she's trying to put those pieces together, but I don't give her a chance. I tip down to press a slow kiss to her cold lips, warming them with my own. Maybe someday I'll be able to find the words, but for now, this will work. It's a language only we know.

With it, I tell her that much like the scarves she painstakingly knits, Georgia has built herself a family, weaving all of us in and out, intertwining our lives. I tell her that I'm thankful to be one of the threads, tethered to something tangible and bright.

Something that won't let me float away.

EPILOGUE

Georgia

Two Years Later

The text doesn't even contain words—it's just an eggplant emoji
—but I'm in a hurry. It's not like it matters. After two-and-a-half
years with Heston, we communicate more and more in shorthand.
He knows what I'm looking for.

His reply is quick: a thumbs-up followed by *see you at home.*

My chest floods with relief. Things have been a bit off since I
spent last weekend at my parent's house, but I've been reluctant to
bring it up, fearing the worst just as much as the embarrassment of
discovering it's nothing.

My level of excitement reaches peak absurdity halfway there. I
would have thought after all this time it'd get a little boring—sex
with the same person, day in, day out. But that's far from reality.
Every time with Heston is just as intense and crazy-making as the
last. Two and a half years, and he's never once given me the chance
to cool off. I struggled with it for a while, this crippling fear that I'd
need more than he could give. But it's never come to fruition. I told

him I wouldn't go to anyone else and I haven't. I haven't even wanted to.

The apartment is in Northridge, close enough to Preston for Heston to get to work easily, and not far from Saint Mary's, the women's college where I'm studying political science. I don't know if I want to go into the world of politics like my dad, but I enjoyed working with him on his campaign, and now that he's in office, I see a pathway to an issue I find important: mental health reform.

I pull into the parking lot, passing Heston's tricked-out Honda, and wonder what today will be like. Maybe he'll meet me at the door and slam me up against it, flipping up my skirt and fucking me with wild abandon right there in the foyer. Maybe he'll take me to the couch and bend me over the arm, slapping one of his handprints into my ass until he pounds ruthlessly into me. Maybe, like he sometimes does, he'll take me to bed and make it soft and achingly slow, forcing desperate pleas from my mouth as he teases me, relentless and deliciously wicked.

By the time I climb the stairs, I already feel fit to burst. My life is pretty structured these days, designed around minimizing any opportunities to fixate on anything detrimental. My compulsions haven't gone away, but I've learned how to better manage them. It doesn't hurt that my boyfriend has an insatiable appetite of his own and is willing to sacrifice to my needs.

Our apartment is my favorite place to be. Even having just spent a weekend at my parents' giant manor, I find that years spent living in dorm rooms has conditioned me for the coziness of places like *this*. Heston and I spent weeks finding the perfect one, because although I'm content with small spaces and a lack of luxuries, he still has a bit of that Wilcox snobbishness.

I wouldn't have him any other way.

I rush into the apartment, breathless from my sprint up the stairs.

But he's not waiting for me.

Sagging in disappointment, I set my bag down and call out, "I'm home!"

Nothing.

I shrug out of my jacket, feeling my chest twinge worriedly by the lack of greeting. "Where are you?"

There's a bang and a muffled curse before his voice responds, "In the kitchen!"

Oh.

Oh no.

I pad carefully into the room, peeking at him around the corner. As I suspected, he's red-faced and sulky, darting from one pot to another, stopping to tell something inside, "Oh, fuck you."

"Babe?" I ask, cautiously stepping inside. "You making dinner?"

He throws me a look. "No, I'm playing soccer."

"Okay," I say, holding my hands up. "Stupid question, fair enough."

He flings a hand at the pot. "The bechamel is all grainy, and I can't find the wooden spoons, and *this*," he throws the whisk in the direction of the sink, "is completely useless."

I finally enter the room, going to the drawer with the wooden spoons and pulling him out a pair. Heston always needs two of everything when he cooks. One will inevitably get chucked somewhere.

Wilcoxes.

"What's the occasion?" I ask, sliding onto the counter.

He gives me a bland look. "Hunger."

"Oh."

More elaborately, he explains, "I spent lunch dealing with a Freshman's menstruation crisis, so now my stomach is kicking my ass."

"Oh my god," I laugh, covering my mouth. "I would have paid money to see that."

"I had to take her to the office and call her dad, who, for the record, was about as prepared to deal with that as I was."

"You're an excellent teacher," I decide, and hey, I should know. I was his first student, after all. Sometimes when he goes to the pool for some laps, I'll even get in with him, clutched tight to his neck as he gently guides me beneath the surface, showing me that his world can be more than an icy, black maker of nightmares. Sometimes, I'll even press my lips to his while we're under there, bubbles of air tickling our noses. The water still scares me. I just know that Heston will always lift me to the surface.

I peer into the pot, making happy sounds at what's happening inside. "You're getting better."

"No, I'm not." Heston looks hopelessly into the sauce. "But it's not like I can help it. My housekeeper always brought me prepared meals."

Wryly, I point out, "You haven't had a housekeeper in like three years."

He shrugs, stirring the sauce, and I find my stomach clenching with unease. Heston always greets me at the door when I send him the emoji. It's not the lack of sex that's upsetting. It's the deviation. How harried he looks. The fact that he tossed and turned all night.

Not for the first time, I wonder if I should call Warren.

"Hey," I say when he passes, tugging him between my legs. "Hi."

He finally stops then, taking a breath to rest his palms on the counter against my hips, bracketing me in. "Sorry." His eyes go soft when he looks at me, eyes slipping closed when I cup his cheek in a hand, searching the lines of his face. "Just a weird day, I guess." He tastes like the sauce when I kiss him, humming into my mouth. It's a slow, testing kiss—a question.

He answers by deepening it, licking hot and wet into my mouth. When he breaks away to kiss down my neck, I at least feel a little better. This is normal. The heat of his tongue. The scrape of his teeth. The way his fingers dig into my hips, hitching me up against his growing hardness.

I trail my hand down his arm, brushing the Devil's mark he tattooed there a year ago. It's placed in the same spot as the scar on my forearm—a pale, jagged reminder that for better or worse, people like us survive.

So long as we have each other.

"Is there something you want?" he asks, reaching down to sweep a palm up the outside of my thigh.

I squirm against him, chest swelling with anticipation. "Only if you want to give it."

His movements stutter for a moment, voice tinged with confusion when he answers, "Always." His fingers play at the edge of my panties, tracing the scalloped edge of the lace as he pushes his nose into my neck, inhaling my scent. "Fuck, you smell good." He punctuates this by wrenching me from the counter, causing my breath to hitch. I love it when he gets like this; all worked up, tossing me around, putting me where he wants me.

Right now, he puts me right in front of him, pressed up against the counter, his lips red and already swollen. His blue eyes search mine, and although I don't know what he's looking for, I'm guessing he finds it. "Fuck it."

He drops to his knees and my eyes slide closed, waiting. For a man who was so apprehensive to eat me out, he's become an old pro now. I tremble in anticipation of the heat of his hands dragging down my panties, the warmth of his mouth exploring me. When it doesn't come, I look down.

He's not on his knees.

He's on *one* knee, a tiny blue box perched in his hands.

I stare down at the box, brain a confusing tangle of want and bewilderment. The blue of the box matches his eyes. That's the only thought I'm capable of.

"I was going to do this over dinner, but obviously that's going to suck, so here it goes," he says, his voice uncharacteristically filled with nerves. "Little Red, we've been through a lot of shit together. Some of it's been good. Some of it's been bad. A lot of it's been really, unbelievably erotic." I take in a stunned inhale and his mouth twitches. "I've waited, Georgia, and I've tried to show you I'm good enough. I don't know if it's worked, because deep down, I'm pretty sure I'm not." Before I can argue, he rushes on, "I know your family still hates me. I can't buy you jewels and treat you like a princess, although I know you well enough to realize you'd hate that, anyway."

"Heston—"

"What I'm trying to say is that I know you, and I love you. You're it for me." He opens the box, and the diamond ring nestled in the center of it makes my hands fly to my mouth. "Will you marry me?"

I look from him to the ring, eyes jumping back and forth, and then it's all just a blur of tears, because I'm an idiot.

I'm an *ass*.

There's a long pause before Heston skeptically guesses, "The crying is a good thing, right?"

"I checked the account," I confess, wiping my cheeks. "I checked it and saw all that money missing, and I was so worried that—"

Realization crosses his face. "You thought I was gambling it."

"I'm sorry!" I drop to my knees, taking his face in my hands. "It's not that I don't trust you, I just got in the habit because you asked me to. Remember? And then I wasn't sure how to ask without..."

Without accusing him of something unfairly.

"Hey," he says, mouth pressing into a tight line as his arms wind around me, gathering me to his chest. "It's okay, I get it. It didn't even cross my mind. That's how long it's been since..." He trails off and I know he's referencing that day a year and a half ago, when he almost had a relapse moment. He sighs into my hair, clutching me close. Quieter, he says, "I still check on you, don't I?"

Nodding, I remember all the times he's explored my body, hiding it with kisses and lingering touches, even though I know he's checking for marks. Keeping me honest. Making sure I'm okay.

Jerking back, I fumble for the box, getting a better look at the ring. It's silver and delicate. Modest. *Perfect.*

"I know it's not much," he starts, but I cut him off with a hard, fervent kiss.

"It's exactly what I always wanted," I assure him, my smile so big that my cheeks ache with it. "Can I put it on?"

"No."

My face falls right before hardening up into a scowl. "Why not?"

He gives me a tense look. "You haven't actually given me an answer."

Shit. *Shit.* Marry Heston Wilcox and all the baggage that comes with it?

Well, he'll have to carry mine, too.

"Yes!" I cry, grabbing his face for another tear-stained kiss. "*Absolutely* yes!"

He snorts, but I can feel the stiffness falling from his body, see the flash of relief in his eyes. "Then I guess you can put it on."

I have the ring on my finger before he even finishes his sentence, carefully setting the box aside before straddling his lap. I kiss the smirk from his lips, rocking against him, so eager to take him inside my body that I end up riding him right there on the kitchen floor.

It's just as amazing as it always is, feeling his hands on my hips, his mouth trailing over my neck. It's not the first time we've made love in the kitchen to the smell of something burning. But it's the first time I've been able to look down into his hooded eyes and know that we both want this to last forever.

For better or for worse.

Devils in the flesh.

AFTERWORD

Readers,

Thank you so much for following us on this journey with the Boys of Preston Prep. What started out as a standalone novel about a terrible jerk named Hamilton Bates, opened up a whole world of tragic sad bois, traumatic romance, angst fueled sex, and happily ever afters.

Hamilton Bates made us accept the thin line between love and hate. Reynolds McAllister taught us that everyone deserves a second chance. Sebastian Wilcox showed us that sometimes under the bruises and impulsive decisions there's just a guy who needs a girl and a box full of kittens. And Heston...well, he pushed our limits. All of them.

For the time, Preston Prep is wrapped up and we are focused on the Royal's series. We aren't totally finished with these characters though, so keep an eye out for special outtakes in the next couple of months.

Your support has been amazing and gave us the courage to up our game with The Lords. For those of you that haven't read book 1, the first chapter is below. For everyone else, make sure you join us in Angel's Antics, our facebook group where we talk about everything from books to kittens.

Thanks!!
Angel & Sam

LORD OF PAIN: ROYALS OF FORSYTH U (TEASER)

Story

Gnawing at my fingernail, I ask, "What about this one?"

Mary frowns through my screen. "Not enough tits, sis."

"Seriously?" I look down at my cleavage. I won't pretend like I've got the biggest tits in the world, but I'm not totally flat, either. Things might be a lot easier for me if I were. "I'm completely hanging out."

"Pfft," she says. "Show some nipple or something, Story. The Daddies cream themselves over a hint of nipple." I tug at the top of my tank and rub my thumb over my nipple. It hardens. Mary, who I'm talking to over video chat, gives me a thumbs up. "Perfect."

"What should I ask for?" I snap a few test pictures, trying to look sexy and far happier than I feel. "I keep getting gift cards to Starbucks, but I have to sell them to get the cash."

"Then start going for straight cash," she says, smacking on a stick of gum. "He's obviously on the line."

I didn't mean to get into being a Sugar Baby, but after posting a photo of myself on the beach in my bikini over spring break, the requests kept coming in on my ChattySnap account. I was curious at the time, but not enough to really follow through with anything.

Not until things got bad enough.

Three months later and I've got quite a following. Apparently, virgins aren't a social embarrassment in the world of Sugar Daddies the way it is at my high school.

"Five bucks for a tank without a bra," Mary lists off, "ten for full cleavage with a little nipple. Twenty for topless, but I think if you change into the pale pink tank, you'll get more money."

I do the math. If I send out five topless pics, that's a quick hundred bucks. That's a bus ticket and a meal. It's not enough to really set me up for The

Plan, but it's a nice start. Just holding the ticket in my hand will be enough to make this all bearable, for just a little while longer.

"Okay," I say, pushing back the nerves that have started building in my stomach. The deeper I get into this, the scarier it is. Scary because it involves exposing myself to strangers. Scary because they'll have a part of me—the same part of me I've been trying so hard to keep to myself. Scary because I need it, and if there's one thing I've learned this past year, it's that needing something means giving in to someone else's power.

"My tank is down in the laundry room," I explain, antsy. "Let me grab it and just get this over with."

Mary hangs up and I leave my phone on the bed. The laundry room is downstairs, off of the kitchen. Even though it's been a year, I'm still not used to the size of this house—my stepfather's house. Before my mom married Daniel, we were living in a two-bedroom apartment that overlooked the railroad tracks. Now we're in a cozy seven-thousand square foot McMansion with a pool and an entertainment room downstairs. For a long time, it felt more like a hotel than home.

Now it feels like something else.

I sneak through the kitchen and eye the discarded pizza boxes on the island. That and the trash talk coming from the basement are a sure sign that my stepbrother and his friends are downstairs.

I pause at the realization, feeling stupid.

Laughter bounces up the stairs, like a sharp warning. Killian and his best friends, Dimitri Rathbone and Tristian Mercer, are inseparable, spending all their time together as the reigning kings of our high school. The three of them comprise the complete royalty of the senior class. I don't need to be living with one of them to really *know* them—everyone just does.

I shouldn't be surprised they're over. It's all around school that Tristian got dumped by his girlfriend the other day. If petty high school drama didn't look like juvenile bullshit from my vantage, I'd probably call it a huge scandal. Being a girlfriend to one of these three is like winning the damn lottery. You get the infamy, the expensive gifts, and what basically amounts to three round-the-clock bodyguards. These three share everything, and they protect what's theirs.

She's obviously smart, though. She probably discovered what all those other girls never will: that it's not worth it. They're cold boys, eyes always watching. There's a certain cast to their faces when I'm around that makes the hair on the back of my neck rise. Luckily, I'm a junior and it's been made very clear that I'm never to look at or address them, and under no circumstances should anyone consider my stepbrother and I family.

Not that I'd ever want to be associated with an asshole like him, anyway. There for a minute, right at the start, Killian had been fine. Not kind, nor warm, nor even cordial, but a lot like a prisoner might treat his cell-mate. It was an acceptance, an acknowledgment, that neither of us had a choice in this. He'd been almost sympathetic, bordering on friendly. Briefly, I'd thought of us as allies.

It didn't last long.

I'm not sure exactly when it stopped, but these days, my stepbrother goes out of his way to make it perfectly clear that he loathes me. His friends alternate between ignoring me and sending me vicious, mocking barbs as their eyes track me, waiting, hoping to get a rise out of me. I used to wonder why, trying to figure out what I'd done to make them so mean to me. Killian and his friends are the kind of boys who are blessed with it all; looks, brains, money, athleticism. They're gods around campus and the attitude doesn't stop when they're at home, especially down in Killian's lair.

I know now that they never needed a reason.

Hearing them is just a reminder of how exhausting it all is, tiptoeing around this house, avoiding all the landmines. There's one at every step, it seems. The whole thing has made me paranoid. I feel like I'm constantly being watched. Or that someone has been in my room. I could handle that, though. For my mom. For security. But once things escalated...

I take a deep breath to settle my nerves. I have The Plan, right? I just need to get the money and then I'm home free. I'll get my shirt, flee back to my room, lock my door, and get my business over with.

There are three baskets of clean clothes in the laundry room—mostly Killian's football gear. The whole room smells faintly of sour sweat and lingering body spray. No matter how many times my mom bleaches his uniform, the stench never really goes away. I bend over and sort through one of the baskets for my blush-colored tank.

"Thank god," I sigh, snagging the cotton shirt in my fingers. "Found you."

"Nope, looks like *we* found *you.*"

My heart leaps up my throat and I spin, hand clutched to my throat. Tristian and Dimitri—Rath, as everyone calls him—stand in the doorway.

"God, you scared me." I exhale, darting my eyes between them. "You shouldn't sneak around like that."

"Why not?" Tristian says, a sharp, lopsided grin tugging at his mouth. From the glassy look in his eyes and the way he reeks of beer, he's clearly been drowning his sorrows down there. I'm not dumb enough to imagine he's broken-hearted from getting dumped. Probably just nursing his bruised ego. "You're the one sneaking around up here like a frightened little mouse."

Tristian is insanely good-looking. He's all blond hair, tan skin, and lean, hard muscle. I know that, out of the three of them, he does best with the girls. Much like Killian and Rath, he's also enormous. Intimidating not just because of his size, wealth, and popularity, but mostly because of *something else.*

His smile never quite reaches his eyes.

They're ice blue and carry a glint of cool detachment. Just looking into them makes me want to wrap my arms around myself.

Rath is the opposite of Tristian, with his inky-black hair, lip piercings, pale skin, and dark eyes. He's quieter than the other two, those intense eyes always watching, tracking. We had a class together for a single semester last year, and it was enough to make me hate even being in the same room with him. A long stare from him always gives me a hind-brain impulse to hide. "Check it out," Rath says, jerking his chin at me. "Story's not wearing a bra."

Just the mention of it makes my nipples hard, doubling my embarrassment.

"Perky little nipples, eh?" Tristian says, taking a step into the small room. My eyes flick to his hand, wrapping around the door jamb, caging me in. His lips part and he wets them with his tongue. "Are they sensitive? Did they get hard just from me talking about them? Or do I need to touch them?"

My jaw drops and I cross my arms over my chest. "You're a pig." I start toward the door prepared to squeeze past them, but they block the exit completely. I jerk back, nostrils flaring angrily. "Get out of my way."

"Answer one question for us, Story, and then we'll let you go," Rath says, propping his shoulder against the jamb. He's wearing a lazy smirk and I can smell the beer wafting off him, too. I try to peer over his broad shoulders, hoping to see Killian somewhere. He can't stand it when I'm around his friends. He'll get them to back off.

Finding no sign of him, I release a frustrated sigh. "What do you want to know?"

Rath's head tilts, eyes taking me in. "Are you a virgin?"

"What?" My cheeks are blistering before the word is even out of my mouth. "That's none of your business!"

They both laugh, the tone deep and mocking. Tristian shakes his head, eyes flashing in something menacing and delighted. "Oh Story, only virgins say it's no one's business. You just gave yourself away."

My mouth forms around a weak denial, but I clamp it shut. "Well, who cares?" I snap. "So what? I'm a virgin. Big deal!"

"Nothing we didn't already know," Tristian says, taking another step forward. I move back and bump into the hard edge of the washing machine. "You have that look. All innocent and clean and pure. The kind of thing that just makes you want to..." He reaches out, ignoring the way I bat his hand away when he tries to stroke my collarbone. "Mess it all up."

He has no idea just how hard his words hit.

Rath rakes his bottom lip through his teeth and I don't like the look in his eyes—hungry and heavy. "There's something about virgins, you know?"

"That nervous energy," Tristan agrees. "It gets my dick hard."

"I like the begging." Rath adds, his deep voice shifting into a falsetto, *"Please don't, it hurts!"*

The anxious butterflies in my stomach turn to stone.

"But my favorite part," Tristian says, blue eyes pulsing and dilating, "is breaking them in. Feeling that tight pussy wrapped around my cock?" He reaches down to...*shift* himself. "There's nothing better than that. Damn, what I'd give to break you in right."

"You guys are disgusting," I say, lifting my chin. "I'm not scared of you, you know. You're just a bunch of socially-stunted shitheads. That's probably the only way you can get it, isn't it? Bullying girls into giving it up? No wonder your sorry ass got dumped."

Tristian's demeanor shifts on a dime, all traces of joking washed away. "What did you just say to me?"

I shrug, shifting my glare to Rath. "Guess *someone* in the senior class has more than two brain cells to rub together." I know from the way his eyes sharpen that he's remembering the class we shared. Looking back to Tristian, I say, "It's not like it's a secret that Genevieve tossed you to the curb. Too bad money can't buy you a personality to go with your micro dick."

I'm trying to hold my ground and look tough, but I can't stop the embarrassing shudder of fear at the way their faces harden, eyes sparking in anger. I sense what's going to happen a beat too late. Tristian moves quickly, darting forward and clamping his hand around my throat. My chest hitches on a panicked inhale, hands grabbing his wrist, but his arm is like steel.

He's not squeezing my throat, but he flexes his fingers, and I read the message loud and clear. *He could.* Roughly, he says, "Pretty shitty way to treat someone who was just giving you some compliments. Isn't that right, Rath?"

"Rude as fuck," Rath agrees.

"Maybe," Tristian says, prying my fingers from his wrist, "we should show her just how small our dicks *aren't.*" He yanks my hand down until it's pressed to the bulge at the front of his jeans. "As you so obnoxiously just pointed out, I seem to be finding myself short of a steady fuck these days. Maybe I'll take you, after all."

I fight to pull my hand away, mouth screwing up in disgust, but he holds my palm there for a long moment, grinding against it. "Fighting will only make it hurt more, baby. I know that's not what you want...or is it?" He tilts his head, like he's assessing me. All he gets is the feel of a hard, involuntary swallow beneath his palm. "Maybe you would, huh? You like it rough? Because we're good with that."

Rath stonily adds, "Crazy good."

I try to speak, but my voice is trapped somewhere in my chest, caught in the irony of the moment. Here I've been keeping my eye on one threat only to walk into another.

This can't happen. Not now. Not like this. Not with these guys. Not when I've managed to dodge worse—so much worse since moving in here. My eyes drop down to Tristian's wrist. The corded muscles in his forearm as he holds me by the throat flex and shift beneath the skin. I test my strength against his other hand, yanking it sharply away from his crotch. I do, but I'm not fooled. He just let me. Even one of these guys would be impossible to fight off, but two? My heart goes from racing to thunderous as I realize how entirely overpowered I am here. I could fight. I could kick, scream, lash out.

Or I could reason with them.

They can't be as bad as all that, can they?

"Come on, let me go." My voice comes out in a whisper. "I just want to go back to my room."

Tristian's lips curl into a sinister grin. "But the fun's just beginning, isn't it?"

A shadow moves in the doorway and my heart leaps. Killian's broad shoulders fill the space. He looks between his friends and me, face blank.

"Killian," I say, eyes pleading, "tell them to let me go."

"What's going on?" he asks casually, like his friend doesn't have me by the throat, pinned to the washing machine. "I thought you were bringing down more beer."

Rath's dark eyes remain fixed to me as he explains, "Story was just telling us how she's a virgin."

My stepbrother's face remains eerily blank. "Was she, now."

Tristian's looking straight into my eyes when he adds, "We were saying how we'd be happy to help her fix that pesky problem."

From the expression on his face, you'd think Killian was being asked whether or not he wanted pepperoni on his pizza. So casual and aloof. Unaffected.

I swallow to remove the dry lump from my throat. "Killian, I don't know why you don't like me, but—"

"You don't know why I don't like you?" He barks a caustic, scoffing laugh. "Your white-trash slut of a mother wrecks my family, and brings her little whoreling with her, and you can't figure out why I don't like you." His eyes slither down my body, lip curling. "I don't give a shit what these two do to you. They could both fuck you at the same time, and you know what I'd do?" His eyes spark and blaze, and there's no mistaking the surety of his words. "I'd *laugh*."

He means it, and for some reason, I'm surprised. I always knew he hated me, but this?

This is fucking evil.

Killian is never going to be my saving grace.

"I'll tell your dad," I blurt, panicking. Normally I'm not a narc. Snitches get stitches and all that. I've never told on Killian for the other things he's done; the weed, the porn, the party he threw a few months ago where two girls left crying. Secretly, I hoped that keeping my mouth shut might make him warm to me, at least a little. Clearly, I was wrong. But the thing about Killian's dad is that he *likes* me. "I'll tell him that you let them do it."

Killian's face shutters, his brown eyes staring blankly back at me. "Just because my dad has some idiotic weakness for sluts doesn't mean he'd choose you over me."

The way he says it, the emphasis on the word slut, makes me wonder if he knows what his father is doing, what he tried to do, but I'm desperate so I continue, "If you let me go, we can pretend this never happened, okay? I won't—I will never say a thing, Killian, I swear."

Abruptly, he barks out a harsh laugh. "You're such a fucking idiot. I really hope your tits get bigger, because that's clearly all you've got going for you. You really think I'd let trash like you live under my roof and not come up with some leverage of my own?"

"Leverage?"

He reaches into his pocket and pulls out his phone. Tristian's still holding my neck and his thumb keeps sweeping up to my jaw, stroking little circles into it. Each caress sends a tremor across my limbs. Nausea rolls in my belly as my stepbrother holds up his phone. I only have to see a glimpse of the screen to know what he's talking about. He smirks when he sees the recognition on my face.

"That's right, *Sweet Cherry*. You say a word about me and my friends, and I'll show my idiot dad, who thinks you're the most innocent little snowflake, exactly what you've been doing online." He flips through the Sugar Baby account I made, including the photos I've posted. I look far from innocent. "Quite the little lucrative business you've got going on, Cherry. You may be a virgin but you're far from innocent. I mean, who's to say anyone would even believe you after seeing this? You, slutting it up just like your gold-digging mother? Tsk tsk." He taps the phone on his chin, eyes full of amusement. "Nah, I think you'll give my boys exactly what they want."

Fuck.

The Plan. I need quick money, and that's the only way I'm going to get it, but worse is the threat of Killian's dad finding out.

"I'll give you a cut of the money," I say, breath coming in frantic gasps when Tristian's grip tightens around my throat. "Whatever I make, I'll give you a quarter. *No.* Half of it!"

Killian barks a dark laugh. "That's fucking rich. You giving me money? You two hearing this shit?"

Tristian smiles and it lights up his whole face. "Oh, Sweet Cherry, we don't want your money. I thought we made that clear." His face tips down into mine and he runs his nose down my cheek. His breath is hot, reeking of beer, and my skin crawls. He looks back at Rath. "How do we want to do this? Who gets to pop this delicious little cherry?"

Do this?

Rath wagers, "You fuckers owe me for last month."

Tristian scoffs. "Eat shit, that's nowhere near equal value. You still owe me for Sophomore year."

"You're still on about that?" Rath complains, face hardening. "Fine. Three thousand and my guitar."

Hot tears spring to my eyes. This can't be happening. They're negotiating over me like a piece of meat. "Please don't do this," I beg. "Don't hurt me. I'll give you whatever you want, just don't...take *that.*"

"Ah, the begging," Rath groans, hand coming down to cup his crotch. "Fine, four thousand."

My knees buckle, but Tristian's hands move to my arms, holding me up. Rath slides behind me, hands cinching around my waist. I make eye contact with Killian again, silently pleading with him. His gaze is cold. Uncaring. It's more than obvious he doesn't give a damn about what happens to me. That's why it shocks me when he says, "Neither of you are fucking her."

Tristian and Rath both freeze, turning to look at him.

"Do whatever else you want to, I don't care, but..." He rakes his fingers through his hair, looking away, jaw tight. "The last thing I need is for her to bleed out all over the laundry room floor. I'm not cleaning that shit up, and I'm sure as hell not explaining it to my dad."

"The biggest value a girl has is her innocence," Daniel told me that night in his office. His words, his hands, made my stomach twist painfully. *"Who you give that gift to, Story, will be the most important decision you make."*

Did Killian get that same lecture? Something tells me he did.

Rath mutters a curse of disappointment in my ear, but Tristian's eyes sweep over me, undeterred. He takes a step back and says, "Fine. Let's see your tits."

It's a demand, and although I should fight back and say no, I'm scared that Killian will tell my mom and Daniel about my Sugar Baby account.

Rath doesn't give me more time to think about it anyway, grabbing the straps of my tank top and shoving them down my arms. He grunts behind me and I feel his gaze over my shoulder. Tristan licks his lips and reaches for me, his fingers grazing the underneath of my breast. "A little small, but soft. Am I the first one to touch them?"

I clamp my mouth shut and glare defiantly, refusing to let them take anything else personal away from me. He grins wickedly and pinches my nipple. I yelp in response and try to twist away. Rath doesn't let me move far, holding me against his solid body. The proximity makes it impossible not to feel the hard bulge in his pants.

"I asked you a question, Sweet Cherry." Tristian's fingers circle lazily around my other nipple, waiting.

"Yes," I grind out, lying. "You're the first."

"Thank you." He tweaks me softly, sending a flare of traitorous sparks down my body.

"Dude," Killian says, "I know you're having a bad week and working some shit out here, but my dad will be home soon. Whatever you're going to do, just get on with it."

Tristian runs his thumb over my mouth, eyes fixed to the movement. "Get on your knees."

There's no mistaking what he wants me to do, and after Killian told him to hurry, he picks up his pace. There's no time to process as he unbuckles his belt and pulls down his jeans. He's not wearing underwear and his penis is just as hard as it'd felt under my palm before. It's big, straining at the skin and pointing right at me. I stare down at it, frozen in shock until Rath's hands bear down on my shoulders, forcing me to my knees.

To my horror, Rath comes down with me, still aligned with my back. I hear his zipper lower while one hand snakes around to grope my breast.

"What are you doing?" I ask, barely recognizing the sound of my own voice.

"Watching," he says, nipping at my earlobe. "Feeling. Getting off. There's more than one way to enjoy a girl."

I take one last look at my stepbrother, one last chance to hope he's come to his senses. There has to be something human inside of him. I refuse to believe otherwise. But I don't find any sympathy there. God, no. I find him in the process of shoving his hand down his shorts and pulling his own cock out. He leans back against the door jamb and takes two long strokes as he watches. The movement is obscene and strangely hostile. It looks like a warning.

Tristian's fingers touch me under the chin, and he redirects my gaze upward, toward his icy eyes. "Open up, Sweet Cherry. I want your eyes on me the whole time. I want to see those pretty lips wrapped around my cock. I want to see it when I come and you swallow it down. I want you to watch me while it happens." He licks his lips, thumbing my mouth open. "Understood?"

I nod, understanding everything. Understanding that no one, not even family, is going to save me. Understanding that this is all life is for me now, one sicko after another, lining up to take something from me. Someone a little more naïve might think it was bad luck.

I know better.

I open my mouth and take him in.

I close my eyes and try to shut everything out, to curl into the back of my brain the way I've learned. It isn't me doing this. This is just automatic. Something else has taken over my body and I'm watching it, locked away somewhere safe.

I can't quite get to that place this time, though.

Tristian makes a low sound, hand fisting in my hair as my lips slide up his shaft. Rath's breaths are loud against my ear and his touch is inescapable, hand cupping my breast, rolling my nipple between forefinger and thumb.

"Never sucked a dick before, have you Cherry?" Tristian's thumb prods at my cheek, and despite his disapproving words, his voice emerges in a pained rasp. "You realize that's where the real money is, don't you? Daddies would pay a sweet penny for some head if you can do it right." He tightens his grip on my hair and thrusts into my mouth.

I sputter angrily around his cock, jerking back.

He holds me still. "I thought I told you to look at me. Not very good at following instructions, are you?"

My hands curl into tight fists against my side, but I do it. I pry my eyes open and wrench them up, meeting Tristian's glazed eyes.

"That's a girl," he says, patting my head like I'm a dog. "I'll make this easy on you."

It's laughable. *Easy.* Nothing about this is easy. I'm trying so hard to ignore the sight of Killian in my periphery, of Rath's hand skating down my ribs, that I'm taken by surprise when Tristian starts thrusting in and out of my mouth. My hands shoot up to his hips, holding him back, but his eyes narrow, grip tightening in my hair.

"Either I fuck your mouth or you get better at this. Your choice, Story."

I hold his hips, glaring up at him even though my eyes are welling with tears. And then I start bobbing my head. I'm pretty sure blow jobs aren't supposed to be like this—bitter and angry in the way I work my tongue against him. I look into his eyes as I do it, watch them dilate, jaw slackening. Now, it's more of a promise than a blow job.

A promise that these boys aren't going to break me.

"Fuck," Tristian breathes, feet shifting. "Yeah, that's it. Shit, she's really doing it."

I can feel Rath behind me, the bounce of his arm as he jerks himself. His hand snakes down my stomach, shoving into the waistband of my shorts, and I know better now than to fight.

Doesn't mean I don't try.

"Shh," he says into my ear. "Relax." Despite what's happening here, his fingers are slow and teasing when they push into my panties, shoulders curling around me. I already know what he's going to find down there, but it doesn't make it any less humiliating when he pauses. He whispers low into my ear, "Should I tell them how wet you are for this?"

My fingers are digging bruises into Tristian's hips, but he doesn't even seem fazed.

"I don't think I will," Rath decides, fingers rubbing tight circles around my clit. "Now we can both have a secret. Keep your mouth shut about mine and maybe I won't tell everyone how much of a slut you are for all three of us. You are, aren't you?" His chuckle is warm and damp against my ear. Loud enough for the others to hear, he adds, "You could be ours, you know. We could take turns. We don't mind sharing if it's with each other."

My angry tears spill over, making hot tracks down my face. Tristian keeps his eyes locked on mine, but brings his hand to my cheek, thumbing them away. "Don't cry, now. We're just having a good time. You want us to have a good time, don't you?" My only response is the way I stare at him, wet-eyed and full of hate. He sighs as I suck him. "I don't get it, Killer," he says, talking to my stepbrother. "Used to be, we could show a girl a little attention and she'd trip over her own feet to be ours. Nowadays, all these bitches do is fuck around."

He fists a hand in my hair, yanking me deeper onto his dick, glazed eyes flashing. It makes me cry harder, because that, combined with what Rath is doing to me, is making my hips want to grind into Rath's hand, and *god*.

It's the worst part of all of this, knowing that Rath could be right.

Maybe this is what I am.

A magnet for creeps, something to be used, and a slut for all of it.

Tristian's head falls back, eyes falling closed, and I'm grateful for the reprieve when the sharp, building ache between my legs reaches a full crescendo, clenching as Rath moves with the movement of my hips. The reprieve doesn't last long. Tristian thickens and pulses in my mouth, his thick, salty release surging against my tongue. He cups the back of my head and presses me close, holding me there as he empties himself between my lips.

Behind me, Rath grunts, yanking me against his chest, and I'm caught in the middle of them, being pulled two different ways. I hear more than see Killian finish, his rough, breathless groan startling me.

Tristian pulls out of my mouth, but not before he grabs my hair and rasps out, "You know what to do now, don't you?"

Rath takes his hands out of my shorts and grabs my jaw, forcing my chin up. "Swallow him down, pretty girl."

It takes me three tries to do it without gagging, but I hold Tristian's gaze as I obey, swallowing his release. I hope it looks like how Killian had before—hostile—a warning—instead of showing this lost, aching thing in my chest.

"Good," he says, stroking my cheek. "You're so good for us, aren't you, Cherry?"

I don't know how I manage to get my feet under me, but I do. I clamp my hand over my mouth as I bolt away, the sound of their breathless chuckles following in my wake.

ALSO BY ANGEL LAWSON & SAMANTHA RUE

Boys of Preston Prep

(M/F Steamy Angst-Romance)

Devil May Care

A Deal With The Devil

Touched By The Devil

Devil Incarnate

Royals of Forsyth University

(Reverse Harem Dark/Bully Romance)

Lords of Pain

Lords of Wrath

Lords of Mercy